# THE WELSH DRAGON

## A NOVEL OF HENRY TUDOR

# K.M. BUTLER

First Firsthand Account Press Edition, September 2022
Philadelphia, PA





Library of Congress Control Number: 2022908028

ISBN 978-1-7376391-2-1 (paperback)
ISBN 978-1-7376391-3-8 (ebook)

Cover design by Cutting Edge Studios

Printed in the United States of America
10  9  8  7  6  5  4  3  2  1

**For my wife Shelby,**
my partner in a quiet life of happiness.

# THE
# WELSH
# DRAGON

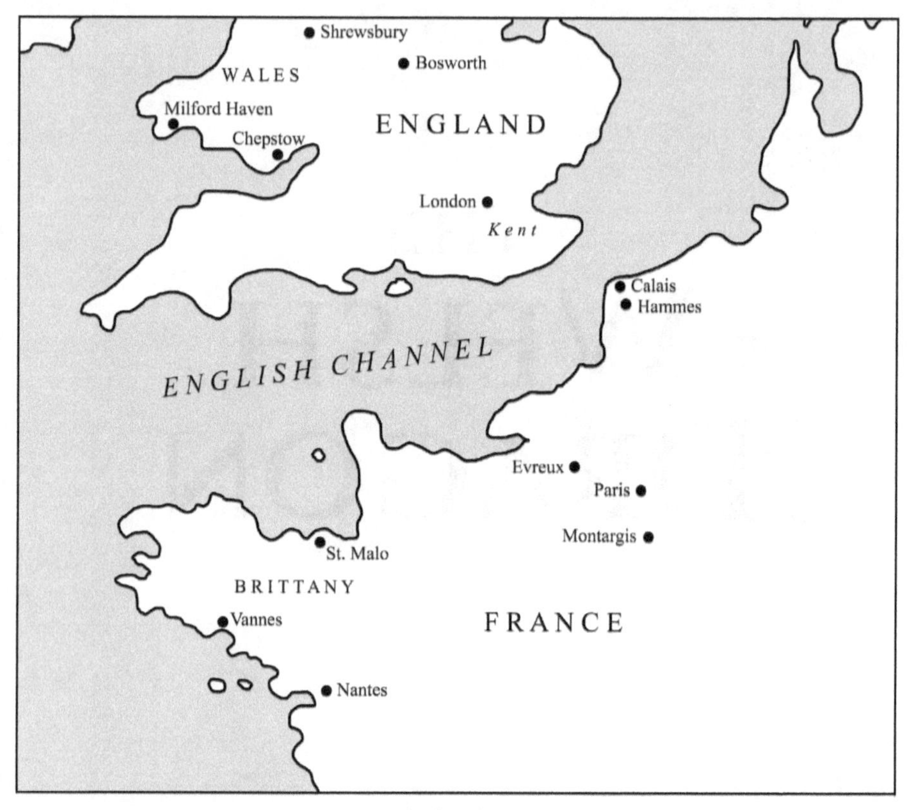


**English Channel**
AD **1471**

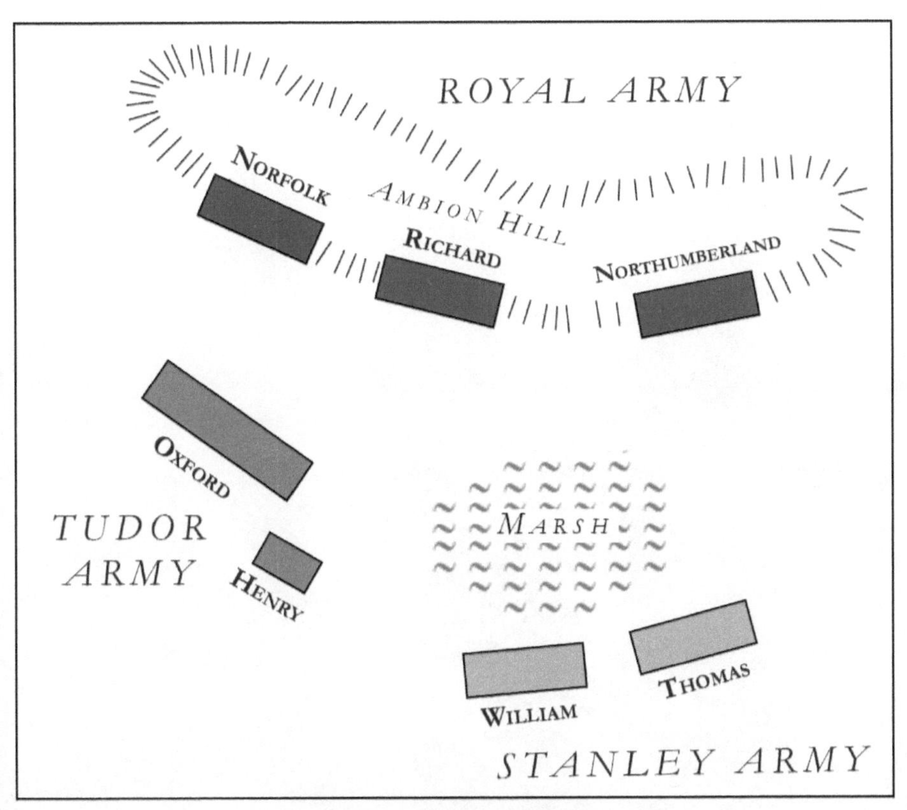


**The Battle of Bosworth**
**August 22, AD 1485**

# I

## FLIGHT

AD 1471

# CHAPTER ONE

## HENRY

THE PILE OF armor in the corner of the room would begin to rust soon. Henry knew he should finish cleaning it before he slept, but his fourteen-year-old fingers were starting to throb. With the excitement of his first battle fading, the aches were beginning to set in, accompanied by his growing comprehension of all the terrible fates that could have befallen him.

Beyond his chamber, his uncle Jasper's insistent footsteps approached with a cadence that warned of another task.

Henry brushed aside a damp strand of dark brown hair and straightened. He would say something this time. Even Jasper's Lancastrians camped in the courtyard were allowed a respite after turning the tables on the Yorkists.

Henry's objection died on his lips when the door opened, revealing Jasper in full armor, his pale blue eyes intense.

"We have to leave. Dress quickly." It was the voice his uncle used on his men. Something was wrong.

Swallowing, Henry reached for his gauntlets.

"No," Jasper interrupted. "I can carry the weight. You can't."

"I don't understand." Henry forced his feet into his muddy boots and reached for his discarded belt and doublet. "Did Vaughan escape?" If he had, the Yorkist commander would reassemble his scattered soldiers and continue hunting them.

Wrestling with his sleeve, Henry nearly collided with a second man wearing armor that was encrusted with mud and something dark red.

"Lord Oxford!" Henry gasped. "We heard you died at Barnet."

John de Vere, the Earl of Oxford and the greatest Lancastrian general, exchanged a grim glance with Jasper. "Many did, but not me. Not yet."

"Come, Henry." Jasper beckoned Henry to follow him down the hall.

Henry's fingers fumbled the threading of his sword belt through the buckle. "I don't… Where are we going?" He wished his height matched his fourteen years; his short legs struggled to keep up. His uncle and Lord Oxford moved so quickly that the torches lining the wall were only brief flashes reflecting off their breastplates. "What's wrong?"

Jasper slowed but spoke only after a passing servant left their earshot. "Do you remember the message from four days ago?"

Henry nodded. After a mere six months' exile, the pretender, Edward IV, had defeated and captured King Henry, the rightful King of England, at Barnet. The news had caused most of Jasper's Welsh recruits to desert overnight.

"After the defeat at Barnet, Queen Margaret and her son marched to join your uncle here at Chepstow," Oxford said. "Two days ago, Edward captured her at Tewkesbury and executed the prince."

Henry swallowed. If Edward had killed the prince, he wanted every Lancastrian dead.

Leaving the hallway, Jasper continued past the row of blacksmiths in the courtyard and the smell of coal floating on the air. "I suppose that's why Vaughan came after us. Only three Lancastrians remain who Edward can't buy."

Henry swallowed. He stood with two of them now. "But we won today."

"Vaughan's a nobody." Hostility flashed in his uncle's eyes. "Edward will send someone else, perhaps his brother Richard."

One evening after Henry had come to court, he had overheard his uncle and mother arguing about his future. While Henry hadn't been able to distinguish all of Jasper's words, he had heard a few: gifted… potential…toughening. His uncle's tone had held clear respect for his nephew's abilities.

It was the same tone he used now regarding Richard, a few years older than Henry.

"Who's the third Lancastrian Edward can't buy?" Henry asked. "Maybe he'll help us fight them."

"Not unless you're hiding an army somewhere." At Henry's blank stare, Oxford went on to explain, "It's *you*, Henry. Edward fears your royal blood."

Henry drew in an unsteady breath. Yes, he was a descendant of Edward III, but that blood came from women and illegitimate marriages. It had never mattered before. He might be the half-nephew of the king, but that connection came through the king's mother, not the half that could claim the crown.

"And, you were marching with Edward's enemies," Oxford concluded.

"I was only obeying my king."

Jasper rested a hand on Henry's shoulder. "Men have died for less. Your youth won't protect you. Edward tried clemency when he took the throne ten years ago. He won't make that mistake again. We must withdraw."

Henry clenched his fists to hide their shaking. Edward and his demon brothers were capable of anything. They'd emptied castles throughout England by the nobles they'd killed, including Henry's own father and grandfather.

"Where will you go?" Oxford asked.

"France." Jasper resumed trudging toward the courtyard. "My cousin the king is still sympathetic."

France. The word conjured images of cathedrals and wide streets filled with people. Henry's French had a terrible accent. His mother had recently arranged for a tutor, but half a year of occasional study hadn't accomplished much.

Oxford smirked. "I imagined you'd stay in Wales, like last time."

Jasper shook his head. "Edward will close the ports the moment he takes London. A Woodville is probably already on the way here. We must leave now, or not at all."

Woodville. That name, Henry recognized. Edward's queen, Elizabeth Woodville, had wiggled into the royal sheets and invited her whole family with her. Her half-dozen sisters tied several powerful lords to the Yorkists through marriage.

Oxford grumbled, "We'll need English allies to free King Henry. Edward will kill him the moment we invade."

Jasper swallowed. The king was his half-brother. "Start with those who supported us before. Not everyone fought at Barnet."

"How useful are they, then?" Oxford snorted. "But, by all means, write to our reluctant friends. Work on your cousin in France. At least he provided soldiers. I'll go north. The Scots hate Edward."

Jasper offered Oxford his hand. "I'll meet you in France, afterward."

"You will. This isn't the end." Oxford turned to Henry. "Good luck, Earl of Richmond. I wish you were indeed hiding an army somewhere."

Henry wanted to say something grand, given the circumstances, but nothing came to mind. Instead, he mumbled, "If I did, I'd let you lead it."

Oxford grinned before rushing over to his horse, a rouncey watering itself at a nearby trough. As many flecks of dirt caked the war horse's torn livery as covered Oxford's armor. For an earl of His Majesty's army, pitifully few men surrounded his mount.

"Come, Henry." Jasper was already heading toward a sergeant who had begun to approach. He saluted the man. "How many are with us?"

The soldier ran a hand along his bristled chin. "Two dozen. The rest are willing to risk staying in England."

Jasper swallowed and said nothing, but his disappointment was plain, even to Henry.

The man cocked his head toward a ring of soldiers to the left. "He's waiting."

Jasper offered a tight-lipped grimace and followed the soldier toward the ring, his posture straightening while he walked.

Seemingly forgotten, Henry followed. "Uncle?" he called out in vain.

The ring of soldiers parted. Within was a chopping block with a broad-headed axe planted into it. Two guards held a bound man in a ripped, white wool tunic. But it was his eyes, burning with hatred when he saw Jasper, that demanded Henry's attention.

Turning to his nephew, Jasper gestured to the prisoner and said in a voice loud enough for the encircling men to hear, "Henry, this is Sir Roger Vaughan, the man who murdered your grandfather."

Henry's eyes shifted to the axe. Executing a noble prisoner ran against everything Jasper had taught him. "He was honorably captured in battle, uncle." He kept his voice low enough that only Jasper could hear. "Should we be doing this?"

"A captive may be held to account for prior crimes." Rising to his full height, Jasper raised his chin to look down his nose at Vaughan. "I, Jasper Tudor, Earl of Pembroke, peer of England, brother to our liege-lord Henry VI, find you guilty of treason against your king and the murder of Owen Tudor, my father. As commander of this army, I hereby condemn you to death for your crimes."

It was not the language traditionally used to sentence a noble. The guards forced Vaughan to his knees.

"My king is Edward," he protested.

"Now, perhaps," Jasper agreed. "But not ten years ago when you committed your crimes."

Vaughan's eyes widened.

Jasper nodded to one of the soldiers in the ring, who extracted the axe from the block while the guards forced Vaughan's head down against it.

"Damn you, Tudor! You and all your kin will suffer—"

The slurping slice of the blade hewing through bone and flesh cut off the end of his threat. Vaughan's head rolled off the block and came to a rest in a growing pool of blood near Jasper's feet.

Jasper turned from the twitching body to face Henry. "When you have the chance to destroy your enemies, take it. They wouldn't hesitate. Neither can you." With that, he marched toward his horse, a thick-muscled courser.

Henry followed toward his squat palfrey in silence. He had, of course, seen executions before. When King Henry had recovered his throne from Edward last November, dozens of lords had lost their heads. But he'd never been this close or been so well-acquainted with person commanding the deed.

During the half-year since Jasper had returned, all of Henry's dreams had been fulfilled. He could see his mother when he wanted. He'd been accepted at court as the Earl of Richmond. He knew he'd be safe in the morning when he fell asleep at night.

That would end now. But he wouldn't be alone, not ever again. Together, he and his uncle would flee to France to continue the fight against the dreaded Yorkists. Jasper had lived like this during the decade of Edward's first reign. Listening to Jasper's stories, Henry had longed for some of his own. Now, he'd have the chance.

His peaceful nights lay behind him, but this would be a wonderful adventure.


## HENRY

The halt in the bobbing of his horse's head roused Henry from his fatigue after the grueling nighttime ride from Chepstow. Jasper had already dismounted and was approaching a two-story building, the tallest of those flanking either side of the wide dirt road. It wasn't as polished as some of the manors in London, but intricate carvings along the doorframe announced the importance of its owner.

So, this was Tenby, the Welsh coastal town Jasper had fortified during King Henry's first reign. Henry doubted the Welsh would hand over their own countrymen, but capturing Lancastrian fugitives would curry favor with the new king. In such desperate times, who knew what men might do?

Henry dismounted. Nearly numb from the long ride, his legs almost gave out, but he managed to support his weight against his horse until sensation returned.

A small man in a checkered black-and-yellow tabard answered Jasper's knock. His alarm showed for only a moment. "My Lord Pembroke?"

"I wish to see your master."

"Of course, of course. You're expected, my lord." He gestured for them to enter.

Jasper squeezed Henry's shoulder until it hurt and met his eyes with an unspoken warning.

Was this a trap?

The steward led them into the building's main room, with Jasper preceding his nephew protectively.

"Oh, my Henry!" a woman wailed from within.

He knew that voice!

Ducking past his uncle, he gasped at the sight of his mother. Margaret Beaufort rushed past a surprised Jasper and squeezed her son so tightly that the ribbing of her bodice grated against his chest. He patiently endured her hands probing his shoulders and face, checking for injuries.

When she finally stood back to look at him, Henry noticed the reddening of her usually fair skin and the puffiness around her grey eyes. Henry couldn't decide whether, at twenty-eight, his mother was a beautiful woman or absence merely made her seem so.

"What are you doing here?" Henry asked once he'd recovered enough breath to form words.

"Your uncle and I agreed to meet in Tenby if the worst should happen."

Henry turned to his uncle in disbelief. Jasper had expected the king to fall? What else had he planned?

Now, he realized Vaughan's execution had been one last act of defiance.

Margaret eyed Jasper. "I see he suffered no serious harm in your care, even if it did take you a week to make a journey of two days."

"I care for him as if he were my own son, Margaret," Jasper replied.

"But he's not. He's mine. My only child."

His uncle's eyes carried the sting of the rebuke, but he held his tongue.

"We heard Vaughan came after you," Margaret continued. "Where is he?"

"Dead." His voice carried unmistakable satisfaction.

Margaret pressed Henry's head to her chest again. "There's that, at least." Pushing him back to arm's length, she pinned him with a withering glare. "Are you happy with yourself?"

"What did I do?" Henry squeaked.

"You just had to go fight for your king. And now…" She blinked away another bout of tears.

He had seen his mother like this only once, when she'd reclaimed him from the Herberts after King Henry's restoration. She hadn't left his side for an entire week. After so long apart, it had felt nice to spend time with her again. But now, he felt hollow, uncertain. So many men he'd met over the past six months had died, while all the demons in Hell had been let loose upon England. And he was in the middle of it.

Gesturing, Jasper turned to Henry. "Henry, meet Thomas White, the mayor of Tenby."

Henry hadn't noticed the other person in the room. A complicated cotton chaperon cap draped behind this elderly man and imperfectly concealed a mop of thin gray hair. He wore an equally long black wool robe with a silver chain of office draped loosely around his neck.

Henry inclined his head a fraction, as the Herberts had taught him.

"My nephew and I are grateful for your hospitality," Jasper said to the mayor.

White held his cap in place as he bowed. "You and your family are most welcome here, my Lord Pembroke. I only regret that the safety of my people requires me to limit my help." This man could be executed for merely conversing with them.

Jasper swallowed. "Have you had any news since Tewkesbury?"

The mayor cast a frantic look toward Margaret before replying. "You, your nephew, Lord Oxford, and even those who died in battle have been attainted. All your lands and titles are forfeit. Edward posted instructions for all Welsh towns to refuse entry to Lancastrian traitors—his word, my lord, not mine." Inhaling, he stammered, "Few Welshmen will obey him, if only to frustrate the English." Henry's own Welsh ancestry caused these men to hail him as kinsman. "But it allows the king to punish those who disobey."

"The only king I acknowledge is my brother Henry." Jasper's tone carried an edge of hostility.

The poor mayor squirmed and split his gaze between Jasper and Margaret.

"Tell him the rest, Thomas," Margaret instructed.

Jasper waited passively, awaiting undoubtedly more bad news. Henry lifted his chin to emulate his uncle.

Thomas picked at the stitching of his top button. "I'm sorry, my lord. King Henry is dead, God rest his soul." He crossed himself. "Edward even had himself re-anointed with Henry's crown."

Staggering backward, Jasper collided with the far wall. Henry was beside him a moment later, offering supportive hands on either side of his torso. Guiding Jasper to a nearby chair, Henry crossed to a pitcher and some wooden cups on a nearby table. His hands shook as he poured the wine, spilling some on the table.

The death of the king meant the dark times would come again. When the pretender had ruled England, Henry had only rarely seen his mother, and never his uncle. Henry swallowed his panic and kissed the gold cross at his neck. He couldn't endure being shut up again in some pitiful castle in a corner of England, sitting idly while his relatives fought for their fortunes.

Steadying himself with a deep breath, Henry returned and offered his uncle the cup. Jasper had not only lost a king, but also a brother. His beloved elder brother, Henry's father, had been dead for fifteen years and his royal half-brother, King Henry, not fifteen days.

"God bless poor King Henry." His mother sighed. "He was ill made for kingship, but he deserved better than his fate."

Henry supposed she meant the words as a kindness, in her own way.

Jasper swallowed the wine and inhaled, straightening as he did. "Thomas, we must reach France as quickly as possible. If we can secure foreign aid, we may yet rally our supporters here in England."

Henry released a breath he hadn't realized he'd been holding.

"A ship can take you tonight, my lord. The tide will be right in a few hours."

Henry had hoped to have a little food and a decent rest, perhaps even a bath. Part of him had even hoped Edward might offer a general amnesty. With King Henry's death, his supporters could transfer their loyalty to the new king without betraying their prior oaths.

It seemed none of that would be possible, though.

Jasper turned to the mayor. "Will you send someone to collect Lady Margaret's possessions?"

"I'm not leaving," Margaret said.

"Mother!" Henry's old loneliness came rushing back. "Why are you here, if not to come with us?"

"A damned good question, Margaret," Jasper added.

"Please understand." She stepped closer to Jasper, putting herself between him and Henry. "I can be more useful at court than in France."

"But you'll have to live under that tyrant." Disgust filled Jasper's face. "Groveling to a pretender."

"As I've done for years. In London, the people will see poor Margaret Beaufort, aggrieved mother and widow, praying daily at the cathedral for her son's safe return." Margaret completed the image by pressing her palms together, a mischievous smirk curling across her lips. "That reminder will reverse Henry's attainder, not your political pressure. I may even gain him the Somerset dukedom. My cousins both died without heirs, and he's next in line."

"You must be careful, Margaret. If anything should happen to you—"

"It won't." She held Jasper's eyes, exuding a confidence that lightened Henry's anxiety. "But I must ask something of you." When she spoke again, it was with compassion. "Jasper Tudor... In the whole world, I hold no man dearer. Please protect my son as your own."

Fear crept into her request, and Henry wondered what ill could befall him in France.

"No harm will come to him, else may God strike me dead."

Thomas and Jasper crossed themselves deliberately, and Henry found himself doing the same a heartbeat later.

Though she didn't join them, Margaret wrung her hands together. "Keep him safe, Jasper. Please." The words were a weak plea.

"I will, Margaret."

Henry straightened to his full height. "I'll be fine, mother."

She smiled at him as Lady Herbert had when he would say something foolish. Taking him into her arms, this time she cradled him as if he would break.

"Everything I've done has been for you, Henry. I know you must've thought I'd forgotten you during those years with the Herberts, but I had to be so careful. All the men of my family died opposing the Yorkists. Even your father. I couldn't let Edward's anger fall on you, even...even if it meant..." She fell silent, shaking.

Behind them, Thomas whispered in Jasper's ear before pushing open the front door and departing into the night.

"I know, mother."

Henry wrapped his arms around her shoulders. He'd always believed the hardest part of his life had been those years of separation, but seeing the tears fall down his mother's cheeks was far worse.

He swallowed his unease. "When will I return?"

She smiled, separating from him to meet his gaze. "A few months." Instead of reassurance, her tone carried only uncertainty. "Yes. Once the fighting is over and the nobles submit, Edward will be generous. I'm certain of it."

# CHAPTER TWO

## MARGARET

HOPING A STIFF posture would restrain her anxiety, Margaret mimed the rigid control of the women she'd encountered in her twenty-eight years. Her mother. The old Lady Oxford. Even Margaret of Anjou.

Newly elevated nobles eyed her hungrily, eager for the continued supply of vacated manors and castles further executions would provide. With her cousin Somerset dead, Margaret was the only heir to the considerable Beaufort fortune. They all wanted a piece of it.

This room held so few familiar faces. Gone were the earls of Wiltshire, Oxford, and Devon and the Marquess of Dorset. Though, she did recognize the new Duke of Buckingham, young Henry Stafford, who had been married off to a Woodville sister.

King Edward sat on his predecessor's gilded throne with the slumped shoulders and sagging mouth that made him seem far older than twenty-nine. He wasn't a handsome man—his dark brown hair was too long and thick for her tastes and his chin seemed weak—but he exuded a sincerity he'd employed to good effect over the previous ten years.

Despite his few years, he had counted nine of them as monarch before King Henry's brief restoration, and the rest learning from his formidable father, the Duke of York. He had seized the crown twice and lost it once. That he had recovered it was because of the efforts of those who stood with him now: his brother Richard, his friends Thomas Stanley and William Hastings, his wife Elizabeth, and her brothers Anthony and Edward Woodville.

Edward raised his chin, covered with thick stubble from his short march. "Almighty God has blessed our restoration by striking down the traitors who opposed us. Now, we must establish order to our realm. We have summoned you today to decide how to deal with you and your son."

Margaret tensed the muscles of her neck at the unfriendly reception.

Richard, much shorter than his brother but possessing the same chin and eyes, leaned forward. He was a fierce warrior in his own right, despite the intense curve in his spine that gave the impression he was forever shrugging. The king loved him dearly. "Has she taken an oath of loyalty, brother?"

Margaret had lived under Edward for nearly ten years while King Henry had sheltered in France. Of course, she had taken the oath. Richard merely wanted to remind her of the fact.

Edward began musing about when she'd sworn allegiance to him all those years earlier. While he prattled on, Margaret reconsidered her position. Richard's interruption suggested she'd have to convince everyone on the dais of her loyalty, not just the king.

William Hastings had always remained loyal, at least in his support of the Yorkists over his true king. Oxford had routed him at Barnet, yet Edward had still trusted him with his armies at Tewkesbury. Hastings might offer his opinion, but he would obey Edward's edicts.

Lord Thomas Stanley, a dark-haired man who styled himself as the King of Mann, was handsome of face, but what Margaret found more seductive was his sheer power. Other than Edward's, the Stanley army was the largest in the realm. He tended to use it only after determining which side would be victorious in any given battle. He had personally captured Margaret of Anjou when the troubles began ten years earlier and had remained loyal to the Yorkists ever since.

Then there were the Woodvilles. Their appearance—an overabundance of embroidery and jewelry, their arrogant postures—confirmed their low birth. Their very presence at court was an insult. Margaret's son was descended from Queen Katherine Valois. Oxford's ancestors had signed the Magna Carta. Yet, they were exiled and the Woodvilles exalted. England had fallen low, indeed.

Queen Elizabeth sat on a smaller throne that lacked the intricate gold filigree of the king's. Her pale gold hair and icy blue eyes made her beautiful enough to tempt a duke's son. Worst of all, Margaret jealously observed, she had endured multiple pregnancies without it ruining her figure. Even now, the child growing in her belly only produced a tiny bump in front. How could such a deceitful woman be blessed with so many children when Margaret's difficult pregnancy had rendered her barren?

Pushing the thought from her mind, Margaret looked instead upon the strong arms and beautiful eyes of Elizabeth's brother Anthony, Lord Rivers. Like the rest of his family, he paid no heed to the enemies he cultivated. Uniquely, he was capable of overcoming them. Fresh bandages poked out from beneath his long wool robe. Margaret wished Oxford had killed him at Barnet.

She took them all in with a glance, missing only the last portion of Edward's response to Richard. When Edward deigned to remember her, she was ready for him.

"Lady Margaret, we wish you to answer for the past six months."

"Which of my actions have offended Your Highness?"

"Your presence at the court of King Henry."

She folded her hands before her. "Upon the death of my husband fourteen years past, I sought the protection of my cousin, the Duke of Somerset. I felt it my duty to obey his judgment regarding my affairs."

"So you obeyed him, even if that meant serving a man you considered to be a usurper?"

This was a trap Margaret had expected. If she agreed that King Henry had been a usurper, she would admit to catering to whoever was in power, harming her credibility. But doing otherwise would number her among Edward's Lancastrian enemies.

"I know little of the causes which promote one king over another, Your Majesty. I merely sought to serve my family, according to the teachings of the Holy Church."

Richard obediently crossed himself, as did Margaret and several of the observing nobles. Edward and Elizabeth were too busy scowling to notice.

Stanley offered a sincere smile. "Obedience to family is much like the duty of a subject to her sovereign."

Why was he defending her?

Startled, Margaret nonetheless bowed her head. "Indeed, my lord. I have always found it so."

Edward leaned back. "Your cousin is a traitor who abused our great affection. Custom grants us the right to strip him of his lands and titles." His pause was too short to allow fear to grow properly. He was out of practice. "However, we do not seek to punish a loyal subject for obeying her familial duty, particularly when she is the last of her line. We happily grant you the inheritance of your cousin's lands as his sole heir, though we maintain our right to the honor of Somerset."

That concession would, no doubt, come at a price. "Your Majesty is generous."

"We are pleased you recognize this fact." Edward folded his hands before him. "Certainly, you know of the love we hold for our beloved cousin, your son Henry?"

The question was filled with implication; she carefully schooled her tone. "I well trust the affection you bear all your subjects, Your Highness." *Including those for whom you hold none at all.*

"And you also raised your son to trust in his king?"

"Yes, Your Highness." This loving king had dispossessed and hunted his beloved subject.

"When did you last speak to your son?"

This was the critical question. The way she answered would decide her future. Too casual of a response would attract attention. They would expect some nervousness. "When last he was in London."

"And where is he now?"

"France, Your Majesty." Gasps of surprise filled the room here and there, but she had witnessed enough such audiences to know not to explain further.

"Your son did not leave alone," Richard interrupted. "Jasper Tudor, and possibly John de Vere, the former Earl of Oxford, went with him."

Margaret paused long enough for Edward to react to his brother's outburst, but no response came. "Your Highness will recall, my son was serving as Jasper Tudor's squire."

"And why did you allow your son to be educated by a traitor?" Richard pressed.

Margaret swallowed her anxiety. "My son was of an age to learn the responsibilities he would one day be asked to assume. Had I not let him go, he would not have gained the skills Your Majesty values, even though they'd been taught by the Earl of Pembroke."

"That traitor and his accomplice, John de Vere, have been stripped of their former titles," William Hastings shot back. That open hostility—and the implications of a toad like Hastings feeling confident enough to venture such a bold opinion—would make it difficult for Jasper to ever regain his earldom.

"Forgive me, my lord," she began, emphasizing Hastings' lower rank. "I have been traveling for many weeks in my haste to reach His Majesty and was not aware." She turned back to Richard. "I have not spoken to them for several months."

Margaret had expected much of the conversation to focus on Henry, but now she realized Edward was far more concerned with Jasper, a proven commander and rebel whose mother had been French royalty. If anyone could convince the King of France to invade, it was his English cousin.

Henry didn't matter to anyone but her.

Stanley cleared his throat. "Then it is entirely possible young Henry merely accompanied Tudor out of a squire's obligation." His tone held the perfect amount of surprise for a sudden insight. "Perhaps the order for his arrest was…precipitous."

At first, she thought him a simpleton. But after noticing the subtle twitching of his cheeks, she understood Stanley's intentions.

Caution still seemed prudent. "It is indeed a possibility, my lord."

"What are the intentions of your late husband's brother in France?" Elizabeth Woodville cupped her growing belly as she spoke.

Beside her, Anthony ran his eyes across Margaret's figure, his thoughts obvious. If not for his wife, Margaret might have considered cultivating his interest. A marriage to Anthony Woodville would quickly secure her son's return.

She addressed her answer to Edward. "Your Majesty knows more about these matters than I."

Richard shifted his weight. "Indulge us."

Damn him. Jasper was the one man she could always trust. Answering truthfully would condemn his chances of ever returning to England. But if she lied, she would undermine her posture as a loyal subject and endanger her son's return.

Mind scrambling, she dropped her gaze to conceal her thoughts from the court. Jasper would never bend his knee to the man who'd murdered his half-brother and whose cause had killed her dear Edmund. Would she really be betraying him by admitting what Edward's council already knew?

She raised her eyes. "I suspect he intends to raise France against King Edward."

The observers broke into a furor of conversation marked by a distinct unease. They knew of Vaughan's execution and the long memory it implied. Margaret privately suspected Jasper would fail in mustering another invasion without an heir to place on the throne.

The king rose to his full height, pulling Margaret out of her thoughts. "We thank you for your indulgence on these matters." He pinned Margaret with a withering gaze.

Never had she felt more alone, standing in a circle of emptiness surrounded by nobles who wanted to profit from her humiliation and a royal family who showed little interest in reconciliation. Her hopes for her son's quick return were vanishing. She should have either approached Edward before news of Henry's flight arrived or delayed until she'd learned whether the French would provide Jasper with soldiers.

"We are moved by your son's plight. We will send an envoy to France to determine whether your son fled as a supporter of our enemies or a victim of his duty. Should your son be proven innocent of treason, we will, of course, allow him to recover his forfeited Beaufort birthright. We would value his addition to our ranks, in whatever capacity we find suitable to his character."

Margaret repeated Edward's pronouncement to herself in stunned silence. How could she have been so wrong? With one sentence, Edward had extended the bill of attainder to Henry's right to the Beaufort lands as well as his Richmond title. Though she'd retained her lands, Henry wouldn't be permitted to inherit them. Edward had stripped everything from a boy of fourteen.

She forced herself to offer an unsteady curtsey. "Your Majesty is kind in his judgment. I am certain he will fulfill your faith in him." Fearing that Edward—or Richard, with that keen mind—would see the shock and anger in her eyes, she fixed them firmly on the floor.

"We also," Elizabeth began, "invite you to remain at court to respond to news from France about your son's case."

Case! As if her son had been prosecuted like a common brigand. "I am Your Majesty's servant."

She bowed deeply as the king and queen descended the dais. No doubt, there would be a festival tonight in honor of the country's deliverance from the corruption of the usurper and his French she-wolf of a wife.

Edward had left open the possibility of Henry's return while stripping him of anything that might encourage him to do so. Was it simply because of his connection to Jasper, who had caused havoc for the Yorkists for fifteen years? By stripping both him and her son of their titles, Edward would limit the danger Jasper presented in France. A commoner could only accomplish so much. That part of Edward's strategy made sense.

Yet, why would Edward allow Margaret to inherit her cousin's lands if they wouldn't pass to Henry? Edward had dispossessed plenty of widows over the past ten years. He could have settled Somerset on a loyal supporter after Tewkesbury. Why hadn't he?

"Lady Margaret?"

Thomas Stanley, with his well-proportioned shoulders and sinewy muscles, studied her with concern. They were almost alone. Most of the court had followed the king's procession.

"Your Majesty," she replied, recalling his title as the King of Mann.

He grinned at her greeting. "My lady, I would be honored should you address me simply as Thomas, your humble servant."

She dimpled her lips into a smile. "Thomas. Allow me to thank you for your assistance during the audience. Or should I call it a performance?"

Smile widening, he offered his arm and gestured to the corridor. "It was unfair of them to ask you such questions." His was a bold reply; criticizing the king or his ministers could cost a man his head in this new England. "A woman's duty is to serve her family."

"The king seems to have recognized that."

They passed a group of young men encircling Richard against the wall of the corridor. With them was the young Duke of Buckingham. Considering how he had spoiled after many years without a father, Margaret was relieved Henry was at least exiled with his uncle.

Stanly continued in a near-whisper. "Though I find it strange Edward is willing to entertain your son's inheritance of your cousin's lands."

"Is it, my lord?"

"Indeed. And unprecedented." He shrugged. "Mind you, I'm certain Henry will be found innocent of the charges. When that happens, I suspect he'll be very pleased with the sudden reversal in his fortunes."

His hidden message became clear. Denying Henry his title, yet offering the hope of inheritance might lure Henry back to England without Edward having to make any firm agreements. It was a subtle, cunning approach. But why?

They had strolled some distance down the main hallway.

Doubts clawed at Margaret's mind. "My lord is perceptive."

"Alas," Stanley replied with a strange inflection, "I cannot take credit for the assessment. The queen was kind enough to enlighten me."

This tangled strategy was something Elizabeth Woodville's devious mind would dream up.

Margaret picked at the embroidery along the edge of her bodice nervously. What advantage would the queen gain from bringing Henry home in such an indirect way?

Tallying the dead over the past ten years, she realized with alarm that, outside of Edward, his children, and his two brothers, the only men who could claim even an ounce of Plantagenet blood were the wastrel Henry Herbert, the young Duke of Buckingham…and her son.

It couldn't be. Henry was disbarred from inheriting by the same law that legitimatized her ancestors, John of Gaunt's bastards. Henry's blood was Welsh and French, peasant and enemy, wholly unsuited by royal English standards. Surely, Elizabeth wasn't that paranoid.

Yet, Edward had lost his throne once. If it should happen again, it would endanger Elizabeth's children by the king. Margaret herself would condemn the entire court to the fires of Hell to keep her Henry safe. Elizabeth would only have to eliminate a select few.

Perhaps the queen intended to bind Henry to one of her sisters the way she'd done with Buckingham. A bride as a bridle was better than a noose for a necklace. The husband of the queen's sister would merit an earldom, at the very least. Perhaps even her cousin's Somerset dukedom.

Margaret remained silent until they were free from the din of the chattering nobles and into the main courtyard. "I must thank you for the pleasant escort, and the insightful observations, my Lord Thomas."

He had helped her twice now. She suddenly remembered that his family had been Lancastrian before Edward.

"It was my pleasure and my duty." He leaned in and kissed the back of her hand.

She could do worse than cultivating a powerful Yorkist. Perhaps that would even reassure the royal family that their devious strategy was succeeding.

"Come, come, my Lord Thomas. Here, I thought you were merely interested in polite conversation. To find you paying me compliments like a wide-eyed youth is a surprise, indeed."

His bellow filled the courtyard, startling a pair of chickens grazing near the stables. It was a pleasant sound. She liked him more by the minute.

"I offer my most humble apologies. Might I show my contrition by inviting you to dine with my family tonight? My household is somewhat neglected since the death of my poor wife. I would like to introduce you to my son, Lord Strange, and my brother William."

It was a kind gesture. Inviting her to dinner would notify the court that he, one of Edward's strongest supporters, believed her innocence. Yet Margaret began to wonder whether his Yorkist sentiments stemmed from loyalty or self-interest. After all, Stanley had remained in England when Edward had fled six months earlier.

She recalled the body of Warwick hanging above St. Paul's Cathedral. Rotting flesh had attracted crows that had pecked at the blood-caked gashes created by Yorkist swords. The sight had nearly sickened her when she had arrived in London. The wars were over, and the cost of defeat had been high.

Her son would need allies, or at least indifferent nobles, to return in some measure of dignity. "I would be honored, my lord."

## HENRY

A storm two days into the Tudors' voyage forced them to seek safety in the Breton port of St. Malo, where they were immediately escorted to Duke Francis at Rennes. Jasper grumbled about the delay but eventually accepted their circumstances with a sigh.

Henry knew nothing about the aging duke standing before him: a white-haired man covered in silk, with eyes that carried genuine pleasure at seeing them. Unlike in England, this duke was a sovereign in his own right, since Brittany was independent of French rule.

He greeted his guests in clear and clipped Breton. "On behalf of my duchy, I welcome my most noble cousins. I'm told your journey has been a long one."

Jasper executed a polite, but not subservient, bow. "Indeed, Your Grace. Despite our eagerness to reach France, we felt it our duty to secure permission to cross your domain."

They'd had no choice in visiting the duke in Rennes; had his uncle injured his wits?

"I appreciate your thoughtfulness and respect, my Lord Pembroke. What is the purpose of your journey?"

Jasper wasted no time on preamble. "The pretender has seized the English throne and executed both the prince and His Majesty, King Henry, most cruelly."

Gasps filled the suddenly attentive court, followed by the whispering. One woman standing in the front row fainted into the arms of her companion—artfully done! Distinct groups of courtiers stood apart, wearing copious amounts of silk. Ambassadors, perhaps? From one group, he heard a few snippets of Parisian, distinguishable from the duke's Breton by its rolled *r*'s. Another spoke clear Castilian.

"We were traveling to my cousin King Louis when a storm forced us ashore," Jasper continued.

Francis himself showed no reaction. "We heard nothing of this."

"It happened five days ago, Your Grace. I and my young nephew were relentlessly hunted by the pretender's forces, barely escaping with our lives. Edward intended to kill us without according us the English right of judgment by our peers."

"So you are outlawed." The duke's eyes darted wildly among his court.

Henry shifted, but Jasper pinned him with a stern glare. This was a tense moment, but why?

Francis met Jasper's eyes and inhaled. "You have suffered greatly at the hands of those who should nominally be friends, my Lord Pembroke. But now, you are safe."

Relief flow through Henry. Thank God and all his angels that the Duke of Brittany was a reasonable man!

Yet, his uncle stared wide-eyed at the floor.

"My lord duke!" One of the courtiers stepped forward and executed a brief bow. "My master, King Louis, has already guaranteed the safety of all men loyal to King Henry VI. Naturally, this offer extends to his aunt's son, Lord Pembroke, and his great-nephew, Lord Richmond." A smirk played across his lips as he emphasized their relationship. "An accident of weather prevented them from reaching France. While my liege will certainly appreciate your gesture, he will insist on their release to his custody without delay."

One of the Breton nobles rose. "Your king guarantees their safety, Philippe? When last I checked, the French king isn't safe in his own palace and has little power in the wilds of France."

"His Highness' people love him," the ambassador insisted, to a smattering of chuckles from the court.

"Were it so, 'tis also true that Burgundians and English litter French shores. I doubt all those sympathetic to Edward of York joined him on his invasion. Can your king protect against all of them, as well?"

"Do you doubt my king's honor, Landais?"

The speaker, Landais, raised a hand. "Not his honor, ambassador, merely his competence. Unlike in Brittany, not every Frenchman honors his liege's promises."

Jasper's head dipped, drawing Henry's attention. His eyes were filled with pain when he turned to Henry.

While Landais and the French ambassador traded barbs, Henry lowered his voice. "Uncle?"

Anguish consumed Jasper's face. "I'm sorry, Henry. That damn storm ruined all my plans."

"Uncle, I don't—"

"Silence!" The duke raised his jeweled hand, and both the ambassador and the Breton subsided. "A duke is obligated to protect all those within his lands. With the disturbing developments in England and doubts about the loyalty of King Louis' subjects, it would be irresponsible to decide anything without more information."

The ambassador began to bristle, but Francis waved a hand at him. "It is no criticism to say your master has enemies. Consider it a consequence of his strength." A few more chuckles accompanied the comment.

Henry had finally arrived at the conclusion Jasper had already reached. Francis had no intention of letting them continue on to France.

Jasper cleared his throat. "Duke Francis, I would gladly accept your generous hospitality in exchange for your oath to protect myself and my nephew against all those who wish us harm."

The French ambassador began to protest but subsided when Jasper snapped his head around to meet his gaze.

"I gladly give it," Francis replied. "I hold my cousins Pembroke and Richmond dear to my heart. You shall be our guests at Rennes until we can arrange lodgings more fitting to your status." Even Henry recognized the ambiguity in the statement. What was their status? "My lords, I invite you to join us for dinner tonight and further discuss events in England."

Jasper bowed. "We would be most honored, my duke."

Smiling, Francis rose and led a procession out of the room.

Once the majority of courtiers had left, Henry turned to his uncle. "I don't understand. Why would you agree to stay in Brittany?"

"Duke Francis has no intention of releasing us." Looking beyond Henry, he called, "Monsieur Ambassador!" He crossed to the Frenchman, and Henry followed in his wake. "Jasper Tudor, Earl of Pembroke. I am thankful for your efforts."

"Phillipe de Commynes, Ambassador to King Louis XI of France." Sighing, he gestured to the throne. "I fear I may have done more ill than good."

"Nonetheless, you have my appreciation. Are you free to convey a message?"

After verifying their privacy, Commynes lowered his chin to listen.

"The Earl of Oxford will be arriving in France," Jasper whispered. "Pray ask my cousin Louis to welcome him as my brother."

Commynes nodded. "He is of your persuasion regarding Edward?"

"He's a dear friend and a talented soldier."

"Is that so?" Commynes offered Jasper his hand. "I am certain my king will not rest in his efforts to see his kin released from the custody of this troublesome duke."

"I remember well the years I spent in his company and welcome the opportunity to join him again." Jasper shifted his gaze to one of the Bretons standing behind the ambassador. "We will talk more when we are able."

Commynes nodded and moved on to exchange pleasantries with another courtier.

Henry watched him leave. "Duke Francis can't resist the king's will. King Louis will help us dethrone the pretender."

But Jasper shook his head. "That man's all we'll see of France."

The simple pronouncement shattered Henry's confidence. He had crossed an ocean and had been labeled an outlaw, and now his uncle was telling him there was no hope of French support? He swallowed a pang of fear. "Are we prisoners?"

"The duke called us his guests," Jasper said. "And guests are free to talk to people. Guests can cultivate allies. And that's exactly what I intend to do."

# II

## EXILE

AD 1476

# CHAPTER THREE

## MARGARET

THE PALACE GUARDS detained two young nobles for dueling over the first rose of the year and brought them before Anthony Woodville. Both wanted to deliver the prize to Lady Elizabeth, the king's daughter. Anthony gave them a tongue-lashing for stealing from the king's gardens but relented when the queen commented how romantic it all sounded. Softening his tone, he settled the matter by offering the rose to his sister, which all parties at least pretended to find satisfying.

The boys probably wouldn't have inflicted any serious injury, but who could tell these days? Margaret would have appreciated the romantic gesture in years past, before nobles had started killing each other.

She settled in for the Easter feast in a foul mood. Her son would have gotten to that rose first. But instead, he was rotting away at Largoët in the Breton wilderness. Though owned by the Marshal of Brittany, it was still a dunghole. Realizing her fretting had attracted attention, Margaret smiled at the couple passing her: Henry Stafford and his wife Catherine Woodville, the young Duke and Duchess of Buckingham.

"My dear Catherine, you look more beautiful every time I see you."

Catherine mustered a radiant smile closely resembling that of her sister, the queen. She clasped Margaret's offered hands, but couldn't keep the contempt from her eyes. Like all her relatives, Catherine considered Beaufort and Tudor resistance to King Edward a personal insult.

Her husband wasn't as skilled at concealing his discomfort. The orphan of a Lancastrian, Buckingham's education had been woefully insufficient to prepare him for the finer points of the false smile.

"And you, Lady Margaret…" She studied Margaret's feminine features as if searching for flaws. Proudly, Margaret waited her out, knowing she would find no crow's feet, blotchy skin, sagging breasts, widening hips… She had cultivated her image precisely. "I only hope I look as well-preserved at your age. You must share your servants' secrets with me."

Margaret smiled in genuine pleasure. Resorting to age? "Oh, it's no secret at all. I live in accordance with the duties of my class. Scheming and social climbing ages us prematurely, don't you find?"

Catherine's face flushed. The barb was as bluntly crafted as the duchess' insult; the Woodvilles were all parasites of royal power.

Turning her attention to Buckingham, Margaret caught him lifting his gaze from her breasts. "Congratulations on your appointment as exchequer for Kent, Your Grace. You have grown into a fine man."

Buckingham offered a smug grin. "I could do nothing else, descended as I am from Edward III and the flower of English nobility."

Catherine shot him a look of shock mirroring Margaret's own. Was he oblivious to the implied insult about his wife's birth?

Margaret recovered first. "You remind me much of my son, also named Henry. Blood tells, does it not?"

"Your son?" He cocked his head toward her. Recognition dawned a moment later. "Oh, yes, the traitor in Brittany."

She resisted the urge to remind him of his own father. "His Highness has cleared Henry of culpability."

"So I thought, but the Duke of Gloucester recently reminded me the order for his arrest remains valid." He met her eyes for just long enough to gloat over the fact. "My dear..." He raised an arm for his wife, who was still bristling at the earlier slight. "I believe your sister awaits us." Raising an eyebrow, he added, "Good day, Lady Margaret."

Margaret considered his words while they departed. So, Richard was still interested in her son's status after all these years. The thought evoked a shiver. Even the velvet of her dress seemed itchy, constraining.

A commotion at the other end of the hall silenced the assembly. "Make way for His Majesty, Edward, King of England, Ireland—"

Edward, wearing the crown and a long fustian robe with an ermine cloak, waved off the remainder of his titles as he strode into the hall toward the head table. Behind him came his brothers George and Richard, as well as Hastings, Norfolk, Northumberland, Anthony Woodville, and the rest of the Privy Council—including Margaret's new husband, Thomas Stanley.

She didn't delude herself into believing Stanley had been taken by her beauty. He was far too shrewd to ally himself with the daughter of his king's enemy so lightly. No, he'd been interested in the Beaufort estates. Margaret had allowed him to draw men and supplies from those lands and use them as collateral while Henry remained in Brittany. Of course, that didn't bother her. Marriage was by nature a business arrangement.

She was hardly a victim. His protection as the King of Mann, the Lord Stanley, would shield her son when he finally returned. He had sheltered her during the first year of her son's exile. For that, she would be forever grateful. Even the news that her steward, Reginald Bray, had arranged means of communicating with her son hadn't softened the pain of parting.

While the new arrivals filtered through the hall toward their seats, the king greeted his wife. The lines of his face were drawn tight as he grasped her hands.

Beside him, Richard offered Elizabeth a stiff, uncomfortable bow. The queen responded with an insulting inclination of her head, fit only for servants.

But, before he seated himself next to his wife, Anne Neville, Richard met Margaret's eyes with a gaze of absolute emptiness. No hatred, no love, no suspicion, no interest… They were simply empty.

She felt as if her soul were slowly draining away.

The connection lasted only a moment before Richard turned to embrace his friend William Catesby.

Freed, Margaret lowered her eyes to the quail and smoked salmon being paraded before her. Just as quickly as it had manifested, the intensity of that moment evaporated. She stole a peek at him again, but this time, Richard seemed lively and indulgent, even slapping Catesby on the back with delight.

Surely her thoughts had made him seem worse than he was. Or, maybe it was that damned Catherine Woodville and her feeble insults. She would have to spill something on her dress later.

"Stop scheming, my dear. It'll give you wrinkles." Stanley squeezed her hand affectionately. She hadn't seen him approach.

"I suspect I'm not the only one scheming." She nodded toward the royal table. "In five years, he's never been late for a feast, particularly when he's paying."

At the head table, a wine steward offered the king his usual over-sized goblet, from which Edward took a long, sustained drink.

Richard shifted his gaze from Catesby to his brother for a brief, telling moment. When he resumed his conversation, concern had replaced merriment.

Stanley sat beside her. "Official business." He reached for the quail. "Brittany."

She gasped. That damned Duke Francis valued his guests like gold. Her son had been collecting dust on a shelf when he should have been managing his estates.

"A new ambassador?"

"Mm-hmm." He popped a piece of meat into his mouth. "His treasurer, a man named Landais, says Duke Francis is beset by petitions to release the Tudors into French custody."

The implication was clear: only further funds and manpower from England could prevent Jasper from escaping to France, where he would no doubt foment an invasion. It was a dangerous game, not the least for her son.

"I imagine the king was not pleased with the reminder."

Sighing, Stanley slowly shredded a piece of quail.

She rested a hand on his forearm. "Tell me."

"The king is furious at this Breton extortion. Jasper's animosity is well known. They assume your son feels the same."

"Which, of course, you refuted."

He hesitated and stole a glance at her. "What would you have me do, Margaret? Suggest Edward ignore the indignities inflicted by Margaret of Anjou and her followers? I'd wind up with my head pinned to St. Paul's."

"You exaggerate. Oxford was caught raiding English possessions and merely locked up in Hammes."

"Only because he was technically in King Louis' employ and England isn't ready for another war with France. I'm an Englishman with a sizeable army at my command and a Lancastrian for a wife. I have to be very careful."

Lowering her head, Margaret admitted he was right.

"There are ways to heal the divisions and restore your son," he continued. "Opposing Edward publicly isn't one of them. I'll not risk the future of my own family for the sake of your son." After a pause, his tone had softened. "Now eat, or you'll attract attention."

She had spent the previous five years cultivating an image as a loyal Englishwoman, attending mass every day, giving generously to the poor in London, and bowing before Edward and his brother. Obediently, Margaret turned to her meal, picking at her salmon just enough to give the appearance of a hearty appetite for the sake of anyone who might be watching.

She accompanied Stanley from table to table, chatting with the other nobles. The Duke of Norfolk's wife greeted her pleasantly enough, for she shared the same pious devotion Margaret projected. They spent some time pitying the poor of London who lacked the character to earn a decent living.

By now, her stomach was growling from genuine neglect. She returned to her own table to devour a plate of cheeses when a shadow fell over her. Following it to its source, she leaned back and offered a poorly covered gasp of surprise.

"Lord Rivers!"

Anthony Woodville seated himself without permission in her husband's seat. "I'm pleased your appetite has returned. I feared I might have to put our cook to death for offending your palate."

She was fairly confident he was joking. "I'm pleased to command such attention." The comment came unbidden. Was it rebellion against years of carefully controlled responses, or his proximity? He was very attractive.

"My lady, you would command the attention of Jesus Christ himself. I am thankful you were not present to ensnare him with the promise of domestic tranquility." For the first time, she recognized the young man fidgeting behind him.

She roused her pious mantle. "It is impolite to blaspheme in the presence of a lady, Lord Rivers."

"Forgive me. Might I make it up to you?" He gestured for his companion to approach. "Have you met my young brother?" He turned to the boy. "Edward, may I present the Lady Stanley, Margaret Beaufort."

"My lady." The young man bowed to a sufficient depth for her rank. His eyes carried none of the entitlement that tainted the rest of his family.

"Well met, Sir Woodville."

"He resembles your son, don't you think?" Anthony asked.

The casual comment transformed the table into a battlefield for her son's future. She had been lulled by Anthony's smoothness and had found herself enmeshed in a conversation she hadn't been prepared for.

Anthony Woodville had no way of knowing whether anyone

resembled her son, of course. Even if he did, no one would claim the two men looked alike. Her son's face was long, with dark eyes and hair, quite unlike this young man's round appearance.

"How is your son, Lady Margaret?" Anthony pressed. "The Breton ambassador says his duke fears my dear brother-in-law wishes him dead." He shook his head too slowly for it to be a genuine reaction. "I don't know where that vile thought came from."

"Perhaps from the summary execution of the Prince of Wales at Tewkesbury?" She regretted the outburst almost immediately.

Anthony didn't appear to take offense. "Surely not. It's well known the king's brother George gave that order." That much, at least, was true. George of Clarence had earned his way back into his brother's good graces with that murder after betraying him to Warwick six months earlier.

"I have no communication with my son in Brittany."

He offered a hint of a sigh. "It must be hard to be separated from your son for so many years while he's at the mercy of a foreign tyrant."

*Not as bad as being at the mercy of a domestic tyrant.* Did he intend to teach his young brother how to insult a noble lady without overt offense? She had little interest in serving as his lesson. "Pray you never experience separation from a loved one. It is a terrible burden."

He leaned an elbow on the table. "Your son's plight rests heavily on my heart. No family deserves the uncertainty of exile. Tell me, what efforts might I pursue to entice his return?"

Finally understanding his intentions, she began to relax. "Surely, that decision rests with Duke Francis."

Anthony dimpled his cheeks. "But the duke's opinion is formed largely by that of Jasper Tudor. Does he not oppose a happy reunion?"

Ah, but would that reunion be with Henry's mother in Wales or his father in heaven?

Margaret popped another piece of cheese into her mouth and chewed while considering her response. Had her patience finally paid off? She was, at least, well-prepared to answer this question, having had five years to consider it. "There's a greater obstacle. Without lands or title, what does he have to return to?"

"The love of his king?" Anthony grinned impishly.

"While my son was overjoyed to be exonerated for leaving England, he remains troubled that the order for his arrest has never been reversed."

"Who told you such a thing?" His sharp reply carried an edge of annoyance.

"The Duke of Buckingham mentioned a conversation he had with Lord Gloucester."

"Richard…" He turned to glare at the man himself at the head table, speaking to the Archbishop of Canterbury. "Surely it's but an oversight. I'm certain it could be corrected."

"Demonstration of the king's affection would speak louder than words."

"Such as the restoration of his lands?" He inched forward.

"Richmond…or Somerset," she prompted.

Instead of alarm at trading an earldom for a dukedom, Anthony pretended to consider the offer. "But the Tudors suffered attainder once already. I don't suspect a man as powerful as Francis would be swayed by such a fickle grant."

Had Anthony broached this topic merely to point out the futility of her efforts? "Do you have a suggestion?"

A little too quickly, Anthony obliged her. "Perhaps a more permanent arrangement will convince Duke Francis of our king's goodwill."

"A permanent arrangement?" She tried to grasp the direction of his mind. A court appointment to keep Henry under Edward's watchful gaze? A marriage to the daughter or sister of some loyal supporter… It had precedent. Elizabeth Woodville's sisters had been married off to important nobles. She tried to remember which Woodville relations were of age and not yet betrothed.

Then again, death was about as permanent of an arrangement as Elizabeth could imagine.

But after so many years, Margaret could hardly believe Edward still wanted to kill her son. The danger posed by the Tudors was minimal considering Jasper's continued failure to gather support. Yet if he truly feared the blood in Henry's veins or held Henry responsible for Brittany's extortion, he would go to any extent to eliminate that problem.

Anthony smiled absently at someone behind Margaret before returning his attention to her. "Princes consider such matters, though their ways are a mystery to their humble servants."

Margaret doubted he felt either humility or uncertainty about Edward's intentions.

He rose. "I'm certain the king and Duke Francis can reach an arrangement. Trust in him and your son will return." Bowing deeply, he strode off into the crowd with his younger brother in tow.

Only then did she realize she'd shared all her hopes for her son's future while learning nothing whatsoever in return.

## HENRY

Henry was adjusting the lay of his doublet when the herald leading him through the palace corridor halted. He barely caught himself before colliding with the man's long silken locks and velvet cloak.

"Forgive me, my lord," the functionary drawled in thick Breton. "There is a delay."

He sighed. It had been one delay after another since his arrival in Nantes. But after five years of waiting, he was just happy to be doing something.

Compared to the octagonal keep at Largoët, Nantes was a sprawling nest of excitement. The landowners and nobles followed the duke on progress, of course. And crowds had gathered around every craftsman's shop dotting the streets leading to the castle.

The trip to the Breton capital had happened suddenly, leaving Henry without enough time to have his new red and yellow padded doublet properly fitted before the Rieux household had abandoned

Largoët for the capital. Nor had he had the chance to write to his uncle for guidance.

His uncle's fears about King Edward's retribution seemed to have been mere fantasy. His mother was working on his behalf, and she wouldn't seek his return if it was dangerous. Their letters would duel; Jasper warning Henry to watch for conspiracy and assassination and his mother encouraging hope for a speedy return.

Yet in all that time…nothing.

"My lord?" The herald gestured toward the clear path into the hall.

Once again, Henry adjusted his doublet and the sword at his side—the same one he'd worn at Chepstow all those years earlier—and approached the entrance of the feasting hall. It had been years since he had attended any event larger than a private dinner, but he could still recall his uncle's lessons. Briefly, he wondered whether Breton customs differed from English etiquette.

The herald tapped his cane against the floor three times. "Henry Tudor, Earl of Richmond."

He'd have to muddle through.

Swallowing sudden panic, he rubbed at a tooth that had been hurting him for several weeks. He carried himself into the reception hall with the straight back his uncle had always emphasized.

Where was Jasper?

The faces studying him belonged to strangers. A few whispered and pointed, while one of them surprised her companion with a hushed comment. Others shifted their focus to his doublet. It was too big, he knew. Or perhaps it was out of fashion—curse the Rieux boys for suggesting it!

While the older men wore long houppelande cloaks that dragged on the floor, the youths his age wore similar doublets. If anything, his hose were a little thicker than theirs, but surely that small detail couldn't possibly matter.

Then, he remembered: this was simply how the court worked. Any new curiosity drew attention. With each person he passed, his excitement rose. One by one, he greeted them with nods of increasing confidence, eventually offering a few words in Breton. He basked in their attention.

A young blonde woman watched him for a moment before arching an eyebrow and running her eyes over his body. Unlike the others of her age, her hair was bound with braids and kept off her neck, though a few tendrils hung down enticingly, teasing her skin. Her light blue dress hugged her lovely curves. Its dark blue embroidery made an intricate vine pattern that perfectly matched her eyes. Those bottomless eyes somehow attracted him and kept him at a distance, all at once.

Caught in her attention, he could hardly breathe.

He recovered only when two men approached. The first, a bishop, smiled broadly. His traditional purple robes of office strained beneath the weight of his potbelly and a large cross the dull luster of solid gold. A thatch of flaxen hair poked out from beneath his purple *zucchetto*.

"My lord Tudor, I am Bishop Stillington, ambassador for His Highness, King Edward." He spoke flawless English and, after a moment's pause, executed a proper English bow, much as Henry himself had been taught all those years earlier.

Henry searched for the woman in blue, but she was gone.

The other man offered a suitably respectful bow a moment later. "Sir William Catesby. We're honored to meet you." He was slightly taller than the round bishop, and far more broadly built. If not for the gold chain of office around his neck, Henry would have taken him for a manservant. Yet his gestures were hesitant. He was assuredly not noble, probably one of Edward's lackeys.

Some of the Breton lords had turned to watch the ambassadors acknowledge Henry as an earl by the quality of their greeting, if not by their overt language. He had to respond appropriately; he couldn't afford to scorn any of his countrymen.

Henry straightened and swallowed his doubt. He was the Earl of Richmond. "Not as honored as I am to meet true and noble Englishmen."

He inclined his head a fraction to honor the bishop according to his status. He delighted in the chance to employ his education again.

"I suspect you don't see many of your countrymen in Largoët. I'm told it's a beautiful town," Stillington continued.

He was thankful for the polite conversation but tried to restrain his excitement. After all, these men were agents of Edward. He would have to be careful, in case his uncle's fears were justified, after all. "It is. You can see for miles from the ramparts."

"But not in the direction of England, if I recall correctly." Stillington's voice carried an odd undertone. Henry had never forgotten the inflection of his uncle's and Oxford's voices the night of his flight, presaging conspiracy. "Are you well?" the bishop asked in a hushed voice. "We hear so little news of you. It weighs on our minds."

"As well as I can be in a foreign land." His skin tingled at the husky tone that escaped his own lips. Whispering amid the court… His heart beat with excitement.

Beside him, Catesby clicked his tongue against his teeth. "It's intolerable for the duke to hold you as a prisoner."

"It's a circumstance my mother and I work tirelessly to remedy."

More Breton courtiers had turned to observe Henry's conversation, adding to his excitement.

"Your mother sends her respects," Stillington added.

Surprised, Henry almost asked him to repeat himself.

The bishop continued, "At Easter, she spoke with pride about your progressing education. You've grown into a fine young man, Lord Tudor."

Doubt tugged at him. Everything Jasper had said seemed wrong. Why would they openly greet him if they meant him harm? "You show me great courtesy, Your Excellency. I'm humbled by your words."

"No, my son. You have endured your circumstances nobly. Your father would be proud." Stillington blessed himself.

Surprised at the compliment, Henry lagged in duplicating the gesture.

"So many terrible things happened during those days," the bishop continued. "That's why we struggle, to justify those sacrifices."

Henry desperately wanted to believe him. Edward and his servants had murdered dozens of nobles, including his father and both of his grandfathers. But how would further hostility benefit him? His uncle had spent half his life as an exile. Henry couldn't live the life a long memory required.

A servant dressed in the same livery as the herald approached and bowed politely to the ambassadors. "With respect, my lords, His Grace is prepared to welcome you to his court."

The bishop offered Henry a curt bow. "I look forward to talking with you further, Henry."

Henry fought his disappointment that these eminently respectable gentlemen had been called away. Surely, he could do worse than cultivating their support. Perhaps his mother was right to hope Edward would let him inherit something of his birthright.

Yet, what would it mean for his uncle if Henry was welcomed back to England? Jasper had kept him safe over the years. Henry's peaceful return would sign his uncle's death warrant. Francis would have no reason for holding Jasper and would repatriate him at once. He'd lose his head the moment his feet touched land; Jasper had opposed Edward too long to hope for clemency.

He couldn't abandon his uncle. Either they'd leave Brittany together, or not at all.

A tall, sharp-boned man with a thin frame strode toward him. The court parted before him with respectful bows and curtseys.

The man offered a mere inclination of his head, reserved for equals. "Lord Richmond, welcome to court."

"Monsieur du Quelennec." Henry clasped his arms in friendship and planted a kiss on either cheek. He and Jasper had stayed with Quelennec for a year before Henry had been relocated to Largoët. "I'm thankful for a friendly face, monsieur. Do I have you to thank for my increased stipend last year?"

Quelennec's grin reminded Henry of Lord Oxford. Both men carried themselves with a military grace tempered by the finesse of nobility. "I felt it would satisfy the French of your good treatment. But you did more than I when you saved Marshal de Rieux's son."

Henry exhaled at the memory. He'd been riding through the forest with the marshal and his sons when Rieux had rushed ahead with young Armand. Poor Philippe had tried to keep pace with his elder brother, but he'd lacked the experience to make the sharp turn and had crashed into the brush. Henry had waded in, only to discover him at the mercy of a bear. He had distracted the animal until the marshal and Armand had doubled back to investigate their delay.

"Your mother wrote a scathing letter to your uncle about the incident," Quelennec recalled. "I never dreamed the saintly Margaret Beaufort knew such language."

Henry couldn't help but laugh, wondering how much her secretary had left out of his transcription.

He sobered quickly, though. "Any news of my uncle? I expected to see him today."

"He should arrive tomorrow." Quelennec hesitated. "I saw you talking to the English ambassadors. What did you think?"

Henry considered. "Polite, friendly. Perhaps they can resolve matters with the king."

Quelennec scowled. "I doubt Edward will ever forgive the brother of King Henry or his nephew. Be careful around them. They, like all courtiers, will use your situation to their advantage."

The warning rang false. At no point had Jean de Rieux behaved like the social climbers in the English court. "You are a courtier too, my lord," Henry ventured.

Quelennec showed no signs of having taken offense at Henry's implication. "While you remain in Brittany, we can extract promise after promise out of fear we'll arm you against Edward. But he'll retaliate against us the moment we turn you over. Your safety guarantees ours, but some here don't understand that."

Henry nodded but privately doubted Quelennec's fears. England wouldn't risk weakening Brittany when it relied upon the duchy to threaten France. But he wasn't going to share that opinion with his only steadfast defender.

"Henry!" Philippe de Rieux ran toward him, blond locks jangling back and forth. "I was worried I wouldn't find you."

Henry gestured to Philippe. "Monsieur Quelennec, do you know Philippe de Rieux, son of the marshal?"

"Hello, Philippe." The admiral nodded. "Last time we met, you were just a boy, refilling my goblet at your father's manor. You've grown into a fine young man."

Philippe beamed at the compliment, but restricted himself to a simple, "I apologize for interrupting, monsieur."

"Not at all." Quelennec offered one of those charming smiles. "You're young enough to appreciate court. Go, enjoy, Lord Richmond." His eyes, though, reinforced his earlier warning.

"Come, Henry. There are so many people you need to meet." Philippe tugged on his arm.

Only as Philippe led him into the crowd did Henry realize Quelennec had used his title, Richmond, while the English had not.

Brittany was a far cry from the English court filled with old men and soldiers. The Bretons trusted in the stability of their realm and duke enough to bring their children. Assuming the role of Henry's guide, Philippe introduced him to a series of young Breton lords who kept aloof at first. Henry asked polite questions about their families and holdings until they softened.

Nonetheless, their chosen topics of conversation—such as the differing social implications of a ruffled cuff versus a straight cuff— sounded naïve and trivial. Henry had survived a court populated by men now dead.

But, where young men were, so were their sisters. Henry tried not to leer at the extremely low cuts of their dresses or allow his internal debate over the softness of their skin to show in his eyes. Nor was he the only one to appreciate the ladies of the Breton court. They flirted terribly with every young man who approached. While chatting with one of Philippe's friends, Alain de Rohan, a group of young women strode past. The conversation fell silent as the young men watched the lines of chin, neck, and shoulders bob up and down in rhythm.

Once they'd passed, Henry noticed the young woman in blue from earlier in the distance, studying him. She smirked faintly upon being caught staring but showed neither embarrassment nor interest in the group of young lords beside her.

Without a word for Philippe, Henry stumbled toward her without the faintest idea of what he would say to this beautiful, strange girl. Executing an awkward bow, he prayed she didn't take the opportunity to run away. He needed to hear her voice.

She was still watching him with those wide eyes when he rose.

"My lady." His voice squeaked.

Rather than comment on his nervousness, she dipped into a shallow curtsey. "My lord."

"I'm Henry Tudor, Earl of Richmond."

"The English exile?" she asked.

"You've heard of me?" He immediately regretted the outburst. The young Breton lords would never react in such a way.

The corners of her lips curled into a grin. "There's hardly a courtier who isn't talking about the Tudors' thrilling flight from the White Rose."

Thrilling… Would they describe it thusly after a life under guard for fourteen years, only to be taunted with six months of freedom before doing it all again?

He managed a passable smile. "As you say."

She gestured to his clothing. "I didn't know the fashions of England were so similar to our own."

He self-consciously straightened his doublet, trying to make the extra material sit more attractively. "I cannot say, I'm afraid. I've spent the last four years in Brittany. This was a gift from friends here."

"Ah, I see."

"I should count myself very lucky if you blessed me with your name, my lady." This conversation was not going as he had hoped.

She shook her head quickly. "Forgive my manners. I am Jehane de Rousson, tailor of Vannes."

"Jehane." Henry savored the sound on his tongue. "A beautiful name for a beautiful woman." His voice, in a register far lower than usual, sounded silly to him.

She offered him no giggle or bashful smile, only the faint incline of her head. The controlled reaction confused him. The other young ladies had all clamored for his attention. Exile or not, he had the blood of English and French royalty in his veins.

"A tailor, you say?"

"Yes. My husband comes from a long line of skilled craftsmen." She spoke proudly, almost defensively.

"That explains it, at least." No wonder she wasn't interested in him; she was already married. His heart sank.

"Explains what?" she asked stiffly.

"Your behavior, your hair, it's just—"

"What's wrong with my behavior?" Louder, she demanded, "What's wrong with my hair?"

His own eyes widened. "No, I just meant that you're not acting like the other girls. They're so friendly, and—"

"And I'm not?" The muscles in her neck tightened.

"No, no, that's not what… I mean the other girls are all seductive—"

"And what, I'm a frumpy peasant widow?"

Had she said *widow*?

"When I first saw you," she continued, "I was intrigued. Every other boy here just wants to bed a pretty girl. I thought I saw something deeper in your eyes. I thought maybe, because of all you've experienced…" She shook her head. "I was wrong. You're just an arrogant fool, looking down his nose at us commoners. Go back to your boar-hunting and servants. I have no time to waste on you." She stormed away, but halted and spat over her shoulder, "And your hose are too thick!"

His cheeks warmed with growing embarrassment. He felt the judgment of the nearby courtiers whose gazes dropped to his legs. Whispered surprise turned into laughter as the incident spread with his shame.

His fury was only held at bay by the inescapable proof that he was a fool. A tongue-tied, clumsy fool.

## HENRY

Henry peeked inside the small room to discover Jasper reading a scroll that curled over from the weight of a thick red seal. He quietly stepped all the way inside and shut the door on the four guards in the hallway.

"Henry!" Jasper tossed the scroll aside and closed the distance to clasp him tightly.

Returning the embrace, Henry basked in the reassuring strength of his one true friend. The lingering embarrassment from the previous day melted away.

Jasper held him at arm's length. "Another growth spurt?" he asked in Welsh. "I can't wrap my arms around you as much anymore."

Henry's tongue easily slid into the familiar language. "In Largoët, my choices are eternal study and serving as Philippe's or Armand's sparring partner."

"Imagine if I hadn't sent you the tutor." Jasper gestured to a pair of chairs around the empty fireplace. A smile lingered on his lips as he seated himself. "Two years. You look well, Henry."

"I am well, though eager to return home in triumph," he prodded. "How have you been?"

Jasper leaned back in his chair. "I had to be careful. I suspected my letters were being read."

"The seals had definitely been re-melted," he confirmed. "But my mother explained the unwritten meanings."

"Lad, if my letters were intercepted, what makes you think hers wouldn't be?" His voice carried a growing alarm.

Henry smirked. "Reginald Bray."

"I remember him; one of her grooms."

"Now her spy. The letters she lets the duke's men see urge me to continue my studies and pray to God for deliverance."

"And the letters you receive by way of Bray?" Jasper asked.

Henry shrugged. How did a person compress two years into a short statement? "She petitions Edward to restore Richmond or her lands, though I can't imagine Edward ever granting me Somerset."

"He doesn't want another Lancastrian duke." Jasper snorted. "A lot has changed in five years, Henry. When we left, I expected Oxford and I to lead an army of Frenchmen and Scotts to overthrow Edward. But Oxford is imprisoned in Hammes near Calais for pirating Edward's ships, and I'm stuck here."

"Our allies are unwilling to help?"

Jasper shook his head. "Brittany needs a strong England to shelter him from France. He'll only support a viable claimant, but we have no one to replace Edward."

"George of Clarence? He helped Warwick dethrone Edward once before."

"He was such an incompetent wastrel that Warwick opted to restore King Henry rather than crown him," Jasper countered.

"What about Henry Holland?" He was a great-grandson of John of Gaunt and a solid Lancastrian.

"Not even I would prefer the Butcher of Exeter to Edward." Jasper grimaced. "Brutes like him pushed the nobility into Edward's arms in the first place. Besides, he conveniently died on the way back from France last year."

"I hadn't heard." Henry had only been familiar with the man's lineage, not his character. "There must be others."

"Only you and Buckingham."

"And my claim comes through the Beauforts." Henry recalled well the deficiencies of that line. Descended from John of Gaunt through his bastards, the Beauforts had been later legitimatized by the Pope but forever disbarred from the crown.

"Buckingham has your claim too, but his father was also a legitimate heir of Edward III's youngest son, Thomas of Woodstock. He's the only one the nobles would support, but he married a Woodville, and I doubt his wife would take her eye off him long enough for him to foment rebellion."

Edward also commanded a fiercely loyal group of knights, lands, and allies, including the Duke of Burgundy. With two brothers and two sons, he was the safe, strong option. Nobles were nothing if not cautious.

Jasper leaned forward. "Henry, you must understand. You may not have enough royal blood to sit on the throne, but he still fears you. You're related to the French king, are beyond his control, and have nothing to lose. Never doubt that he'll see you dead if he gets the chance."

"We should watch the ambassadors closely," Henry replied at length.

"Quelennec told me the duke already gave them a private audience." It was a telling fact, but surely Jasper's friends would warn of any concerning developments.

"I saw Quelennec yesterday. It was nice to find a friendly face."

"He's a good man and a great comfort when things seem bleak." Jasper's eyes brightened. "What did you think of the court?"

Henry remembered Jehane's golden hair and those angry eyes. "Complex." He tried to banish her image from his mind but couldn't forget her bold scrutiny, or that temper. "What kinds of people are invited to court?"

"Nobles and large landowners. The duke calls them counts and marquises, but Pembroke and Richmond were larger than their holdings. Knights, merchants, bishops, moneylenders—"

"Moneylenders?"

"Sometimes. If the French invaded, Duke Francis wouldn't survive without loans."

Henry nodded. "And merchants would have to be successful, right?"

Jasper nodded. "Otherwise, why would the duke keep them nearby?"

"What about tradesmen? Say, tailors?"

Jasper's eyes narrowed. "Not usually. Each lord who hosts the court would have his own on staff. I suppose a few might follow the court if they provide some special skill the duke may need, but that's rare."

"Interesting," Henry muttered absently. "If a craftsman died, what would happen to his shop, his workers?"

"Why all the interest in craftsmen?" Jasper asked.

"I'm just trying to understand how things work here in Brittany. The people at court, and all that."

"Ah." His uncle leaned back. "It would depend. If he had children, it would pass to them. If not, a male relative. Barring that, a wife could inherit, but there would need to be some special condition. A will, a ducal writ, a contract, or an ecclesiastical decree."

"So it is possible for a woman to inherit a tailor shop?"

Jasper snapped his fingers. "A girl."

"What? No…" When the smile spread across his uncle's face, Henry surrendered. Perhaps Jasper knew something of her family. He'd need merchant connections to equip an army, wouldn't he? "Yes. Jehane de Rousson, a tailor from Vannes. A widow."

Jasper stroked his chin, but after a moment, he merely shrugged. Henry tried to hide his disappointment.

"Better a widow than a girl intent on a marriage you can't deliver. You'll have time for wooing, at least. The duke will stay in Nantes all autumn. That means festivals, dinners, balls, maybe a joust."

Henry could imagine himself rushing headlong in full armor, with Jehane worrying from the seats. No, she'd be relegated to the railings. But that would be a much better place to see him unhorse his opponent. The breath caught in her throat, the shower of kisses when he stood victorious—or even better, her careful attention to his wounds if he lost.

"If only we hadn't left your courser in Tenby," Henry mused.

Jasper barked a laugh, but Henry didn't hear him. He was already debating the best way to convince Jehane to speak to him again.

# CHAPTER FOUR

## HENRY

HENRY ACCOMPANIED JASPER to his private interviews over the next several days. Each man they visited greeted them as earls and expressed sympathy for their plight but offered no tangible assistance. After a few meetings, Henry noticed a trend in his uncle's behavior.

"You talk about their families and lands but never about contributing to our purpose. Why don't you ask for support directly?"

"How many times could I ask you for money before you'd start avoiding me?" Jasper yanked on a fold of his houppelande in frustration. "If they won't support us now, nagging only guarantees they never will."

Henry's obligations as an exiled earl denied him the chance to apologize to Jehane at the duke's St. Bartholomew's feast. She met his eyes only once early in the evening before ignoring him for the rest of the night. Forced to sit with a Breton family Jasper hoped to impress, Henry watched helplessly while Jehane admired the doublets of endless courtiers.

He was certain she did it to spite him. Consumed by jealousy, he nearly severed a finger while carving a haunch of roasted pig. He was fortunate, both for the mildness of the wound and the pain that interrupted his obsessive thoughts.

Jasper had insisted time would cool her anger, but Henry felt only his own anxiety. How could he endure court if he was forced to watch her fawn over arrogant Breton lords?

His chance to speak with her came four days later during St. Augustine's feast. Few lords took notice of his entrance into the sweltering hall. The scent of fish and a fragrant beef stew rested heavily on the air. The aromatic dishes had probably been selected specifically to counteract so many nobles sweating in their layers of brocade.

Jasper was standing near a window with Quelennec and a St. Malo port official. Though his uncle beckoned for him to join them, Henry ignored the summons. He had spent the previous two weeks obeying Jasper, but now he had to address greater concerns than an invasion of England.

He searched for Jehane's face among the passing women until her found her. She wore a black dress with a gold gown peeking out from the joints. She could change her hair and wear a gaudy, four-layered dress and he'd still recognize her; her image had haunted him for weeks.

The crowd's chatter and the occasional barks of laughter faded.

Ambling between clusters of courtiers, he circled to her left, hoping she would catch sight of him. But when she turned in his direction, it was only to greet a passing friend. He was close enough to hear her laughter as she placed a hand on her companion's sleeve.

His sliding feet stubbed against something hard, and he fell forward, crashing into a nearby courtier with a loud grunt.

"Hell's hounds!" a young man cried in a low tenor. "Watch yourself, cur. Do you know who I am?"

Henry had no clue who he was. Few men in Brittany outranked an earl, and this boy was not one of them. But, Henry noticed the young woman standing nearby and recognized indignant posturing when he heard it.

Having more important concerns than quibbling with an arrogant lordling, Henry fell into a low bow. "I do indeed recognize you, sir, and beg pardon for my rudeness."

Mollified, the young man raised his chin and offered a curt nod before turning back to his companion, muttering something about inconsiderate youths.

When he turned back, Jehane was watching him with a pinched expression. Taking his chance, he gestured to the large windows facing the courtyard. She spared a glance for her companion before drawing off toward it.

Henry darted through the shifting mob. Many of the nobles had clustered beneath the chandeliers, but the open balconies running along the second floor blocked out some of the light, casting the colonnade beneath them in long shadows. Only the light of the moon, cascading through the windows, overcame them. His hands started to shake in nervous anticipation.

Jehane stood by one of those windows, with the pale moonlight casting her figure in a wash of white light and shadow. She looked almost angelic.

Remembering her temper, he needed a moment to find his voice. "My lady."

"*Lady*, now?" She arched an eyebrow. "I'm honored to have risen in your esteem so quickly."

The edge of annoyance was too much for him after a week of torment. "I'm such a fool."

She snorted. "That's one way of putting it."

Her reaction was hardly encouraging, but at least she had agreed to speak to him. "I'm very sorry for my insult. I didn't mean—" He sighed, forgetting all his careful words. "That night, I meant to say the other girls looked so very desperate. They fawned over every young noble. They barely fit in their dresses. Parts of them didn't."

Her eyes softened, but she studied him carefully. He welcomed the scrutiny as a necessary step toward her forgiveness, even as the hammering in his chest began to frighten him.

"When I first came to Brittany," he continued, "I was like them. I thought this would be a grand adventure. But most of the people I knew in England are dead now, and my uncle and I are hunted. In your eyes, I saw depths, the experience of life. You had this intensity about you that sets you apart." He swallowed. "I didn't know about your husband. I'm sorry for your loss."

"Thank you." She smiled, but her eyes were pensive. "I never thought to be complimented for my lost innocence."

The window was pointing north, to England. He turned to gaze out toward home. "I prefer to think of it as having the strength to continue on despite hardship."

He could feel her studying him. "I think I like that better, too." Gone was her animosity from the other night. "You're thoughtful. I didn't expect that from your reputation."

Given the opening, he grinned. "But still a fool?"

A chain of light laughter escaped from a place high in her throat. The sound soothed his racing heartbeat. "Yes, a fool. But not quite as arrogant as I thought."

He swallowed. "And I don't look down my nose at you. That one was hurtful." He sighed. "I'm an exile with nothing. You're by far my superior."

A mischievous smile tugged at her mouth. "Now *that* is a much better way to compliment a woman. I see you can be taught."

His response was immediate. "I pledge never to be so tongue-tied again."

She gasped. "Are you saying I no longer leave you speechless?" Her bright smile uncoiled the knot in his stomach.

His eyes were moving across her shoulders, her chest, her waist, before he could control himself. "I wouldn't say that."

A crash sounded across the room, followed by laughter a few seconds later. The wine had gone to someone's head.

"Will you walk with me?" He gestured down the hall.

"I'd be delighted." She took his offered arm.

A faint breeze carried cool air through the windows, offering blessed relief from the stifling heat in the hall. Yet, even through the fabric of his doublet, his arm tingled from the warmth of her hand.

"A beautiful night, isn't it?"

Jehane smiled and glanced up at the moonlit sky. "On nights like these at home, you can see for miles. The moonlight reflects off the waves and breaks into a thousand tiny lights."

Her words let him picture it. He hadn't seen the water in years. "Home is Vannes?"

She tilted her head. "It is now, but I meant St. Malo, where I was born. It's a port town, nothing like Nantes. My sister and I would sneak away to watch the ships unload. Merchant caravels, Venetian galleys, Dutch cogs… We'd guess what was in the crates and where they came from."

"And your father is a tailor, as well?"

"He's the largest cloth merchant in the north." Her voice swelled with pride. "Trading with the Dutch made him very successful, but it requires him to watch events at court. That's why I'm here."

Henry grimaced. "I'm sorry, I don't understand."

She smiled faintly. "International trade is risky. A war or embargo with the Dutch, French, or English could isolate him from the Channel and ruin him. At court, he can learn about trouble soon enough to sell his contracts, perhaps even to a competitor, before they become worthless. But he needs to run his business, so I attend for him."

A similar reasoning motivated nobles in England. "You said it serves your interests?"

She nodded quickly. "My husband specialized in men's clothing. Doublets, hose. I'm expanding to dressmaking. Here at court, I can see the latest fashions and materials. And if I make connections and gain new customers, all the better."

He remembered when she'd felt the sleeves of the other young nobles. Perhaps that had simply been professional curiosity.

She accompanied him through the doors leading into the

courtyard. "I'm sure it's terribly boring listening to me prattle on about business."

"No, I'm genuinely curious. The kind of life you describe is new to me." When she raised an eyebrow, he explained further. "The past five years, I've been a guest of one Breton lord after another. Ten years before that, I was locked up in English castles while my uncle made trouble for Edward. I'd talk with the castle blacksmith, stable master, and servants, but they were all part of my keeper's household, not proper tradesmen." He smiled faintly. "My jailor planned to marry me to his daughter, so I did spend some time with her."

"Another of those silly girls in pretty dresses?"

She'd been a sweet girl and a genuine friend. "Well, I was a silly boy."

Jehane lowered her eyes to find her footing on the cobblestone path. "What changed?"

Whether she meant his situation or personality, the answer was the same. "King Henry was restored, the Yorkists were thrown out, and I came to court. Suddenly, I was free. I could see my mother and uncle for the first time in a decade. It was wonderful." He swallowed. "For six months. Then, I lost it all."

"I'm so sorry."

He smiled to acknowledge the kind words. "I do sometimes wish for memories of a home like you describe."

They continued to walk toward a pair of guards flanking an ornate stone gate.

Her hand tightened on his arm. "Where are we going?"

"I thought we might view the gardens."

Nantes hadn't been attacked for decades, and some nature-loving duke had damned up the moat and filled the wide trench with the finest garden paths Henry had ever seen. In an emergency, the moat could be flooded with the nearby river, but he couldn't fathom the loss of such beautiful paths.

"We can't." She clasped his arm. "It's forbidden to any but the ducal household. We'd be banished from court."

"My uncle and I are the duke's wards, and you're my guest."

Her hands continued to tremble as they passed the guard flanking the outer gate. She stumbled when they descended the ramp leading to the gardens, and Henry held her waist tightly to keep her on her feet. Steadying herself, she brushed her hand down his shoulder, sending a surge of delight across his body.

He met her eyes. She had felt it too. He fought the urge to kiss her. That would be unseemly—roguish, even.

She broke the connection, turning instead to the delicately shaped shrubs flanking the path. In areas, the grass popped up between the cobbles. Whole sections of the path were covered in the dark canopy of wide branches from drooping trees. Henry guided her toward a torch near a stone bench in the distance.

"Beautiful." She sighed through an exhaled breath.

Henry had to agree. "Being a ward does have some advantages." Movement in the distance alarmed him, but it was only a ducal guard.

Seating herself on the bench, Jehane meticulously arranged the folds of her beautiful gown. Henry wondered if she'd designed it herself.

Once he was confident she had finished, he took his place beside her.

"Lord Tudor—"

He raised a hand. "With you, I'm just Henry."

The torchlight illuminated her smile. "Very well, then. Henry."

The sound of his name on her lips entranced him with a wave of excitement. He was glad of the relative darkness, for it hid the childish grin quickly spreading across his face.

"When you think of home, what do you imagine?" she asked.

All he remembered of the days before his wardship with the Herberts were a few brief images—his mother stuffing the blanket around his body and kissing him goodnight, the feel of the gnarled hardwood banister in her castle, a memory of chasing chickens in someone's manor farmhouse. The few months of King Henry's second reign hadn't even seemed real, except for his uncle's lessons.

"They say home is where you feel safe," he answered carefully. "But everything I had was taken from me. So many people think a fief is the solution to all their problems. They imagine the lands and positions. But they never think about the fragile desperation and whispering alliances. It can all vanish, even if you satisfy your obligations and serve your king."

He met her eyes. "When I think of home, I think of my uncle. He fights so hard for a life I barely remember, even when the rest of the world has abandoned him. He's a pennant stiffened by the wind. He gives me my bearing when I'd have lost it years ago."

"You must love him dearly."

His lip curled up. "I suppose I do. My father died before I was born, and my uncle pledged to protect me. He kept his word. Of all the Lancastrian nobles, we're virtually the last ones left."

She pressed her lips together and studied him. "I've met plenty of men who speak passionately about hatred of the French, or the beauty of a woman they want to bed." Jehane took his hand. "But rarely do I meet someone who speaks about an uncle's love."

The tender comfort of her fingers threaded through his offered a balm to a soul left weary by so many years of uncertainty. This one, perfect moment could sustain him for another five years. "Do you miss your husband?"

She lowered her eyes to her dress. "I miss his kindness. We were married only a year, but he taught me how to run the business. He was my father's age, one of his business partners. He had no family and hoped for a son to inherit his shop. But then he caught a chill one night and never recovered."

Henry had always thought commoners could marry for love, but it seemed they were as bound by duty as the nobility. "Do you think of marrying again?"

"Absolutely not."

He lowered his eyes. "I'm sorry. You must feel his loss terribly." Perhaps the brevity of his acquaintance with King Henry's court before Barnet was a blessing; he had been spared the pain of losing close friends.

"Would you think me wicked if I said I did not?" She raised a hand. "He was no mean husband, and I wished him no ill. But while maidens are subject to their fathers and wives to their husbands, as a widow, I'm free. My shop is mine by law. I direct my future. I couldn't do that with a husband." She shook her head. "I won't give that up easily."

"You've gained the freedom I desire. I envy it."

She offered an affectionate smile. "I'm glad I decided to speak to you tonight."

The thought that this night might have never happened terrified him. "Why did you? I was such a fool."

"I wasn't going to. But then I saw you give way to the man you bumped into."

He gasped. "You saw that?"

"Yes. The arrogant man I thought you to be would never have done that. I thought perhaps I was wrong about you."

A moment later, the deeper meaning lifted his anxiety. "You were watching me?"

Her cheeks dimpled in the torchlight. "I've never been so angry at someone. But to feel such passion…"

Her hand was warm and smooth when she squeezed his. Her bodice rose and fell with each rapid breath.

He felt more vulnerable and exposed than in five years of exile. That terrified him, even as her proximity exhilarated him.

Bereft of words suited to the depth of his feelings, he simply sat with her in the pale torchlight, cradling her hand and basking in the happy moment.

# HENRY

Henry's happiness only grew as autumn matured. He and Jehane strolled through the gardens after court receptions and explored Nantes, accompanied only by the ducal guards who followed him everywhere. From how she ate salmon to a story of her family hunting rats in their cloth warehouses, everything Henry learned about Jehane revealed a life strikingly different from his own.

When the obligations of her trade would not wait, Henry accompanied her during negotiations with suppliers and customer visits. She patiently explained the nuances of pricing for different sewing techniques and styles. He absorbed it all, amazed at the complexity of a trade that was supposedly beneath the attention of his class.

He even acceded to his uncle's request that he attend church as much as possible, since it offered another opportunity to be with her, even if from a distance.

She was the first person he'd met who hadn't care about his status or blood. Indeed, mention of his debatable future in England only produced a worried silence. But most of all, he loved the laughter that began deep within her chest and the smile that filled her cheeks. She had suffered as he had, and through her vibrancy, he could see a better future for himself. Her appreciation for life replaced the hollow expectation of the past five years with excitement and hope.

His confidence had risen so high that he resolved to enter the final tournament of the year in late November. He would ride one of Quelennec's stallions, use his uncle's armor, and rely on Jean de Rieux's training. Though Jehane said nothing overt, she clearly worried about how he'd fare. He couldn't blame her, nor anyone who wagered against him. It was, after all, his first joust.

Yet his interest was in participating, not dying. So as he made his rounds of Breton nobles during the pre-tournament feast, he bowed deeply and spoke politely, determined not to insult in the evening those he might face on the morrow.

Those exchanges of empty pleasantries kept Henry from Jehane for more than an hour. She had carefully chosen a pale green dress to match the tunic poking out from beneath the new, black doublet she had designed herself. She'd even offered him a discounted price.

He had thought it was too tight. Eyes sparkling with a curling grin that had reminded him of a cat with a saucer of milk, she had insisted it was perfect.

Just when he saw the chance to sneak away, his uncle ushered him to his seat for the obligatory speeches before the meal exhorting honorable combat.

"Henry, try to pay attention," Jasper whispered. "Study the words of those around you. The duke could let something slip about his negotiations with the ambassadors."

Henry tore his attention from a pair of young men seated perilously close to Jehane just long enough to notice the proximity of the English to the orating duke. They'd been creeping closer with each feast. Leaning back, arms folded over his broad belly, Stillington looked too pleased for comfort.

A restrained bubble of laughter drew his attention back to Jehane. One of the young men grinned hopefully at her reaction to his drivel. And how could she laugh at what was probably an awkward, stale muttering barely passing for wit?

Swallowing the flare of jealousy, he admitted that his doubts were at fault, not her behavior. She wouldn't encourage a hopeless suit.

When she felt the material of the courtier's doublet, Henry realized she was simply drumming up business.

Of course, he knew the cause of his unease. She was a self-reliant tradesman who could do anything she wished. Why was she spending her time with a penniless exile at the mercy of others?

He glanced at the ambassadors anxiously.

Once the half-dozen toasts praising the duke's speech concluded, a line of servants paraded the plates past the ducal table. The Tudors and Quelennec were seated close enough to smell the offerings.

Quelennec turned to him. "You'll have your work cut out for you tomorrow, Henry. I only wish I could be there to see it."

This drew his full attention. "You'd leave your prized courser in my keeping?" The thought of being solely responsible for the magnificent animal terrified him more than a collision with a lance.

But Quelennec simply laughed. "I trust you, Henry." He paused. "He's not the fastest, but he's steady, and that'll serve a novice jouster better. Only experienced jousters should use faster horses. Ride him as gently as if he was Jehane and I'll have nothing to worry about."

Henry reddened, a reaction that only widened Quelennec's grin.

Jasper furrowed his brow, ignoring the rowdy exchange. "You're leaving the city?"

The admiral studied the first dish the servants presented: thin-sliced venison with truffles. "The fleet is at Paimbœuf for the winter. I need to inspect how it fared this season." He plucked a few pieces from the communal plate. "I'm off tonight."

Rallying from his embarrassment, Henry noticed the concern in his uncle's eyes.

"The burdens of title." Jasper mustered an unconvincing smile.

"Burden, indeed. I loathe leaving the city to Landais and his cronies, but my men will watch him, just as his men watch me when he leaves to count the duke's money."

Jasper took a deep swallow of wine. Henry could smell the strength of it from where he sat. "Have the ambassadors progressed with their suit?"

Quelennec shook his head. "Not to my knowledge. If they're interested in you, Jasper, they're being very circumspect."

Henry shared a moment's relief with his uncle. After England's short war with France a year earlier, they both had expected Edward to return his attention to Brittany. But perhaps the pretender had lost interest after Jasper had failed to convince Duke Francis to fund an invasion while England's armies had been occupied in France.

As much as Edward's interest threatened him, it also encouraged the duke to maintain him with a generous stipend. While he could do without the importance, how could he survive without his only income?

He had eaten very little by the time the servants circled back to clean the tables. Quelennec only snorted when Henry wished him a safe journey. He'd travel with enough guards to scare a contingent of professional soldiers, let alone the bandits roaming Brittany's forests.

Though Jehane was still sitting beside the same young man, her interest in the conversation had clearly ended. When Henry approached, her face brightened like a blossom opening to a spring day. Gone was the uncertainty over his future. With Jehane beside him, he was luckier than Duke Francis, King Louis, and King Edward combined.

He kissed her hands. The smile on her face faltered as if she sensed his troubles. He couldn't hide anything from her.

"My dear count, will you excuse me?" she asked her companion.

The young man handled the dismissal with grace, and Henry bowed in appreciation.

The weather was too cold for a stroll; besides, the moon was only a half-crescent and not bright enough to navigate by. But the palace boasted plenty of lightly occupied corridors.

Guiding them out of the hall, Henry teased, "My dear count?"

"Why, Henry, are you jealous?"

"Jealous? No, no, of course not."

"Then I'll have to think of some other punishment for taking so long to greet me." At his surprise, she grinned. "I'm teasing you. We were discussing a doublet he wanted to order."

"I could tell." He sighed. "I'm just tired of playing the outraged noble to remind the duke and his ministers why they're spending so much on my upkeep."

Catesby, speaking with Pierre Landais nearby, faced Henry and offered a courteous bow. Though Henry thought Catesby might engage them in conversation, he and Jehane passed without interruption.

She noticed the attention, though. Once they were safely out of earshot in the corridor, she asked, "Do you have to? Remind him, I mean. Wouldn't you rather enjoy a quiet life?"

"I've dreamed of giving it all up." He sighed. "But a dream is all it can ever be. No matter what I do, I'll always be descended from French, Welsh, and English nobility. I'll always be a reminder of the murders that gave Edward his usurped crown."

Biting her lip, she slowly shook her head. "I don't understand that kind of thinking."

She had shown him her world, and he wanted to do the same. "Noble blood has a long memory, Jehane. It's not something easy for an outsider to comprehend." He paused, struggling to put this instinctive truth into words. "My mother, Edward, Duke Francis... We've lived according to our abilities. We would sooner cut off our hands than live as commoners. It's what sustained Edward when he fell from power. It's what sustains my uncle. We know the terrible sacrifices necessary for rank and position, yet we pay the price gladly. The alternative is too...small."

"But you've tolerated it for years," she insisted. "I see a good, kind man before me, not a soul-sick one."

"Only because of you, Jehane." He caressed her cheek. "I'm capable of nobler pursuits than hawking and riding as a guest of a Breton noble. Edward understands that. He's been in my position before. He'll always expect me to strike at him to reclaim my old life. Even if I ran off into the wilds of Europe, he must come for me."

"He hurt you terribly, Henry." She spoke slowly, deliberately. "But Edward isn't a demon who can see into every dark corner of Europe. You could disappear beyond his reach."

He shook his head. "I'll never really disappear. Not with my court manners, my accent, even the confidence in my eyes. Let's say we buy a bit of land and try to live quietly. Eventually, I'd come to the attention of the nearest noble. Maybe it's a dispute about boundaries or a demand for additional taxes. But it'll happen. Any lord would view me as a threat to his power or as a pawn to bargain. And I wouldn't have Francis's protection."

He inhaled a shaking breath. He'd only contemplated such concerns in private before. "The thought of standing alone before that Plantagenet rage terrifies me. I need my position, even if it forces me to scrape at Francis' feet. It's my burden and my best advantage, all at once."

"I'm sorry, Henry, I don't understand." She placed a hand on his forearm as a gesture of sympathy. "But I do know there's more to you than your birth."

"How can you know that, Jehane?" He needed the reassurance that only another could give.

She caressed his cheek. "You're a good man, kind and honest. And you accept people as they are. You're not like the other nobles."

"Oh, I'm different," he grumbled. "I'm a guest taking advantage of his host's hospitality with nothing to offer in return. No respect, an empty title—"

"Thank Jesus and all the saints for it," she interrupted. "I'd rather have the man in front of me than a greedy lord coveting me for my assets. How many English nobles spare even a moment's attention for a tailor, let alone cultivate her love? Nor would you have, if not for your past."

"Your love?" His voice wavered at those precious words. "Oh, Jehane…I…I have nothing to offer you!"

Jehane raised her hands to his cheeks and lowered his head, gently touching her lips against his. He had imagined the experience as a passionate embrace, but the feather-like touch reminded him the bond between them was a delicate thing meant to be cradled and treasured. Up came his hands to her waist, then up her back.

She lowered her lips, snuggling deeper into his embrace. "You truly are a fool sometimes, Henry." He'd heard those words a hundred times, uttered by Lady Herbert or Madame de Rieux to their children and servants. Now, they were filled with tenderness. "The events of your life—even your dispossession and exile—brought me the man I love. I can't condemn them, and neither should you. We're here together. That's cause enough for joy."

As an earl, his future involved a political marriage to a dull girl, conspiracy, and endless worry. The rest of his squandered hours would be spent in loneliness, lacking companions who weren't interested in exploiting his affection for their own benefit.

But with her, he was just a man. And his worth to her wasn't in his wealth, his protection, or his name. She had what she needed. It was his heart she valued, a heart that would love her the way she wanted.

"So stop sulking, my dear Henry, and indulge a young lady's desire to dance." She raised an eyebrow. "Unless you'd rather be the arrogant and lonely Earl of Richmond?"

Following her back into the hall, Henry encircled her hand in his and met her smile with one of his own.

Later that night, with the exchange of their tender affection fresh in their minds, they made love. He held her in his arms, feeling her chest rise and fall with her excited breaths. He rejoiced in their closeness, yearning to leap into her soul. She was a fire that would encircle him, yet leave him unconsumed. He could never let her go.

"Stay with me, Jehane," he whispered just before they nodded off to sleep, still entangled. "I'm home."

## HENRY

Jasper pushed aside the flap of the tent assigned to Henry for the tournament. "It's William Catesby." He spared a glance for the ducal guard watching Henry. "I imagine Landais thinks a tilt between the exile and the ambassador would please the crowd."

Balancing himself on the shoulder of the servant helping him into his armor, Henry frowned at the news. "I'll have to lose."

"You'll do no such thing." Jasper leveled a frightful gaze upon him. "This arrogant, grasping upstart fights in the name of your king's murderer. You're going to teach him his place."

Henry waved the servant away from his adjustments and turned his full attention to his uncle. "He's the English ambassador. He'll already be insulted at facing an exile. You want me to compound it by beating him? At best, I'll only attract Edward's attention. At worst, Catesby will convince Francis to repatriate me."

"Francis won't release us to that man," Jasper insisted. "He swore an oath."

Henry fell silent. A ruling duke might renege on vague promises but never a solemn oath. Doing so would call every agreement into question, including those with his nobles.

Still, Henry had an ominous sense that defeating Catesby would turn Edward's eye to him. "You assume I can win. He's a veteran and I've never jousted before."

"Focus on the basics. Expect to be hit. Ride smoothly. Make small corrections. Cradle your lance against your body. Don't force it into your opponent, let him ride into you." Jasper offered a reassuring smile. "Your cause is just, you've practiced with Marshal de Rieux, and you have the finest equipment in Brittany. You will win." After clasping Henry about the shoulders, Jasper ducked through the tent flap.

The salutation gave him no peace. As his servant led him to his waiting charger, chewing on hay at its post outside Henry's tent, he weighed his options. He had entered this tournament to prove his worth, not to lose. Jasper was right that defeating a Yorkist would justify his ducal stipend. It might even enable their release to France. So many possibilities relied upon an enhanced reputation.

But those possibilities would all lead Henry away from Jehane and the Breton court: more time occupied with negotiation and travel through Brittany, perhaps even France. And that Plantagenet eye turned toward him... He had been honest with Jehane about his fears. Jasper might be content spending his life arguing matters of honor and nurturing grudges, but Henry was happy with the life he had.

He had to let Catesby win.

The servant guided Henry and his horse down the dirt path running between the knights' tents and the lists. Henry bobbed up and down, balancing his lance on his sabaton. Though it had rained through the early hours of the morning, the boy—one of Quelennec's, of course—could tell puddles of rainwater from horse piss and piles of mud from dung. Every few steps, he danced around a section of the path with the grace of an acrobat.

The competitors entered the lists through a temporary gap in the railing. When Henry entered the tiltyard, the spectators offered a polite round of applause stemming more from curiosity than support. The court was watching him.

His heart began beating faster.

Henry's horse trotted forward along the railing, a familiar route Quelennec had no doubt ridden many times. His progress carried him past the ducal family before he realized he was expected to bow respectfully.

As promised, Jehane was waiting for him in the blue-on-blue dress from their first meeting. Of course, he would lose. He would do nothing to threaten his time with her.

She smiled at him, just as she'd done the previous night. But instead of kissing him, she silently reached up and pulled his lance down. When she released it, he stared. Wrapped around the tip was a silk ribbon that matched her dress.

She had left him with something much greater than a simple kiss: her favor. Eyes widening, Henry very nearly lost his grip on the reins.

When he lost, he would shame her.

Henry maneuvered his horse into position without remembering having done so. Across the yard, Catesby saluted him with a raised lance, and Henry did the same. His servant placed his helmet in his free hand.

"Thank you, Girard," Henry muttered before positioning it over his head, thankful that the closed visor would hide his sudden panic.

The court had seen him dote on her and would now assume their time together involved more than just conversation. But she had bestowed her favor regardless of the message it sent.

He could not shame that gesture. He must try to win.

So, when the groom between the riders lowered the flag, Henry stiffened his determination, kicked his horse into a gallop, and pointed his lance straight and true.

Catesby's wild horse bolted forward, yet its rider easily controlled the speed and kept his lance slightly elevated.

Henry muttered his uncle's warning aloud. "I will be hit." He couldn't allow anything Catesby did to affect his own performance.

As his horse hit its stride, he tried to remain balanced and steady his breathing. His legs were clenching his mount's back too tightly, so he loosened them enough to allow his body to absorb the shock of the gallop.

Within ten strides, Henry began gradually lowering his lance to shoulder level. Too fast, and he'd be chasing his target the whole way. In his mind, his uncle's voice screamed for him to aim for where Catesby would be, not where he was.

At the last moment, Henry leaned forward and angled his lance. Catesby was aiming for his upper shoulder just near his neck—a difficult target that would cause a devastating blow if well-aimed. He had to deliver a similarly devastating blow, so he clenched to weld lance, rider, and horse into a single, charging object.

The hammer blow of their collision forced a grunt from Henry. Catesby had over-compensated for Henry's leaning forward, and his strike had rolled off.

Henry's lance struck the ambassador squarely, right in the crevice between his neck guard and shoulder. The tip tore cleanly off without splintering. Recovering from the collision, Henry looked up at it in frustration. He thought he'd placed it perfectly.

When he reached the other side of the list, he turned back. Catesby was lying on the ground with his back and helmet caked in mud.

An unhorsing…on his first ride!

The court erupted into applause. More than a few courtiers pointed in surprise. Henry raised his lance to acknowledge their acclaim.

But, perhaps there was still time to prevent further damage. Cantering over to the downed knight, he lowered himself to the ground, feeling the ache in his shoulder from the blow as he did. With a hand beneath the ambassador's arm, he helped a servant lift his opponent to his feet.

"Well met, Sir Catesby. You are a skilled competitor and struck true."

Catesby studied Henry with an unsettling expression. For a moment, Henry expected the ambassador to spit at him.

But after a cleansing breath, Catesby extended his hand. In it was the broken tip of Henry's lance, with Jehane's favor still attached to it.

"Perhaps the love of a beautiful woman made all the difference, Lord Tudor."

Accepting the favor, Henry held it within his mailed palm. Catesby had spoken true. A simple strip of cloth had changed his fate.

# CHAPTER FIVE

## HENRY

THE JOUST INSPIRED an official summons from the duke five days later. Henry had met Francis only once this season, during an audience that had lasted only a few minutes. While this latest audience probably presaged a fatter stipend, Henry's thumb itched, an ill omen.

The year's first winter chill had descended upon the capital. Philippe de Rieux warned that the castle would stay cold until the servants scrubbed a year's neglect from the fireplaces. The temperature forced Henry to spend the paltry remainder of his yearly stipend on a quilted houppelande originally made for a count who had defaulted on his order. Fortunately, Francis valued Henry's title, not his fashion sense.

The servants pushed aside the heavy oak doors of the duke's audience chamber. One of them beckoned him forward with a reverent nod. That was also a change from a week before.

Rising, Henry straightened the lay of his clothing. When he walked through the doors, he would be Henry Tudor, Earl of Richmond, ordained by his birth and anointed under the eyes of God.

At least he'd be spared the scrutiny of the court during this private audience.

Only now did Henry recognize how much his title meant to him.

It was the last piece of his father, a warm blanket that had encircled him, even during the Herbert years. A day earlier, he'd been afraid of offending Francis or facing Edward. Now, he wished he could settle this matter with the pretender without another moment's delay.

But Edward wasn't awaiting him. Nor was Duke Francis.

Instead, a group of nobles—too few to be the entire council—surrounded the empty throne, with the English ambassadors standing off to the side. Catesby, whose forehead and cheek bore the half-healed marks of his rough landing, seemed tense.

Landais approached with arms outstretched when Henry took a few tentative steps into the chamber. "Earl Richmond, we are honored to receive you."

Francis would not be coming.

Belatedly, Henry studied his surroundings. Around the perimeter, the duke's private guards stood motionless. Henry felt their presence like a heavy hand on his shoulder.

His mouth had suddenly gone dry. "Seigneur Landais. The messenger reported that His Grace requested my presence."

A few of the nobles murmured until Landais shot them a hostile gaze.

"Unfortunately, Duke Francis has taken ill, and cannot attend." He paused long enough for a breath but not an interruption. "We, as his council, are empowered to handle the duke's business until he is fit to resume his duties."

They were watching him with a scrutiny bordering on suspicion. The shifting of weight from one foot to another, the nervous rubbing of hands or scratching of noses… This meeting was about more than a casual inquiry into his health.

By comparison, the English seemed calm.

He cleared his throat. "I remain in Nantes at the duke's pleasure. I'm content to wait until he has recovered."

Landais drew his lips into a strained smile. "Certain matters are too important to be delayed until the duke's mind is strong enough to address them."

Henry could hear the beating of his heart in his chest. How could no one else hear it? "What matters are those?"

"The disagreement between yourself and King Edward, as well as our very serious concerns for your safety."

Repatriation. Henry's mind slid into ruthless clarity.

Stillington raised his chin to project his voice. "My king is saddened by the persistence of old hostilities and longs to welcome all his subjects back to England in honor. He desires nothing more than the mending of old wounds so he may direct his full attention against France, our mutual threat."

"My uncle and I have heard these assurances before," Henry noted, "when Edward returned to depose King Henry with an army of Burgundians. What followed was the brutal execution of the prince and many other nobles."

Stillington shook his head. "After a hard-fought civil war, those actions seemed necessary. His Majesty desired to secure the prosperity of England."

Always before, Edward had blamed his brother George for the prince's murder. He had never before personally accepted responsibility. That shift seemed…ominous.

"We remind you that Henry Plantagenet also committed egregious crimes to maintain his throne." Stillington folded his arms over his belly. "But His Majesty now regrets those decisions. As king, his responsibility is to heal his country. He wishes to reconcile with those who loyally served the last king. It pains the king that the former Earl of Oxford elected imprisonment to *rapprochement*."

Henry lowered his head to conceal his surprise. Had his mother been correct, after all? Could his uncle's interpretation of Oxford's imprisonment and their continued exile merely reflect his own hostility and not the king's animosity? Surely, Edward's ambassadors wouldn't openly lie to a foreign court. Deceit would threaten Edward's alliance with Brittany, his only staging ground for an invasion of France.

Was it more reasonable that Edward wished to solidify his rule before his children came of age or that he would hunt down his enemies regardless of the damage to his realm and international reputation? Despite his faults, Edward was no fool.

"The ambassadors have presented an interesting offer to us, Lord Tudor," Landais prompted.

Catesby strode forward, addressing the council as much as Henry. "His Majesty respects Duke Francis' concern for his guest's safety. Surely, no prince in Europe deserves his afflictions less than Duke Francis. King Edward yearns for the day that his brother might recognize him again."

From the sound of it, the duke suffered a malady of the mind. Why hadn't Henry heard rumors of mental instability before?

Catesby continued, "His Majesty regularly discusses your situation with your mother and wishes to prove his love for you once and for all."

At least his mother's efforts had borne more fruit than his uncle's. But why now, after five years? "In what way might King Edward"—he carefully inserted the proper title—"prove his affection?"

"The king and your mother have agreed to a marriage between you and whichever of his unmarried daughters you find most agreeable," Landais explained. "Rightly, your mother expressed concern over your uncertain status. King Edward has agreed to restore your former title, along with suitable lands to maintain a princess of England in proper state."

A royal marriage. Though the pretender had anchored himself to political enemies through marriage in the past, he'd always used the queen's relatives, not his daughters. Naturally, Henry's choice would be Elizabeth, Edward's eldest. As part of the royal family, he might even persuade Edward to reverse Jasper's attainder, given enough time.

One thing was certain: this offer must have preceded the joust. A message from England would have taken weeks, plus time for negotiation. His victory over Catesby hadn't threatened his status, after all.

And then, as the shock of the offer began to fade, he remembered Jehane.

While Edward lived, Henry would likely never be permitted to leave England. Would Jehane make the crossing? Her business, her life, was here in Brittany. Though she hadn't desired marriage, would she really accept being the mistress of a married man?

Even if she did, how could he spend time with her, under so many hostile eyes? The daughter of Edward Plantagenet wouldn't be satisfied with an unfaithful husband. How long would it be before she offered proof of imaginary treasons to avenge herself on him?

He would lose Jehane forever. Yet this might be his only honorable opportunity to ever return home. Refusing could anger both Edward and Francis, and only Francis' oath prevented them from concluding a private arrangement.

"The Duke of Clarence currently holds Richmond," Henry reminded. "How can I recover my former title while another holds it?"

Stillington waved his hand. "King Edward will compensate his brother for the loss of those lands, and a duke has no need for an inferior title."

George would likely strip the lands of portable wealth before handing them over. Impoverished lands, a hollow bequest… It held the ring of truth for a reconciled enemy. Edward wouldn't empower someone he didn't trust.

"A most generous offer. How can I be certain it's genuine?"

Neither ambassador seemed outraged by his suspicion. "This scroll from His Majesty details the terms." Catesby handed him a curled parchment with a complicated seal. "You'll find everything in order, including plans for the presentation of his daughters for your perusal, proposed dates for your restoration and marriage, and provision for expressing his thanks to Duke Francis for his long care for your person."

Henry forced a casual tone. "Provision for Duke Francis?"

"Four thousand English archers to preserve the independence of Brittany against the depredations of France." Turning to Landais, Catesby added, "His Majesty wishes to prove his serious dedication to both Richmond's restoration and the Breton alliance he holds so dear."

"The Archbishop of Canterbury has also written." Stillington raised a second scroll. "He affirms the king's oath before God to conclude this marriage in good faith." After a moment, he added, "I can confirm the authenticity of the seal."

So, the cost of Breton assent was four thousand archers. It was beginning to look like Francis wasn't mad, after all, only avoiding responsibility for handing Henry to the English. That possibility was troubling.

If he had paid more attention to Jasper's conversations with the Breton nobles, perhaps he'd know how to respond without giving offense. Jasper had warned against trusting promises, but Edward was offering something tangible: his own daughter.

It was all happening too fast. He needed time. "I will need time to review the offer in more detail."

"Of course, of course," Landais pledged. "You can review it at your leisure on your way to England."

Landais' words struck Henry like a cold Breton wind. The change that had overcome him in the corridor had been irrelevant. His fate had been sealed long before he'd entered this room.

But he had changed, and the new Henry was formed from the passion of an exile and the dignity of a noble. "I surely will, when that time comes. I'm pleased to know Brittany endorses the offer. I'm certain that, after consulting with my uncle and mother, I will be pleased to accept. God willing, I will return home early next year."

Landais met Stillington's eyes and licked his lips. "Why would you consult with them?"

Catesby furrowed his eyebrows ever so slightly; Henry only noticed it because the wounds on his forehead shifted.

"To confirm the validity of the offer and seek their experienced counsel."

"As to the former, the bishop and this council have both recognized the king's seal. And the Archbishop of Canterbury, God's highest representative in England, recounted King Edward's oath. Do you doubt the word of such esteemed and venerable men?"

Naturally, he doubted it. Edward had never before offered such generous terms. And Canterbury and Stillington owed their positions to the Plantagenets. Henry now began to understand why only a fraction of the council was present. Landais had gathered only those who would support him.

Yet, if it were genuine… "What is Duke Francis' opinion on the matter?"

One noble shot a nervous glance at Landais. Even before the treasurer responded, Henry knew it would be a lie.

"Duke Francis did not have time to consider this matter before his affliction struck. Seeing an opportunity to achieve a happy reunion of his ward, honor our English alliance, and strengthen ourselves against France, we have concluded this arrangement." There was the truth slipping out: they were informing him of his fate, not presenting an offer. "No loyal subject could refuse such a reasonable offer. We have already arranged passage to England. You will leave immediately."

Behind the assembly, metal struck metal as the ducal guards shifted, probably preparing for action.

Inhaling stiffened Henry's posture. "I must gather my possessions." Somehow, he had to get word to Jehane.

Landais waved a hand. "That won't be necessary. Your possessions were purchased with ducal funds and will remain in Brittany for His Grace's use. The king will provide for your needs until your holdings are restored. Riders are assembling to escort you to St. Malo, from where you will finally return home after so long away."

"Congratulations, Lord Tudor." Catesby clasped Henry's forearm in a strong greeting. His wooden smile filled Henry with unease. "I should say, Earl Richmond. Finally, this long ordeal is over."

Henry knew better than to believe his words. It was only beginning, and he would have to face it without the woman he loved or the uncle he trusted.

## JASPER

Half an hour after the lad's meeting with the duke, Jasper lost patience and went looking for his nephew, with his ducal guards falling into step behind him. However, he found no sign of Henry's escort near either his room or the audience chamber. Jasper sighed and trudged toward Jehane's townhouse.

Surely, the boy knew he'd worry. These meetings were important, even if Henry couldn't see it. Though Jasper could sympathize with his nephew's infatuation, Henry should have at least updated him before running off to that woman.

Though not large, her house had a back entrance that would make it impossible for the ducal guards to watch Henry from outside. Jasper wasn't surprised to find the front door unattended.

Jehane answered with a curtsey. "Lord Tudor. To what do I owe the pleasure of this visit?"

"My nephew had an audience today, and I much desire to know the results. Please call him forth."

"He told me as much." Of course, he did. "But I haven't seen him since early this morning." Her cheeks dimpled into a faint grin. "I'm surprised my home is the first place you'd search for him."

Jasper frowned. "I was sure he'd be here." Where could the boy be, if not with his lover? "You haven't seen him since the audience?"

"No." Her eyebrows creased. "Is that worrying?"

"Yes, it is." He hadn't passed Henry or his escort between his room and the audience chamber. "If you see him, tell him to return to his room immediately."

"My maid can do that," Jehane said. "I'm coming with you."

"That's not necessary."

"Your concern has made me concerned. I may be of some help."

"I don't see how." Jasper nonetheless stepped aside for her to join him.

"Then perhaps I can educate you," she countered with an edge of annoyance. After relaying instructions to her maid, she fell into step beside Jasper on the walk back to the château.

The weather had turned cold, but the brisk walk warmed him. Beside him, Jehane shivered.

"You really didn't need to come."

She eyed him. "Is there some reason you don't want me here?"

It was best to discuss this now. "That depends on what you expect from my nephew."

She halted. "Pardon me?"

He stopped a step later. "He can never marry you. You must understand this."

Emotions crossed her face in a surprisingly quick succession. Disbelief, outrage, anger, and finally…amusement? "Because he's an earl and I'm a tailor?"

"Yes."

She shook her head. "Perhaps it is best he spent only six months with you in England, if that's your opinion."

"Excuse me?" He scoffed. "That is not your business."

"No, my business is tailoring." She crossed her arms. "Allow me to disabuse you of your fears. I have no intention of marrying your nephew."

His eyes widened. "But…he bore your favor at the joust. I thought—"

"I spend time with your nephew because he pleases me."

"He pleases you?" Jasper grunted. "He's an earl."

"A fact I choose to overlook." She paused for a moment, after which her voice had calmed. "He is a good, kind man. I have his company and his heart. That's all I desire."

Jasper fell silent. Every woman at court hungered after title and luxury. It was how they assured their security and prosperity. Jehane was a mystery he didn't understand.

"Now, unless you wish to insult me further, we should find my Henry." Emphasizing the last few words, she trudged forward through the château gates without waiting for a reply.

Jasper matched her rapid pace through the corridors. "I thought you meant to ensnare my nephew."

"Is that an apology for your arrogance?"

This time, he bit back his irritation. "Perhaps."

She curtseyed to a passing lord. "I don't want marriage, but nor do I wish to be alone. I love him, but have no desire for a master."

Jasper never had the chance to respond. They rounded the corner to discover Henry's door half-open and unguarded. Skin tingling with warning, Jasper pushed through the portal.

Inside, a servant was rummaging through the oak cabinet beside Henry's bed.

"Explain yourself!"

The man poked his head out from behind the wooden door. Recognizing Jasper, he bowed. "Lord Pembroke." He straightened. "I was instructed to inventory the contents of this room."

"By whom?" This was unprecedented. He'd have someone flogged for this insult.

"By Lord Landais." His eyes darted toward the door. "He directed me here specifically, said I was to catalog these possessions since Earl Richmond has no further need of them."

"No further need of them?" Jehane shouted with an intensity that far outmatched a battlefield commander. "Where has Earl Richmond gone?"

Possibilities rolled through Jasper's mind: an assassin's blade flashing in the candlelight, the young man insulting some hotheaded noble.

No, if that were the case, the court would've been tittering about a duel or a scandal.

"To England, *mademoiselle*."

"Impossible!" Jasper's cry carried more certainty than he felt. He recalled how pleased the English ambassadors had looked the previous night. "If that were true, I'd know of it."

"M-my lord, 'tis true. I swear."

He had failed. He had even begun to believe arriving in Brittany had been a blessing in disguise. But, despite so many years spent cultivating men like Quelennec who recognized the value the Tudors offered, he had broken his oath to Margaret.

"England…" As he uttered the word, his resolve hardened. Henry's audience had begun an hour earlier. Even with horses waiting, they couldn't have gotten very far, and that assumed they would trust Henry with a horse. More likely, they'd use a slower carriage to keep him under control.

Jehane tenderly took the man's hands. "Tell me what happened."

The man knew only the basic details of the marriage offer, but that was enough to terrify Jasper.

He ran his hands through his hair. The ambassadors were certainly lying. Edward's men could have easily found the archbishop's discarded seal. Stillington was Edward's creature. And the way Landais had excluded Quelennec's supporters…

Most concerning was Duke Francis' absence. A timely bout of madness would neatly exonerate him for violating his oath of protection.

But none of that mattered if Henry's head adorned London Bridge.


## JEHANE

Gone. Her Henry was gone forever! All hope deserted her, replaced by a hollow agony as the tears fell.

Jehane hadn't expected to feel this way about someone, not so soon. In fact, not ever again. The past few months had been a dream.

Of course, she knew he could be restored at any time. But she hadn't been prepared. She had expected to have more time.

Everywhere her eyes fell, she recalled memories of their time together. That bed, oh, that bed and its delights. He had whispered that just being with her filled him with all the happiness he could ever imagine. She had believed him.

By the cabinet, she remembered his adorable fussiness when she had tried to stow his doublet. He had always kept one and a pair of boots beside his bed in case of trouble.

But now, he was off to marry some silly girl whom he hadn't even met.

As suddenly as they began, the tears stopped. Something seemed wrong with this room, and not just the open door. Wiping her nose on her sleeve, she scrutinized it further.

The cabinet door was ajar, and his clothes were still hanging within. Retrieving one of the doublets, she could swear it had been on the floor the night before when she had reached for her gown.

His desk still held the sealing wax, quill, and parchment. He wrote constantly to his mother and the sons of the men he'd stayed with over the years. He was always working on something. He'd never leave without his quill.

The sword he had brought to Brittany all those years ago was sitting partially unsheathed on the bed. The blade had rusted years earlier, yet only she had known that. He had carefully avoided duels through these long years.

Henry hadn't been back to this room.

Her mouth fell open in a silent gasp. "He didn't leave willingly."

"What?" Jasper turned on her with a desperation bordering on panic.

"He was taken from Nantes against his will." At least she could comfort herself that he hadn't hidden his departure from her. But, oh…what did it matter?

"How do you know?"

She gestured around the room. "He didn't bring any of his things. This was done quickly."

"Edward will kill him."

"Why now?" She frowned. "The ambassadors have been here for months. Why do this now?"

Jasper's eyes widened. "Landais had to act while Quelennec was gone."

"Why would that matter?"

"Quelennec opposes repatriation. We provide leverage to maintain English support for Brittany. If the support stops, Duke Francis can finance our rebellion against Edward. If we're repatriated, that support will go away as well. But Landais thinks it's too dangerous."

She nodded and fell silent. "Could the duke change his mind and recall them?"

Jasper sat on Henry's bed, slumping forward. "He could, but I'll never get an audience."

"Who would?"

"Quelennec, but he's in Paimbœuf reviewing the navy. I can't get to him because of my escort."

At this time of year, the galleys would be making their way to Spain and Portugal, fleeing the winter squalls that could damage their hulls. Perhaps, if she were lucky, the ambassadors would have to wait for a suitable ship bound for England. There was a chance.

"I can retrieve this Quelennec."

"What?" Despite his cry, Jasper's voice carried excitement.

"You can't leave the city. I can. Paimbœuf is on the way to Vannes, beside the Loire. I know the route well."

"He won't see you," Jasper insisted.

She pointed to the desk. "Write me a letter of introduction."

"You'll never make it. A carriage is too slow."

She smirked. "Who said anything about a carriage?"

His eyes widened. "You ride?"

"Of course, I ride." She sighed. "God's blood, you really are naïve. My father is richer than many nobles, and a stable is a minor expense."

He was already crossing to the desk. "You would do this for me? Even after what I said?" He dipped the pen in ink and began writing.

"I would do this for Henry. And for myself."

Half an hour later, after changing into riding clothes and choosing a hardy palfrey, Jehane disappeared down the road to Paimbœuf to save the man she loved.

# CHAPTER SIX

## HENRY

HENRY GREW MORE uncomfortable in the company of the two English ambassadors as the party—accompanied by a dozen ducal guards on horseback—made their way through the forest paths of Brittany. His stomach twisted in anxiety with each tree rolling by his window. This was all happening too quickly.

Catesby chatted pleasantly at first, but Henry's efforts at conversation increasingly seemed to offend him over the course of the day. Stillington, on the other hand, grew ever more talkative. Forest animals, court fashions, the differences between French and English manners, the preferred size of candles at mass… He babbled endlessly. Like Catesby's silence, Stillington's ebullience only increased Henry's discomfort.

When the party came across a tree trunk obstructing the road and Henry opened the carriage door to stretch his legs, Catesby darted over to slam it shut.

Henry snatched his hand back in surprise. The eyes he met contained a cold disdain bordering on accusation. The iron grip and immediate anger made his scalp tingle.

After darting a look to Stillington, Catesby released the door and swallowed. "Bandits have been seen in the area."

Outside, the guards worked to remove the split tree. What bandit in his right mind would attack a heavily armed carriage?

Henry turned to Stillington. The portly face softened a moment too late to hide the shadow of concern.

The guards made short work of the downed tree and set the carriage back on its way. Henry even contributed to a developing conversation about the state of the roads in Brittany. Nonetheless, his thoughts lingered on the exchange.

After another hour's silence, he requested the scroll detailing Edward's offer. Henry skimmed the flowery language. Perhaps Landais had genuinely believed its authenticity and had simply feared Jasper's prejudice would spoil an honest offer.

"It says I'll be greeted by the princesses upon returning to England." Lifting his eyes, he looked not at Stillington, but at Catesby. "We're taking the first ship to England, yes?"

"That's correct."

"I'm sure the king expects his new son-in-law to be suitably dressed when he meets his future wife. Will clothes be waiting for me?"

Stillington interjected himself into the conversation. "His Majesty anticipated your assent and has prepared a new doublet and tunic, which you can change into when we arrive."

"How will the king know where we'll land?"

"What?" Stillington asked with more than an edge of alarm.

"The vessel we take could be destined for any port from Tenby to London. How will the king know where to send the clothes?"

"Oh, I see." Stillington chuckled nervously. "When I said they would be available when you land, I meant they'd be waiting outside London, because of just those difficulties."

Henry nodded once. Though possible, the explanation wasn't plausible. "Then the princesses will be waiting in London, where I'll be presented to them?"

"That's correct."

The sun was descending as they reached the town of Héric a few hours later. The party halted at a ramshackle inn on the edge of town.

While one of the guards negotiated lodgings, Henry tested the limits of his escort's patience. "Surely, you don't intend to stop here, gentlemen."

Stillington and Catesby turned to each other in surprise. Huddled within his cloak, Catesby recovered first. "Why not?"

Henry swept his hand in a gesture encompassing the peeling paint of the doorframe and the shrubbery ruined by the temperature change. "It's not seemly for a future prince of England to stay in such a…a…flea-ridden establishment." He mustered all the hauteur he had observed at the Breton court. "It is beneath my dignity."

Catesby sighed loudly but spoke with his usual reservation. "The horses are exhausted. If we don't rest them, we risk their health over the next few days."

"If we expend our horses, we can simply acquire more. Surely the Earl of Richmond and two ambassadors may appropriate anything we need."

"It isn't seemly for an ambassador to infuriate his host by seizing his subjects' property."

Thwarted once, Henry tried again. "Then claim them in my name. They will not risk offending a noble of my stature."

"To the world, you're an exiled commoner and the son of a traitor." Stillington's words rushed forth. Like Catesby's movements in the carriage, they carried the ring of truth. "While Sir Catesby and I know of the king's generous accommodation, the wilds of Brittany are unaware of your impending…restoration." He stumbled on the word. "Surely you cannot expect them to treat you as you deserve whilst they labor under this misunderstanding?"

Henry inclined his head to Stillington, both to concede the point and to conceal the alarm in his eyes.

Though it had taken most of the day, he had finally verified that they viewed him as an exile and traitor. Oh, they were leading him somewhere—probably the block, not a princess's bed. No, not the block… Affording him the courtesy of beheading would acknowledge his noble birth. He'd have a hangman's noose.

The guards emerged from the inn and nodded. Henry let himself be guided into a back room with a window that overlooked a stable. No opportunity to escape there; the Bretons would stay with the horses, only a few feet away.

Henry declined a meal with the ambassadors. He couldn't risk them realizing he had discovered their intentions.

He could not allow himself to be taken from Brittany. Edward wouldn't offend his ally by executing a man in Francis' realm, but Henry's life was forfeit the moment he left the duchy. He needed to escape, or at least delay his return. Time might let him send word to his uncle about his dire situation.

He remembered Vaughan's reaction when he'd realized Jasper had intended to kill him. Panic. Absolute terror. After the isolation of five years in exile, Henry refused to meet his end at Edward's hand, even if he died in the process of avoiding it.

But he had no method of escape, no weapon to give him an advantage. Nor could he offend God by taking his own life. The behavior of ordained villains like Stillington only called the Pope's judgment into question, not God's commandments. And Henry's death would only give Edward what he most desired.

His eyes drifted to the window. Henry couldn't command the elements to dash the Breton ships to pieces or summon a gale to make sailing impossible, but they could still be useful.

He was supposed to be returning home in triumph and safety. But, if he wasn't healthy enough for a sea voyage, embarking would be a death sentence on the rough seas. Those Breton guards might pause at that prospect.

Crossing the room, he tossed his houppelande on the bed and loosened his doublet. When he pushed the window open, the cold night air forced a shiver. It wouldn't be enough, though. Crossing to a pitcher on a table beside the bed, he cupped his hands and splashed some of the water on his bare chest. After a few more splashes, he returned to the window and inhaled the cold air, feeling his chest constrict beneath the frigid dampness.

## JASPER

The next seven hours were the most terrifying ones of Jasper's life. He tried to remind himself it would take at least that much time for Jehane to reach Quelennec and return, perhaps longer. And all that was assuming she was as skilled of a rider as she claimed. If she wasn't, she could have fallen or gone the wrong way.

Oh, why had he entrusted this mission to a mere tailor who had known his nephew for a few short months?

But as he sat at the entrance to the château watching for signs of a mounted party, he knew the answer. He had no choice but to trust her. The two ducal guards standing at a respectful—but actionable—distance would never permit him to leave. He was helpless to prevent Henry from rolling ever closer to his death in England.

At eight hours, his joints were stiff and his control over his panic was slipping. What if Stillington and Catesby had instructions to kill Henry upon leaving Nantes?

He buried his face in his hands again. He couldn't believe that. No, Henry was still alive. He had to be.

*Damn these guards, and damn Brittany.* He should have fought harder to remain on the boat five years earlier. He should have never allowed himself to be taken to the duke. This was all his fault. He had failed in his pledge to keep Henry safe.

"Jasper."

Raising his head, he wiped his tears. Approaching him was a very dirty Quelennec, a half-dozen ragged soldiers, and Jehane. She was the most haggard of the bunch, clothes and hair caked with mud.

She had done it.

Ignoring the pain in his knees, Jasper rose. "Jean, my god, Jean."

The admiral nodded stiffly. Quelennec's face remained stone-faced, but Jasper recognized the subtle signs of fury. The matter of the Tudors was only one aspect of his war for dominance with Landais, and the treasurer had stolen a march on him.

Befriending someone as powerful as the admiral was supposed to prevent things like this.

"Jehane, may God bless you." Jasper squeezed her hands. "Thank you."

Her arms felt heavy. She was using his grip for support. "I have to change, then I'm off to St. Malo." She took a few deep breaths. "I've already sent word to my father from Paimbœuf to do everything he can to delay them."

"You need to rest. You've been riding all day."

She shook her head. "I can rest in the carriage. I'll swap for a horse when I'm recovered."

The admiral pushed past him.

"Thank you, my dear. Thank you a thousand times." Releasing her, Jasper rushed to follow.

Quelennec galloped up the stairs leading to the ducal palace, forcing a path through the sea of milling peasants. "Out of the way!" He gestured to one of his escorts. "Tell the duke I bring tidings of treason from Paimbœuf."

Eyes widening, the man nodded and jogged into the palace.

"Treason?" Jasper asked.

"It should get his attention."

Quelennec plunged into the castle, with Jasper and the other guards trailing in his wake. A host of servants swirled around them, reaching for Quelennec's riding cloak and offering wine. Putting a goblet to his lips, Jasper drank deeply. Warmth spread throughout his body, replenishing him after a day of anxious anticipation.

Francis arrived a few moments later in a nightgown looking his usual, lucid self. "What news of my fleet?"

His grooms hastily carried his throne in from the antechamber where it was stored. Jasper and the admiral fell to their knees long enough to pay proper respect before rising.

"The fleet is in excellent condition and should weather the winter well," Quelennec explained. "Other than some new sails and reinforcement for the hulls of two ships, no significant repairs were necessary. My full accounting should arrive next week."

Francis waved a hand. "To my ears, this is good news. How is it treason?"

"Forgive me, Your Grace. The treason comes from news I received in Paimbœuf. I deem treason to be anything that diminishes Your Grace's reputation."

The duke rolled his eyes. "Explain, Quelennec."

"I regret to report that decisions made by your council during your affliction have tarnished Your Grace's honor and respect. In light of the dire consequences, I must conclude those responsible are traitors."

In a sign Jasper took to imply his culpability, Francis narrowed his eyes. "You refer to the joyous news of the *rapprochement* between Henry Tudor and our ally, England?"

Biting his lip to suppress a scream, Jasper reminded himself that Francis cared only for his duchy's safety, not Henry's life. Quelennec's smooth words, not a tantrum from a petitioner, would save Henry.

"I refer to Treasurer Landais bullying of the council into handing Lord Tudor to men determined to murder him, without regard to the cost to our duchy." He shook his head. "But that they would jeopardize my liege's soul is, to me, the greatest offense."

Francis' troubled face betrayed his wavering confidence. "I remember my oath quite well, Jean." Finally seating himself on the throne, he smoothed his expression and relaxed his shoulders in an approximation of regal authority. "I'm told the king's terms address my reservations about Lord Tudor's repatriation. The council was confident of his safety. And they secured four thousand English archers in appreciation for our care of him." He raised an eyebrow. "I fail to see how such an agreement tarnishes my reputation."

With his ascendency at stake, Quelennec remained undaunted. "Edward's agents demanded the return of his adversaries when young Henry and his uncle first arrived. Oath-bound to protect them, you could not comply while they remained attained and charged with treason. Despite five years of false claims of forgiveness, the order for their arrest remains valid. Treasurer Landais knew this. You expressed concern over this very point this past summer. Yet Landais nonetheless handed this innocent young man to a king who had murdered his predecessor."

"Is it certain King Edward was responsible for Henry Plantagenet's death?" Francis was clinging to Edward's title with uneasy desperation.

"His men held King Henry under guard at Edward's palace. No one can strangle a king without the consent of his captor. Let us not forget the massacres at Barnet, Tewkesbury, and Towton. He acquired his throne through blood and will shed more to preserve it against a man with claims to the English and French thrones."

Jasper listened nervously. To suggest Henry could claim either throne was patently ridiculous. Yet the duke seemed to accept the argument. And with France's increasingly forceful demands to release the Tudors to them, Jasper could understand why.

"Two bishops testified that the king's offer was genuine. Do you doubt their honor?"

"Canterbury's seal was already broken when our ministers received it. Its validity rests on Stillington's word." Quelennec let the truth of the comment sink in for a moment. "A loyal subject must be willing to sacrifice his honor, life, and very soul for his lord. I would do the same for Your Grace. I'm certain King Edward named Stillington ambassador for his loyalty."

Quelennec had started as a natural ally, but after five years of cultivation, the admiral had grown into a stalwart defender. Jasper couldn't have framed the argument better himself. Nor did he suspect Francis would respond as favorably if he had.

"Your Grace, consider the very absurdity of the offer presented to Landais. Would you ever marry your daughter to a traitor?"

"A concern…" Francis muttered, deep in thought now.

"Why would Edward spend four thousand archers if not to eliminate a threat? It's a high cost for the pleasure of a man's presence at his court." He shrugged. "Of course, now that Edward has what he so long desired, I suspect we'll never see those archers. He may even punish us for extorting him over the years."

Francis' eyes were wide and wild now.

"With Edward freed from the risk of young Tudor's rebellion," Quelennec concluded, "nothing prevents him from conquering us to secure his foothold in France."

The admiral had evidently spent the long miles from Paimbœuf well. His argument was an effort worthy of Jasper's years of friendship. The treasurer had wanted to end Breton involvement in English affairs, but too much had happened for such an easy resolution. Quelennec, son of a noble Breton family, understood this. But Landais, a court lackey elevated by Francis for his service, did not.

Francis had seen opportunity when he had obstructed Jasper's progress through Brittany. Now, Quelennec had reminded him of his obligations.

Fingers picking quickly at a seam of his gown, those obligations were filling Francis with obvious discomfort. "But what can be done? I've given my consent. The consequences of violating my word would be dire."

Anger burning, Jasper lowered his eyes. Francis had admitted it. He'd made the agreement after all, in direct violation of his oath.

"The council spoke in your name, but not with your consent," Quelennec reminded neatly. "Surely every king in Europe can relate to those circumstances."

When Quelennec didn't add anything further, Jasper finally spoke up. "You possess all within your domain, Your Grace, as my nephew and I recognized five years ago. Henry remains in your custody while he remains in Brittany."

Quelennec shrugged. "Your Grace cannot be charged with reacquiring that which you have not yet relinquished."

Francis pressed his lips together. In addition to being forceful, Quelennec had also spoken the truth. The Tudors' value to Francis rested in the threat of letting them loose on Edward. No king appreciated extortion.

Finally, the duke rose. "The issues you raise deserve further consideration. We must verify that the bill of attainder and warrant for Henry Tudor's arrest have been withdrawn." He met Quelennec's gaze. "Admiral, travel to St. Malo to retrieve young Tudor and remind the vessels in port of the consequences for disobeying their duke."

Though his face was vacant, triumph flashed in Quelennec's eyes. He had re-established his influence and had given Jasper a chance to save his nephew.

But, as he and Quelennec rushed off to find new horses, Jasper wondered whether it would matter. He had lost a day already. Unless the tide conspired against the ambassadors, he'd never reach St. Malo in time to prevent Henry from sailing.

## HENRY

A burning fever set in during the third day, leaving Henry so weak that two guards had to hoist him into the carriage for the last leg of the journey. His joints throbbed with each jostle of the wheels on the uneven path. One of his last lucid memories was the guard captain, cantering beside the carriage, ordering Stillington to donate his cloak to his passenger. Its warmth spread slowly but banished the chills enough for him to slip into a thin sleep.

When the carriage broke through the forest and approached St. Malo, the road transformed from a jagged dirt path into a smooth, straight cobblestone road guiding them in comfort to the town. Henry woke at the transition, feeling a little refreshed by the brief rest. Poking his head out from the cloak, though, proved disastrous. The cool breeze rushing past the carriage tickled his nostrils and threatened to reawaken his chills.

One thing was certain: with such a fever, he could not sail.

By no means a rival to Nantes, St. Malo nonetheless had substantial walls and stout stone buildings. The large iron cross atop the city's cathedral reached above the other buildings. Pillars of smoke rose from chimneys somewhere in town, and chimneys meant prosperity. Surely he could acquire paper to write to his uncle. Jasper would know what to do.

Flashing the ducal seal, the carriage passed through the guard post just outside the main gates. Dust from the stream of traffic entering the city invaded the carriage, and Henry made a grand show of distress by coughing up a clump of phlegm and spitting it out the window. The effort attracted a look of concern from Catesby.

The fever was more genuine than Henry had hoped, and even the simple act of leaning forward left him winded. His lungs wheezed as he tried to catch his breath, surprising even him. Were his eyes ringed with circles? Were beads of sweat forming on his cheeks? He couldn't be certain, but Stillington's apprehension suggested they were.

The argument started the moment the carriage stopped.

"This is not the port." Catesby unlatched the door and stepped onto the street.

Henry risked opening his eyes a little further.

"No, it isn't," the guard captain replied gruffly. "My orders are to see Lord Tudor safely bound for England. Look at him."

Henry adjusted the cloak, letting just enough fresh air into his cocoon to trigger a shiver.

The captain grunted. "He's not fit for a voyage."

"It's only a slight fever. He'll be fine. Take us to the port." Catesby's voice carried a dangerous edge, reminding Henry of his first impressions. A soldier preparing for battle.

The carriage jostled roughly as Stillington disembarked, shaking

Henry enough that he had to free his hands to brace himself. The movement sent his stomach reeling. Forgetting the chills and the ache in his bones, he vomited on the ground clear of the cabin, in full sight of Catesby and the guard captain.

"Yes, just a slight fever." The captain sneered. "Aubrey, take some men and find a physician." A pause. "And a priest."

A priest? Did he really look so ill?

Henry heard galloping somewhere beyond the cabin. The door on Stillington's side sat tantalizingly open.

"Captain, surely you understand the delicacy of our position." The bishop's voice carried from behind the carriage to the other side, near the guard captain and Catesby.

Henry quickly assessed the square beyond Stillington's door. Plenty of residents milled about, but he didn't see the livery of either city or ducal guards.

"And you can understand my position," the captain insisted.

"Of course, of course." Stillington used the same sickeningly smooth voice that had lulled Henry into believing these ambassadors might actually aid him. "But Treasurer Landais is a very precise man. Is this not so?"

"He is a careful and wise man." This guard captain would naturally be loyal to Landais; otherwise, he wouldn't have been trusted with this task.

"Then I must assume the wording of your mandate was deliberate. Landais knows full well that King Edward wishes Henry's return. He would be extremely angry if young Tudor dies without ever seeing his beloved homeland again. That anger would be unfortunate for Brittany."

Though Henry couldn't see them, the captain made no immediate response. That silence shouted his doubt. With enough time, he would relent before Stillington's smooth words.

The ploy of his sickness would fail. He had to risk more extreme efforts.

Summoning every scrap of control he could manage, Henry ignored the aching in his bones and smoothly shifted his weight to his left foot. The carriage didn't move. Good.

Which would give him more time? Should he dart out of the carriage even though it would draw attention, or should he move slowly, avoiding notice until he was farther away? To pursue him, they would have to circle the carriage, but Catesby and the captain were both fit, and Henry's rasping lungs would fail long before theirs.

Mustering his last reserves, sapped by the rattling of his bones during the long ride, Henry pushed himself through the open door and ran, slapping his feet down in the mud before him. He hadn't thought of that; he'd leave a trail. But it was too late to reconsider now.

Four…five…six steps at a dead run…already halfway across the open square. Before him, the side street beckoned. His body was fatiguing faster than he'd expected. His legs were starting to burn after only a few dozen feet.

Someone cried out his name, followed by a commotion from behind.

He reached the side street, but its blanket of traffic deserted him. St. Malo wanted nothing to do with ducal guards or an escaped man. The crowds parted to both afford him a clear path and isolate him in his own clearing.

Continuing forward, Henry spared a glance behind. Dangerously close, heads were pushed violently aside amid cries of protest. The crowd left enough room for a single man, but not Catesby and the guards. He doubted Stillington could keep pace.

Faces rushed past as he ran. He ducked down a random side street, hoping it had an outlet. His breath came out in hot wheezes. His muscles throbbed as if he were carrying sacks of grain. And all the while, the roar of the crowd's outrage marked his location to his pursuers.

The brightness of the open streets gave way to dark alleys hidden among the closely arrayed buildings. His feet came down one after another, slapping into puddles of filth dumped from upper-story windows. Each step splashed more of it onto the bottoms of his breeches. The odor nearly overcame him, and he struggled not to vomit.

Searing pain shot up his leg as his foot landed awkwardly on a rock, but he bit his lip and kept going. His spirits sank when the final alley opened into an open square. Squinting, he tried to focus on the shapes he was rushing past. Booths of some sort sat along the sides. He crashed into a beggar and sent his wooden cup flying.

It was too exposed, too easy for his pursuers to track him. He'd never reach the alley at the other end before Catesby and the guards emerged and saw him. They were just around the corner. But he didn't have time to retrace his route.

Panic overcame him. He'd be sent back to England this time—illness or not. Would Catesby and Stillington kill him on the voyage out of fear of another escape? Or would they tie him down and give Edward the satisfaction of doing it?

Did he deserve to die because of his blood? Buckingham was legitimately descended from Edward III, but he had married the queen's sister. King Henry might have done something to deserve his death, but Henry had been a boy. It wasn't fair.

As his eyes adjusted to the brightness, the giant cross materialized before him. The cathedral!

Wheezing heavily, he pushed aside anyone in his path. No longer did he care about the commotion. Muscles threatening to rebel against the exertion, Henry focused on the great carved doors before him.

He rushed inside. The slapping of his feet on the stone echoed through the cathedral. All heads turned toward him, including a young priest with a protest on his lips.

All the years of scheming…those meetings lasting well into the morning…all his posturing and presumption as the Earl of Richmond…the diplomatic wrangling across the seas…the separation from his mother…the death of so many allies… It all counted for nothing. His uncle's anxiety had been justified, after all. This was no grand adventure. Nothing had prevented Edward from reaching out his hand to claim him. Only the frail hopes of an old institution stood between him and death.

"Sanctuary!" Speaking agitated the irritants in his lungs and sparked a deep, wheezing cough. "I am the Earl of Richmond. I beg you…"

Surrendering himself to the agony of the long run and even longer ride, he fell to his knees, then to the ground, and lay motionless in a hazy fog. Several pairs of hands lifted him, and someone called for blankets.

A Latin prayer faded in and out. A cry of shock. The hands shifted him in their grasp.

Cracking his eyes open and willing them to focus, he turned to the figures clustering near the entrance.

The English were just outside, with only one small priest barring the threshold.

"Henry Tudor is a fugitive from Brittany and your duke." Catesby didn't even sound winded. "We will have this man."

"Who are you to demand anything of the Holy Church?" came the piping reply.

"Who am I?" Catesby's voice carried a dangerous inflection. "I am Sir William Catesby, Ambassador to King Edward of England. I carry a mandate to recover this fugitive. Stand aside."

"This man has asked for the Church's protection. He's too ill to move, let alone be manhandled by your soldiers. I have granted him sanctuary in God's name."

"Like hell you have. Get out of my way." Grasping the priest by both shoulders, Catesby tried mightily to dislodge him.

The Breton guards did nothing to aid him. One even tugged at his shoulder to stop him.

Stillington's voice rang out. "Sir William, no!"

But his warning was too late. While Catesby clearly held little reverence for the protections of sanctuary, the citizens of St. Malo took the religious custom much more seriously. A few men surged forward to defend their fragile priest, then a few more. Before long, the entire square rushed to protect their shepherd. Pummeling Catesby, the hesitant Breton guards, and each other, they turned the cathedral entrance into a riot.

Catesby tried several times to break through, but in the priest, he found a worthwhile adversary. Every time he rushed for the breach, the priest drew the attention of enough nearby citizens to throw him back again.

Henry remained conscious just long enough to see the ambassador draw off in defeat, nursing a bloody lip and a swollen eye.

## HENRY

Henry remembered the odor of the alley, so pungent that it couldn't simply be a memory. Was he lying there, bleeding to death?

Voices…the feel of hands on his shoulders…the scent of horse carried by his shallow breaths… It all seemed so long ago. How long had he been here?

He remembered a woman. His heart thumped in his chest as he thought of her, that cascading hair, her alluring smile. But the image that drifted across his mind seemed hollow, bereft of something vibrant.

Jehane. Jehane was her name. He loved her. He needed to see her again, at least to say goodbye properly.

Eventually, he managed a deep breath, though his lungs labored under the strain. The effort took more strength than he had, and it wasn't until some time later that he could take another. Then another. Each one became a little easier.

Once he could open his eyes, forms materialized slowly in the pale light. But the wheezing in his chest told him this wasn't a dream. And he was alive.

The bed beneath him was too comfortable, free of lumps and

lice, for him to be in the cathedral. To his surprise, his arms and legs obeyed him. Shifting, he tried to prop himself up on one elbow, but a hand restrained him.

So, he wasn't free after all.

He turned to face its owner, expecting to see either Stillington or Catesby looking down at him with smug satisfaction.

"Uncle?"

Surprise drew him fully awake. Drawing his legs beneath him, he propped himself up despite the restraint. He actually felt quite well now that he could stretch his muscles. They were sore from disuse, not disease. He delighted in the difference.

"How long?" His voice sounded scratchy, and he reached up to rub his throat.

Jasper handed him a cup of wine. The liquid tingled as it slipped down his throat.

"Five days."

Five days.

He looked around the unfamiliar room. It didn't look like a cathedral. "Where am I?"

"We moved you to the mayor's house two days ago, once we convinced the townsfolk we wished you no harm." Jasper squeezed Henry's hand. "When I heard you were ill, I hoped it wasn't true." His expression softened for only a moment before he restored his composure. "I was so worried."

"I exposed myself to the cold once I realized the English were lying. Sea air is too dangerous for an invalid. I needed a real fever to prevent them from taking me to England."

"It was quick thinking in a difficult situation."

Henry shook his head. "It was stupid, and it failed." He lowered his eyes. "I squandered all my money on a new doublet, so I had none to bribe an innkeeper or a servant. I should've secreted a knife on myself months ago." He paused, mustering the resolve to form the words. "I was useless. And I very nearly died because of it."

He hoped his uncle would disagree with him. The expanding silence said more than any chastising litany ever could.

"Am I still going to England?" The panic slipped into his voice despite his restraint.

Jasper shook his head. "Quelennec made the duke see that releasing you isn't in Brittany's interest."

"Francis handed me over in the first place. Landais would never make a decision like this without his support."

"Never speak of it again." Jasper leaned forward. "We still need his protection, and though his feigned madness nearly condemned you, it's also his excuse for wiggling out of his agreement with the ambassadors. If we undermine that, he'll be forced to send us home."

Jasper had always warned against trusting Edward and his minions. Well, Francis was Edward's ally, and an ally was almost the same thing.

"Our continued safety has a price," Jasper said. "The ambassadors were furious. Francis had to promise to bottle us up."

A close watch or a distant one; did it really matter? Henry had been a prisoner for five years. "So we're headed back to Nantes." Back to the court politics and all the comforts that had filled him with hollow hope. All the things that had counted for nothing.

"No, not to court. There, we could speak to ambassadors and gain allies." Jasper's lips drew tight. "Nonetheless, Francis genuinely wants to protect us now that he realizes reconciliation isn't possible."

Henry drew in a breath. "Then where—"

"Vannes, a naval base on the southern coast. There, Francis can control who comes and goes. Though no one could take us from there by force, nor will we be able to leave." Inhaling, he mustered an unconvincing smile. "At least all us exiles will be together."

His uncle's eyes revealed the death of his dreams. After struggling for fifteen years, the Lancastrians had finally been defeated, not by Edward but by insignificance.

They would be a community in exile, bottled up far from the watchful eyes of everyone who might help them overthrow Edward.

No longer would he waste his time chatting with nobles who wielded no power and cared little for the fate of an English exile. Perhaps now he could live in peace with Jehane.

"Jehane! Does she know I didn't abandon her?"

Smiling, Jasper rose and straightened his doublet. "I'll send her in."

"She's here?" Joy banished his residual lethargy.

"You don't hear her?"

Freed from the final shackles of sleep, he recognized a faint sobbing from beyond the door. It was noticeable now that he knew to listen for it.

Jasper slipped out, leaving the door open. A few soft words followed by a gasp of surprise sounded from the other side.

Then, all of a sudden, she was there, not quite as pristine as his vision. Her eyes were red and frightened, and her hair was unkempt from her vigil. For him.

Even in distress, she was more beautiful than he remembered.

She wrapped him in her arms with a half-sigh, half-moan. The soft embrace, the feel of her hot breath on his neck, the chest carefully constricted within her bodice… Henry squeezed her, desperate to hold her as long as possible.

"I thought I'd never see you again." Her tears began to moisten his cheek.

"Oh, I'm sorry, Jehane. I'm so sorry."

"They took you away from me. Curse Landais!"

He pulled back to meet her eyes. "No, not about that." Fumbling to find her hands, he clenched them. "When I met Catesby and Stillington at court, I was excited to be the Earl of Richmond again."

She stroked his cheek. "You just wanted your due."

He shook his head. "Edward planned to have me killed once I reached England. That's what my title earned me. Pain and death."

Sobering, she leaned back, opening some distance between them. "Then I suppose you need to decide what kind of life you want. You can remind everyone about your title and accept the suffering along with the possibility of restoration. Or, you can let everyone forget you and live as you wish."

There it was, stated plainly. His uncle had made his choice decades earlier and had suffered terribly for it. Was that his future?

Thoughts of Jehane had brought him back from the edge of death. She had saved his life. His title had nearly killed him and promised only to take her from him forever.

He pulled her closer. "Exile isn't exile if I have you with me."

She leaned against him, nestling against his chest. "In Vannes, we can be together, just as we were."

"You heard about that?"

"Oh, Henry…" She raised her head again to meet his eyes. "I spent hours on the road with Lord Quelennec. Do you think we were silent all that time?"

He gasped. "You convinced him to send me to Vannes?"

"Certainly not." Her mouth dimpled into a delightful grin. "I'm sure the admiral thought it was his idea."

His uncle would be furious, but she hadn't done it for Jasper. She'd done it for him.

For the first time since setting foot in Europe, that knot of unfulfilled desire uncoiled. He was no longer the Earl of Richmond. In his heart, he knew he'd never really own that title again. But he had his Jehane, and that was all that mattered.

# III

## INTERLUDE

AD 1478

# CHAPTER SEVEN

## HENRY

*Lord Richmond,*

*I've attempted to write you several times, but my captors are skilled at detecting my letters. Gone is any pretense of privacy.*

*Carry no doubt that we will supplant the usurper. It took ten years last time, but we succeeded, nonetheless. Our mistake was failing to kill the Yorks when we had the chance.*

*We will prevail, so long as one of us remains alive. I'm working on something that might help, but it's too soon to talk about it. Until then, be assured of my friendship.*

*John de Vere, Earl of Oxford*

SIGHING, **HENRY SET** the letter aside and brushed the stray pieces of broken wax onto the floor. How could Oxford hope to organize resistance when all of Edward's enemies were either imprisoned or dead? Until that changed, here he would remain.

The old Henry would've itched for freedom and made plans with his uncle and the other exiles. But dinner conversations filled with Lancastrian hatred no longer interested him. A hot passion for the woman who loved him had replaced the old fire to reclaim his lands. Two years with Jehane had soured him to the obligations of his birth. He had no room for Edward or the Lancastrian cause anymore.

And then there was his mother, who still clung to hope of his return. Her latest missive bore the elegant script of her scribe. Breaking the seal revealed anecdotes and gossip about the court, included to expand the pool of words from which she could build her hidden message. Henry began translating the hidden code as Reginald Bray had taught him, looking for the casual strokes identifying key words.

> *You are not forgotten. George, the king's brother, was executed yesterday for treason. Stillington was also implicated and has been arrested. Edward can once again grant you Richmond. Remember, you are an earl, not a tailor.*

The last line provoked a grunt. While he was a poor excuse for an earl, he had discovered a natural skill for accounts and negotiation. After Jehane had shown him how, he had thrown himself into managing her books. Though his ducal guards prevented him from joining her in Nantes to view the latest fashions or St. Malo to negotiate with her suppliers, he kept the business running while she was gone.

Her shop was thriving, partly due to the addition of a master dressmaker from Rouen who had fallen on hard times. But Henry had also left his mark, both through his keen eye for irregularities and by introducing Jehane to the English exiles, who hadn't brought their households with them. Most now used Rousson tailors to outfit themselves. And that brought a sense of satisfaction. For too long, he'd been an idle petitioner. It was fulfilling to finally do something worthwhile.

He supposed he should've been grateful for his mother's efforts on his behalf, but her letters only reminded him of traumas he preferred to forget.

Yet, the Duke of Clarence's death stirred something within him. The villain deserved to burn in the fires of Hell, but the king had probably afforded his brother a painless death. What a waste of a perfectly good opportunity for revenge.

Wearily, Henry realized this was the first time he'd genuinely thought of Edward as king. Did it matter what he called Edward? St. Malo had shown him the truth of his prospects. Why couldn't his uncle and mother understand that his life was here with Jehane?

He tossed the paper onto the desk. It landed sloppily on the otherwise neatly arranged surface.

The familiar warmth of lithe arms wrapping around his shoulders interrupted his thoughts.

"Jehane."

Her hair tumbled over his forehead, and he looked up. Even upside-down, he recognized her strained smile. She must have seen the letters.

"What news from England?"

He dared not share his assessment of the Lancastrian cause. If his doubts ever reached Francis, his stipend and protection would end. He couldn't take that risk, even with Jehane.

He swiveled around to face her. "Nothing of importance."

Though she nodded, her concern didn't fade.

"Lord Oxford is in good spirits despite his captivity," he continued. "There's nothing like good news from a friend."

Her eyes lowered at that. She assumed the same expression she'd worn when she'd greeted him on his sickbed.

His sense of danger roused, he stiffened. "Something's wrong, isn't it? Is my uncle—"

She stirred. "No, no, your uncle is well."

"Then, what?"

She held a breath. "It's Quelennec. A fever set in two weeks ago during a hunt. It took him four days ago."

He sucked in a breath. Without Quelennec's golden tongue,

Henry would have likely died at St. Malo. Such a dear friend and good man, gone forever.

Who was left in Brittany to support him? Jean de Rieux had cared for him out of obligation, not affection. Despite their affinity, the Rieux boys were compelled to follow their father's lead.

His throat felt dry. "How did you hear this?"

"One of my agents." She passed information gained from her court-watchers to her father in exchange for discounts on the cloth her tailors used.

He didn't relish the idea of telling Jasper this news, but the Tudors would need permission to travel to Nantes for the funeral before they could start assembling horses and escorts.

But Jehane's eyes carried concern for more than logistics; she saw the danger.

He smiled faintly. "Once we reach Nantes for the funeral, everything will be fine."


# HENRY

Jasper lived in a well-furnished building a few streets down along the main avenue through Vannes. When Henry arrived, his uncle was scraping his pen furiously over parchment.

After two decades on the run, Jasper had grown old. Henry would have to proceed carefully or risk his uncle's health.

"What are you writing?"

The pen froze. Jasper stared hard at the table between them. "A letter to my half-brother, Owen, asking for the support of the Welsh clergy."

"He didn't give you an answer the last time you wrote."

"That's why I'm asking again." He resumed his writing. "Your mother said she would write to you. Has she?"

Henry nodded.

"Then you know about George of Clarence. He and Richard

neutralized each other's influence on Edward. With George dead, Richard will squeeze the border provinces for taxes and levies. The Welsh and Scots have both written asking my intentions."

"Would Richard move so fast?"

Jasper shrugged. "Landais did when Quelennec was absent. The English court closely resembles that of Brittany."

Pressing his lips together, Henry broached the unpleasant subject. "I've had news from Nantes, and—"

"You have contacts in Nantes?" His eyes widened in surprise.

"Jehane does."

He sighed. "At least *she* watches events."

Henry chose to ignore the jab at his own inattention. "I received some bad news. I don't know how to tell you this, but I'm afraid—"

"Quelennec is dead." The comment spilled out casually while Jasper drew long strokes on the bottom of the letter.

"You knew? When did you hear?"

"Just this morning." Jasper folded the letter and dropped some wax over the edge.

"And writing a letter was more important than telling me?"

Jasper sighed. "Frankly, yes. You'll be here tonight. The boat taking this letter won't." He imprinted his seal on the paper. "Robert," he called over Henry's shoulder.

One of Jasper's servants poked his head through the door.

"There's a ship in port bound for Ireland. Take this to the captain immediately. He'll know what it means."

Robert accepted the letter and, bowing, withdrew.

Watching him go, Jasper muttered, "It takes four weeks for a letter to reach Wales by way of Ireland. If that boy misses the ship, it'll take another two."

"We need permission to travel," Henry said.

"Why would we travel?"

"To attend Quelennec's funeral."

Jasper seated himself wearily and rubbed his writing hand. "We're not going."

Only the feel of the chair's arms against his palms convinced Henry he hadn't imagined the response. "For God's sake, he was your ally."

"He was my dearest friend!" The depth of Jasper's loss poured out with the anguished cry. "He saved your life when I stood helpless. Can you imagine how that felt, to know I'd failed to protect you? Quelennec helped me keep my sanity."

He hadn't thought Jasper blamed himself for what had happened. "I'm sorry, I didn't—"

"But I don't have the luxury of friendship," his uncle interrupted. "If I attend his funeral, it'll remind his enemies that he supported me. Before I can win their support, they must forget I knew him. And the English ambassador would report our presence in violation of Francis' oath to keep us in Vannes."

Henry made no attempt to repress the scowl forming on his lips. "You're forsaking your friend's memory."

"Quelennec is dead, and his use to our cause died with him. Wailing, wringing my hands, or lamenting God's will won't bring him back, only threaten our future."

"This is wrong, uncle, just as it was wrong to kill Vaughn so many years ago." Hadn't Jasper fought against men who had abandoned their oaths of friendship and fealty?

Jasper bolted to his feet. "Don't sit there and judge me. You know nothing of the world, St. Malo notwithstanding. I've been sacrificing for our cause—for you—for decades. My family has been destroyed piece by piece. I've agonized over the tough decisions that could doom us. And now, I have to find new allies. I'd appreciate if you didn't fight me at every turn."

Startled, Henry straightened. "What do you mean?"

Jasper grunted. "Oh, wake up. Henry Herbert is dead. George of Clarence is dead. You're the only royal claimant Edward doesn't control. The exiles here look to you for salvation."

The anger of so many suffering years rose to the surface. "What has seven years bought us? There's no one left to fight for us. Resisting Edward further will only destroy us, and I refuse to be the cause of that."

"Is that why you waste your time with that woman, pretending to be a tailor?"

The comment struck Henry like a sword blow. "Excuse me?"

"You have French and English royal blood in your veins," Jasper reminded.

"An illegitimate drop."

"Nonetheless, doing sums and"—his lips twisted into a scowl—"negotiating prices is beneath you."

Henry's fists tightened at his sides. "How can you still look down on her? You act like she's the dirt beneath your boot."

"I don't look down on her. She's a skilled tailor and a good woman. I'll be forever thankful to her for saving you at St. Malo." The response surprised Henry into silence. "But she diminishes you. You should be working to reclaim your title. Instead, she teaches you to be content with a small life." He shook his head. "Your father would be ashamed of you."

"My father is dead, and so is the cause he died for," Henry spat. "I can't waste my life on the vain hope of somehow recovering my title. But I can learn how to make my way in the world. Why won't you let me be happy?"

"So you'll just sit comfortably in Brittany and hope Edward doesn't remember you?" Jasper asked. "He won't forget, regardless of how much you work at Jehane's trade."

"It's over, uncle. We've lost."

"It will never be over," Jasper hissed.

"Our titles are gone, and I don't see any way to recover them." He crossed his arms. "Until something changes, I'm going to start living my life."

Jasper gestured to the papers beside him. "As king, Edward makes a hundred decisions a day, and each one harms someone. Each day, more of our peers lament his preference for common merchants over his own class. The discontent is growing. One day, they'll realize they've lost too much. Every king starts his reign surrounded by allies and ends it surrounded by enemies. Our chance is coming."

"Regardless of whether I want it to?" Henry spread his arms wide. "This is my life you're playing with. I barely survived St. Malo, and you want me to jump into the fire again? Why would I even want that if it means becoming just like Edward? It starts with forsaking a friend. Where will it end? Will I have to execute my family and friends like he did?"

"You're taking your fears to absurd extremes." Jasper scoffed. "We're walking a thin path through a dark wood, Henry. Make too much noise and Edward will sacrifice everything to destroy you. Make too little and Francis will withdraw his protection and the stipend you depend on." He let the words hang in the air. "You're not a child anymore. Disabuse yourself of the belief that your actions—or inactions—have no consequences."

"I refuse to be the type of man who harms his friends."

"No one's asking you to," Jasper growled. "But Quelennec is dead. Whether he resides in paradise or torment, he won't care whether you attended his funeral. But he would grieve if his death contributed to yours."

## HENRY

The trip home took a fraction of the time. Shock over his uncle's words lingered long after Jasper had revealed the dark reasoning governing them. It was callous and calculated, more suited to a Plantagenet than the uncle who had protected him all these years. Henry had believed Jasper had executed Vaughan out of grief and anger, but now he realized Jasper had acted with brutal, unfeeling reason to warn the traitors of a reckoning.

And yet, it had failed. Executing Vaughan had been insignificant compared to King Henry's murder. The English feared Edward, the man who had seized the crown twice. He held the hearts of the nobles in the palm of his hand.

Henry tried to control his wild thoughts and wilder breathing before opening the door to the simple townhouse that had been his and Jehane's home for the last two years.

She promptly abandoned the fabrics strewn about the bed when she saw his expression.

He loosened the laces of his doublet and rubbed his neck, billowing his shirt to let in some cool air. "You should have heard him, Jehane."

As Henry recounted the conversation, she listened with such calmness that Henry's outrage seemed embarrassing. She spoke only when he had finished, out of breath and still angry.

"I'm sorry for Quelennec, Henry." Her voice carried the same serenity she always ascribed to important decisions. "No man deserves to be forgotten by his friends." She folded her hands on her lap, her muscles relaxed. "Is your uncle correct about how the court would interpret your attendance at the funeral?"

He sighed. "Probably." Uttering the word felt like a betrayal.

"Would any of Quelennec's allies feel abandoned if you did not attend?"

Another calm question, this time one Henry hadn't yet considered. "The court knows Francis restricted our movements."

"Your uncle told you it'd be dangerous."

"That wasn't all he said." He hesitantly recounted his uncle's opinion about her effect on him.

Rather than become angry, she simply sighed. "I assumed as much."

"Really?"

She nodded. "He said something similar in Nantes. I suppose the question is what you want, Henry."

He shook his head. "There are too many obstacles to reclaiming my title."

She studied him closely. "But if there weren't?"

He lowered his eyes. "Everything I told you when we met remains true. Without my title, I've lost a part of myself. But these years with you have shown me a part I never knew was there. Here, I have a different life, a safer one that I genuinely enjoy. And I can be with you."

She nodded slowly. "Then your uncle made the correct decision about the funeral."

"I can't just abandon my friend."

She laid a hand on his shoulder. "Edward would hear of your attendance and try to take you away from me again, just like St. Malo." A few stray tears broke free to drip down her cheeks.

What he had mistaken for calm had actually been tight control. The thought of his returning to court terrified her.

"Oh, Jehane." Twisting, he kissed her forehead gently and cradled her head against his shoulder. "You're right. Oh, my darling, I'm so sorry, you're right."

Neither of them could suffer another St. Malo.

He had pledged to never again cause her pain. He would keep that promise. Traveling to Nantes would borrow trouble. Unless something changed in England, his safest course was to keep his head down. His life was Jehane, now.

# IV

## POLITICS

AD **1482**

# CHAPTER EIGHT

## MARGARET

THE SLEEVES ON Margaret's new brocade dress, commissioned in the Burgundian style preferred by the queen, felt oppressive. Despite the February chill outside, they were too thick for the stifling heat of the feast hall. The flaring, floor-length sleeves got in the way of everything from eating to needlepoint. Not that the queen, who championed the fashion, ever sewed anything herself.

Margaret hated this dress. But, it was necessary to conform in Edward's England, and she had done so with remarkable skill since his restoration eleven years prior. Even now, she was as fit as a woman half her age and kept pace with the ridiculous fashions most women pushing forty had long abandoned.

So, as she stood with her husband's brother awaiting the arrival of the royal couple at another wine-soaked celebration, her expression remained the same serene, humble visage she had cultivated for years. The court ladies respected her as a proper matron, loyal to her husband and obedient to her king despite the unresolved matters between him and her son. Little did they know that beneath that calm exterior, she'd long ago exhausted her patience for such drunken revels.

Finally, Elizabeth escorted Edward into the hall. The king's eyes, though paler than when he'd been a young man taking the field against Margaret's father, still darted from one noble to another, acknowledging each in turn. Most of the court still adored him as much as ever.

In recent months, the train following him had grown from only their children and nursemaids to include all of the Woodvilles, their families, children, and servants. Anthony and Edward Woodville left little doubt about the longevity of their ambitions by each escorting one of the king's sons. As difficult as it was to believe the Woodvilles could worm themselves any deeper into the royal apple, here was the proof.

Then there was Richard, whispering furtively to the old nobility at the back of the train. Buckingham and Hastings nodded occasionally as he spoke. Richard's omnipresent glare at the back of the queen's head suggested the topic of their conversation.

His wife stood beside him, engaging the men with equal force and commanding equal attention. Clearly, Anne Neville had spent her childhood learning from her father, the Kingmaker, who had orchestrated every change in monarch over the past thirty years. While her family retainers were the backbone of Richard's power, they supported him only to honor his wife, a fact not lost on the young lady. She could directly command more men-at-arms than any woman in the country and exerted more influence than any but Queen Elizabeth.

Buckingham had only joined Richard's circle of acquaintances recently, even though his marriage to Catherine Woodville had been cooling since he'd reached an age to realize his wife had been a yoke, not a gift.

It was a wonder the Woodvilles could walk calmly with their backs turned to so many powerful men who loathed them.

Suddenly self-conscious, Margaret wished her husband was here to remind her to govern her thoughts with a playful pinch. But he was surveying his lands for damage from the harsh winter and wouldn't return until the embassies arrived and the spring tournaments began.

Edward assumed his seat and immediately downed a full goblet of wine. With the usual symbol to start the revelry now completed, the court broke off into smaller groups. The women found their friends while the men clustered with their allies.

But the warmth within the room was taking its toll on Margaret. Fanning herself, she politely declined a few greetings and made her way to a corridor leading outside.

On the way, the newly appointed bishop John Morton began to approach, but he halted when his eyes shifted to the hand waving cool air toward her face. With a look of sympathy, he simply bowed and left her to her recovery.

After so many years at prayer, she'd come to know much about men of the cloth, and kindness was not one of their more common qualities. He was the exception. Though an ardent supporter of King Edward, he was also a compassionate man.

The cool breeze from the opened doors offered blessed relief from the stifling heat of so many packed bodies. As she began to recover, the French ambassador approached along the perimeter of the great hall. It was a poor time for conversation, but opportunities to speak were rare.

"*Bonjour, mon duc. Comment ça va?*"

"*Je vais bien, madame.*" He offered a light bow intended for close quarters and discreet situations.

Understanding the gesture's meaning, Margaret strolled farther down the hall so her voice wouldn't carry. "It is good to see you, Monsieur Beaujeu."

"And you, my lady. Though, I wish I brought pleasing tidings."

She recalled their last conversation. "Lord Oxford?"

Beaujeu nodded. "Edward will not consider his release at any price. When I presented King Louis' proposal, the king warned that further discussion would forfeit Oxford's life."

"Then, by all the saints, please let the matter rest, Peter." Oxford was the only Lancastrian left who she could both trust and rely upon in a battle. "He must be preserved at all costs." All costs except her son's life, of course.

"Take heart, my lady. It seems Oxford dines regularly with his jailer, Sir James Blount, and they have become quite friendly. I do not fear for his life. Nor should you, madam."

Smiling, Margaret nodded. Over the years, she had grown to trust this man, son-in-law to the French king. So long as her son could punish Edward for his war against France a few years prior, the ambassador would continue to pressure Brittany for his release.

Beaujeu and his wife, Anne, had persuaded King Louis to move troops to the Breton border in the wake of St. Malo. Despite Stillington and Catesby's protests, the Breton duke had realized the French would overrun his country long before his English allies could arrive. Henry was convinced Quelennec's influence had kept him in Brittany; Margaret and Jasper knew better.

"And the other matter?"

He made a quick sweep of the corridor before answering. "My wife and brother are sympathetic to your cause, but matters in France have changed."

She furrowed her brow. His wife was King Louis' favorite child and the sister to the heir, while his brother was the powerful Duke of Bourbon. She needed their continued support. "If I can help—"

"Alas, madam, you cannot. You see"—he again checked that they were alone—"King Louis is dying."

She crossed herself out of habit, though the familiar company didn't require it. "Peter, all of Europe is aware of that." Over the past few years, King Louis' influence had been declining with his health. If this was his reason for refusing assistance, she would have to reconsider his worth as an ally.

"This is different. Always before, he suffered sudden bouts but recovered within days. This time, it crept up on him slowly. Our enemies in court don't yet realize it. We have an opportunity to position ourselves for the impending struggle."

"For the throne?" Swallowing, she contemplated the possibilities.

France's laws didn't permit a woman to rule in her own right. Pressing the claim of Beaujeu's wife would lead to civil war.

"No, my wife and her brother Charles are very close. The fight will be for his regency until he comes of age."

First Quelennec, then Francis' health, now the possibility of a French power struggle. Elizabeth Woodville was related to the Duke of Burgundy, the other powerful faction in France. Should Anne and Peter lose, Henry would be surrounded by enemies.

"I will continue to pray for your safety."

"As I will for yours, and for your son's."

"Have you any news from Brittany? My secret letters go through Wales, and the rough seas have kept the ships in port." She would have happily traded all her Welsh allies for one trustworthy Englishman with a port on his lands.

"Our ambassador reports murmurs of discontent over Landais, but he is still the undisputed master of the old duke. Quelennec's son is not as forceful as his father was. Those who hoped he would build on his father's legacy must look elsewhere."

All around him, her son's support was eroding. The more his position weakened, the more forgettable he became and the more careful he needed to be.

St. Malo had changed much. No longer did Jasper urge Henry to present himself before the duke and the ambassadors. Nor did Henry himself even seem interested in currying support from the other exiles, now numbering several dozen. Of course, she could never ask them whether they were beginning to believe Henry would never again set foot on English soil. It was not a conversation easily had from hundreds of miles away.

"Fear not, my lady." Beaujeu clasped her hand. "My wife and I will not forget your plight, and will do all within our power to aid you."

Margaret curtseyed as the ambassador took his leave. She put little stock in his words. Promises were easy.

No, that wasn't fair. The ill tidings were affecting her mood. She would need another way of appealing to Edward, to find something he wanted badly enough to overcome the embarrassment of St. Malo.

"Now, what would you possibly have to say to the French ambassador?" a husky voice asked behind her.

Mind flashing, she resumed her usual serene expression. The speaker was intelligent enough to spot a lie, so she calmed herself for a moment before turning to face Richard of Gloucester.

She lowered her eyes in feigned reverence. "I wished to convey my deepest sympathy to his wife for the continued illness of her father."

He smiled without humor. "And no doubt you met him in a private corridor out of…a bashful nature? Surely, pious Margaret Beaufort would never dream of conspiring with the French."

"It must be so, my lord. After all, I have complete trust in His Majesty's efforts to resolve my son's situation, for he has acted in good faith in all things."

She regretted the words immediately. Richard's smug smirk only reinforced the foolishness of her insult. She still hadn't restored the control shaken by Beaujeu's news. That was worrying. She'd have to be extremely careful to avoid further indiscretions.

"Efforts that, until this point, have proven fruitless." Richard casually circled her to lean against the far wall. "We have tolerated uncertain loyalties among the nobles for far too long. The time for negotiation is over. The king wishes to finally put an end to the divisions in his realm."

The king had mouthed this same comment many times over the years. "I wish it as well."

"I'm pleased to hear that." Richard's tone indicated anything but pleasure. "My brother has instructed me to present one final offer for your son's repatriation. You would do well to heed me."

Mind whirling, Margaret folded her hands in front of her. For a few weeks, she had been discussing the possibility of a marriage to one of his daughters, the very same offer falsely offered before St. Malo. But she had expected Elizabeth Woodville to reject any proposal involving her girls. Her family hated everything Henry stood for, from the shame of losing the throne once to the enduring reminder that they hadn't fully stamped out resistance to their rule a full decade later.

"In exchange for your son returning from Brittany, His Majesty will allow him to inherit enough of your lands upon your death to live comfortably. The charge of treason will be removed, and he will be welcomed back to the kingdom as a loyal subject. His Majesty will even grant the land as a fee simple freeholding. Your son will own the land, rather than hold it in the king's name."

Margaret bit the inside of her lip. "What does 'live comfortably' mean?"

"Two hundred pounds a year," he replied, tight-lipped.

His tone suggested an opportunity. "Comfortable for a country squire, perhaps. His birth alone merits at least a thousand."

But Richard didn't allow himself to be drawn into a negotiation. Instead, he simply stared at her for an uncomfortably long time in silence. He stirred at a celebratory shout from the king's table. "Four hundred, but not a gold piece more."

"And my son's title?"

Richard barked a laugh. "Was lost when his father opposed the king years ago. His Majesty does not see fit to grant that honor again."

"Then what of the Somerset title?"

"Don't test me, Margaret." He balled the fingers of his misshapen arm into a fist before relaxing them again. "You have no prospects save this concession. Only because your son has shown no aggression is the king even tendering this offer."

In some ways, it was less than she had hoped for. Without the honor of Somerset or Richmond, no longer would her son be a noble, and that in itself was a great loss. He couldn't hope for a marriage to a family the equal of the Beauforts, let alone one of Edward's daughters.

However, this could be a first step. In exchange for an oath of fealty, Henry would regain the knighthood that had never been stripped from him. And by granting a fee simple freeholding, Edward couldn't hold

Henry hostage over these lands as he could a title. Her son could do what he pleased with them.

But why now?

"It is a most generous offer. I shall offer my prayers that the duke recognizes its merit."

"I very much doubt that." Richard's voice contained a twinge of humor.

When Richard was amused, all other considerations became secondary. "My lord?"

"We both know Francis isn't keeping your son a fugitive. It's that whispering uncle of his. And Catesby told me how sneaky your son is." His mouth curled into a grin. "I think you keep him well-informed about your efforts here, and I know for a fact such information isn't contained in the letters you let us intercept. The two of you are more alike than you want us to believe."

The leaden words filled her with a terror unmatched even by her son's narrow escape at St. Malo. Richard had known, all these years, that she'd instructed her son to ignore her letters supporting Edward's offers. Perhaps Richard had even whispered in his brother's ear, undermining her every conversation with the king. Had it all been for nothing, or had he only now discovered her distrust of Edward?

"I've known how cagey your son is for quite some time."

*Damn this man.* Her confidence in every action over the past decade shattered. All she could do was stand in silence and debate the moment he had started to thwart her. Everything was suspect.

Richard's face wore naked satisfaction. Peeling back his teeth, he stepped closer. He looked more like a feral animal than a mildly attractive duke. "If I were king, neither you nor he would be in a position to contemplate this offer today."

She did not doubt his meaning.

Never before had a Plantagenet expressed such naked hatred of her and her son. Those words, spoken by a man a foot away from her, terrified her.

But her father had been a Duke of Somerset, and she had been trained from birth to survive this world. She would not let an enemy intimidate her.

"But you are not king."

"Tch." It was an odd reaction from a man who had always faithfully supported his brother. A few courtiers standing near the corridor would probably debate the significance of that reaction in the coming days. That in itself was a victory, albeit a small one.

The reaction also drew the attention of the king's young son and heir, Edward, who ran up to his uncle. A mop of golden locks bounced atop his head. "Uncle, uncle!" He would have collided with Richard if the duke hadn't halted him. "Papa said you were fighting the Scotts by York. You told me you would take me with you." Though he tried to maintain a hurt expression, his curiosity overtook him. "What was it like?"

A pang of agony struck Margaret as she recalled her own son's eagerness to travel with Jasper. She had finally reclaimed him after all those years, but he had been a young boy used to being on his own. She couldn't have borne him resenting her for refusing to let him go.

If she had, he would've been safe in England.

"Your uncle is in the middle of a conversation. I will tell you later." Richard turned back to Margaret.

"No!" Prince Edward stamped his foot. "I am your prince. You will do as I command."

Whirling on the young man with eyes wide, Richard inhaled to put him in his place.

Before he could speak, Margaret interrupted, "I see mine isn't the only son who resembles his mother."

As if struck, Richard bit off his prepared retort. In a shockingly short time, the hostility painted across his face shifted to concern. He was contemplating the implications of her loaded statement.

Elizabeth Woodville had raised her children herself, rather than relegating them to nursemaids. And for all those years, the queen had been teaching them to trust her family above all others. Despite her unpopularity, Edward had named her as his son's guardian in his will, rather than his own brother. Where would that leave Richard once Edward, ten years his elder, died? Surrounded by his Woodville enemies, his nephew would sit on the throne with his mother whispering in his ear.

Compared to that realization, making Margaret feel uncomfortable must have seemed meaningless.

Richard salvaged the situation by bowing to the young prince. "You are right to chastise me, nephew. This woman is nothing compared to my prince." Richard strode off with the prince, excited again now that he had his uncle's attention.

Margaret grinned as they withdrew. He could insult her all he liked: she now knew how to hurt him. She'd forced him into a full retreat with only a few words. A Lancastrian hadn't done that to a Yorkist in a dozen years.

Activity around the king's table was bustling when Richard and young Edward arrived. They joined Hastings and Buckingham at Edward's right, who were obviously discussing something dull, based on Edward's expression. The mood lightened when Richard arrived and took over the conversation. That was the effect he had.

The excitement in the room gradually increased. Everyone here loved Edward, and while many simultaneously hated his wife's family, they tolerated the grasping Woodvilles out of loyalty to him. How long would that coalition last when Edward was gone?

The queen sat beside her husband with her brothers and sisters arrayed to her left. Unlike Richard's group, the Woodvilles leaned toward each other occasionally and whispered in hushed tones. None of the other courtiers made eye contact or approached them for conversation.

But it wasn't the two clearly divided noble factions that caught Margaret's attention. Instead, her eye dwelled on Elizabeth, who watched her husband with visible concern. At first, Margaret didn't understand what had caught the queen's eye. Edward was known to spend plenty of time in his cups, but his eyes never dulled from intoxication and he never missed a word of the conversation. He was a typical man: a heavy drinker who could manage the alcohol.

Then, she saw the unmistakable twitching of his muscles.

It took a quarter-hour of discrete observation before she was certain. They were definite signs of intense muscle spasms, and concerning ones at that. He was taking extreme care to hide them, too. Perhaps he drank so much to dull the pain.

Having stamped the seeds of insurrection throughout his realm, he was facing the one opponent he couldn't brutalize into submission: his own body.

The concern on the queen's face as she surreptitiously studied her husband announced her fears. She believed Edward was dying.

Stunned by the realization, Margaret stumbled into a country knight's wife. The woman was dipping into a reverent bow when Margaret shocked her with an apology and escaped into a side corridor. Leaning against the wall, she inhaled several deep breaths to still her sudden dizziness.

If the queen knew, so would Anthony Woodville. Hardly a family to let sentiment crowd their scheming, the Woodvilles would be preparing, just like Beaujeu was doing in France.

Gossip hadn't said anything about the king being ill. From their mannerisms, not even Richard or Hastings suspected. They would be caught entirely unprepared.

Now she understood why Edward had ordered Richard to extend that generous offer. He didn't want his son to inherit old grudges. War followed successions as the princes of Europe tested new rulers. If Edward died while his son was still a minor, the threat would only intensify.

Any fool with the sense to find his nose at the end of his face knew Richard and the Woodvilles would battle over the regency. Though the Woodvilles were hated, they had too much to lose. They would be desperate for support. They would look for allies wherever they could find them…including the last of the Lancastrians. Margaret could even play them against Richard. And that presented a tremendous opportunity for Henry.

Margaret's despair transformed into hope. With luck, the king would die soon, and his coalition of supporters would crumble. Perhaps there would even be a civil war.

It was exactly the kind of delightful news she so desperately needed.

## HENRY

As Jehane wiggled in the steamy water of the washbasin, Henry remembered the delights of the previous evening. The very thought brought a smile to his face and an awakening of his body.

She knew he was watching. Teasing him, she poured water over her shoulders and ran her hands along her skin in a long stroke from neck to navel.

Laughing lightly, he knelt beside her and brushed aside a stray lock of her hair. "You're as beautiful as the day I met you."

"I should hope I've only grown lovelier after all these years."

"True." He twisted his lips into a wry grin. "You were a shrew the first time we spoke."

Giggling, she splashed him with her far hand. He reached down to tickle her hips and she shifted, dumping him into the basin with her. He could only resist her body, glistening with moisture, for a few seconds before succumbing to some mid-afternoon lovemaking.

Half an hour later, they draped themselves over the bed in exhaustion with a drying path of water between them and the basin. The red of his doublet was staining the floor.

A few years prior, they would have been more careful not to conceive a child. She had remained steadfast in scorning the shackles of marriage, and he refused to inflict the bastardy of his ancestors on his children. But despite their care, she had fallen into the increasing way two years earlier. They had kept it secret while considering how to react, but the miscarriage so early in the pregnancy had rendered their plans unnecessary.

She had suffered terribly and languished with weakness for some time. At first, his only thought had been for her physical health. But after she had recovered, the emotional pain had lingered. A desire they hadn't expected had awoken. The loss of what could have been haunted them. Before they'd realized what they had, it had gone.

For days at a time, she hadn't looked at him. At first, he'd insisted they talk through the pain, and though he had talked, she had said nothing. She spent weeks at Nantes, and again at St. Malo visiting her family. He'd thrown himself into his work. Eventually, he had stopped talking, too.

But one day, the terrible pain had subsided just enough for them to eat together. Slowly, they'd rediscovered the joy of each other. And then, without words, they'd decided to try again. There had been many interrupted baths and early departures from friends' homes. In all that time, though, no child had come. It was now out of their hands; God would do what he willed.

No longer did Vannes seem like a prison. Henry saw little reason to go anywhere, even if he could. He had Jehane and his uncle. What else did an exiled Englishman need?

If a part of him occasionally whispered its protest over the loss of his title and old life, he quieted it with good, hard work. After contributing to the success of Rousson tailors for seven years, he was a part of the business. He occupied his mornings with suppliers and his afternoons in front of Jehane's books, tallying every last ducat and florin.

Jasper still insisted that he attend dinners with the exiles, but with Jehane at his side, he used those meetings to make introductions that would see them prosper. Englishmen needed doublets and wives needed dresses. More than a little of the money Francis distributed to his growing community of exiles made its way into their pockets.

And the nights were reserved for them alone.

His mother saw him as a title wrongly stolen. To his uncle, he was a symbol of Lancastrian honor. The duke saw him as a shield against aggression from all sides. Oh, they all cared about his safety and prosperity, but none of their dreams would satisfy him like a quiet life in Vannes with Jehane.

What a fool he'd been to believe he needed his title and homeland to be happy!

That thought returned his attention to the reason he'd come to find her. "I've had news from England."

"Oh?" She was still lounging naked on the bed.

The play of light and shadow on her skin started to arouse him again and made him regret his news. "Edward offers to restore my status and grant me a freeholding worth four hundred pounds."

Jehane pushed herself onto an elbow. "Can the offer be trusted?"

He shrugged the thought away. "My mother instructed me not to give an answer yet."

They had discussed Margaret's desires many times. For her to advise against the proposal could mean anything from it being another deception to her being worried he might accept a settlement beneath his status.

"Four hundred a year isn't much."

"More than enough for a simple life far from the upheavals of court." He shook his head. "The price isn't the problem. If I accept, I'll no longer be a noble."

"Would that be so bad?" Always before, the risk had been that the Yorkists wouldn't believe Henry had given up his claims. "It could all truly be over."

He smiled faintly to conceal his pain. "If it were so, we'd return to England tomorrow, my love. But without my title, any noble in the realm could have me charged with a crime in the morning and executed by dinner."

Her eyes glazed over as she contemplated his words. At length, she shrugged. "I see why he proposed it."

Henry nodded. "He offers me a way to return in safety without limiting himself." He purposely avoided mentioning his mother's report on Edward's health. After a decade hunted by the Yorkists, he couldn't believe a timely death would solve his problems.

"Will you answer?" Her voice carried more curiosity than anxiety.

He grunted. "No. I agree with my mother's advice, for my own reasons."

"Then we have time for dinner. I'm starving."

They had worked up quite an appetite.

## THE PUBLIC

By the time it was clear Henry had no intention of answering Edward's offer, the king's health became public knowledge. A squad of wine stewards ensured the king's goblet never emptied, and even Richard acknowledged the need to dull his brother's near-constant pain.

The mood of the court changed. No longer did nobles align themselves by the maturity of their Yorkist sentiments, but rather by whether they supported Richard or the Woodvilles. Shunned dinner invitations and seating arrangements set the battle lines.

Already, the Woodvilles controlled the king's navy, armies, and royal purse and were responsible for the care of the crown prince, safely kept at Ludlow Castle.In Richard, the older nobles—Hastings, Buckingham, Norfolk, Northumberland—saw a strong hand capable of turning back the tide of arrogant upstarts the queen's family was appointing as fast as possible. Quietly, the old guard began appending powers to their supporters' positions.

During Easter, while Richard was away dividing the north with the Earl of Northumberland, the king coughed up blood. He died nine days later, having accomplished his father's dream of obliterating the Lancastrian half of his family.

Despite his love for Elizabeth, Edward hadn't been as wine-muddled or love-struck as some believed. A new will recognized the widespread unpopularity of the Woodvilles and named Richard as regent during his son's minority.

The court braced for civil war among former allies. Meanwhile, Anthony Woodville moved quickly, convincing the Privy Council to restrict Richard's role to that of head of the regency council, not regent himself, and hastened the new king's coronation. Anthony himself was dispatched to Ludlow Castle to retrieve the new king. After Edward V's coronation, the public reasoned, Elizabeth would turn the new king against Richard once and for all.

A few days later, Buckingham proposed that the court historian prepare a summary of Edward V's lineage for the coronation. No one saw any reason to object.

Shortly afterward, Richard sent an elegant letter from Middleham to the queen offering his condolences on the loss of her husband and pledging to uphold the succession of Edward's heir.

The court was astounded until someone mentioned how pragmatic Richard had been the previous year when dealing with northern nobles who hadn't supported his invasion of Scotland. He was a reasonable and intelligent man. Why had they been so worried?

# CHAPTER NINE

## MARGARET

MARGARET FEARED SHE'D seriously miscalculated the consequences of Edward's death. After so many failed plans and years of frustrating ineffectiveness, Margaret's hopes required a struggle between Richard's faction and the Woodvilles. Richard considered Elizabeth a succubus who had stolen his brother's vitality with her sexual perversions, while the Woodvilles feared Richard for his birth, ability, and inveterate hostility to their power. Neither had any choice but to destroy the other. Surely they understood this.

Margaret needed bloodshed and murder in the streets. Why were they doing nothing?

Cultivating a reputation as a devout and proper noblewoman had made her a desirable companion for the ladies of the court. Her son's status, on the other hand, kept her on the political periphery, so she could do little to precipitate open conflict. All she could do was maintain the regimen that had served her so well, which meant being seen praying for Edward IV's soul in Westminster.

Or, at least, kneeling with the other ladies who were offering prayers for Edward IV's soul. She was convinced a vengeful God would find her punitive prayers quite justified. The dead king's crimes assuredly justified Hell's finest punishment, while his victims—including her father—watched from Heaven above.

It was still early in the morning, perhaps an hour after dawn, when the polished doors of the abbey burst open. A host of soldiers wearing the Woodville livery fanned out through the chamber and began to secure the exits.

They had come for her.

A group of women rushed in, headed by Queen Elizabeth and accompanied by her son by her first husband, Thomas Grey, who ordered the doors locked. The queen's daughters and her only son in London, the Duke of York, clustered around her, huddling together in blind terror.

Some of the guards had gashes across their faces.

They hadn't come for her, after all. The dam had finally broken.

Seeing the girls whimpering and clutching their mother's hands, Margaret felt a pity she did not expect. They were innocent of their father's crimes.

Only Elizabeth of York, the oldest, remained composed as she cared for her younger sisters. She was comely, though not beautiful. Her fine, smooth complexion and the chestnut hair so akin to her mother's could only partially mitigate her weak Plantagenet chin and mulish resemblance to Edward.

The other girls were their mother's daughters—beautiful with delicate features, strong chins, and thin necks. They cast occasional glances toward their eldest sister, copying her gestures and poise.

And then there was eight-year-old Richard, the Duke of York, whose long golden curls more resembled his sisters than his half-brother Grey.

This was her opportunity. Margaret turned to the others who had been at prayer, who were watching the arrival in stunned silence.

"Ladies, your queen has need of you." Crossing the distance, she smiled at the young girls and offered the queen a quick curtsey. "My lady, allow us to care for you and your family."

"Lady Margaret?" the queen asked breathlessly. Like her daughters, she still wore her nightgown. The Woodville girls weren't early risers like Margaret. "I thank you for your kindness."

"What has happened?"

"It was all so fast…" Fury filled her cheeks and burned through her eyes. "He'll pay for his treachery!" Her fervor fled a moment later, and she dropped her head into her hands. "My son!"

Grey had finished issuing his orders and was now approaching. The other ladies had already drawn the children away to soothe them. The three of them were being given some privacy.

Margaret curtseyed to him, as well. "My Lord Grey, I pray you forgive my impertinence, but it appeared your sisters could use soothing."

His eyes carried his suspicion. "I thank you for your compassion."

She stepped closer. "What has happened?"

"Gloucester," the queen growled.

"Has he sent word from Middleham?"

"Oh, he sent word," Elizabeth replied with venom. "Kind words to lull us into complacency while Buckingham, Richard, and his northerners intercepted my brother and son." She had to have been referring to Anthony Woodville and Richard Grey on the way to London with the king.

"Was there a battle?" The king had an honor guard of three thousand.

"If only. Anthony greeted them as friends, only to be arrested. Richard took possession of them all, including my son the king."

"When was this?"

"Yesterday," Grey answered. "Had my brother's groom not stopped to relieve himself, he too would have been detained. I'd have heard nothing of this, and we'd all be caught now."

"Caught?"

"Catesby's men came for us. 'For our protection.' He said Earl Rivers and my brother had committed treason against His Majesty."

The queen glowered. "He issued warrants against all the men of my family."

The Woodvilles had no reason to conspire against the young prince—now the young king—when he was their surest protection against Richard's reprisals and the animosity of the rest of the kingdom.

Richard's actions astounded her. In one stroke, he had acquired the young king and cast a net to snare the entire Woodville clan. He'd have had to coordinate intricate actions from hundreds of miles away with such clarity that even Buckingham couldn't misunderstand. And, he had done it all in complete secrecy.

He would need to delay the coronation until he'd neutralized every last Woodville. Even afterward, who could say what the young king would believe of his relatives with Richard pouring reports of treason in his ear?

But the Woodvilles were still alive, even those in captivity. "Will you rescue Lord Rivers?"

The queen shook her head. "Richard convinced the king's escort of my family's treason. We cannot rely on their loyalty. And I don't know where they're being held."

Margaret considered. "If Richard is wise, he would remove them to one of his strongholds, surrounded by men he trusts. That means the north."

The queen relaxed visibly at the sensible conclusion. "Without my brother Edward's fleet, we would have to traverse all of England to reach them."

"You cannot risk it, mother," Grey said. "If Richard should lay hands upon you…"

"Your son is right, my lady," Margaret agreed. "While no one would believe you capable of conspiring against your eldest son, Richard would surely use your brother's and son's captivity to force you to support his regency."

The queen scoffed. "Not even Richard would threaten the new king's stepbrother and uncle as a mere regent." Yet, her voice quivered with uncertainty. Richard had already arrested them.

"We must take every precaution to ensure he acquires no further captives," Margaret said.

The queen narrowed her eyes. "What do you suggest?"

"I propose you follow my example, my lady," Margaret said. "When your husband hunted my son and brother-in-law, I remained in England to effect a reconciliation. My own father was the king's enemy, yet my sex protected me from retribution."

"But you've failed in your efforts, Lady Beaufort."

Grey's clumsy bluntness drew an irate glare from his mother.

"Nonetheless, I was safe in England, as your mother and siblings will be. And my task was much harder. I had to express my son's affection for a king he'd actively fought against. Your mother need only convince the young king to hold his relatives to trial. The charges are outrageous, and Richard cannot possibly present credible evidence. He will have to free them."

The queen chewed at her lip. "We were harried all the way here. I don't imagine we could escape London even if we wished to."

Grey straightened. "Richard is pious; he will not violate sanctuary."

The queen sighed. "So I must remain a prisoner in every way but name while Richard hunts down the rest of my family."

"Think of the safety of your daughters and son, mother," Grey said.

"And from here, you will hear news to benefit them," Margaret added. "Your family will need as much information as possible to rescue Master Grey and Lord Rivers."

Elizabeth Woodville smiled at Margaret with a surprising warmness. "I never considered you to be trustworthy, Lady Beaufort. I see now how wrong I was."

Pressing her lips together, Margaret considered her response. This was a rich opportunity to cultivate the queen's friendship, but she refused to be accused of breaking faith.

"On your husband's orders, my husband was detained until his death. My cousin died fighting against him. But revenge is a man's pursuit. My only desire was to restore my son to his rightful rank and position. My son's life is more important to me than past deeds."

It was a more honest assessment than she'd ever offered in this Yorkist court.

"Rest assured that we will not forget your kind counsel," the queen answered with more sincerity than any Woodville had ever offered a Beaufort. She gestured for the abbot, who had been hovering at a respectful distance, to approach. "Abbot, I throw myself upon the mercy of the church. I and my children are but humble sinners persecuted for our relationship to His Majesty. I ask for the safety and sanctuary of the Holy Church."

The abbot cast his eyes across the assembly of soldiers, worshipers, and ladies. "In the name of our Lord Jesus Christ, I grant you His protection."

"Mother," Grey piped, "my duty is to assemble our retainers to release my brother and uncle."

"Against Richard?" Elizabeth's eyes widened. "His agents and vassals fill the north. They'll pin you down long enough for Richard and his soldiers to arrive. You're no match for him on the field."

Though Grey began to bristle, Margaret anticipated his outburst. "My lord, while your skills are formidable, recall that the Duke of Gloucester's victories extend beyond this past summer against the Scots. Even his enemies admired his skill at Tewkesbury and Barnet."

The queen was probably overstating the risk—it would take four weeks to assemble and march an army north—but Margaret needed to delay them until her son could profit from this opportunity.

To Margaret's surprise, the blatant flattery satisfied his outrage.

The queen muttered, "I will not gamble with the lives of my kin. We must not antagonize Richard until my son Edward is crowned. My boy knows I desire only his happiness." She pressed her lips together. "Then, we will strike Richard down."

Margaret licked her lips. "Where will you gather your forces?"

"England isn't safe with charges of treason hanging over our heads," Grey warned.

Elizabeth nodded. "France would extract too severe a price, I fear."

"Scotland has no cause to love Richard," Grey suggested.

"But the bulk of Richard's loyalists would rest between you and London, or even you and your captured relatives," Margaret reminded.

"What option remains? The Welsh would rather watch us destroy each other," Elizabeth spat on the floor at mention of that hated race. That was a pity. Some of the Welsh lords still wrote Margaret with tender remembrances for her husband's family.

Regardless, Margaret had an even better alternative. "Brittany."

"Brittany." Elizabeth scowled. "Duke Francis is a wily old goat incapable of giving a straight answer to anything."

"Which is exactly why he's your best protection," Margaret explained. "Recall, he has some experience protecting English fugitives. I'm sure he would do so again. And in Brittany, my son can unite your forces with the Lancastrian exiles to eject Richard."

"In exchange for your son's restoration to Richmond." Grey scoffed. "Now your purpose is clear."

"I have been honest about my desires, have I not?" The remark elicited only begrudging silence. "My son has long yearned to return to the safety of his old title in his home country. Surely that's a fair price for aiding the young king's mother and her family?"

The queen studied Margaret for several heartbeats. If she sought duplicity, she would find none. For the first time since Anthony Woodville had teased her objectives out of her before St. Malo, she had spoken the unmitigated truth.

But the suggestion also made sense, and Elizabeth Woodville was no fool. Brittany provided access to ports that could disembark soldiers anywhere along the English coast before an alarm could be raised. That possibility had tormented her husband for twelve years.

The queen nodded. "I will write to my family, urging them to shelter in Brittany until the time is ripe to crush Richard."

She and Grey began to discuss the last-known locations of their family members. Edward Woodville was at sea with the English fleet, fending off French corsairs at the request of the king's council, and would have to be intercepted before returning home. Richard Woodville was in France.

Margaret gave them their privacy. Some of the ladies had already left, either to spread this gossip or out of fear of associating with the beleaguered queen. Margaret cared little whether they mentioned her aid to Elizabeth Woodville. She had cultivated a reputation of piety and compassion. No one would remark on her aiding a family in need.

Hopefully, Elizabeth wouldn't tarry before writing to the other Woodvilles. Richard had them reeling. He would use each moment to hunt them down with both royal forces and his own. The Woodvilles needed to collect their strength. They needed allies. Her son could provide both.

Richard would probably scorn any offer of support Margaret made now that he had the young king in his possession. If she was wrong and Richard sought to entice Henry to his side with his old title, that would be acceptable, too.

Everything was falling into place.

She had a letter to write. A swift ship would take one of Reginald Bray's men to Brittany on the evening tide.

## HENRY

Though the port of Vannes was some distance to the south beyond the ramparts, many points in the city offered a clear view of the bay. While meeting with Jehane's lace supplier, Henry spotted Edward Woodville's ship on the horizon.

Henry could do sums in his head, keep a ledger, and rattle off supply costs. His real skill was in staring down a partner and understanding him, his desires, and his fears. But, he would never be a merchant. His past refused to let him go.

Bray's agent had prepared him for this ship, though not when it would arrive. His mother had thrust him right back into the middle of another civil war. Having long since stopped wasting thought about what might be, he simply sighed, sent a warning to his uncle, and returned home to change into his finest doublet.

He, Jasper, the Lord of Vannes, the other Lancastrian knights, and two contingents of Breton soldiers had assembled by the time the English ship glided into port. It felt strange to be beyond the walls after being constrained by them for so many years.

Jasper leaned closer. "Just relax. Respond to Woodville as you would to Quelennec or Rieux." A moment later, he added, "But, no matter how arrogantly he acts, don't bow or abase yourself. He's the son of a commoner and brother to a whore. You're descended from Edward III and the King of France."

Henry silently searched for a way to avoid the next few minutes. Perhaps Woodville had fallen ill and died on the passage. Or perhaps he would act so insufferably arrogant that Henry and his uncle could reach no honorable accommodation.

When Edward began to descend the gangplank, those hopes vanished. This fresh-faced man in his late twenties lacked the proud tilt of chin that Henry expected from the Woodvilles. The precision of his movements and the way he balanced the weight of his sword suggested he knew combat. In that, he reminded Henry of Catesby.

He could deliberately spoil this conversation. Edward would probably assume Henry had forgotten how to conduct himself during all his time away from court. If he lived up to that expectation, he could still stay with Jehane.

But no, that was foolish. Beside him, the Count of Vannes shifted, grunting slightly and rubbing the knee permanently maimed in an accident some years earlier. Duke Francis would hear of it if Henry acted like a fool. Already, there were whispers that the Tudors' value had diminished. A new English king provided an opportunity for

Francis to rid himself of his pesky guests, a fact Jasper had repeated endlessly over the past two days.

Edward Woodville stopped before them and studied his greeters with a hawk-like intensity. His clothes smelled of salt and sweat. After a brief hesitation, he offered Henry a shallow bow. "My Lord Richmond."

Beside him, Jasper gasped.

Henry could not believe his ears. The queen's brother had greeted him by the title her husband had so long denied him.

"Sir Woodville." Henry inclined his head a fraction. Though he was the brother of a queen, Edward was still simply a knight. An earl—at least, a man greeted in the style of an earl—vastly outranked him. "We heard about the trouble in England. I'm pleased to see you're well." He paused for a moment, as Jasper had demonstrated in their preparations for this meeting. "What brings you to Brittany?"

They had debated this opening for some time. Though Henry had wanted to let Woodville begin, Jasper had insisted that Henry set the tone. The Yorkists had committed enough crimes against Henry in particular to justify suspicion. Eager to end the debate, Henry had relented.

"What exactly have you heard?"

Jasper had instructed Henry to ask the questions, but he had to be certain of the facts first. "Edward IV is dead. Gloucester will preside as head of the Privy Council until the king's coronation, and he has arrested Lord Rivers."

Woodville pressed his lips together. "Then you have not heard the latest. Once he arrested my brother, Richard had himself named Protector of the Realm, with all the powers of a king."

Richard could do whatever he wished.

Henry flicked his eyes to Jasper, whose deep stare suggested he was already considering the ramifications.

"Has he attainted your family and their supporters?" Jasper asked.

"No." Woodville's lips curled into a smirk.

Jasper drew in a quick breath. "No?"

Turning to him, Woodville bowed his head. "My Lord Pembroke."

"Sir Woodville."

"Much to Richard's surprise, the council has forbidden it. Nor have they allowed him to execute my brother and nephew."

"Unbelievable." Jasper shook his head.

Many of those same men had done nothing when Edward had deposed King Henry because of the vile conduct of Queen Margaret and her favorites. The Woodvilles were just as bad, yet now they chose to intervene?

"Richard may have the position," Woodville explained, "but the new king will one day be a man. While he may not avenge himself upon his uncle, my nephew will certainly punish those who supported him." He sighed. "They fear to execute us but are content to see us humbled."

They feared the new king more than Richard. After so many years evading the sons of York, Henry could scarcely believe it.

Years earlier, Henry had told his uncle their cause was dead unless something significant changed. This was it. His uncle had been right all along. The Woodvilles only needed to survive until the coronation.

"I'm pleased you reached Brittany safely, my lord." Henry craned his neck to survey the horizon. "When will the rest of your fleet arrive?"

Woodville's brow furrowed. "There will be no further ships. The majority chose to put in at Calais until they received new orders."

"I see." Henry suspected the other captains had lacked confidence in the Woodville cause. Commoners, even insightful ones like Jehane, often struggled with the consequences of the close-knit relations among nobles.

"Lord Tudor?" Woodville gestured to the side. Once they'd drawn off from the main party, Edward continued in a whisper. "Let us speak plainly, Henry. My family is on the run, our forces are scattered, and Richard is free to poison my nephew's ear with claims of our treason. Everyone wearing the Woodville crest is a marked man until Richard is removed from power. But the king's coronation will cure all our ills. We simply need to survive until it takes place. Then, we can return."

Margaret had written about how Elizabeth had spent every available minute with the boy, and Anthony Woodville had doted on him, too. Once he was king, young Edward could overrule his uncle, recall his mother from sanctuary, and restore her relatives. Richard would have been better served by killing Anthony Woodville and Richard Grey outright.

"My mother agrees," Henry acknowledged. "I admit, it sounds like you require Brittany more than Henry Tudor."

Woodville shrugged. "What if Richard doesn't step aside easily? Stanley, Northumberland, and Hastings will support the king's decisions, but can that be said for Richard's wife's family, the Nevilles? What about Buckingham, who arrested my brother alongside Richard? And what of Norfolk?" He jutted his chin toward Henry. "You can bring loyalties we lack. The Lancastrians would follow you and your uncle if you align with us, and your Tudor blood would help recruit the Welsh."

"Buckingham controls the Marches," Henry reminded.

"How many men would follow a Buckingham when a Tudor asks for their loyalty?"

Henry conceded the point; Welsh lords wouldn't regularly be writing of their continuing affection for the Tudors if Buckingham had been so beloved.

Woodville shrugged. "With York, Lancaster, and the Welsh allied against him, even Richard's famous strength at arms would falter."

"And in exchange for my support…?"

"Richard's lands are vast," Woodville said. "Those under attainder who fight for the king will see their holdings and titles restored."

It was a rich offer. While Richard would become more vulnerable with time, it was still a dangerous gamble. The duke had pulled himself out of trouble before when he'd maneuvered his brother George into treason. Could Henry ever consider Richard to be beaten whilst he drew breath?

But more than just his fate depended on this decision. Some Lancastrians might follow Woodville anyway, but the story of St. Malo had become almost legendary. And there was that business of his blood claim to the throne through his bastard of an ancestor. If Henry was willing to put aside his grievances, the rest of the Lancastrians would follow him.

His choice would alter the fate of a great many men.

Woodville had detailed a solid strategy. If Richard submitted to the young king's wishes, nothing more would be required of Henry than lending his name to the cause. It was a small price to pay to recover his title. He could be whole again.

"You have my support." He forced himself to smile as he extended his hand.

Woodville shook it eagerly.

With four words, he had committed himself to a cause as dangerous as that which had brought him to Brittany. He only hoped he was making the right decision.

## MARGARET

While Londoners of all classes seemed delighted to see the Woodvilles fall, suggesting that they would commit treason against one of their own was going too far. Why would Anthony Woodville conspire to depose a nephew who would be even more susceptible to the queen's influence than King Edward? But Richard must have had compelling evidence to have acted so boldly, let alone convince Buckingham, married to a Woodville, to support him. Apprehension in the capital grew.

Margaret had told her husband about the queen entering sanctuary. A skilled survivor, he knew his safety rested in ignorance and had asked no questions about their conversation. But he had seen the sense in ordering his brother William to quietly equip a few hundred of his most loyal men with arms and rations for two weeks.

Though Stanley would not risk taking sides, he continued to accept invitations for private dinners, offering Margaret opportunities to identify potential allies without jeopardizing his neutrality.

Nonetheless, Margaret spoke little when Bishop Morton joined them for dinner. The bishop repeatedly asked probing questions, but Stanley offered no opinions about recent events beyond expressing hope for a joyful coronation. She refused to openly undermine her husband's efforts, but she shared more than one meaningful look with Morton throughout the night. By the time he departed, she felt confident the bishop understood her feelings didn't align with her husband's.

The following day, Morton entered the pew next to her at morning prayers and crossed himself. "My lady," he whispered into his folded hands.

They were alone except for a pair of altar boys going about their duties too far away to overhear them.

"Your Excellency." From dinner, she had gathered he was a loyal Yorkist, but that definition ceased to be sufficient. "Have you heard the latest rumor?"

He abandoned his illusion of pious prayer. "I have not."

"Apparently, the Scots are planning to dig up Robert the Bruce and invade England with an army of ghosts."

He allowed himself a faint smile, though the tension in his fingers remained. "The people are surprisingly inventive."

"No more than when King Henry was deposed. They're uncertain and afraid."

"They have much to be uncertain about," Morton admitted. "Such as why the king has not been crowned, despite his arrival in London more than a month ago. Such as what Richard will do now that his request to execute Woodville has been denied. Such as why Catesby visited Hastings last night and what they might have discussed over dinner."

Margaret turned at that, abandoning her own pretense. "Catesby and Hastings?"

He nodded. "Indeed. He stayed for nearly two hours."

At St. Malo, Catesby had proven himself a deceitful minion, albeit an intelligent one. On the other hand, Hastings was an honorable man who had rebelled out of genuine revulsion at Margaret of Anjou's policies. The difference in their birth alone would render Catesby too common to share Hastings' table. The only reason they could have possibly dined together was to discuss Richard.

"How do you know he stayed so long?"

Morton offered a patient expression of indulgence. As a member of the Privy Council, naturally he had his peers followed.

"What is Richard planning?" she muttered.

Morton rubbed at one of his knuckles. "All of Europe is asking the same question. The Scottish ambassador asked me directly if Richard intends to seize the throne."

"He said that?"

"The very words."

"How did you reply?"

"I told him I had no idea what the protector planned. Only later did I realize my poise revealed more than I'd intended."

Margaret understood his meaning. Shock and outrage would have suggested the thought had never occurred to him. Mere surprise would suggest he had previously contemplated the matter. But calmness indicated well-conceived fears.

"So, you believe the rumors?"

"I told the ambassador the truth, Lady Beaufort. I truly don't know what Richard intends. He insists the coronation will occur. The people seem to believe him."

"The people *want* to believe him," Margaret corrected. "They want stability. Fears that Anthony Woodville may have conspired against his nephew are ridiculous, though widespread."

Residents who could afford to leave London had already fled to their country estates. Even the beggars had gone elsewhere. Merchants were making arrangements to ship their goods out of the city to their storehouses in the ports. Many nobles had spread retainers along the coast to give warning of a Woodville invasion.

"They're not alone in wondering," Morton said.

"When you broached this subject last night, you didn't share such opinions."

He shrugged. "Your husband seemed unwilling to discuss it."

"He is skilled in keeping his own counsel," Margaret admitted. "Yet you share freely with me?"

"I cannot believe you're as uninterested in the matter as your husband. Your son's status may very well be affected by it."

How far could she trust this man? Though his family had Lancastrian roots, Morton had supported Edward. Revealing too much about her desires for her son to Anthony Woodville had nearly gotten him killed at St. Malo. But that had been when Yorkist meant only one thing. The concerns Morton had raised suggested he didn't support Richard now.

"I take interest in any venture that may see my son restored. Richard is no friend of my cause."

"Any venture?" Eagerness edged Morton's tone.

"Yes."

He nodded deliberately. "A dangerous situation is developing, Lady Margaret. Richard has gone too far for the Woodvilles to forgive. If his request to execute Lord Rivers without trial is any indication, Richard realizes his mistake. His only choice is to destroy them utterly." He swallowed once. "This will end in blood."

He had rightly assessed both the situation and the Woodvilles' fury. Margaret had heard as much from the queen herself.

Despite the risk, Margaret found herself trusting this bishop. "Why would Richard send Catesby to meet with Hastings instead of going himself?"

"To keep the meeting secret, I imagine," Morton replied. "Catesby took great pains to avoid being followed. I discovered the meeting only because my men were observing Hastings, too."

"What does he need from Hastings specifically? It can't be soldiers. He hasn't approached my husband."

"Sending a cretin to ask a man like Hastings for military support would be an insult." He sighed. "I can think of only one reason."

If he meant to execute the Woodvilles, Richard needed royal authority. "He truly intends to depose his nephew."

"And Catesby was gauging Hastings' support," Morton concluded.

She swallowed the lump in the back of her throat. "If only we knew what they said in that conversation."

"Indeed, Lady Margaret. But take heart; two hours is perfectly suitable for dinner, particularly among men who do not share affection."

"I don't follow you, my lord."

Morton's lip curled into a smirk. "If Catesby and Hastings had come to an accord, the pretext of dinner would not be necessary, and Catesby would rush off to inform Richard. That he stayed for the duration indicates he needed to maintain the pretense."

She'd never before made that observation despite having accepted many invitations. However, neither had she the kind of authority that attracted supplicants. "Where do your loyalties lie, my lord?"

Morton swiveled his head, searching the corners of the church. "The Lancastrian cause is dead. Edward IV established a claim through conquest. Who can I support but his son?"

Disappointed to hear that another Lancastrian had resigned himself to Yorkist rule, Margaret nonetheless could not blame him. "And if Richard claims the throne?"

Morton straightened. "All true Englishmen must resist him."

She released a breath in relief. "Who supports him?"

"His northern Neville retainers. Buckingham, though I'd have never guessed it, considering his wife." A moment later, he added, "Northumberland and Norfolk would support the stronger side. If he has Hastings, no one could resist them, even your husband."

They fell silent. The sounds of the altar boys muffling their laughter in the vestibule echoed through the church. They had long since finished lighting the remaining candles in the abbey. It still seemed darker than when she'd entered.

Morton shook his head. "I can't imagine Richard would risk another civil war."

"If he knew he could win, Richard would risk a great deal more than that. He has no choice but to destroy the Woodvilles."

"The court wouldn't stand for it. The people wouldn't stand for it," Morton insisted.

"My cousin and the king died from that delusion. The people want stability. Richard would make a strong king."

"Once the heads ceased to roll," Morton muttered.

She was a survivor of a defeated faction. It had been almost three decades since her first husband Edmund had died, and twelve years since King Henry. Though the pain had dulled, she still carried the memory.

Morton was only now beginning to feel the ache of a world on the wrong path. Yet, pain was a tremendous motivator, and she needed allies that would fight with her.

"And all that stands in Richard's way is Hastings' honor," she mused. "It provides me little comfort, since he was so flexible with it fifteen years ago."

"Then we must prepare other means to ensure that Richard upholds his nephew's succession." He swallowed. "Will your husband support the young king or Richard?"

Despite his kindness, Stanley would not risk his own safety. "He will support the young king until doing so becomes dangerous."

"Let us hope more lords feel the same way. Particularly Hastings."

"But if he's in league with Richard and Buckingham—"

"I will press for the young king's immediate coronation. How the council responds will reveal their loyalties." He crossed himself and began to rise. "Meanwhile, inform your son and Edward Woodville to ready themselves to defend their king."

Margaret crossed herself as well. "Let us pray it won't be necessary, my lord bishop."

## MORTON

The next day, Richard called a meeting at the Tower of London to discuss the coronation, inviting Stanley, Hastings, and Buckingham as the preeminent lords of the realm, as well as Morton and Archbishop Rotherham of York, both of whom would have significant roles in the ceremony.

Despite the heat, Morton chose to wear the full garb of his position, including his purple robe, *zucchetto*, and the chain and rings of his office. Dangerous though he might be, Richard had always deferred to the church and continued to honor the queen's claim of sanctuary. Morton wasn't too proud to appeal to Richard's piety for his own protection.

When he reached the small room in Beauchamp Tower, the group was already conversing. A few of them snacked on sweet cakes in the center of the small table.

"Before considering precedence, we must determine the date," Richard insisted. "The Woodvilles emptied the royal treasury when they fled. I fear it may be in sanctuary with Lady Woodville."

Morton suspected that only her relationship with the young king justified Richard using the humble term 'Lady'.

Richard turned. "Rotherham, did you see any gold?"

Eyes widening, Rotherham darted his gaze from one noble to another but found no one willing to aid him. The night the queen had fled into sanctuary, she had demanded the great seal from him, and he'd unfortunately obeyed.

"No, Your Grace." He quickly added, "Nor did I see any when I corrected that error and retrieved it."

Richard shrugged, apparently letting the matter drop.

"The people need to be awed by their monarch," Buckingham

added with remarkable insight. "After all the plots, it will settle their minds and re-establish order."

"Then we are agreed to bestow the full majesty of his position on the next king?" After the briefest of pauses, Richard added, "Without the coffers, we must tax to pay for the coronation."

Hastings and Rotherham shifted in their seats at this news.

Richard threw a hand up. "We cannot possibly have the coronation before late July."

"We need not have the funds in advance," Hastings retorted. "If a man won't accept a pledge of repayment from his king, he is a traitor."

"Well said," Stanley added. "A secure succession is the strongest way to douse the flames of dissent. You've dealt with the Woodvilles, but how long will the Welsh or Scots wait before interpreting our lack of a king as weakness?"

"Planning a coronation takes time," Buckingham said.

"We cannot wait until July. England needs a king now." The room fell silent at the speed of Hastings' response.

Morton swallowed. The moment had come.

Hastings leaned forward and stabbed the table with his finger. "Edward V must assume the throne immediately." He gestured to Rotherham and Morton before raising his hand to the heavens. "As soon as is religiously auspicious, of course."

Morton simply gaped at him. He had been certain Hastings would propose Richard as king. He had clearly misread the alliances brewing. That concerned him deeply.

Rotherham shifted through his papers. "The soonest auspicious date is June seventeenth."

"It'll take twenty days for the lords in Wales to reach London," Stanley reminded.

The bishop consulted his documents again. "The twenty-second is also acceptable."

"Then June twenty-second it is," Richard agreed.

Satisfied, Hastings plucked up a sweet cake and popped it into his mouth.

"The venue will be Westminster?" Rotherham pressed.

"The witch still abides there," Buckingham added with surprising confidence. "We must deal with her."

Patting him on the shoulder, Richard rose. "Now that we have a date, I will go presently and appeal to her desire for a peaceful beginning to her son's reign." He casually claimed one of the cakes. "If that convinces her not, I'll remind her I still have her brother in my custody. Gentlemen"—he bowed—"I leave the remaining preparations in your capable hands."

Stanley started to rise out of respect, but Richard left too quickly to see the gesture.

Once he had departed, Buckingham and Hastings began arguing about which of them deserved to be closest to the king in the coronation procession.

"I will not walk beside a mere baron," Buckingham insisted. "As a duke, I should precede all but the royal family. And I am married to the king's aunt."

"A Woodville aunt," Hastings reminded with a sneer.

"Let's ask the young king if he sees a distinction," Buckingham countered.

"Let's ask if Richard has room on the block for another Woodville relative."

Overcome by some unknown sentiment, Buckingham began laughing.

"Enough!" Stanley shouted. "You walk together. Hastings, you're only a baron. And Buckingham, your father was executed for treason. Be content that you walk before the King of Mann."

Morton almost grinned at seeing Stanley put these two nobles in their place as only one of the oldest nobility could.

As they began to put the knights in order, the door burst open with a violent crash.

"Sorcery. Treason!" Richard stormed into the room. "I am beset by traitors!"

The sudden outburst left everyone speechless, helpless to do anything but watch Richard pace with heavy steps.

"Damn that Woodville succubus! She poisons me with her sorcery." Meeting Hastings' eyes, Richard crossed and lifted his shirt, showing the deep twist in his spine. "Do you see, William, what she has done with her charms and incantations?"

Hastings, stunned by the bizarre claim, looked around for help, but the others were just as surprised. Richard had borne that deformation all his life.

"She thins my blood, leaving me light-headed. And always, the evil eye." The duke fingered the hilt of his dagger.

Hastings paled, in stark contrast to the flush during his argument with Buckingham. "Richard, what has happened?"

Stopping, Richard shook his hands near his head. "I have just heard proof of her sorcery. Her confederates bring ingredients for dark rituals to her in sanctuary."

Morton exchanged a glance with Stanley. Richard meant to absolve the protections of sanctuary with this claim of sorcery.

"You must present your proof to the Church," Hastings ventured. "Sorcery will not be tolerated within our holy places."

"Bless you, my friend." Richard collapsed into his chair. "Oh, how can a man defend against witchcraft?"

"It must be truly awful," Hastings stammered. His eyes searched wildly. Like Morton himself, the baron was struggling to comprehend this strange turn in Richard's demeanor.

"And the punishment, William? What is the punishment for sorcery?"

Hastings smiled. "My friend, the punishment for sorcery is death."

Richard brought his supposedly afflicted fist down on the table with a shattering crash. A dozen men bearing the Neville crest burst through the doors and rushed for the assembled lords. Rotherham and Morton didn't have time to stand before the guards gripped them tightly on either arm.

Stanley released a shrill cry and tried to duck beneath the table, striking his head and falling to the floor in a daze. Hastings—face pale and eyes dilated by the sudden invasion—backed up until he bumped into the wall, at which point he froze and was surrounded.

Buckingham, however, sat calmly during the commotion. Once the others were secure, he rose to stand beside Richard.

The guards hauled Stanley to his feet. Blood trickled down his forehead and cheek.

Richard stalked forward and halted before Hastings. "I arrest you, traitor, for sorcery and conspiring with the queen." He jabbed a finger in Hastings' face. "You wish the young king to be crowned so the witch can manipulate him again. You conspire to destroy me with charms and works of the Devil."

"Richard, I swear I have never—" Hastings began.

"Silence!" Richard thundered. "You, who claimed my friendship, only to have your mistress Jane Shore cast charms and spells on me."

"Wh-what? Jane Shore has no allegiance to the queen."

"See!" Richard turned to face the rest. "He persists in calling her queen, despite her family's crimes." He snapped his head back toward Hastings. "Villain, I will not tolerate treason in my midst."

"Richard—"

The duke brushed his arms across the table, knocking its contents to the floor. "By St. Paul, not another word." The plates clattered before eventually coming to rest. Richard pointed to the scattered food. "I will not dine until I see thy head off!"

In the time it took Hastings' eyes to dilate in awareness, two of Richard's men hauled him out of the room.

Richard glared at the other guards and slashed a hand across the remaining lords. "Take these men to the highest room in the tower until I determine the extent of this treason."

As he was being dragged away, Morton turned to protest his

innocence, but he fell silent when he saw Richard exchange a look of smug delight with Buckingham.

Hastings' pleas reached them from Tower Green until the sickening thunk of an axe burying itself in wood and the unmistakable thud of a body falling to the ground silenced them.

Baron Hastings, the second-most-powerful man in England and a staunch supporter of Edward IV, was dead.

## THE PUBLIC

The claim was shocking. Pious, good Hastings, guilty of witchcraft against a dear friend? Reports even implicated Lord Stanley and members of the clergy. Of all the claims tossed back and forth—the Woodvilles' treason, Richard's devil's mark, reports of Henry VI's queen sailing to England with French fleets—this one had to be false.

But Richard's agents among the crowds whispered that Stanley and Hastings had ancient blood. Perhaps they had designs on the throne themselves. Stanley had even married a Lancastrian, whereas the Duke of Gloucester had stalwartly defended his brother from all challenges, including exposing the treachery of his brother George all those years past.

Then, the heralds announced Hastings' execution. His guilt, they declared, had been self-evident, and Richard had acted within the rights of the royal authority he possessed as protector.

No one chose to mention the limits placed on Richard's authority that had been intended to prevent exactly this sort of abuse. Schemes to rescue the captives in Pontefract were abandoned. In the next four days, six more Woodville retainers were betrayed to Richard's agents. Hastings' death had shown how Richard would deal with men he considered enemies.

Margaret only learned of her husband's incarceration when her maids returned home in a panic after hearing the second reading of the proclamation. Fighting down the rapid beating in her chest, Margaret wrote to her husband's brother William. They needed to act before more of Richard's northern Neville retainers arrived.

## MARGARET

Margaret paced in the empty, hot room, adjusting the positioning of her sleeves yet again. Richard had kept her waiting for over an hour now. And unlike Westminster's main audience chamber, there was nothing for her to occupy herself with except thoughts of the impending confrontation. Nor did it have windows to mitigate the stifling heat.

If he meant to impress upon her the treatment due to the wife of a traitor, his point was unnecessary. She well-remembered the uncomfortable scrutiny when Edward had called her to account for her family after Barnet and Tewkesbury. At least she had the chance to save this husband from sharing her father's fate. The last time, the executions had already occurred.

Hastings had died for reasons no one understood. That made her course a dangerous one, particularly considering her tactics. One never knew how Richard would react.

But she had no choice. If Richard executed Stanley, he would not hesitate to do the same to her.

When Richard finally entered, the thunder of him pulling the door open and slamming it shut again startled her. Without as much as a greeting, he eased himself into the throne with an imperious pose. "Lady Margaret, what do you want?"

Of course, he knew what she wanted.

Margaret offered a mild curtsey without moving to the center of the room. She didn't need to defer to him in private. "I want you to release my husband."

"Request denied. Anything further?"

She remained undaunted by the speed of his reply. "Why are you holding him?"

He casually buffed at a scratch on the arm of the throne. "I'm investigating reports that he conspired to undermine my regency and restore the Woodvilles."

She swallowed nervously. "Thomas Stanley is known for many things, but boldness and treason are not among them."

He barked out a laugh. "No, I supposed not. He is a dithering old man, isn't he?"

That was why no one would believe Stanley was guilty of treason. Yet, Richard had chosen to maintain the lie, which meant he still feared someone discovering his real reason. His plans weren't finished yet.

"Please release my husband. You know he is innocent."

"I will do no such thing."

Her approach wasn't working. Richard had always preferred open threats to innuendo. She had to risk more. "His brother William will be unhappy to hear it."

"Yes, where is the Stanley with a spine?" Richard asked. "I expected him to petition me, not you."

"Perhaps he would, were he in London. Since he is out of the city, the duty fell to me."

"Out of the city?" A hint of curiosity slipped into his voice. "Where?"

"I cannot say." Furrowing her brow, Margaret feigned contemplation. "When last he wrote, he and my husband's retainers were marching from Lathom. I imagine he's somewhere between here and Birmingham by now."

Richard bolted to his feet. "Your husband's retainers? How many?"

"I should think all of them." Margaret widened her eyes in mock surprise, if only to hide her pleasure at his reaction. "I believe the last count was six thousand men armed and ready to follow their lord's orders."

"Impossible." Richard's eyes darted back and forth. "No one can raise a force that quickly. Your husband was arrested only yesterday."

"It is the obligation of every loyal lord to defend his liege in times of trouble. When he heard of the Woodville conspiracy, my husband made provisions to raise his forces." Margaret kept her voice even. She wanted to remember her tone and behavior when speaking the truth, so she could lie convincingly later.

"Treason!"

"Not at all." Treason was his excuse to justify anything he liked. She forced herself to remain relaxed, despite her anxiety. "My husband recognized that your few men were not enough to protect His Majesty. Many could seek to profit from your brother's death. Not only the Woodvilles, but also the Scots, French, and Welsh. All loyal lords must do their part to protect the realm." She was reasonably sure he understood the implied threat.

Seating himself again, Richard tried to project calm. His blood was up now, though, and he scratched absently at the arm of the throne.

"I'm sure Sir Stanley and my husband's retainers will be alarmed to find their lord arrested, particularly after so much rumor. Please, allow him to greet them and explain what has happened." Though Richard had encouraged this confusion, she could exploit it, too.

In a frighteningly short span of time, the duke worked through the consequences of facing the Stanley armies. When he spoke, his voice carried the resolve and authority lacking only a few moments before. "Thank you for sharing this news with us, Lady Margaret. Surely, a man who would rise to defend the realm and his liege with such zeal cannot be guilty of treason. I will naturally arrange for his immediate release." After a moment, he added, "I trust Lord Stanley understands how misunderstandings can cause rash—and irreversible—consequences."

Margaret curtseyed. The charge of treason had already been made. Richard could always manufacture enough evidence of his involvement with Hastings' supposed conspiracy to execute any whom he'd previously pardoned.

"I trust that will be all, Lady Margaret?" He rose.

Emboldened by success, she decided to push further. "I understand you've detained Bishop Morton as well."

"Indeed."

"He is an honorable man and has always proven loyal to King Edward. It would be a shame to tarnish such a respected member of God's clergy without cause."

Margaret couldn't recall a king—let alone a regent—ever executing a consecrated bishop. Surely, with Hastings dead and her husband released, keeping Morton prisoner served no further purpose. She needed the bishop.

"Fine, fine." Richard waved his hand. "But he is a commoner, only freshly acquainted with the duties of title and position. The Duke of Buckingham will oversee him until I can be assured of his loyalty."

Though a prisoner, Morton might learn something useful from Buckingham.

Richard was studying her with a strange intensity. At first, Margaret thought he was waiting for her to comment about her son, but she would not use her husband's retainers that way without his permission.

Then she realized what he wanted. And he was right to expect it, she concluded. Regardless of her feelings, Richard was effectively the king's regent.

Lowering herself in a deep curtsey, Margaret forced the appropriate words out of her mouth. "I thank you, my lord, for your wisdom and kindness in this matter."

Richard peeled his lips back into a feral smile.

*Let him take what satisfaction he can.* Her husband was free.

"You may go, Lady Margaret." When she turned to depart, he added, "Rest assured I will remember your conduct today."

She mulled over that warning while waiting for her husband in a carriage outside the Tower later that day. When he entered and sat beside her, he was wearing the sleeve of someone's tunic as a makeshift bandage. He insisted he hadn't been put to torture.

But neither of them could comprehend the reason for Lord Hastings' death.

# THE PUBLIC

Richard wasted no time making use of the fear he'd generated. On the sixteenth, two days after his meeting with Margaret, the Archbishop of Canterbury and the Bishop of Lincoln persuaded Queen Elizabeth to release her son to their care. With honeyed words, they claimed the young king was lonely and desired the company of his dear brother. Elizabeth had little choice but to comply or risk defying her son's command.

Margaret felt a shiver of dread when she learned of the churchmen's assurances; Henry had received similar pledges before St. Malo. She marveled that the queen hadn't demanded to hear the request from the king's mouth.

Then, June 22 arrived, the day of the coronation. Assembled that morning in their finest regalia, nobles from across England attended Sunday mass, officiated by Dr. Ralph Shaw, the renowned preacher. But, instead of the usual biblical passages, Shaw treated the congregation to a diatribe against bastardy that made the celebrants wonder if the good preacher had gone mad.

Then, Shaw made his final pronouncement: Edward IV and his younger brother George had not been the legitimate sons of the Duke of York.

The declaration produced the shocked silence of utter disbelief.

The claim seemed to benefit no one since Edward IV had taken the throne by conquest, not descent. Why had Shaw staked his life on an irrelevant point? Everyone agreed that Richard would have executed the man on the spot like Hastings if he'd been present.

Though wagons of finery and food continued to arrive, there was no coronation. In a rare partnership between their networks of agents, Stanley and Margaret worked together to determine Richard's plans, but they only succeeded in confirming the arrival of a large company of armed men from York.

And then, on the 25th, the lords of the realm received an official summons from Buckingham. Finally, someone in the government would respond to the wild charges about Edward IV's legitimacy. But why was the wrong duke calling them into session?

As soon as they were seated, Buckingham announced another unbelievable discovery: Edward IV's children by Elizabeth Woodville, including the young Edward V, were not legitimate.

With an eloquence that sounded strange on his tongue, Buckingham explained the discoveries the master of the king's library had made while preparing young Edward V's lineage for the coronation. Apparently, twenty years earlier, a woman named Eleanor Talbot had petitioned Edward to recover lands repossessed by her father-in-law. Taken with her, Edward had wanted to bed her, but she'd resisted until he'd signed a pre-contract of marriage, officiated by Stillington himself. Considered a full marriage according to church law, this pre-contract made Lady Talbot the king's legitimate wife. He and Elizabeth Woodville, therefore, were not legally married, and all their children were bastards, including the new king and his brother.

And because Edward's other brother, George, had been declared illegitimate, his son could not inherit either. Richard of Gloucester was, therefore, the only remaining claimant and next in line for the throne.

Richard's retainers began whispering among the crowd. Didn't this explain why Edward and Elizabeth Woodville had married in secret so many years earlier? Perhaps Anthony Woodville had known Edward IV's bastards had no right to inherit and had planned to seize the throne before the truth was discovered. And Hastings, loyal to King Edward, would do anything to protect his friend's children.

Opposition was pointless with Richard's northerners present in force and Buckingham absorbing Hastings' retinue in full. With little alternative, the council unanimously confirmed the bastardy of everyone in line for the throne ahead of Richard.

And so, Richard Plantagenet became King of England, acclaimed by the unanimous—if reluctant—decision of his peers.

# HENRY

*The twenty-eighth day of June, Anno Domini 1483.*

*My dear Henry,*

*I was so terribly wrong about Richard. His arrest of Anthony Woodville seemed to put him in an impossible position, but only if Edward V would eventually be king. Richard was counting on us all making that mistake. He cared little for future retribution from Edward's son because he never intended to allow a Woodville boy to sit on the throne. The taint of the unclean witch ran too deep.*

*Hastings would have used his extensive lands and resources to defend the young king and turn the nobles to his side. But the execution of that fine gentleman preemptively crushed any resistance.*

*Shaw was evidently following Richard's orders to remind the public of the importance of legitimacy so it would readily accept Richard's unimpeachable weak Plantagenet chin and flaxen hair.*

*He fooled us all. Why should he seize the throne when he could arrange for it to fall to him naturally? If intelligence and cunning were the sole requirements to rule, I must confess Richard's suitability.*

*The people see his strength as protection against chaos and uncertainty, even though he created that uncertainty himself. They fear civil war more than a usurper. His coronation will take place on July 6.*

*Anne Neville is delighted at becoming queen. I'm to hold her train during the coronation. Many are not pleased. Bishop Morton is horrified and is cultivating those who might agree with him.*

*Lastly, I'm afraid I have sad news for your companion*

*Edward Woodville. Anthony Woodville and Sir Richard
Grey were executed on the 25th of June. I am told Anthony
Woodville conducted himself as a gentleman and met death
with dignity. I know not how Sir Grey met his end. I offer
my sympathies.*

*The wheel of fortune has turned against us. Have faith
that it will turn again.*

*Your loving and faithful mother,
M. Beaufort*

Having finished reading, Jasper raised his eyes. "This changes nothing. The King of England wished your repatriation before, and he wishes it still."

Henry knew better. Their fortunes depended on a factional struggle in England. "Edward, his sons, and George's son… That's four fewer claimants to the crown."

"Not necessarily," Jasper reminded. "The princes may be bastards now, but that can change with a stroke of the pen." After a pause, he repeated, "This changes nothing."

Nodding meekly, Henry inwardly sensed a change, a heightening of his risk. Richard had managed to claim the throne as the next legitimate heir. What else was he planning?

Upon hearing the news, Edward Woodville sequestered himself for the next three weeks. When he returned, he carried himself with a solemnity that contrasted with his usual charming disposition. Henry recognized it as the same shadow that veiled his uncle's eyes at the mention of the Yorkists.

This damnable throne was ruining good, honest men. It had to stop.

# CHAPTER TEN

## ROGER

Scowling, Roger glanced behind him upon hearing the muffled laughter of children through the solid oak door. Squeezing the haft of his pike, he repressed the familiar urge to sweep the butt across these spoiled brats' jaws.

Guarding a pair of princes in the Tower of London wasn't why he'd come to London. He wanted to loot something.

His partner, Will, tugged on his collar one more time.

"Quit yankin' it," Roger hissed.

Twisting his neck back and forth, the other man grunted but said nothing.

Footsteps echoing up the stone stairwell focused his attention. "Tut," he signaled. They straightened to attention with both hands on their pikes.

Two men wearing ornamental cloaks in the livery of the royal household emerged from the spiral staircase. They approached casually with their arms at their sides. One of them, a few fingers shorter and more thickly built, held a scroll of some sort. Neither wore any gold chains of office, jewelry, or weapons.

"State yer business," he declared with an approximation of calm control.

The shorter visitor presented the scroll. "We come on behalf of the king to assess the health and general state of the princes." His voice initially sounded local, but hints of a Yorkshire accent bled through the last few words. He must have been one of those prissy up-and-ups who tried to hide his heritage to claw for all the really comfortable assignments.

Roger studied the scroll for all the proper indicators. The seal was definitely a royal one, though not the king's personal seal. The paper felt like the same smooth blend used in official commands and had the right weight. He'd been taught enough to recognize certain key words, even if he couldn't read the entire document.

"Very well. Submit to a search."

Both men twisted their cloaks up and around their shoulders. Will approached and patted their jerkins and breeches for concealed blades, but he found none.

Nodding, Roger unlocked the door with the key at his belt and stepped back.

The two men dipped their heads in a brief salute as they passed. The taller man greeted the two princes when the boys bounded toward the door.

The other man turned to Roger. "You may hear some odd sounds, but fear not. My companion is a doctor. He will be assessing their health with tests he learned on the continent."

Roger shuddered, recalling his own experience with the surgeons on the battlefield. But, if the king trusted this doctor with the princes, who was he to question?

When they closed the door, Roger stowed the royal edict in his tunic. He'd have to deliver it to his captain when he reported the visit at the end of his watch.

A harsh thump sounded from within the princes' room, followed by some clattering. Something had fallen. Hushed voices followed, and then a muffled cry. Then another.

Roger met Will's concerned gaze. He felt the bulge of the scroll beneath his tunic. It was authentic. He was certain.

The latch clicked once. Roger gripped his pike tighter. The solid oak door swung open and the two men stepped through again, smiling.

"The princes are in excellent health," the shorter one announced. "Don't be surprised if his grace the Duke of York complains of a bruise on his hip in the coming days. He collided with a chair while we were attending them."

"They are taking their rest," the second man added in thicker Yorkshire while latching the door. "They must sleep until dawn." With that, he bowed and the two men approached the stairwell.

Biting his lip, Roger gestured for Will to level his pike. "Hold."

Instead of stopping, the men began rushing down the stairs at a run.

"After them!"

Will disappeared down the stairwell while Roger opened the door and stepped through.

At first, he saw only a ragged pile of books knocked off the table and the two princes lying in their beds with the covers pulled up.

"Pardon the interruption, my lords," he muttered.

Studying the floor and furniture, he saw no blood or signs of foul play. The linens were orderly and smooth, and the boys were sleeping peacefully. He turned to leave.

Then, he halted. Something was wrong. They lay too still, with no rise or fall of the chests to indicate breathing.

Dropping his pike, Roger charged up to the closest bed and ripped the covers off. Horrified, he did the same to the other.

Breathing heavily, Will stepped into the room. "They were too fast, and my pike got caught on the steps."

Roger staggered backward, bumping into the table and knocking the remaining books to the floor. It wouldn't matter that he had the edict in his hands or that the two men had said all the right things. It was all over.

"What is it? Why did you have me chase them?" Will asked, furrowing his brow.

"They're dead." He stared at the still forms on the beds one last time. "And so be we." Without another word, he rushed out of the room and down the stairs.

## MORTON

Morton rolled the wine along the inside of his goblet, watching the candlelight reflecting off the rippling pool of reddish liquid. The vintage was just like everything else in this estate: desperately elegant. The meals consisted of five different kinds of meats. The gardens had been intentionally designed around centerpiece trees imported from the Levant. The pillows had the finest brocade woven into them.

Of course, those meats also paired poorly with the wine, chosen for its expense more than its bouquet. Those foreign trees needed to be changed often as the harsh English climate claimed its victims. And the brocade, while beautiful, was often made of wool—not silk—and scratched the skin so badly that it was best to toss it to the floor rather than sleep on it.

Like everything about the Duke of Buckingham, depth rarely extended beneath the surface.

Morton selected a topic pleasing to his host. "How do you find your new lands?"

Buckingham leaned back and licked the guinea fowl from his fingers. "They seem profitable, but Hastings didn't watch his men as carefully as I intend to."

"I have no doubt the profits will expand under your careful attention, my lord." Morton predicted Buckingham's new tenants wouldn't appreciate his means of achieving it. "I'm told Lord Hastings was much-beloved."

"He was rich and powerful," Buckingham corrected, a small smirk tugging at the corners of his lips. "While his son inherited his title, I will put his wealth to use."

"It still unsettles me to think of how he was executed."

The duke stared at his own goblet without responding. This topic always made Buckingham uncomfortable. While the duke had obviously conspired with Richard to arrest Hastings, Morton doubted he had known Richard would execute the lord.

"We must trust the king's reasons for such an odd action," Morton continued. "Though, the public considers it an act of murder, what without there being a trial."

They sat in silence broken only by rushed conversation and pacing footsteps from outside the door.

At length, Buckingham finally replied, "I hope the king finds no treason lying in the hearts of any more of his subjects."

A month earlier, the comment would have been a veiled threat. But now, the duke's voice held too much uncertainty for it to be more than a window into his host's mind.

"As do I," Morton added. "If he is willing to behead one of the most passionate supporters of his family, I doubt he'd hesitate to do the same to anyone else. Especially someone like, oh, Henry Tudor, a Lancastrian with a claim to his throne."

"I have the same claim," Buckingham fired back. "Our mothers were cousins, and my father has an additional, legitimate claim through Thomas of Woodstock."

"Quite so. I had forgotten," Morton lied. "That would give you a stronger claim than even Tudor."

Buckingham nodded in agreement before returning to his wine. His eyes assumed a distant expression that had become all too common recently.

Time to push further. "I heard a rumor recently."

"How do you hear rumors? You're not supposed to have any private correspondence."

"I must still perform my duties. If my priests choose to report events in my bishopric, I can hardly stop them," Morton replied easily.

"Naturally, you may read all my correspondence to be reassured of its contents." His host would never waste his time with such a task.

Shrugging, Buckingham accepted the explanation. Morton waited patiently until the duke asked, "What was the rumor?"

Morton deliberately delayed by sipping his wine. "I'm told the king is granting his friend William Catesby three additional royal estates."

"Three more for that peasant?" Grimacing, Buckingham finished off his wine, about half the goblet, and tugged at his collar.

"I suppose he is one of our king's oldest friends," Buckingham muttered.

Morton struck. "I'm certain His Majesty will reward your loyalty, as well."

"The only reward I need is the rest of the Bohun estates." Buckingham licked his lips.

Morton injected a hint of confusion into his voice. "The Bohun estates?"

Buckingham leaned forward and nodded eagerly. "My great-grandfather Thomas Woodstock married Eleanor de Bohun, the eldest daughter of Humphrey de Bohun, the Earl of Hereford. He was fabulously wealthy, but when he died, his lands were divided up between both Eleanor and Mary, his younger daughter. This was an outrage. It should have all gone to the eldest daughter."

"And the younger married Henry Bolingbroke, who became Henry IV."

The duke nodded. "But Richard will restore them to me. He promised."

"You have an august lineage. Thomas of Woodstock granted you both your right to those lands and your claim to the throne," Morton reminded. "I'm sure Richard will reward you once his reign is secure."

In the distance, Morton thought he heard a cry from somewhere.

Buckingham inclined his head and raised his goblet in a silent toast. "Which estates did Catesby receive?"

"My priest didn't know their names, but they were in Herefordshire,"

Morton replied innocently. "Perhaps you and Catesby will be neighbors once the Bohun estates are restored to you."

Buckingham leaned forward. "The only royal estates in Herefordshire are the Bohun estates."

Morton pursed his lips. "Are you certain?"

"Quite certain." Buckingham bit at his lower lip as tenaciously as if Morton had hooked him there. "I must speak to Richard about this. Thank you for sharing this information."

"It is the least I can do for your kindness and consideration through—"

"Murder!" The doors burst open and Buckingham's wife, Catherine Woodville, came storming through. "He's killed them, the bastard." Tears streaming down her cheeks, she collapsed into her husband's arms.

"Now, wife, what's this?" Buckingham held her at arm's length. "Compose yourself in front of our guest, woman."

Catherine looked from her husband to Morton. Upon recognizing him, she inhaled a fortifying breath and straightened herself. The sudden change was remarkable. "Bishop Morton." She looked at him with an intensity that suggested some meaning, but Morton, still recovering from the outburst, could not divine it. "I've had a visitor from London, husband."

That must have been the noise Morton had heard in the hallway while he'd been manipulating Buckingham.

"Yes?" the duke prompted.

"Roger, come in here," she shouted to the open door.

A sweat-caked man wearing a dirty tunic stepped forward and snapped to attention. "Your Grace." He executed a low bow, suggesting a familiarity with protocol.

"Who is this man?" Buckingham demanded.

"He is a guard at the Tower of London." Her voice wavered. "And he says my nephews are dead."

No one spoke for some time.

Morton recovered first. "Start at the beginning, my child."

Nodding, the guard Roger recounted the visit by the two strangers, the sounds of struggle, and the lifeless princes.

"Why did you come here?" Morton asked when Buckingham did not.

"I couldn't reach their mother in sanctuary, so I rushed to the closest Woodville I knew." He glanced at Buckingham's wife, who simply nodded. "They summoned me and Will, and that didn't feel right. If the king wanted them boys done in outright, he'd have done it openly." The man's eyes darted wildly. He was terrified. "When lords be killed in quiet, our kind takes the blame."

"The king would never do such a thing," Buckingham said.

"He killed my brothers," Catherine hissed. "He claimed his own brother was a bigamist. He called his mother an adulterer."

"I won't have this treasonous talk in my house." Buckingham turned his back on them.

When he did, Morton met Catherine's gaze and acknowledged the silent plea. Alliances were made in such moments.

"What if it is true?" Morton asked delicately.

"Silence!" Buckingham rounded on him.

"Can you say it's impossible?" Before Buckingham could reply, Morton crossed himself, a subtle reminder that he was a consecrated bishop. "God rest his soul, Edward IV left two sons to follow him. Yet now the king is Richard, not Edward V. He murdered Hastings—"

"Executed," Buckingham corrected.

"Murdered," Morton insisted. "Hastings was a member of the Privy Council and a nobleman in good standing, not in active revolt. He should have been tried and convicted first."

"There is no proof but this man's word." Buckingham swallowed. "I do not support men who murder children."

"There is proof," Catherine cried. She turned to the guard. "Show him."

Swallowing, Roger retrieved the scroll from his tunic. "The men who done the deed gave me this." He extended it to the duke.

When Buckingham made no move to take it, Morton did. The paper, the script, the ink, the seal… He swallowed. This was it. God forgive him, he was about to turn the murder of two young children to his advantage.

*The boys are already dead,* he told himself. *And not by my hand. It has to be done.*

"The seal is correct," he announced.

Buckingham stirred. Accepting the document, he began to study it.

With a nod, Catherine dismissed the guard. Her steward was waiting at the door and escorted him farther into the house.

The duke shuffled to the fireplace, studying the scroll by the flickering light. Morton exchanged a nervous glance with Catherine. She saw the danger, too. With a gesture, he could reduce the proof of Richard's worst crime to ashes.

"Your Grace, consider what this means," Morton said. "It's one thing to execute Lord Rivers. Richard had to remove the Woodvilles to protect the rights of true noblemen." Catherine stirred at this, but Morton waved her off. "But consider Lord Hastings, who did everything both Edward and Richard asked of him. Did he deserve his fate? Is that what you agreed to?"

"Never." Weakly, Buckingham shook his head. "I wanted his lands, not his life."

"Hastings helped depose the Woodvilles, and his reward was execution. He served his purpose, and Richard discarded him as soon as he could."

Buckingham hadn't moved. It wasn't working; this wasn't personal enough. He had to try a different tactic.

"He murdered two innocent young boys who were already dis-barred from the throne. Such an act is abominable. Amoral. The shame of this will taint all those who stand by him." Morton let the thought sink in for a moment before asking, "Did you agree to the death of children when you helped him seize the crown?"

"Of course not." As he turned, his hand dropped to his side, placing the scroll dangerously close to the fire.

"Of course not," Morton agreed. "You helped Richard because you are loyal. Much like Hastings."

Buckingham's eyes widened.

Morton shook his head. "I wonder when Richard's men will come in the night to reward you for your assistance."

Catherine rallied. "My husband, I do not want to see you executed. This king fears the power of his supporters. He does not reward them."

"Except for Catesby, the commoner." Morton twisted the knife. "Who is to receive three estates in Herefordshire."

"My estates," Buckingham corrected.

"Bohun estates," Morton said, "going to the son of a country knight instead of the legitimate descendant of Humphrey de Bohun."

"Husband, my nephews are dead by this monster's hand. Will you wait for him to dispose of you, too? What will happen to your children and your family name?"

"My priests write to me constantly about the unease Hastings' murder has caused throughout the country," Morton said. "The people believe we live at the whim of a tyrant. That the rule of law and privileges of position mean nothing. They cry out for someone to save them."

"My nephews are dead," Catherine repeated. "My family yearns for someone to deliver the justice they deserve. Avenge them against this usurper and they will support you."

"No one has a stronger claim to the throne than you." After a moment, Morton added, "I was a Lancastrian once. I would proudly follow the House of Stafford. I'm sure other Lancastrians would, as well."

"The people will flock to your banner, my husband," Catherine added. "Unite us against him. Woodville, York, Lancaster, Hastings."

"And do not forget Henry Tudor and the Bretons," Morton said, adding the final piece of the puzzle.

That roused a response. "What value is Henry Tudor? An exile without rank these past twelve years cannot help me."

"But Henry Tudor is the key to his stepfather, Thomas Stanley, and his six thousand men," Morton said. "As well as Jasper Tudor, beloved of the Welsh. They can be had for the price of a few titles."

Morton could almost see Buckingham contemplating himself as the first king of a new dynasty. Finally, he would live up to the promise of his blood.

The duke laid the parchment on the table, far from the consuming fire, and reached for his goblet. "Tell me more about the forces that will make me king."

Morton spared a glance for Catherine Woodville. They had been Lancastrian once, before Elizabeth Woodville had married Edward Plantagenet. All three of them had once been Lancastrian, in fact.

It was time for the House of York to fall.

## RICHARD

"The boys are dead?" Richard's mouth fell open.

Catesby swallowed. "Two men presented a royal edict to evaluate their health and strangled them in their beds."

For a moment, the king simply offered a bleak, absent stare. "They will blame me." The statement was a simple declaration of fact. "Even though I have no reason to kill bastards with no claim to the throne." He shook his head. "My own nephews."

"The guard we interrogated said the men had clear Yorkshire accents."

"Surely, someone recognized them."

Catesby frowned. "I can inquire. I wanted to keep this quiet until you instructed me further."

"Until you determined whether I ordered this, you mean?" Richard demanded. "I did not!"

"Not at all, sire. I simply wanted your guidance."

Richard ran his hands through his hair, forcing himself to think. Then, all at once, his face contorted into a mask of rage. With his strong right hand, he grasped the closest candelabra and slammed it again and again into the nearest table. Only when it was a wreck of twisted silver did he stop.

"Now, husband, that's enough of that," came the sweet voice of Queen Anne from the doorway.

The candelabra thudded when Richard dropped it. "Out, woman. This is crown business."

"I can see that." She made no effort to move. "Or, rather, hear. The entire castle can hear you. Show some discretion."

"Show some discretion?" He scoffed, nearly choking on his disbelief.

"Yes, discretion." She stepped fully into the room and closed the door behind her. "Lest you want the entire kingdom to know those Woodville bastards are dead."

Catesby narrowed his eyes.

Richard met his friend's gaze before turning back to Anne. "What?"

"You heard me."

"How?" He licked his lips. There was no point in lying to her. "How did you know?"

Anne Neville raised her eyebrows. "Because I ordered it."

Silence.

Slowly, Richard staggered to the closest chair and settled himself into it. A dozen questions flooded through his mind, quickly followed by the obvious answers. Who had written it? She had; all the Neville women knew how to read and write. How had she secured the seal? Its keeper had been a Neville man. The parchment? Likely retained from the stock her father had kept during Henry VI's reign.

Only one question required an answer. "For God's sake, wife, why?"

Anne folded her hands in front and pressed her lips together. "While they lived, they posed a threat. The surviving Woodvilles would have never stopped using them to unseat our family. A king loses support as his decisions affect his subjects, and you are not starting your reign with a surplus of popularity. Every noble is a feckless wretch who believes he's owed more than he has. With an alternative to the crown, they would turn on you like sharks. I have removed that alternative."

"I cannot believe this." Richard shook his head. "You have no authority here."

"That's why I forged the edict. I had to wait until I could retrieve samples from my father's chests. Otherwise, I'd have had them killed the moment you were crowned. You obviously weren't going to handle it."

"I declared them bastards."

"By an act of parliament that can be reversed," Anne said.

"They are my family. You can't simply kill them!"

"You did the same by arranging for Edward to execute your brother George for treason. And you shared his blood, while the princes were diluted by the Woodville taint." She scoffed. "You could see it for yourself: the tantrum prince in training."

"Have you no faith in me?" Richard shook his head. "I executed Rivers to scatter Woodville resistance and killed Hastings to crush those who would fight for the princes' claim. Why didn't you trust me to deal with two young boys?"

Anne stared at him, her mouth falling open. It was the first time her expression had changed. "You think I did this for you?" She barked a dry laugh. "I did this for our son."

"What?" Richard breathed.

"Our boy will face the sons of the men you've killed. Your brother George's boy, Hastings' son, and all those who died at Barnet and

Tewkesbury. His list of enemies will be staggering." She inhaled a deep breath. "I won't see him saddled with the actions of his father and uncle. If everyone else with a claim is dead, he will rule peacefully."

Richard spread his fingers across the table, feeling the wood grain against his skin. "You used my seal to murder two innocent children in an attempt to spare our son trouble decades from now?" He raised his eyes to stare into his wife's. "When the country has had to accept the illegitimacy of three claimants to the crown in front of me? When not two months ago I purged two powerful families? You thought that *now* was the best time to handle a problem that won't be a threat for thirty years?"

"What happens if you die tomorrow?" She asked. "Who would protect our son? My family's retainers can protect a northern duke, but we don't have the strength to uphold a regency alone." Flexing the muscles of her neck, she restored her calm. "They had to die, for the sake of our son."

"They will blame me for this!" Richard shouted. "Do you think I hadn't weighed the threat they posed against such a despicable crime? I can't even claim it was an accident or blame anyone else. They were locked in my tower, the most secure place in the country." He turned to Catesby. "Who has access to that tower?"

Catesby cleared his throat. "The king's guards."

He glared at his wife again. "The king's guards. Not every Englishman with a doublet. One house. One person. Me." He paused long enough for another thought to come to him. "Didn't it occur to you they might do something in the next fifteen years to justify my executing them? As you said, they're arrogant Woodvilles. It was only a matter of time before they hanged themselves. But not now. You've robbed me of that."

Anne, however, remained unconvinced. "That's all well and good if you live that long, husband. Your brother died young. We've been warring with our nobles for thirty years. And you…" She eyed him up and down. "Let us speak plainly. You are reckless in battle. You barely survived Barnet when you could have easily avoided the thick of the fighting. One revolt could see the end of you and leave my young son alone among enemies."

"You are very well-acquainted with events you didn't witness," Richard remarked.

"I should be," she countered. "You speak of it endlessly."

"Get out of my sight."

Anne bowed her head. "After you promise to kill the young Duke of Clarence."

This time, Catesby gasped as well.

"Absolutely not. What has my brother's son ever done?"

"I would do it myself if I could reach the boy. You'll be blamed for the princes' deaths. Why not finish it all at once? Your brother George's boy. Henry Tudor. You might as well finish off Buckingham, too, since you dispatched Hastings. Extinguish everyone with a rival claim."

Richard clenched his hands into fists and said in a dangerously quiet voice, "Catesby, if the queen is in this room ten seconds from now, I want you to kill her where she stands."

Swallowing, Catesby nodded. A calm Richard terrified everyone.

Eyes widening, Anne offered a quick curtsey and backed out of the room, but not without grace.

What could he do? The only way to deflect the blame was to reveal his wife's guilt and subject her to a trial and execution. But that would cost him the support of her family's retainers. They were the only forces he could rely upon.

He needed time to buy the loyalty of the other nobles, appoint his men to key positions, and secure the most vital areas of the country. His reign was too new, too unprepared to absorb this catastrophe.

But so much had changed in the past two months. Perhaps an opportunity would present itself to clear himself of blame. "William, who knows the princes are dead?"

"Us, the two tower guards, and the two of my men who discovered their bodies." Catesby, it seemed, had recovered from the queen's shocking revelation.

"Can you trust your men?" Richard asked.

"As much as I trust anyone but you, sire."

"Kill them. And the two tower guards as well. Have the one lot do the others in, then take care of them yourself." He leveled an unblinking gaze at Catesby. "You're the one man I trust, William. No one must know of this."

Catesby bowed. "I am your loyal servant, sire."

Richard offered a curt nod. "Thank you, William. Remain true and I swear I will ennoble you and your children."

With a bow, Catesby ducked through the door to attend to his grisly business, leaving Richard to contemplate the ramifications of the two murders he hadn't committed.

# HENRY

Four weeks later, a fast ship delivered a pair of letters to Henry Tudor. The one from his mother contained all the secret indications that it was genuine—the edge markings, the staining along the top corner, a seemingly jagged tear at the right spot—but it was uncoded.

*The seventeenth day of September, Anno Domini 1483.*
*My dear Henry,*

*Buckingham will write to you proposing rebellion. Agree to join him. You are an earl, not a merchant. This is your chance. Reclaim the life that was stolen from you.*

*Both Buckingham and Morton are convinced Richard murdered King Edward's young sons. Strangled, I'm told. I suspect Buckingham is finding his own future uncertain enough to rouse him from his complacency.*

*My confessor, Christopher Urswick, also ministers to Elizabeth Woodville and has passed messages between us. I told her of her sons' death, and she is more committed than ever to destroying Richard. Loyal Woodville men have been preparing for this rebellion since June. With Buckingham, success is all but assured.*

*Morton and Buckingham have agreed not to reveal the death of the princes until the eve of the rebellion. Public outcry is fickle, and sustaining it will be difficult. We need it to be at its peak when we strike.*

*Hasten to join this cause and I will see you in London before Christmastime.*

*M. Beaufort*

Henry had to read the middle portion twice before believing it. Richard had likely arranged Henry Holland's murder. He had assuredly arranged his brother George's execution. He had killed Hastings, Anthony Woodville, and Thomas Grey, but all those murders had been necessary to claim the throne.

Those boys had done nothing. They had been innocents. Worse, Richard had pledged to keep them safe under his care. It was abhorrent.

Henry tried to imagine Elizabeth Woodville's reaction upon learning her children were dead. She had even enabled the deed by delivering one of them into his murderer's hands.

Disturbed, Henry dropped his mother's letter onto the table and turned his attention to the second one, bearing Buckingham's seal.

*The fifteenth day of September, Anno Domini 1483.*
*My dear cousin Henry Tudor, Earl of Richmond,*

*By the common blood of our ancestor John of Gaunt and my noble predecessor Thomas of Woodstock, I greet you as a fellow peer of the realm and faithful Lancastrian. On October 18, Kent will rise against the tyrant, drawing his attention east of the city. Elizabeth Woodville has pledged the support of her kin for insurrections within London itself, and I will muster retainers from my considerable Welsh lands.*

*I invite you and any loyal Englishmen in Brittany to join my rebellion. Petition your host, Duke Francis, for his support. Reassure him that, under my rule, England will increase its defense of his duchy against the French. Land in Devon and swell your ranks with recruits. Meet me in Bristol on October 16th. For your assistance, I will restore your and your uncle's titles when the tyrant is dead.*

*Convince Lord Stanley to raise forces from his lands as well. He will be greatly rewarded if he can contain the Neville soldiers in the north.*

*Henry Stafford,*
*by the grace of God, Duke of Buckingham*

Henry studied the letter. The corners where the crisp folds met were rumpled and worn, suggesting damage during the long journey. The hand that had poured the wax had been unsteady and unpracticed, dribbling some across the paper. The duke had probably sealed the letter himself, probably not trusting it to a servant.

The seal. He rubbed his fingers along the indentations. Buckingham's father had been executed as a Lancastrian traitor, and yet the young duke had never lost possession of his father's signet. How did it feel, to carry that constant reminder of his worth? Even the mere imprint of its presence carried the weight of rank.

Henry had never seen his father's seal. It had been lost when he'd died, even before Henry's birth, and his affairs had all been handled by others during his time in England. In the few brief months of Henry VI's restoration, so much effort had been spent assessing the damage of ten years of Yorkist rule that something as simple as a seal for a minor hadn't been a priority. Jasper had promised to cast a new one when they returned from securing Wales. Before Barnet and Tewkesbury.

This wrinkled, poorly signed letter could mean the end of all his troubles. He would never have his father's seal again, but he could have a new one. He could finally live without fear of a Yorkist king wanting him dead.

"Matthew?"

His servant popped his head through the door.

"Send for my uncle. Tell him to wear his finest doublet. Then call for Edward Woodville. I have tidings for him."

# CHAPTER ELEVEN


## HENRY

HENRY RETURNED HOME late that evening. A single candle still burned in the upstairs window. After taking a deep breath, he pushed open the door and ascended the steps.

Jehane rose from the bed when she saw him. "Henry…" Beside her was the knife he had told her to keep near her ever since they'd moved in together. But the point, not the hilt, was facing her.

"Hello, love." He managed a faint smile as he removed his boots and doublet and slid into bed next to her. She was half asleep, and her hair was tousled. The image brought a smile to his face. "How was your day?"

"Fine, fine," she said through a yawn. Pushing herself upright, she rubbed her eyes, forcing herself awake. "I tore the seam of my blue dress today. I must have caught the sleeve on something."

Henry frowned. "The one you wore the first time I saw you?"

"You remembered." A smile crawled across her face. "Can you believe the shop was entirely out of blue thread?"

"I'll see to getting some more tomorrow," he promised.

"No need. Alais had some." She nuzzled against him, offering a contented sigh.

He raised his chin to make room for her against his chest. "One of my finest memories is of you in that dress. Despite my foolishness."

She filled the room with pleasing laughter. "You were a hopeless courtier." After a long silence, she prompted, "How was your day?" Her voice had drained of its lightness.

Things would change between them after he shared his news, and he couldn't predict whether she would be delighted to end the uncertainty or terrified at the risk. Yet, his news could not wait.

"I've had a letter from the Duke of Buckingham. He's inviting me to join his rebellion." She tensed against him. "The Woodvilles have already agreed."

She absorbed the news for a few moments. "Are you… Will you have to fight?"

The catch in her voice nearly broke his heart. "I don't hunger for military glory, love. I may have to march, but I'll stay safe in the rear with the commanders."

She remained still. "It sounds like a very great risk."

"He'll have us, the Woodvilles, and both his and Hastings' lands to draw from. I'm going to petition my stepfather as well. The king can only draw on half of Edward's strength. If all goes well, it'll be over before it starts."

She drew herself up, turning to face him. "What if Buckingham fails?"

"He won't," Henry began.

"But what if he does? If Richard puts down this rebellion, it will bring trouble. We've been happy here. Why risk all that?"

"I don't really have a choice." He sighed. "Duke Francis expects me to participate. It's why he kept us all these years. If I don't join Buckingham, I'll show him he was wrong, and my stipend and protection will go away. Whoever wins, I'd lose everything."

After all the years of trying to reconcile his feelings, only now, when he had no choice at all, did he understand. "Every royal decision, every rivalry, every rebellion forces nobles like me to make choices.

The wrong one costs us something, maybe everything. So we have to keep improving our position, keep collecting lands and holdings for the moment we need them most. If we don't, our families could fall into ruin." Quietly, he added, "Like mine has."

"Your father and uncle didn't have a choice. They were brothers of the king."

"I know," he answered simply.

"But you can have another life." She lowered her eyes. "With me."

Henry brushed a stray lock of hair out of her eyes. "I'm living on a duke's charity, love. We can be together only because Francis allows it. He can take it away at any time." Swallowing, he forced the cheer into his voice. "But this is my chance to end the uncertainty, to take control of my life. I can end the threat hanging over us. I won't have to worry about being dragged off in the night anymore."

She lifted her hand to his cheek. "I hear your cries at night, love. I know how you fear another..." She couldn't bring herself to finish the sentence.

"Another St. Malo," he supplied. "But my drop of royal blood won't matter anymore. Buckingham has the same drop and an ocean more. He's Lancastrian twice over. With a Woodville wife, he brings together all the factions. I can just be the Earl of Richmond."

She pulled away from him. "If Buckingham succeeds, you'll be leaving forever." She uttered the words with a toneless certainty.

He took a deep, steadying breath. "But not alone, I hope. Not if the woman I love would agree to be my wife."

Her eyes widened. "Henry, are you asking me—"

"I know you feared to lose your independence to a husband, but I thought, perhaps after..." The miscarriage had changed them, brought them closer; perhaps this, too, had changed. "We could set terms for the marriage contract. You would maintain sole control over your interests here."

She lowered her eyes, but the faster pace of her breathing gave him hope. "My tailors are here. How could I monitor them from England?"

"Albert has been hungry to take more of a role for years. He's trustworthy and has a way with the journeymen that's rare in a master tailor." Quickly, he added, "Perhaps you could even expand with a shop in London, or near my lands."

"Can an earl's wife do such a thing?"

"She can do whatever she wants if it means she'll stay with the earl."

Her posture eased a little. "Wouldn't you need a noble wife?"

He smiled. "If I have my title, I can marry anyone I damn well please." He pressed his lips against her forehead. "You're all I want, Jehane. After this rebellion, I'll never have to care what anyone thinks of me ever again."

"What about this Buckingham? Wouldn't he want you to marry one of his supporters?"

"He'd be delighted if a man with a claim to the throne married a Breton tailor instead of a duke's daughter." He offered a tentative grin. "At least until he got to know you."

A light laugh escaped her tight control. She leaned against his shoulder. "Lady Richmond," she muttered, testing the sound.

"Elizabeth Woodville's father was a chamberlain's son, and look how high they rose."

"Did you just compare me to the wife of the man who haunts you?" she asked hotly.

"And whose brother-in-law stood at my side before Duke Francis today."

"So that's where you were. Was it difficult to gain the duke's support?"

He raised an eyebrow. "How do you know he agreed?"

"We'd be having a different conversation if he hadn't."

Henry grinned, impressed. "Buckingham's letter convinced him. He's offering five thousand men and ten thousand crowns."

She sat up again, wide-eyed. "So much!"

Henry nodded. "Richard is making enemies of men like Buckingham. That instability troubles Francis. He needs a strong England to defend against France." She would hear about the princes soon enough; he couldn't bring himself to mention that atrocity.

She picked at the edge of his doublet. "When do you leave?" She always hated when he traveled to meet the duke, and this trip promised to be considerably longer.

"My uncle and I are leaving in a week with five hundred men. The rest will follow later."

"So soon!" She paused. "How long will you be gone?"

"It's hard to say." If they could catch Richard unprepared, it might only take a few weeks. If not... "It may be some time."

She lowered herself down again, holding him tightly. "I wish I could go with you now."

"Does that mean... Will you marry me?"

Jehane burrowed deeper into his embrace. "Let me see the text of that contract first."

"You can write it however you like, my love."

She smiled and tilted her head, kissing him on the lips. "Then let's enjoy these last few days of living in sin before we become an honest couple."

## HENRY

In early October, Henry's flotilla of seven vessels left the harbor at Vannes and began the long journey through the English Channel. After passing Brest, the flotilla slowed to round the cape. The winds were picking up, and the captains sought to avoid both hitting the shoals and drifting too far out to sea. Nonetheless, two ships nearly ran aground, and while the first was able to adjust its tack and navigate around the cape smoothly, the other captain was inexperienced and over-compensated. They spent two hours holding position while he caught up with the fleet.

As they left Brittany behind and let the wind fill their sails, dark clouds appeared on the horizon behind them. When dawn should have broken the next day, instead they were met by angry black clouds.

Worry darkened the captain's face after studying the sky. "This will be a bad storm."

"What do you recommend?" Henry asked.

"Spread the ships out and have them meet us at Plymouth. We'll need room to maneuver if we're to avoid crashing into each other."

"As you advise."

The rain, when it came, fell in sheets, obscuring their view of the other vessels' quickly receding silhouettes. The captain struggled mightily simply to keep the vessel upright. All of them—Henry included—pumped water out of the hold in shifts.

During one particularly bad wave, Henry was sent careening into the mainmast. He managed to grab a rope at the last moment, and while he survived, the sleeve of his best tunic caught on a cannon and tore completely off, disappearing over the side with a cascade of water.

The storm lasted for ten days, causing them to miss the rendezvous with Buckingham. If the duke had raised enough men and surprised the tyrant, then the decisive action had already happened. And if he hadn't, Richard would already be preparing his response.

Two days after the storm broke, Henry's battered carrack reached Plymouth. Seeing none of his other ships on the horizon, he retreated below deck, fretting. With a few more men, he could at least attempt a landing. But while Uncle Jasper had been confident with five hundred back at Vannes, the few men on Henry's ship simply weren't enough.

On the eighth day at anchorage, a small party on horseback signaled them from shore.

Some of his men reported back after rowing out to investigate. "Buckingham has Richard in his custody in London and invites you to march to him there."

Henry narrowed his eyes. "Captain, have your men seen much activity from Plymouth?"

"The terrain obscures the far side of the city, but we've seen nothing near the shore."

Henry rubbed his chin. He was no expert in such things, but he would expect the leaders of a town to be loyal to the king; if not, they'd be replaced. Yet were that so, he should have seen more activity if the king had truly been overthrown.

"Tell them we will join them after our other ships arrive. Tonight, discretely send some men to shore. I want to know what they hear in town."

The captain nodded and arranged the shore party. Before dawn, they returned.

"There are rumors of unrest in Kent, but no news of any armies in the west country."

Henry turned from the officer and studied the shore. The riders had erected a simple camp while they waited for Henry. Nothing about their behavior seemed suspicious, but they left Henry feeling unsettled, nonetheless. Could the Yorkist threat really have been eliminated in a single week?

If he turned back now, when his goal was in his grasp, he would become an enemy—or at best, an object of cowardly contempt—to the new king as well as the old one. If he only took a few more steps, he could put all the hardship of these many years behind him.

Everything he'd ever wanted was so close.

Suddenly, he realized why those men camping on the shore filled him with unease. A small band of soldiers wouldn't camp so casually in contested territory. Even if Buckingham had defeated Richard, he couldn't have pacified the entire country. Those riders had to be lying.

"Captain, return us to Brittany. Buckingham has failed."

## HENRY

Henry's ship progressed from port to port along the Breton coast, collecting the remainder of his scattered fleet. Each ship he recovered brought more detail about the rebellion. Kent had indeed risen, but it had done so eight days earlier than planned upon learning of the princes' murder. The Duke of Norfolk had been on hand with his soldiers and had responded decisively. Several of the tortured survivors had revealed the extent of the plot, including the involvement of Henry's mother.

The same storm that had scattered Henry's fleet had prevented Buckingham from crossing into England over the Severn. Frustrated by the flooding of the great river, he had demanded that his army attempt a crossing, nonetheless. Not nearly as loyal as the duke's letter to Henry had suggested, they had deserted in droves. One of Buckingham's retainers had even betrayed him in Shrewsbury. Richard had refused to even see the duke before ordering his beheading, just as he had done with Hastings five months earlier.

So, as Henry's battered ships limped into Vannes two weeks after turning around, the exiles praised Henry for his caution. The rebellion had been over before any of them had come within sight of land.

He suspected that despite his failure, Duke Francis wouldn't discard him so easily. With Buckingham's death, Henry had become the last remaining adult with a competing claim to the English throne.

Jehane was waiting for him, a cloak wrapped tightly around her to banish the November chill. Behind her to the north were the confining ramparts of Vannes he'd hoped to have left forever.

His chest tightened as it had on the road to St. Malo. He had failed to bring her to England and would have to fail her again. He couldn't marry her, not in light of his new vulnerability from this debacle.

Meeting her eyes, he confronted the twisted reflection of those promises and dreams. Even when she offered him a gentle smile, he could discern the lines of tension in her forehead and read the disappointment in the puffiness around her eyes.

Weakly, Henry leaned his head against her shoulder. "Oh, Jehane," he whimpered. "I'm…I'm so sorry."

The words broke his fragile control. The tears fell freely, shed not for the collapse of a rebellion or a lost title, but for the pain he had caused a woman who had trusted him with her future.

As his tears disappeared into the lining of her cloak, Jehane stood motionless. Slowly, ever so slowly amid his fears and regrets, she raised her arms to encircle him. "It will be…just fine, Henry."

He raised his own arms to embrace her, desperately searching for something in her tone to convince him of the truth of her words.

## MARGARET

Richard did not conduct audiences as his brother had. Instead of making them wait, he had his servants bring Margaret and Stanley to his audience chamber without delay. Nor did he care to clothe himself in the protection of his position. He wore a simple black tunic with breeches, boots, and vambraces, not the royal robes one would expect from a king.

He still displayed the signs of royal power, though. Fifty Neville guards surrounded the room, holding their pikes in a menacing repose. Tightly gripping the folds of her dress to hide her apprehension, Margaret dipped into a deep curtsey. Her husband offered a low bow.

"Lord and Lady Stanley." Richard's wooden greeting offered no indication of his mood.

Stanley rose. "Summoned, we present ourselves, Your Majesty."

Richard shifted his weight to relieve his curved spine. "I've brought you here to answer for your actions during Buckingham's revolt and determine whether you are guilty of treason."

Stanley's mouth fell open, but he closed it quickly and cleared his throat. "I played no part in the duke's treachery, Your Majesty. Indeed, I cannot comprehend his actions."

"Nor can I," Richard agreed. "Be assured that my investigations have unequivocally revealed the extent of your involvement." He fell silent, drawing out the moment.

Behind him, one of the guards shifted, causing two pieces of armor to tap together. In the distance, the hollow ringing of bells tolling the hour bled through the stone.

"I have found you to be innocent of all conspiracy." He waved his hand limply. "Indeed, not a single one of your soldiers showed any signs of mustering. I will assume you were unaware of the insurrection, rather than that you deliberately chose not to come to my defense."

In hindsight, Margaret was grateful her husband hadn't trusted someone as arrogant and inexperienced as Buckingham to defeat a seasoned commander like Richard. Stanley's tendency not to take chances had saved them.

Richard waited patiently while a waiting servant handed Stanley a scroll.

"For your loyalty, even as your stepson joined my enemies, I hereby grant you the lands I seized from the traitor Sir Thomas Arundel."

The tension drained from Stanley's posture as he unfurled and read the scroll. "Thank you, Your Majesty." When he bowed again, his motions were much more graceful.

Margaret loosened her grip on her dress. Her arms were starting to ache from holding her curtsey for so long.

"The involvement of your wife, however, is another matter entirely."

Blood pumped through her ears, and her hands began to shake again. She straightened out of her curtsey; though it was rude, it permitted her to still her hands by folding them before her.

When she raised her head to meet Richard's gaze, she arched an eyebrow. "My actions, Your Majesty?"

Richard grinned wolfishly. "Oh, I remember you interceding on good Bishop Morton's behalf when you came to plead for your husband's release, and I know you communicated with him in the weeks leading up to the rebellion."

She needed to encourage doubt. "Your Majesty—"

"Be silent," Richard whispered through clenched teeth.

Margaret swallowed. Any response faded like mist within her mind. A calm Richard was a dangerous Richard.

Leaning on his right elbow, he watched her for a time while his lips worked in and out. With surprise, she realized he hadn't planned her punishment beforehand. Quickly, she tried to recall whether an English king had ever executed a woman for treason.

When Richard finally inhaled, the sound filled the silent room with an echoing hiss. "Previously, your son was merely an annoyance. But now, he proves himself the traitor I always believed him to be. There will be no reconciliation between us. He has chosen his path, and will know only ruin."

Margaret closed her eyes to hold back the tears. All those years of watching her had taught Richard exactly how to hurt her.

"I will not reward Lord Stanley's loyalty by depriving him of a wife," Richard continued. "But you have proven yourself untrustworthy. I take your lands from you, and give them to your husband to use as he sees fit." Richard directed his attention to her husband. "Lord Stanley, do you pledge to use these lands in service of the crown?"

Stanley hesitated for only a moment. "I pledge to do so."

Margaret lowered her gaze. Now that the blow had come, she was both surprised at its lightness and buried by its implications. Her inheritance was lost to her and her son but not to her household. It was a mild punishment compared to the dozens who had been attainted or executed. Nothing but her gender had saved her. Of that, she was certain.

But it had saved her, and she had survived yet another lost crusade. She forced herself to take a slow breath to calm her nerves. Nothing had really changed. Henry had been disbarred from inheriting her lands twelve years prior, and though Richard had declared her son a traitor, both Edward and Richard had already viewed Henry as an enemy and a threat.

Only, everything had changed with Buckingham's death. No one else could press the Lancastrian claim to the throne, and no Yorkist would contest Richard. Her son was Richard's only remaining threat.

"You are both dismissed. I expect you to attend Christmas court this year."

"Of course, Your Majesty." Stanley bowed and took two steps backward.

Margaret did the same and took his arm. They headed for the door.

"Oh, one more thing," Richard interrupted. "Your son, Lord Strange, also refrained from joining this rebellion. I wish to reward his loyalty with a position at court. Tell him to attend me by the end of the week. He will be at my side at all times."

Her husband's arm stiffened beneath her hand. Richard would hold his son hostage for Stanley's continued good behavior.

When he made no response, Margaret took a step forward to acknowledge the command, but the King of Mann managed a quick, "As you wish."

"Excellent. That will be all." Richard waved his hand dismissively.

They walked out of the audience room and continued down the hall in silence. Though Thomas Stanley was normally a quiet man, when he maintained his silence through the full length of the palace, Margaret grew nervous.

"Thomas, say something."

Only when they were back in their carriage, returning to their lands, did Lord Stanley finally speak.

"I have tried not to interfere with your efforts to restore your son, Margaret. I trusted you to understand how to exert pressure without crossing the line." He gazed out of the window at the endless streets and alleys rolling by. "But you went too far."

She released an irritated sigh. "Buckingham had all of Hastings' retainers and his own. Elizabeth Woodville's supporters were ready to rise, and all of Kent was ready to cut Richard off from his support in the north. It seemed infallible."

"But for a little rain," Stanley added in the same, calm voice.

"Weather!" she cried, loosening her frustration. "And now my son is back in Brittany, with those who would have been allies in England dispossessed and fleeing for their lives."

"But it's not your son who you've placed in Richard's clutches." He turned to face her. "It's mine."

Without the revenue from her lands to pay for the gesture, Margaret resisted the urge to smash the carriage door and storm out. He could be coldly practical, but he'd never before been unfair.

"Was it I or Richard who made your son a hostage?" she demanded. "That devil crawled over a pile of bodies to become king, including a young boy to whom you owe your allegiance. And his brother was no better. Edward was a usurper. He relentlessly tormented my son for years because Henry had the audacity to remain loyal to the rightful king. Something you yourself failed to do." Pausing for a moment to catch her breath, she leaned forward. "I didn't put Richard or his brother in power. Look in the mirror for that culprit."

He had supported the Yorkists for over twenty years. And from the shadow that fell over his face, he was starting to realize it.

Irritation still blistering, she added, "Don't blame those of us who are trying to do something about it."

# CHAPTER TWELVE

## HENRY

THEIR CARRIAGE JOSTLED when it rolled over a rough cobble, and Henry almost hit his head against the frame. Annoyed, he tugged again at the shoulder of the tunic poking out from beneath his doublet. He felt like he was being squeezed and pinched everywhere at once.

"Stop fussing with it," Jehane demanded. "I spent a lot of time making your tufts look just right."

Henry frowned at the slits in his doublet that exposed the tunic beneath in billowy puffs. They were all misshapen and crumpled. "I'm sorry, it's this tunic. It's too big." His own tunic had been ruined in the expedition three weeks earlier.

Growling, he reached for the dagger at his hip to cut it to fit.

She slapped his hand away. "Be grateful I had one lying around the shop." With a sigh, she turned to look out the window.

"I am, truly."

He squeezed her hand, but the affectionate gesture evoked only a quick smile. He watched her carefully, subsiding only when he was satisfied that the muscles of her neck were relaxed. He hadn't yet stopped searching her face for signs of either frustration or anguish. Surely, she felt the loss of their hoped-for future as much as he did.

Work had kept them both busy, though. Ships had begun to arrive with men fleeing Richard's retribution. First had been the knights Giles Daubeney and Robert Willoughby. Each had raised small forces in southern England with the intention of combining with Buckingham and Henry. Discovering that Norfolk had intercepted some of their letters, they'd fled to the one place safe for Richard's enemies: Henry Tudor. Many more followed.

Feasts had been planned to parade the newcomers among the Breton elite. Tonight's was at Edward Woodville's residence. The trip should have been a short one, but an oxcart with a broken wheel had required them to take a longer route.

"Woodville's hosting Jean de Rieux tonight, isn't he?" Henry studied the passing streets.

Jehane nodded quickly. "Do you know him?"

"I stayed with him shortly after arriving in Brittany." Henry couldn't help but grin. "I saved his son's life, actually."

"His son?" She adjusted her posture to give him her full attention.

Henry nodded. "We were riding in the woods when the marshal and his second son—his heir was out for fosterage at the time—made a sharp turn at full gallop. His youngest son was thrown. I saw the whole thing behind them."

"Why did he do something so dangerous?"

Henry shrugged. "Maybe he wanted to push them, toughen them up."

"Maybe he didn't really care what happened to a third son."

Henry considered the possibility. "I don't think so. Those boys were fated to become knights of Brittany. Sparing their training would have endangered them when they were older."

The carriage passed through a square. A monk was holding an impromptu sermon that had collected quite a crowd in one corner.

Henry studied a group of children on the periphery. "I wonder how many of the nobles who died at Barnet and Tewkesbury were coddled as children. From what I gather, Buckingham certainly was."

Jehane sighed and adjusted the lay of her cloak. "Henry—"

She never finished the sentence. The carriage rocked violently, sending her crashing into him. The horses whinnied outside, drowned out only by a series of cracks from splintering wood. The wheels on the left side shattered, dropping the cabin at an awkward angle.

Jolted so hard that his back throbbed with a stinging pain, Henry braced himself on the frame with one arm while helping Jehane right herself with the other. A large, dark object pressed against the right side of the carriage.

Henry heard shouting that he couldn't understand. Whatever happened had drawn attention, though.

Then, the crossbow bolts pierced the carriage.

The first tore through the cloth roof and embedded itself in the seat far to the right. The next two came from the left, passing over Henry's shoulder. The last one came through the roof again, narrowly missing his thigh.

This was an attack, an assassination.

He needed to draw them away from Jehane. "Stay here!"

He slid his feet through the damaged left side and grabbed his dagger. The shards of the splintered wheels strewn across the cobblestones prevented him from gaining traction. His feet kept sliding against something slick. Blood? Probably of the driver and ducal guard that had been riding in front.

"He's running!" The voice came from above.

A burly man rushed in from a side street. Without the time to stand after freeing himself from the carriage, Henry rolled to the side as a broadsword flashed past him. Having opened up some distance, he stood and brandished his dagger.

A dagger… How was he supposed to fight off a broadsword with a dagger? But the man stood perilously close to Jehane. He had to protect her.

The man came at him again with a wide slash. Henry jumped out of the way. Frantic, he dropped to the ground and grabbed a spoke from one of the shattered wheels.

His attacker was bringing his heavy sword around again for an overhead swing. When the sword reached the top of its arc, Henry threw the spoke at the man's head. Shouting out a curse, the assassin freed a hand to cradle the fresh wound.

Henry charged forward. Though his thrust with his dagger barely nicked his attacker's ribs, his shoulder slammed into the man's midsection and knocked them both off balance. Behind him, the broadsword fell to the ground with a loud clang. He kept hold of his dagger until his hand slammed hard into the cobblestones, forcing his fingers open.

They landed in a tangled heap. Rolling on the ground, they twisted and tried to wrestle the other into submission. Henry reached for the assassin's neck but missed. The other man tried to lock Henry's elbow, but Henry squirmed free.

Scrambling to his feet, Henry heard the thunk of another crossbow bolt and turned to find the source.

Atop a nearby building, Partially washed in the moonlight, stood William Catesby.

Gone was the calculated composure of the man who had faced Henry across the lists or in the court at Rennes. Carrying more shadows than the night itself, his face seethed with hatred and anger.

And he was reloading his crossbow.

Henry's attacker advanced again, but as he was about to grapple with Henry, he halted. Eyes widening, he instead turned and disappeared into the concealing shadows of the alley.

Only then did Henry hear the ragged cries of a crowd gathering to investigate the commotion. At the vanguard was the monk from the square.

When he turned back toward Catesby, the roof was empty. As suddenly as the attack had begun, it was over.

Catesby. And that meant Richard. Henry hadn't dreamed he'd go this far, but Jehane had been right to worry about the king's reaction.

*Jehane!*

Whirling, Henry ran to the carriage. The crowd had cleared the cart that had collided with them and had propped up the side with the splintered wheels. The inside of the carriage was concealed in shadow. She was sitting motionless, terrifyingly still.

"Jehane!" His voice dripped with panic.

"I'm here. We...I'm fine." She pressed her hands against her stomach. A crossbow bolt had dug into the seat, pinning her dress, but she herself was unharmed. She raised her eyes. "Are you well?" Her voice sounded thin, fragile.

"It was Catesby. I chased him off."

She nodded slowly, eyes losing her focus. "Richard. The rebellion."

He swallowed. It had only been a few weeks since the disastrous landing, but the timing could not had been an accident.

"We should move." She spoke with the same flat tone. "Before they return."

She ran her fingers along the smooth shaft of the crossbow bolt for a moment before tugging at it uselessly. It was too deeply embedded in the carriage. Grabbing a fistful of fabric, she yanked hard, ripping a jagged tear down the edge to free the dress, and abandoned the carriage.

With an odd sense of dread, Henry watched the torn edge of her dress wave loosely as she walked down the streets of Vannes.

## HENRY

At first, he thought the warmth on his face was simply dawn spilling through the window across his cheek. But when the heat shifted, his eyes snapped open.

Jehane watched him intently, her outstretched hand stroking his cheek. "I didn't mean to wake you. I couldn't help myself. I...I wanted to remember your face, just like this."

"Jehane?" He pushed himself up onto his elbows. The bruises and cuts from the attack stung. He nuzzled her, and she gave a soft moan of delight before stiffening and pushing him away.

"Henry…" Her eyes had changed. Where they had been welcoming, they now seemed distant.

He pulled himself upright to sit on the bed.

"I almost died." She smoothed the folds of her dress. "It may sound selfish or naïve, but in all our time together, I never expected that."

"I'm so sorry, Jehane. I didn't think Richard would respond so quickly. And that he would resort to assassination?" He swallowed. "I'm so sorry."

"Why should he not try to kill you?" she asked. "You have royal blood."

"A drop," he insisted. "And tainted by bastardy."

"It was always enough." Her voice was calm, so calm that it frightened him. "Richard and his brother just had larger concerns. But now, with Buckingham dead, you are his greatest threat." Her eyebrows knitted together. "For you, Henry, I would risk my heart."

She pressed her lips together. An unshed tear sparkled in the corner of her eye.

"But not my life, Henry. Oh, I do love you, but I'm not willing to die for you."

The words struck Henry like a raindrop on a puddle, sending a rippling shiver across his body. "What?"

"No, that's not quite right," she muttered as if to herself. "If it took my life to save you, perhaps I would give it. I don't know for certain. But if I'd died in that carriage, I wouldn't have died for you." Her eyes softened as she swallowed. "I'd have died because of you. Because someone wanted to kill you and I happened to be in the way."

This had to be a nightmare. This could not be happening.

But rather than being dull and ethereal, his senses were on fire. He heard the blood pumping through his veins, and his fingers could make out every flaw in the weave of the blankets he grasped to anchor himself from pitching over.

"I swear to you, I will never allow this to happen again." His words came in a rush. "Now that I know how far Richard will go, I can protect you. We can prepare for—"

"You can't make that promise. There will always be something you don't foresee, and the people around you will suffer for it. I can't live every day of my life wondering if the person I love is going to get me killed." She lowered her eyes and ran her hands along her abdomen. "What of our children? What if they're inside the carriage the next time it's attacked? If the castle holding them is besieged and they fall to illness or an arrow? Is their fate to die by poison intended for you?"

"We won't have children until it's safer, until things are better."

She flinched. "Things will never be better. Englishmen have been killing each other for decades. Your life will never be safe. There will always be another battle, another threat. You told me yourself before you left. A noble has to keep pushing or risk losing everything."

The words stung. Clasping his hands to his head to shut out the battering of her voice, Henry searched for the right phrases to convince her they needed to be together. But his mind was numb.

"I never meant for you to come to any harm."

"I know you didn't, Henry." Still, her voice was maddeningly calm. "And it isn't fair. I don't know how much of your fate you chose and how much was thrust upon you. I really don't. But you are the last man with a competing claim to Richard's throne. That endangers everyone around you."

Henry shook his head, clasping her hands in his own. "This is fear talking, Jehane. The attack was so sudden. You haven't had time to think this through."

But rather than defend herself or recant, she simply pressed her lips together and lowered her gaze. "It sounds so romantic to say you would die for someone until you face that choice." When she raised her eyes again, they were guarded. "I can't do it. I can't live every day of my life for someone else's cause."

"Jehane, don't do this," he pleaded. "I...I need you."

She straightened with a deep breath. "And my heart needs you too, my love. But I have a life to live, and a future to think of. If it isn't a crossbow bolt or a vial of poison, the fear of that fate will ruin me day by day, until all that you love is gone. And I won't do that. I'm sorry, Henry. I won't." She bent to kiss his hands.

He pulled back, pushing himself off the bed and onto his feet. Her touch taunted him. A part of her had closed off to him, and the terrifying thought that it would never open again left him shaking.

"Henry…" Her voice warbled.

He fought a wave of tears. Warding her off, he rushed for the door and stumbled.

He couldn't do this, couldn't look at her face and see something other than love staring back at him.

Nowhere was safe for him anymore. He had lost his last refuge, the one place where he felt at ease. Agony washing over to consume him, he rushed out into the blinding dawn, exposed and alone.

## HENRY

As the Dutch cog slowly maneuvered toward the dock, sailors tossed the bow and stern lines to shore.

Watching them from the end of the dock, Henry straightened his posture and pulled down on his tunic. The lace was too tight and tugged at his neck. His valet Matthew always tied it too tightly. Jehane used to loosen it after the young man left.

"You should say something," she would tell him.

But he never would. Otherwise, she wouldn't have had to adjust it.

Jehane wouldn't be adjusting his tunics anymore. He would have to mention the lace to Matthew.

She had left her master tailor in charge of her shop before visiting her family in St. Malo. Her instructions to Albert had been clear: while Henry was welcome as a customer, he was no longer a part of the business.

Though the Rousson servants had collected her possessions weeks earlier, the scent of her favorite perfume still lingered in the empty trunks and blankets. Henry sometimes knelt before the open trunk and breathed in the aroma, hoping something of hers might inspire the words to win her back. Or, at least, let him feel close to her for a little while longer.

He had spent a lot of time before that open trunk, and the comforting perfume was all but gone. Soon, he would have nothing left of her but the painful truths of their parting.

York and Lancaster… Who of sound mind would choose to insert herself into that mess? His mother had yearned to restore her son's title after already losing a husband, a father, a brother, and a birthright. His uncle had lived as a fugitive, watching his dreams turn to ash as friends and family died one by one. A turncoat Lancastrian queen had married a Yorkist and gained everything she had ever wanted, only to watch from sanctuary while her brothers and sons had been massacred. And those boys… Like Jehane, they were innocents.

*Richard.* Henry began wringing his hands together, wishing that bastard's throat was between them. Richard had taken Jehane from him. He had to die, and Henry was the only one who could do it because he had a drop of John of Gaunt's blood in his veins.

It wasn't much, but that drop had induced ardent Lancastrians like Edward and Piers Courtenay and Sir Richard Edgcumbe to flock to Brittany. But not only them. Turncoats who had thrived in Yorkist England like Edward and Richard Woodville, Sir Robert Willoughby, Thomas Grey, and Thomas and William Berkeley. Even loyal Yorkists had joined him: Edward Poynings, Sir John Cheyne, and his brothers. And they had brought their servants, retainers, soldiers, and influence. Hundreds of men who could petition their friends and allies. The start of an army.

*My love.* He had held onto the dream of a life with her so tightly, but now it was gone. Richard had stolen it from him.

Henry inhaled the morning air, watching the sailors pull the cog against the dock. The sailors had lowered the gangplank and had finished tying down the lines. Already, the man Henry had come to greet was starting to alight in a plain black houppelande that concealed the contours of his frame. Henry suspected he was not hiding a brawny build. Not that he would expect that from a man of God.

As the visitor approached, Henry pinned back his cloak to reveal some of his new red dimpled doublet, assuming a confident pose to make a good first impression.

When the man stopped, he lowered himself into a deep bow Henry didn't expect from Englishmen. "The whispers of the past surround the deaf man."

"And the mute shall shout their anger once more," Henry replied, satisfied. "Father Urswick. It's a pleasure to meet you after all your efforts on my behalf." He had been one of his mother's most loyal agents for many years.

"My Lord Richmond, it's an honor to serve you." It was the confident and proper greeting of one familiar with nobility. "I greet you on behalf of your mother."

"I'm pleased you weren't implicated in Buckingham's revolt. Your efforts are vital to us." Smiling, Henry gestured for Urswick to accompany him, and they fell into a comfortable stride.

Urswick inclined his head to acknowledge the sentiment. "You do me too much honor, Your Grace. I merely delivered letters between your mother and Queen Elizabeth while she was in sanctuary."

Henry halted. "While she *was* in sanctuary?"

"The very day I left London, King Richard persuaded Queen Elizabeth and her daughters to leave. He has taken them under his protection."

Henry's mind reeled. What could possibly induce her to trust in Richard's mercy? That man had murdered her children.

Urswick looked around before adding, "Have you received word from Lady Stanley?"

It was strange to hear his mother referred to by her title. "She told me to expect something so important that it couldn't be trusted in her letters."

Urswick brushed aside the folds of his houppelande and produced a letter from his belt. "This comes to me by way of a priest at Westminster, a man I trust with my life."

Henry accepted the letter and studied the seal. Elizabeth Woodville. It was unbroken, and the paper beneath it showed no signs of tampering. Only when he read the date did he realize it had taken some time to reach him.

*The thirteenth day of November, Anno Domini 1483.*
*To Henry Tudor, Earl of Richmond,*

*I am writing to you upon your mother's advice. My sons are dead, murdered by the Duke of Gloucester. I have shed my tears, but I still have five daughters whose future I must consider.*

*Present circumstances demand that I look beyond the past hostilities. Henry Holland and the Duke of Buckingham are dead. Both his son and my husband's nephew, the young Duke of Clarence, are children. My daughters' virtue and safety cannot wait for them to mature. Only you can challenge Richard for the throne. Our futures depend on us coming to an understanding.*

*I propose a pre-contract of marriage between yourself and my eldest daughter, Elizabeth. She is a virtuous girl and the eldest daughter of King Edward. Loyal Yorkists will battle to assert her rights.*

*You require the support of my loyal followers. I require protection for my daughters. This alliance may save us all and bring down the tyrant.*

*Elizabeth Woodville*
*by the grace of God, Queen of England*

Henry lowered the letter. So, that was why she had left sanctuary. Her daughters had no future while she remained, and Richard had taken no steps to punish the women associated with his enemies. Buckingham's Woodville wife and his own mother had been spared, so why not his brother's widow?

She was correct, of course. While the Yorkists had come to Vannes out of desperation, he would need to bind them permanently to keep their loyalty. But a pre-contract was a sacred oath, one he could not break without mortal hardship. Taking that oath would make Richard into an intractable enemy, but then he already wanted Henry dead.

Accepting would mean losing Jehane forever.

"My Lord Richmond?" Urswick asked.

Henry had forgotten him. "Do you know the contents of this missive?"

Urswick shook his head. "If I knew the content and delivered it still, not even my holy orders would protect me from Richard."

Henry could refuse. No one need ever know. But in time, Richard would prise away the most important of the Yorkist exiles and find husbands for Edward's daughters. He would grow stronger and Brittany would increasingly regret sheltering this colony of English dissidents. This maddening uncertainty would continue until eventually Richard succeeded in repatriating or killing him. And the tyrant who had cost him Jehane would be allowed to endure.

Jehane, who had abandoned him.

Why should he not accept this offer?

He would need to decide before Elizabeth and Richard came to a separate agreement.

Swallowing, Henry adjusted his cloak. A stiff northern wind had brought the winter chill to Vannes a week earlier. He took a deep, cleansing breath of the cool air. The comforting embrace of warmer days was gone.

He turned back to Urswick. "Thank you for bringing this. I should like to introduce you to Edward Woodville and my uncle, the Earl of Pembroke. We have much to discuss."

# HENRY

"I, Henry Tudor, by the grace of God the true and rightful King of England, hereby pledge on my honor before the eyes of God that as King of England, I shall, with all due haste, marry Princess Elizabeth of York, daughter of Edward IV, or in case of her death or previous union, her sister Cecilia. In honor of this pre-contract, on this Christmas Day I give my oath to defend and protect the honor of the Princess Elizabeth, her mother Elizabeth Woodville, and all of her relations, both living and dead, so help me God."

The final words echoed off the high ceilings of the gothic cathedral of Rennes and showered the hundreds of assembled Lancastrian exiles, loyal Yorkists, Breton nobles, bankers, merchants, mercenary factors, ministers, priests, scholars, and ambassadors with the clear, stentorian voice Henry had practiced. He removed his hand from the Bible and bowed his head as the Bishop of Rennes made the sign of the cross.

It was done. He thought back to his Latin lessons. *Alea iacta est. The die is cast.*

The anxiety of the past few days of preparation lifted almost immediately. They had chosen the words carefully to counter any plans Richard might have had for the Woodville daughters.

Landais stiffly made his way to the center of the apse. Before kneeling for his part of the ceremony, he shot Henry an angry glance. Duke Francis had fallen ill with a dangerous fever— genuinely, this time; Henry had confirmed it with his own eyes—but had sent Landais in his place over the treasurer's objections. Ignoring the hostility, Henry instead bowed to Francis's duchess. She would faithfully report if the man deviated even a word from the approved script.

"I, Pierre Landais, Treasurer of Brittany, pledge on behalf of my lord, His Grace Francis, Duke of Brittany, second of his name, to acknowledge the claim of his cousin Henry Tudor to the throne of England and to support him in pursuit of his rights and honors."

If he stomped back to his place among the Breton delegation a little too quickly, no one noticed. The cheering had begun, started by Edward Woodville and King Edward's remaining Yorkist supporters. The tumult soon spread until the entire cathedral was awash with applause.

One man who did not join in was Jasper Tudor. He had opposed this tactic from the start. "You'll be declaring yourself a Yorkist champion if you marry her," he hard argued several times over the past few weeks. "You'll be joining the very bastards who sent us into exile."

Henry had answered sharply. "If I have to ally with the Devil himself to kill Richard and put a stop to this never-ending exile, I will."

Listening to the deafening tumult, Henry felt vindicated. It had been more than thirty years since Yorkists and Lancastrians had joined together in a common cause. Some of the men here had suffered at the hands of others in this very cathedral. But, at least for this moment, they were united.

Henry stood before the purple velvet knighting stool Duke Francis had loaned him. Edward Woodville was the first to kneel. "I, Edward Woodville, pledge my loyalty and fealty to Henry Tudor, rightful King of England. I swear to become his liegeman in life and limb and will defend his and his heirs' rights and honors against all who oppose him, so help me God."

One by one, the English exiles approached. It was a simple oath, but in the eyes of God and before the ambassadors of Europe, it was enough.

Henry had paid the price for his blood for twelve years. It was time he started reaping some of the benefits.

And those benefits lay before him, in the hundreds of men streaming past, declaring their allegiance. He had outmaneuvered whatever Richard had hoped to achieve by his *rapprochement* with Elizabeth Woodville.

*I'm coming for you, Richard.*

# V

## RIVALS

AD 1484

# CHAPTER THIRTEEN

## HENRY

HENRY SHIFTED HIS weight onto his back foot and rested his hands on the new sword hanging from his left hip. It had been years since he'd carried one, and his back hadn't yet adjusted to the extra weight. The half-dozen Breton guards in the chamber wouldn't mind him relaxing.

Finally, the doors to the reception hall opened. Predictably, Landais entered, not Francis. "Ah, Tudor. I'm hoping you can explain this."

A page took a rolled parchment from the treasurer and handed it to Henry. The paper was considerably more creased than he remembered. Henry couldn't help but smirk as he read aloud.

*To the beleaguered people of England, enduring under the
tyranny of Gloucester:*
    *Richard the usurper has visited damnation upon the souls
of all who follow him for the unforgivable and despicable
slaughter of the young Prince Edward and his brother the
Duke of York. This pretender has wantonly discarded the lives
of his loyal subjects with his pointless war in Scotland and
made vile oppression commonplace. His northern soldiers with*

*strange accents daily trample the privileges and rights of peer and burgess alike.*

*This evil tyrant is as twisted in visage as he is in spirit. Now, God has deprived him of his heir in punishment for his wicked ways and vile deeds. England will not know peace until all faithful Christians stand united in opposition to sin and devilry.*

*An oath to a usurper carries no weight before God or man. I, Henry Tudor, descended from Edward III through his son John of Gaunt, Duke of Lancaster, call upon all faithful, true, and noble Englishmen to join me in liberating our good, sweet land. God be with you, all.*

*H.R.*

Henry allowed the parchment to curl back up. "Which part is unclear?"

Landais leaned forward. "The last bit. The *HR*. What does that mean?"

"Why, *Henricus Rex*, of course."

"King Henry?" Landais translated. "You've taken to calling your-self king, now?"

"It stands to reason. If Richard is not the rightful king and all those who might claim the title are either attainted, ineligible, or dead, then the throne falls to me."

"Even if you haven't been crowned?"

Henry smiled faintly. "A coronation is a spectacle. It does not impart divine right."

"You cannot do this," Landais thundered. "You cannot cause this trouble right now."

"Why?"

"You know what's happening in France. The Duke of Orléans is arming to assert his rights as regent for young King Charles. And he will win. Burgundy and England are both supporting him. We must do so as well, or he'll crush us. We cannot undermine Richard of England right now. We need his forces for defense."

Many of the court, including Henry's old guardian Jean de Rieux, had gone into voluntary exile with Anne of Beaujeu to protest Landais' abuses of power. The treasurer really had no choice but to support the Duke of Orléans or risk having his power stripped by angry nobles.

"There is another side in that conflict."

"Anne of Beaujeu? Pah!" Landais scoffed. "What woman can fight against a prince of the blood with a dukedom at his back?"

*Margaret Beaufort*, Henry thought. *Elizabeth Woodville. Margaret of Anjou. Jehane de Rousson.* "What are you asking of me?"

"Stop these inflammatory tracts at once. Richard cannot commit his forces to France if he must put down insurrections in England."

Henry remembered another conversation seven years earlier in this very room. Landais had announced he was sending Henry to St. Malo with the English ambassadors. Guards had been present then, too. But now he had a fresh promise of Breton support and the loyalty of over four hundred Yorkists and Lancastrians, reinforced by a marriage pre-contract.

"No."

Landais stared at him in disbelief. "What did you say?"

"No," Henry repeated. "I do not believe Duke Francis would ask this of me, were he of sound mind."

Landais growled. "I'm giving you an order, Henry Tudor."

Henry sighed. "If I were to stop, I would be acknowledging Richard as king, which would violate my oath in Rennes. Worse still, I would make it impossible for Duke Francis to fulfill his own oath to defend my claim to the throne. I cannot do either."

Landais opened his mouth to protest, but no words came out. The argument was neat, tidy, and absolute. Landais could not force him to violate an oath his own Duke had taken.

"You dare to defy me?"

"I dare to obey the Duke's wishes."

Unwilling to be put back in that helpless cage, Henry turned and walked out of the room before Landais could respond.

## MARGARET

Regardless of the fever afflicting her usual seamstress, Margaret could do no more mending today. Margaret's fingers simply weren't up to the task.

Folding the gown and setting it on the table, she flexed her fingers wearily. Her eyes drifted over to her desk. The inkpot sat frustratingly closed beside her clean pen and a stack of blank parchment pages. Not even a single grain of sand was out of place.

As a young girl, she had yearned for her own pen and parchment set. She had pleaded with her father, promising to keep it tidy and clean. Paper was expensive, and she had pledged never to waste it, to always think carefully before writing.

She had done more than her fair share of thinking over the past few months. At first, none had interrupted her confinement for fear of Thomas Stanley reporting them to Richard. Only after he had repeatedly mentioned his good wife's pious behavior and obedience to the king's wishes at Christmas did a trickle of letters begin to arrive. But they had been too few for her taste. More often than not, that pen and ink remained dry and clean, far too clean.

At least she still had Urswick, and while he didn't commit any of his news to paper, he did report on whispers and rumors. Paired with the court gossip Bray's agents brought her, it was enough to keep her reasonably informed. At least, as reasonably informed as possible in prison.

Nonetheless, she had endured worse in her life, and she would endure this.

Rising, she crossed to the broad windows of her sitting room and threw open the curtains. She regretted the action immediately. The sudden rush of heat would spoil the room for the rest of the day. The summer had been a harsh one, and she was glad it was almost over.

She turned at a knock on the door. "Enter."

Bray bowed, and his dark green houppelande parted to reveal brown breeches beneath. "Lady Stanley." Though he smiled, he nervously tugged at the edge of his sleeve.

"Reginald. How do you fare today?" She hoped using his first name would ease him.

He fell silent for a time, running his eyes across the room and craning his neck to listen. "Are we alone?"

She straightened; this was how he reported an important discovery. "We are."

He had defied a king's embargo to run secret messages that would mean his death if discovered. What could worry him so?

"One cannot be too careful these days."

"Reginald, what is it?" Her voice wavered.

"I received a letter from Lord Stanley. The Privy Council is keeping him in London, and he will not be returning as usual." This was common enough; Richard cared little for the plans of his nobles. But Bray's eyes carried an intensity that suggested something further. "He asked me to prepare five hundred archers, fully equipped and outfitted. His Grace explained that they would be part of eight thousand being gathered for the king."

Margaret caught her breath. Eight thousand archers. "For what purpose?"

His eyes pinned her without blinking. "His Grace would only say that I was to prepare them for a long stay. And that their captains needed to speak Breton."

"Breton…" She rose and paced to the window. This was St. Malo all over again, while she was trapped in this manor, isolated from anyone who could help. "Richard's trading them for Henry, isn't he?"

"That is my suspicion, my lady. Lord Stanley chose to deliberately mention the total number and nature of their assignment, which I do not need to know to assemble his portion of the levy. I believe he intended it as a warning."

She nodded absently. "Did he say when they were to depart?"

"In six weeks, from Portsmouth."

Six weeks. She had known about the alliance with Brittany and Burgundy against France, but why would Duke Francis surrender his only leverage against Richard?

It didn't matter why. If Thomas Stanley was risking even a well-hidden warning, the threat was genuine. But what could she do in just six weeks? Bray and Urswick had few international contacts.

She needed to consult someone who knew which courts of Europe might aid her son. Who had both the contacts and the desire to thwart Richard openly?

She drew in a breath as it came to her.

Morton.

When she turned, she had restored her calm. "Call for my confessor."


## HENRY

"Bishop Morton agrees with Lady Stanley's interpretation of the warning," Urswick explained to Henry and the assembled lords. "He believes you have no choice but to flee."

Henry rubbed his shoulders, recalling the aching ride to St. Malo. The panic began to wash over him, just as it had so many years earlier. With an effort, he forced it back down. This time would be different. He had a warning.

Only now, facing the prospect of leaving it forever, did Henry realize he had started thinking of Brittany as home. England was a dim memory. He truly belonged here, among the streets of Vannes.

That had been because of Jehane, of course. Their tears, their words, their sweat, and their joys had seeped into the wooden walls and floorboards of this townhouse. Even though she hadn't returned to the city, he could smell her perfume in the streets.

Now, he would have to leave it forever.

"I thought the increase in soldiers was because of the French," Henry said. "All this time, they've been tightening the noose around us."

"So much for the word of a duke," Jasper grumbled.

"Since December, the duke can hardly form a sentence," Henry murmured, more to himself than his uncle. "He may never recover. Landais is the most powerful man in Brittany."

"The most powerful man left," Jasper corrected. "Landais is doing in Brittany what Richard did in England."

"Regardless, Brittany is no longer safe. If the archers are gathering on the first of October, we have little time." He turned to Urswick. "Where does Bishop Morton recommend we go?"

"To Anne of Beaujeu in France."

"The Duke of Orléans is forming a coalition to unseat her," Henry reminded. "Is her regency stable?"

"She has endeared herself to both her brother and the realm. Her policies have proven popular." Urswick blushed in obvious admiration. "Morton believes she will prevail."

"It would be nice to finally reach France, after all these years." Jasper leaned against the wall with a sigh. "There really isn't another option. The Spanish are fixated on Granada, and the Empire, Burgundy, and the Italians would never aid France's enemies."

"But will she have us?" Henry smirked at his inadvertent use of the majestic plural.

"The bishop instructed me to visit Montargis and ask the regent, prior to coming here." Urswick pressed his hand to his chest. "Time was short, else I'd have never spoken on your behalf."

"You did well," Henry assured. "Her response?"

"She provides this personal letter inviting you to her court." Urswick offered Henry another folded paper. "She sends writs of passage and promises of payment for any horses, carriages, or ferries you may need to commandeer when you reach France. She also provided a purse for any bribes necessary to escape Brittany."

Urswick handed Henry the small purse. A few gold coins glinted within.

"That purse represents more than we ever received from Francis," Jasper said.

"It's not his fault. But good intentions cannot defeat an army or claim a throne." Henry shook his head. "I will not suffer another St. Malo." Clearing his throat, he added more loudly, "We have no weapons. How can we extract our supporters under the eyes of so many soldiers? We'd have to seize the whole city first."

Urswick's eyes darted to Jasper, who never took his gaze from his nephew.

"Henry," his uncle began, "while I appreciate your integrity, we cannot take anyone with us."

The argument with Jasper after Quelennec's death swirled in Henry's mind. "I won't abandon men who pledged their allegiance to me. Landais would turn them all over to Richard, and they'd certainly be put to death."

"You have no choice," Jasper answered quietly. "We cannot keep an exodus of hundreds secret from the Landais' informants, and if he discovers your intentions, he'll keep you in chains until he delivers you to Richard. You cannot reason with manacles."

"I will not abandon these men to their deaths."

Urswick coughed politely. "Richard's terms were quite clear. The offer is for you and you alone. Not even your uncle was mentioned."

"This isn't about reclaiming a title anymore, Henry," Jasper explained. "Your blood makes you the only remaining threat to his throne. He will stop at nothing to kill you."

"Edward Woodville? The Courtneys, Daubeney, Willoughby, Edgcumbe, Arundel?" He shook his head. "Some of the exiles have been with us for a decade."

"Some of these men are my dear friends. And if we lose them, our cause will suffer," Jasper admitted. "But if we lose you, our cause is lost. King Henry lost several armies, hundreds of nobles, and thousands of soldiers, but only his death allowed Edward to solidify his rule."

Henry turned from them, disgusted that he was considering this cowardly course. He had dined at many of these men's homes. They had stayed with him through dark years when hope had been a thin thread barely kept from fraying. How could he reward that loyalty with abandonment? When Quelennec had died, Henry had sworn never to be the kind of man who discarded his friends for his own ambitions.

He ran his hands along the rough grain of the wall. He had no means to defend himself, let alone the other exiles. If he stayed, he would be choosing to die without helping their circumstances.

And Richard would never pay for the things he'd done.

He turned back to the two men urging him to flee and saw concern mingled with apprehension. Jasper would do anything, had done everything, to protect him. But Urswick had risked treason before ever meeting him. He believed in the idea Henry represented, not Henry himself.

In the cathedral, all the Englishmen in Vannes had sworn their allegiance not to him but to an England without Richard. They had supported the restoration of their lands and the chance to punish Richard for his crimes. Men would lay down their lives for what he represented.

But for those dreams to have a chance, he needed to survive. At any cost.

Henry sighed. "We tell only those we must. How do we accomplish it?"

## HENRY

Four days later, as the setting sun painted the horizon in varying hues from bloody reds to vivid violets, Henry, his manservant Matthew, and Christopher Urswick made their way through a minor gate in the walls and into the Breton wilds. Henry had selected his finest doublet, a dark maroon madras with the fashionable slashes that allowed tufts of his expensive pure white tunic to show through.

The road to Rennes was faster than any other course, so Henry decided to follow it as long as possible before turning southeast toward the French border.

An hour into their journey, they heard the unmistakable drumming of heavy mounts riding fast behind them. Nervously, they pulled several dozen strides off the road and into thick foliage. The horses, unhappy with the uneven terrain, only calmed a minute before the riders darted past. The moonlight illuminated the ducal coat of arms—a black cross on a field of white—even in the darkness.

Henry chewed on his lip. In moments, the guards would examine the road again and double back to look for where Henry's group had departed it. Without other options, Henry made his decision.

When the ducal guards back-tracked their course, two riders in black burst out of the woods noisily and rushed back toward Vannes. The guards pulled their horses around to follow. A moment later, the rider in maroon kicked his horse in the ribs and sped down the road, east toward Rennes.

But the same moonlight that had illuminated the well-worn livery of the Breton guards shone twice as brightly on the fresh, new white tunic exposed beneath the maroon doublet.

The first guard pointed to the lone rider in maroon. "Forget the servants. After Tudor!"

Pulling so tightly at the reins that their horses cried out in dismay, the guards turned and pounded down the road after the white tunic, ignoring the others.

Forgotten, the riders in black pulled up and watched the figures recede. When the cry of a whinnying horse and commanding voices pierced the silence, they exchanged a glance before turning off the main road and disappearing into the brush.

## LANDAIS

Landais' fine wool slippers slapped against the stone of the reception chamber with each step of his pacing. Widening his eyes to banish the sleep that had consumed him ten minutes earlier, he nodded to the doorman.

A pair of ducal guards entered, escorting a bound man in a maroon doublet between them. Mud caked his right arm and leg, ruining the white tunic beneath. The prisoner's head sagged as the guards dragged him in.

*Serves the arrogant prig right. At least he has the good grace to look humiliated.*

"You interrupted my sleep for the last time, Tudor," he growled, omitting the false title. "Richard and I have come to terms, and you'll no longer be my problem."

The young man gave no reaction.

Landais narrowed his eyes. "I said you're going back to England in chains, and my men will be instructed to throw you on the boat this time—fever or not."

Still, the arrogant pretender was silent.

"Is he dead?" Landais asked the guards.

"No, my lord, he is awake." The grizzled guard to his left jabbed the prisoner in the ribs, eliciting a groan.

Relieved that his half of the English bargain still breathed, Landais nonetheless frowned. After all the expense and political annoyance the young man had caused, the treasurer had hoped to enjoy this moment more. "Did you hear me, traitor?"

Still, no response.

"I'm sending you back to England, where your death will buy me eight thousand English archers. I intend to use them to kill your good friend Rieux and his arrogant allies."

But the prisoner merely hung limply between the two guards. Storming over to him with robe flapping and slippers slapping daintily against the stone, Landais clasped his hair in his hands. At the very least, he wanted to watch this exile's spirit crumble. Tudor would not—could not—deny him satisfaction.

But when he jerked his head back, he stared into unfamiliar eyes.

"What?" He released the hair and backed away. "Who is this?"

The grizzled guard shifted. "It's Henry Tudor. His clothes, the way the others sought to protect him—"

The young man between them grinned. "Matthew Baker, servant to the Earl of Richmond, at your service."

The guards exchanged a nervous glance.

"Fools!" Landais grabbed at the guard's collar.

Surprised, the man released the prisoner, who took the opportunity to run for the door.

"Find Tudor!"

He had imagined rank after rank of English soldiers hunting down the rebel Breton nobles who had escaped his grasp, but it was all slipping through his fingers.

Landais shouted after the guards scurrying away. "Send everyone! Bring me Henry Tudor, no matter the cost!"

## HENRY

"Just a little farther, my lord."

Urswick's words sounded faint on the wind rushing past Henry's ears as his mare cantered through the thick forest. The poor beast was nearly blown from the grueling day and a half. Every few hundred yards, he had to goad his horse to keep pace.

While he sympathized with the creature, they couldn't stop. Landais would eventually learn of his deception and send men after him. Henry had no way of knowing how far behind they were. They could appear at any moment.

A horse whinnied behind them, and they kicked into a gallop.

His mount barred its teeth, either at the new pace or the tension of her rider.

Ahead, a carriage was rolling along the narrow road, bound by a tangled mass of oak, ash, and chestnut trees on both sides.

Henry's hoarse voice cracked in French, "King's business. Move aside, move aside!" When they did nothing, he reached into his pocket and waved a writ of passage wildly before him. "By order of the king, let us pass!"

Finally spurred to action, the carriage driver veered off the road and into the brush. When Henry passed, he caught the flash of a fleur-de-lis on the door. They had to be close to France.

This forest was nothing like the one he'd explored with the Rieux brothers at Largoët. Where that verdant wood had been airy and bright with shafts of sunlight cascading through the foliage, this tangled forest felt ominous. Every shadow was a ducal rider set to interdict them.

And then the road bent and revealed the breathtaking reflection of the noon sun on the shallow Loire. Beyond, atop a round hill, sat the tower of an abbey and the buildings of a small town.

St. Florent-le-Vieil. The French border.

*Goodbye, Brittany. Goodbye, Landais and Francis.*

*Goodbye, Jehane.*

They had been warned that this part of the Loire could vary from a few feet to more than twice a man's depth, but a quick look at the current and the rocks visible along the bed told Henry they could ford it fairly easily.

"Quickly." Henry plunged his horse into the water. The flow of cold across his skin forced a shiver. Beneath him, his gelding neighed at the refreshing relief after the long journey.

The little settlement had no wall or palisade, so Henry and Urswick rode unimpeded toward the main square. The squat buildings and thatched roofs looked no different from the small towns dotting the Breton countryside. The faces that studied the travelers with suspicion amid the setting sun wore the same expressions given to strangers in any country Henry had seen.

They had attracted the attention of the local townsfolk by the time they reached the town square abutting the local church. From a side street, half a dozen soldiers with halberds slung over their shoulders approached. Henry didn't recognize their green-and-yellow livery.

Henry turned to Urswick. "You must have seen Anne's guards when you visited her. What did her coat of arms look like?"

"Three fleurs-de-lis on blue, with a red bend across the upper right."

Henry cursed quietly and gestured to the approaching soldiers. "What if they're the Duke of Orléans' men?"

"She directed us here specifically. I don't imagine she'd lead us into harm."

Henry, though, could certainly imagine a besieged regent seeking to neutralize one of her enemies by turning a rival over to him. Looking around, he saw nothing to serve as a weapon but a farmer's hoe leaning against a nearby building. Hopefully, the church's doors weren't locked.

"Henry?"

Relief washed over him at the familiar voice. He turned just in time for his uncle's broad arms to surround him in an embrace.

"Uncle! We were supposed to meet in Angers."

"Yes, well… I arrived to learn the regent had moved on to Chartres, so I decided to collect you myself. Plus, the ride served me well." Indeed, Jasper smiled as he hadn't since Chepstow, all those years earlier. "Ah, to ride out freely!"

"Are these friends or enemies?" Henry gestured to the soldiers.

"Enemies?" Jasper asked in confusion. "They're our bodyguards."

"Bodyguards or jailors?"

"Bodyguards," Jasper reassured. A change came across his uncle's face after he counted Henry's party. "Matthew?"

Henry shook his head. "He lured the ducal guards away an hour into our journey."

"So Landais knows you've escaped."

Henry nodded. "What do you think will happen to him?"

"We can't be certain." Jasper sighed. "You knew this was a risk. But all of us—myself included—would sacrifice ourselves to keep you safe."

"I know." *God protect you, Matthew.* "So, on to Chartres?"

Jasper nodded. "But first, you're probably exhausted and hungry. How about some food?" He sniffed the air near Henry. "And, perhaps a bath?"

While Henry and Urswick ate and washed their hands and faces, Jasper prepared a comfortable carriage for their long journey to Chartres. They had several hours of daylight left and could make it to the next town at least, penetrating deeper into the safety of France.

Shortly after the party disappeared down the road, a pair of riders quietly cantered into town, asked a few questions, and hastily returned to Rennes. They had missed Henry Tudor by less than an hour.

Landais would not be pleased.

## HENRY

He noticed the blue first.

After a life spent beneath the black-and-white crest of Brittany, he wasn't prepared for the sea of azure splashed across the plates, banners, pennants, carriage doors, tabards, and table runners. It was built into mosaics on the floors, was inlaid into the hilts staring back at him on rapiers and daggers, adorned the signs of every tavern and shop, and imprinted every available chair and surface. It was overwhelming.

But the effect diminished while he awaited his audience with the French regent. In its place grew an odd sense of comfort. Perhaps it was his French blood through his paternal grandmother, or perhaps a decade among Bretons had diluted his natural English suspicions. Or, maybe those red and yellow coats of arms had sought his death for too long, while the blue and gold of French royalty had been his dream of salvation.

A page bowed to Henry more deeply than any in Brittany ever had. "My lord, the regent requests your presence."

Rising, Henry straightened his new red doublet and adjust the tufts of his white tunic beneath. That pair of colors would remind the regent both of Henry's Lancastrian claim and his pre-contract with Elizabeth of York.

Matthew had worn the same colors when he'd sacrificed himself to enable Henry's escape. Matthew, who might have died for his efforts.

With a nod, he fell into step with his escort. Unlike in Brittany, that escort included no soldiers. As far as he could tell, Anne wasn't even bothering to have him watched. It was an odd feeling after years of constant surveillance.

The page came to a pair of solid oak doors and knocked, a dull thud echoing through the room louder than he would have expected.

When they opened, Henry hungrily absorbed the splendor within the chamber. Fleur-de-lis banners hung from either side of the back wall, framing the large, high-backed walnut throne that served as the centerpiece of the room. The throne demanded Henry's attention, not for the nuanced carvings of roses but for the delicate body contained within.

Back straight and chin slightly elevated, Anne of Beaujeu exuded power without moving, by her mere presence. She was framed in a square-necked dress of goldenrod with black roses and vines embroidered along the lower half. Her fine hair—somewhere between dark brown and chestnut—was bound by a matching snood with pearls and golden stitching along the band. Her dark brown eyes studied him while he approached.

He could understand why Urswick admired her. He suddenly felt very self-conscious of his own flaws. His teeth were starting to go bad and the years in exile hadn't given him the chance to ride or practice with a sword as much as he'd wanted. His calves were not very muscular, and his eyebrows were too thin to be attractive. Compared to her, he was at best uninteresting.

The king beside her was much the same. His eyes drooped, suggesting a perpetual lethargy that his long nose only accentuated. A non-entity, Henry decided. Anne was the real power in France.

He bowed deeply, waiting to be addressed according to the court's custom.

Anne, not the king, greeted him in a clear tone. "Your Highness, it is a pleasure to see you at our court after a delay of so many years."

Though it was presumptuous for her to claim ownership of the court, Henry was more surprised at being acknowledged as the rightful claimant to the English throne, and by the regent of France, no less.

"Your Royal Highness. I thank you for your welcome and the tireless efforts of yourself, His Majesty"—he bowed to Charles—"and your father." Licking his lips, he dared a little familiarity. "I do apologize for my tardiness. We got a little lost on the journey from England."

Laughter danced from her lips, a pleasing sound all the more comforting for its instinctive release. "You are our modern-day Odysseus."

Her eyes hinted that this was a test of some sort. "Only, my journey took thirteen years to his ten," he answered, remembering his Latin lessons. He'd always found it odd that the poet had written in Latin, and not Greek.

"Quite right." Her lips pursed into a satisfied smile.

"Like that king, I must deal with troublesome lords. Will you help me dethrone the traitor Richard of York?"

Charles looked to his sister with interest. Apparently, the young man was following this meeting, after all.

But Anne ignored him. "May we dispose of the formality?"

Intrigued, Henry nodded.

"We know Richard conspires with the dukes of Orléans and Brittany to unseat our regency. I am strongly inclined to support your cause, Lord Tudor. Richard has made himself my enemy, and I will not forget or forgive that." Her posture relaxed. "But we are not in a position to invade England for you, not when we need our soldiers and money to prepare for Orléans."

"If you know he threatens you, why not simply arrest him?"

"He has given no offense yet," she replied simply. "But we hear whispers. It offends him that a woman would hold influence in France." She paused for a moment. "Does that fact bother you?"

The laughter began deep and erupted out of his throat. "You've clearly never met my mother." After a moment, he remembered his place and sobered. "Forgive me. But after Margaret of Anjou, Elizabeth Woodville, Margaret Beaufort, and even Catherine Woodville, who stirred Buckingham to revolt… To me, a woman wielding power is as natural as the wind blowing through the trees."

"It doesn't bother you that my power comes from a position usually held by a man?"

"Power is power. I appreciate its effects, not its source. If your position helps me depose a tyrant and murderer, I welcome it." As he met her gaze, a silent understanding passed between them. He liked this woman immensely. When he spoke again, his tone was more casual. "Would you help my cause, if you could?"

"I would. Richard seizes our vessels and threatens our people. He must be stopped."

Recalling the exiles he had abandoned in Brittany, exposed to retaliation by Landais, he appreciated her desire to protect her people. "Then my interest lies in doing all I can to help you solve that problem."

She raised an eyebrow. "What is your meaning?"

"When I fled, I was forced to leave hundreds of Englishmen in Brittany who preferred exile to serving Richard. We are bound together, they to help me claim the crown and me to restore their honors. Would four hundred loyal men aid you against the Duke?"

Her eyes widened. He had come to her court as a refugee, but now he offered an alliance as an equal. Four hundred men who could wield arms was valuable, even if it cost her some power over him.

"An agreement, then?"

Henry nodded. "My men and I will strengthen your rule against the duke if you provide men and money to invade England."

"You may need to take arms against fellow Englishmen."

Henry raised a finger. "Against Ricardians. The same men we would face eventually."

She rose and descended the dais. She was smaller than the force of her words suggested. Extending her hand, she smiled, showing a set of bright white teeth. "We have an accord."

Henry smiled as well, but he self-consciously kept his lips closed as he clasped her hand. "Will you help me secure the release of my men in Brittany?"

"I will do what I can. My ambassador reports they have not been mistreated." She released his hand. "You have spent some time with Pierre Landais. What leverage would work best with him?"

Henry considered. "Bypass him entirely. Write to Duke Francis. He is an honorable man and can be reminded to do his duty."

Anne looked uncertain. "That has not been my experience. I've found him to be a wily one. He maintains an alliance with a king he extorts."

Henry considered his previous dealings with Francis, the mouse caught between two lions. "If I write to him, could you smuggle my letter past Landais?"

"It can be done, yes." She hesitated. "However, you must be prepared for Brittany to refuse to hand your men to its enemies. I give you formal royal permission to recruit from among French subjects and the mercenary brokers at court."

"I have no funds; I left everything in Brittany." In fact, he'd had very little to lose; the money he'd embezzled by over-reporting his expenses hardly amounted to much. "I would need to provide arms and armor to any I recruit."

"My problem is loyalty, not money." She offered a casual wave. "I will provide funds to outfit your men and place royal surety behind your loans."

Henry nodded, quite satisfied. "Thank you, Your Highness."

Anne smiled and resumed her position on the throne before ending the audience. Henry bowed and exited the double doors, reviewing the conversation with increasing satisfaction.

When he summarized the meeting for his uncle, Jasper wasn't nearly as pleased. "You've involved us in the wrong civil war."

Henry rolled his eyes. "I did what was necessary. I need an army to invade England, and I'm done waiting for someone to give me one." He sat on a nearby bench. "We won't get any support while civil war is brewing, and if Anne loses, we won't get anything at all. So yes, I offered to help her. And in exchange, I can recruit and outfit my own men, and maybe gain a little experience in warfare before I need to fight for a crown."

"Perhaps even blood your soldiers against Frenchmen." Jasper subsided, evidently recognizing the value.

"In one day, she provided more than Francis did in thirteen years. She gave me the freedom to build my own future instead of living at someone else's mercy."

"Yes, you're right." Jasper sighed. "I'm just eager for this to be over." He might have still looked imposing in his new doublet, stitched with silver thread in a diamond pattern over his muscular frame, but his uncle suddenly seemed so very tired. "For so long, I've hoped France would be the answer to all our struggles."

"It will be."

His uncle met his eyes. "You have a good mind, Henry. I'm proud of you."

Henry smiled at the compliment from the only man whose opinion he valued.

Stirring suddenly, Jasper rose with a murmur, leaving Henry alone to draft a letter that could determine the fate of over four hundred men and their families.

# HENRY

*The fifth day of October, Anno Domini 1484.*
*My dear friend Francis, Duke of Brittany:*
*Please forgive my rudeness in departing without your leave. I cannot blame your council for watching out for your interests, yet I must do the same with mine.*
*Faithful duke, you showed me courtesy and kindness when no one else would. Your protection and friendship have meant much to me over the years. In your realm, I had my share of joys as well as sorrows. For that, I thank you.*
*Please be reassured of my love and respect. I hold your treasurer Pierre Landais responsible for the circumstances leading us to this sad state of affairs, not you. I shall always fondly remember my time as a guest of your great duchy. When the usurper is dead, I will honor your courtesy by protecting your realm from those who seek its destruction.*
*May God bless you and protect you from all threats, both from without and within.*

*H.R.*

# CHAPTER FOURTEEN

## HENRY

ENRY HEARD NOTHING from Brittany for nearly a month, though he did hear from Bretons. The many nobles who had chosen exile over submission to Landais were present at the French court, as well. While Henry appreciated the reunion with Armand and Philippe de Rieux, their laughter sounded strained. Exile had already begun to change them in ways Henry understood all too well.

Seeing friends from Brittany only reminded him of the Englishmen he had abandoned. They could be dead now, or nearly so on a ship to England. So many men, wives, and children… William Brandon's wife had just given birth to a young boy, Charles; did he yet live?

And then, the first horses arrived.

A courier and a light escort trotted into Montargis wearing the black-and-white of Brittany, bearing papers to explain their presence. A letter from the Duke—consisting of a few short sentences in his own, shaky hand—offered regrets for Henry's plight and appreciation for his kind words.

Soon after came a caravan of wagons bearing the women and children, flanked on all sides by pack mules, ox carts, and the exiles themselves riding fresh horses.

"Duke Francis granted us everything we had," Edward Woodville explained upon greeting Henry and Jasper. "And he provided funds to pay for our journey." He offered Henry a moderately sized purse.

Henry clasped Woodville tightly, relieved to see so many familiar faces. "Do they know why I left?"

Woodville nodded. "They do."

"How did they take it?"

Edward shrugged and glanced toward the riders. "It was a shock to all of us. Most understood why you had to go."

"Most?" While not unexpected, the news spoiled some of his happiness. "And you?"

Edward shook his head. "My brothers died for misjudging Richard. I begrudge no man for escaping his grasp."

"I am gratified to hear that."

"We'll have to keep an eye out for troublemakers," Jasper added dryly, "in case they feel more than a lack of appreciation."

Henry waved him off. "First, see to everyone, uncle. Having made the trip once, I suspect they're tired and hungry."

Jasper and Edward bowed and went to attend to the exiles, leaving Henry alone. He wished Urswick hadn't already departed for England. This news would help win over the nobles.

But, he supposed it was better to keep his lines of communication secret, and the fewer men who recognized the priest, the better.

Jasper's concern about troublemakers stuck like a splinter in his mind, though. With Henry under guard in Brittany, Richard hadn't needed to place spies in his ranks. But now, Henry would have to watch for false friends.

Two days later, he forgot about that fear and leaped into paroxysms of joy when John de Vere, the Earl of Oxford, came cantering into Montargis with two companions as casually as if returning from a hunt. Both Henry and Jasper wept openly at the reunion. They hadn't seen each other since Chepstow thirteen years earlier.

"How?" Henry asked once he'd recovered sufficiently from the good news to form words. "We were told you were under guard in Calais these past nine years."

"Hammes, actually. And I was a prisoner until about two weeks ago," Oxford supplied.

"Tell on," Jasper prodded.

"When you slipped through Richard's fingers, the pretender decided it was time to settle accounts and ordered my transfer to England. Very likely, to my death, just like Henry Holland."

"Or like me, if not for fortune's favor." Henry decided against mentioning Stanley's warning, even to Oxford.

"That my head does not adorn St. Paul's is due entirely to these men." Oxford gestured to his companions. One dressed simply in riding attire, but the other was adorned as a gentleman. "Allow me to introduce John Fortescue and Sir James Blount, the commander of the Hammes garrison."

Henry included his head respectfully when the men bowed. "You have my most sincere thanks for your role in Lord Oxford's escape."

"Blount once served my sister-in-law," Oxford explained, "who was married to Lord Hastings."

"A good man who did not deserve his end," Blount added. "His poor widow was left with nothing. It's not the sort of thing one should do."

Oxford gestured to the other man, dressed simply. "And Fortescue shares my outrage at the murder of those poor princes."

Though Fortescue remained silent, he crossed himself. The rest followed suit a moment later.

Yet, even reference to the Tower murders could not dim Henry's delight. While Jasper had led companies, Oxford had commanded armies. Anne had granted Henry the authority to raise soldiers. Oxford would train them to confront Richard.

"What happened there?" Jasper pointed to a jagged, healed scar on Oxford's face.

"Took an arrow to the face at St. Michael's Mount when Edward caught me." He brushed a finger against it. "But we need to discuss more recent events." He grinned broadly enough to show his teeth. "The entire Hammes garrison wishes to join your cause."

Henry's eyes widened at the thought of gaining both a general and a company of seasoned soldiers. "They are most welcome."

Oxford shook his head. "Not that easy. We had to escape into the night when Richard's men came for me. Blount here shut the gates on them, but they intended to return with the Calais garrison to seize the fortress."

"Does Calais have enough men to storm the castle?" Jasper asked.

Fortescue shook his head. "The garrison is a hundred, and Hammes is designed to repel a much larger force. They'll lay siege."

"How long can they hold out?" Henry asked.

Fortescue and Blount exchange a glance before Blount answered, "A month, perhaps two."

"We're in no position to relieve them," Jasper warned.

"My wife and child are still in Hammes," Blount explained nervously, taking a step forward. "We cannot leave them to Richard's mercy. You have to help them."

"And I will." This was Henry's chance to wipe clean his shame at abandoning his supporters in Brittany and restore their faith in him.

"How?" Jasper asked. "We have no soldiers or weapons."

"Many among the exiles are soldiers," Henry corrected. "And we can use the rest of Francis' gift to buy arms."

"Henry," Jasper muttered, "those men only just returned from Brittany. Most of them don't even have somewhere to live. They have families to think of."

"Then we take who we can," Henry declared. "I need soldiers like those in Hammes to contest Richard. This is happening, so let's find a way to do it." He met the faces of each of the men before adding, "I welcome any suggestions."

Oxford grinned and eyed Jasper. "No longer the boy running to catch up with us in Chepstow, eh, Jasper?"

"No, indeed." Jasper's eyes carried a respect that had been absent in St. Florent-le-Vieil a month earlier. "Now, he's thinking like a king."

## HENRY

Anne immediately saw the value in diminishing the English garrison on the continent by a hundred men. Though offering French soldiers would instigate a war well before she was ready, she happily opened the French royal armory to Henry and whatever men he could convince to join him.

While he gladly accepted horses from the royal stables, Henry insisted on supplying his own arms. "What I own cannot be withheld," he later explained to Oxford. "I'm through being beholden to others."

Recalling his lessons from Jehane's shop, Henry ignored the armorers who followed the French court and instead sought out second-hand sources. While he spent nearly every coin he possessed, he acquired a hundred serviceable sets of arms, each procured at a fraction of their normal cost. Though some of the swords had uneven fullers and pieces of armor had irreparable dents or rumpled edges, they would serve their purposes.

The effort took some time, but it kept Henry occupied. The walls of Hammes were strong and holding well, and it kept Henry's mind occupied. While Henry delivered batches of arms and armor to them, the exiles trained. Fortunately, nearly all the men who had joined him in exile were former soldiers.

But the Calais garrison consisted of experienced—if slightly indolent—veterans. Word came in mid-December that the besiegers had been bolstered by newcomers from England. Henry had run out of time.

And so, he and his hundred exiles marched through the northern gate of Montargis toward Hammes, a few miles southwest of Calais. The journey took ten days and passed Paris, where Henry flashed a command from the regent and traded in his rounceys for coursers more suited for battle. Each of his men pawed and petted at the fine steeds, and Henry had to prod more than a few to finish swapping their tack and return to the march.

When they reached the outskirts of the Pale of Calais after the turn of the new year, Oxford deployed outriders and scouts. While the former found no ambushes, the latter reported that the castle still stood but was badly damaged on its northern side, with enemy camps in each direction guarding the approaches.

"They'll intercept us if we rush the walls," Jasper explained to Henry and his advisors, frowning over the map Woodville had drawn in the dirt. With them in a poor camp a short ride from Hammes were Oxford, Blount, Grey, and Thomas Brandon. "They have at least four hundred men."

"Are they sapping?" Blount gnawed at his lip.

Jasper shook his head. "It doesn't appear so."

Woodville stood and crossed his arms. "That isn't surprising. If they undermine the fortress, they leave Calais vulnerable to the French."

Oxford nodded. "They seem content to starve the fortress out."

"I've been trapped before, and it's not easy to endure day after day," Grey added with a distant stare. "It's not the lack of food but the hopelessness that will break them."

The group fell silent, contemplating either the situation or Grey's words.

"If we reinforce them, we'll show the Ricardians that Hammes can hold out indefinitely," Henry said at last.

"My brother and I can lead some of our men into the fortress to shore up their defenses," Brandon offered.

Henry bowed his head in appreciation.

"I'll go with them," Blount added.

"You won't stand a chance," Grey cried. "They'll intercept you before you reach the walls."

"Not if we distract them." Oxford offered a broad grin. "We have cavalry. Let's use it."

Once Oxford had explained his intentions, Henry gave him

command of the diversionary force, pleased to divide command between a Lancastrian and the Yorkist Brandon.

Brandon and his men loaded their horses with all the food they could carry as Oxford sent a rider to shoot a messenger arrow over the walls of Hammes. Once they received a response acknowledging the plan, Brandon took his thirty men to wait in a copse of trees just south of the fortress, while Oxford's sixty riders disappeared into the woods.

Though Henry yearned to join them, his advisors were unanimous in keeping him far from the fighting. Jasper and a handful of others stayed with him, ostensibly to protect the royal claimant. After so many years left to his own devices, being coddled felt awkward and unnatural.

Aware that they vastly outnumbered the besieged, the Calais Ricardians had settled into comfortable camps. While they'd set sentries, those men stood along the side facing the fortress. After all, the pale was surrounded by Frenchmen who were disinclined to interrupt Englishmen from killing each other.

So, when Oxford's riders breached the picket lines of the western camp, swinging their swords and torching the tents, the eighty Ricardians were taken by complete surprise. The exiles vanished before their victims could mount a response, disappearing back into the woods and leaving confusion and broken bodies in their wake.

Having believed they would face no cavalry, the Ricardians had no pikes to repel a charge. But the men of Calais were professional soldiers. The camp commander shouted instructions and dispatched messengers to the northern and southern camps for reinforcements while the rest of the men formed a line of battle.

When Woodville led the second half of the cavalry a few minutes later, they met stiff resistance and had to content themselves with picking off the occasional straggler. As a trio of his riders went after an isolated group of Ricardians and risked being surrounded, he blew his horn for the retreat. They rallied at the tree line, where Woodville reformed them for another charge.

Before he could strike, though, another horn blew from the north, and a company of soldiers in formation came jogging toward the western camp, sliding into position alongside their shaken and mangled brothers.

The reinforcements from the south, however, rushed for the safety of the camp in a blind panic, pursued by Oxford's horsemen. For, after his first charge, Oxford's unscathed men had retreated to the forest and had shadowed the messenger running to the south. When the company of soldiers deployed by the southern commander passed them by, Oxford's men had exploded out of the woods and fallen upon their flank. Terror had taken over and eroded whatever discipline the Ricardians had, sending them fleeing for safety in all directions.

And then, as quickly as they'd come, the exiles had gone. The Ricardians converged on the relative safety of the western camp and tended to their wounded while the uninjured eyed the woods, vigilant against further sorties.

Their attention was soon drawn back to the battlement of the fortress, where men stood shoulder-to-shoulder, waving and whistling. Foremost among them were Thomas and William Brandon and James Blount. Hammes had been reinforced.

Bloodied, battered, and beaten, the Ricardians settled into an uncomfortable night's watch.

The next day, Blount and Brandon called for a parley in the field just outside the walls of Hammes. They offered the captain of Calais a selection of sweetmeats and fine French cheeses from the fortress supplies and shared news of Henry Tudor's arrival with his army.

When Brandon mentioned he'd acquired their fine coursers from the French royal stables, the captain cast a pensive gaze toward the French border. Shortly thereafter, he agreed to allow the garrison to join Henry in France in exchange for surrendering the fortress.

Henry now had an army, and it had proven itself the equal of Richard's veterans.

# HENRY

Henry started the leisurely return to Montargis in a delighted reverie. Marching at the head of an army had been the wish of the boy who'd ridden off with his uncle so many years before, and age had not cured him of the excitement.

He rode along the column for most of the day. The eyes that looked up at him were hardened by military life. At first, he doubted they would follow him. But then he recalled his flight from England, fourteen years of exile, and escape at St. Malo. He hadn't endured as much as they had, but he'd repeatedly risked his life, nonetheless. When he met their gazes, more than a few nodded with respect.

Surprised, he struggled to maintain a grave expression and simply nodded back, even as his heart soared at the tacit acceptance implied by that simple gesture.

His good mood, however, was not to last.

Once he had sorted the newcomers and updated their captains on procedures, Jasper rode up. "We had a good day."

"And lost none in the process." Though it didn't make up for abandoning the exiles in Brittany, it helped.

"Lord Oxford was impressive."

Was this the old Lancastrian sentiment raising its head? "As were Woodville and Brandon."

"That's true." Jasper added in a quieter voice, "Not all are pleased."

"Trouble?"

Jasper nodded. "Thomas Grey was glowering when you gave Oxford command of the cavalry."

"He was upset I didn't share his doubts."

"It's more than that, and not the first time," Jasper warned.

Henry turned to study his uncle. "Why am I just hearing of this?"

Jasper ignored the question. "With all the newcomers, I asked some of my men from Chepstow to keep their ears to the ground.

Some of these new exiles could have orders to report our movements, or even to kill you."

Henry thought of that night in the carriage.

"The crown gives Richard the power to pardon, to make peace, to offer many kinds of incentives—"

Henry waved off a lecture. "What did they hear?"

"Grey said that with so many Yorkists among us, one of them should lead your army."

"And which of them has even a tenth of Oxford's generalship?" Henry asked louder than he'd intended. It was too early for politics to start worming its way into his ranks. He hadn't even landed in England yet.

"If he can convince the Yorkists to refuse Oxford's commands, you'll be forced to exclude the Lancastrians. My guess is he favors Woodville, as the brother of your intended."

Henry sighed. "Is Woodville himself behind this?"

Jasper pressed his tongue against the inside of his cheek. "I don't believe so. He and Oxford are becoming fast friends. They're both military-minded. I haven't heard him whispering like Grey."

"But you can't be certain," Henry concluded. Woodville might simply be trying to learn as much as he could from the man he intended to replace.

"What are you going to do about it?" Jasper asked.

"Nothing."

"Nothing?"

Henry nodded. "If I want to dethrone Richard, I need everyone who's willing to fight for me. This can't be about York and Lancaster. I need both."

"I noticed the men have started referring to Richard's forces as Ricardian."

"I've encouraged it when I can," Henry explained. "We can't think of the men we oppose as English, nor can we forget our objective."

"Will you continue to rely on Woodville? This is the kind of thing his family does."

Henry shrugged. "If I remove him now after how well he fought, I lose the Yorkists and a good commander. If he's truly conspiring, he'll go too far and give me cause."

"Weave the rope to hang himself?" Exhaling, Jasper shook his head. "A dangerous strategy."

"Dangerous times." He kicked his horse into a trot and pulled away from the shadow of conspiracy.

Up ahead, Oxford and Woodville rode beside each other, gesturing frequently. Only after watching them for some time did Henry realize they were recounting the battle, punctuated by nods and occasional laughter. The scene before him looked like friendship, not intrigue.

"My lord?" Thomas Brandon sidled up, pulling Henry out of his thoughts.

Henry offered a polite smile. "How are the men after your daring maneuver?"

Brandon raised his eyebrows. "Impressed we managed it with so few injuries, actually."

"Oh?"

"Aye. A sure sign of God's favor for our cause."

Henry inwardly groaned at the conceit. Where had God's favor been these past fourteen years?

Outwardly, he blessed himself. "You wished a word?"

Brandon nodded. "When the fortress surrendered, the Ricardians returned some intercepted personal letters unrelated to the siege. One, from a sergeant's wife, may interest you." He handed a creased letter to Henry.

The paper was a coarse grain, and while it did have a broken wax seal, the ornamentation was simple. Henry unfolded it and noticed that the ink had bled slightly. The letter was dated a week prior.

"Halfway down, it talks about Richard's behavior at a recent feast," Brandon explained.

*His Majesty began drinking deeply, ranting about the
traitor Henry Tudor. Is it true young Tudor is in France now? I
hope that does not mean you will have to fight him. Please stay
safe, for our sake, if not your own.*

*Everyone noticed Elizabeth of York when she entered with
her mother, mostly because of her beautiful white lace dress.
White! We all knew it had to be a gift, what with her family
being dispossessed. With the way the king fawned all over her, it
didn't take us long to realize the dress came from him. He kept
leering in the most unnatural way—his own niece! Every chance
he had, he touched and complimented her. It was shameful.*

*Worst of all, she seemed to enjoy his affections. She batted
her eyes as if he was her suitor, not her uncle. The whole court
is scandalized.*

*And it was all done in front of his poor wife, who still
grieves for the loss of their son this past spring. Apparently, this
has been going on for some time in private, or so I gather from
the angry whispers of the Neville men.*

Henry lowered the letter. He felt surprisingly calm despite the
implications. The contents had to be mostly true; if it had contained
lies about their king, the Calais garrison never would have returned it
after the siege.

Was Richard merely trying to shame Henry by proving he could
flirt with his rival's intended with impunity? Richard depended on his
queen's Neville power, yet he had humiliated her by fawning over his
niece right in front of her. Why would he risk alienating his most
loyal supporters?

Both his intended bride and his future mother-in-law had obviously raised no objection. That alone would signal that they didn't
blame Richard for the princes' murder. And if their mother and sister
did not, how could the lords and knights of England blame him?

Both he and Elizabeth Woodville had realized Elizabeth of York might be married before Henry claimed his bride. That was why he'd included Cecily in his pledge. But losing her—or the public believing she encouraged her own uncle's advances—would cost him some of his Yorkist supporters.

Perhaps even Thomas Brandon, who watched Henry even now.

"Thomas…" It seemed prudent to address him in the familiar. "Have you read this letter?"

"I have, my lord."

"What do you think?"

Brandon shifted his weight to keep his horse in step with Henry's courser. "I think your betrothed lost a father, two brothers, and two uncles, watched another uncle destroy everything her family built over three decades, and spent months trapped in a cathedral. She does what she must to survive."

The words were a balm to his anxiety, but Henry appreciated the unflinching certainty in Brandon's eyes the most. "Indeed so." Folding the letter, Henry studied it for a moment. "Thank you for your courage at Hammes."

"Those men deserved rescue, my lord. You didn't have to risk coming to their aid, yet you did. That counts for much with us."

"Do you mind if I keep this letter?"

He nodded. "The soldier who gave it to me owes you his life."

Henry smiled, suddenly feeling very vulnerable. Loyalty was a precious thing, built and lost by subtle decisions. A military maneuver could build it, or an indiscrete courtship could threaten it.

Brandon began to maneuver his horse to leave him with his thoughts when Henry called out.

"Thomas?"

"Yes, my lord?"

"Would you mind keeping the contents of this letter to yourself?" The last thing he needed was gossip about Elizabeth's apparent eagerness for her uncle's affections.

"Of course, my lord."

# CHAPTER FIFTEEN

## HENRY

THE EXILES SETTLED comfortably in Montargis. As January faded into February, Henry still hadn't resumed his defamation campaign against Richard. The safer topic for his letters was to condemn Richard for seizing French and Breton ships as punishment for allowing Henry to escape. Both states had responded in kind. Richard—king of a maritime island country—found himself beset on all sides by angry merchants.

Unfortunately, the nobles and knights Henry needed cared little for commercial complaints. Such a missive would change few of the minds who mattered.

A brave man would write about Richard's incestuous intentions with Elizabeth and his deplorable treatment of his wife. But that course could suggest Henry was too weak to protect the honor of his betrothed. And what if the report of Elizabeth of York's reception of her uncle's advances had been accurate? The reputation of a Woodville among the English was an already delicate thing.

Someone shouted from beyond the tent.

His uncle peeked in to deliver an urgent, "Henry, come quickly," before disappearing through the flap again.

Frustrated, Henry pushed back his chair and obediently followed.

The light of the noonday sun stung his eyes despite his efforts to shield them with a hand. Arrayed around him were camp tents, except for a clearing where his soldiers practiced their drills. Rather than settle the men into comfortable homes, he had no choice but to keep them in camp. The Duke of Orléans had besieged Paris. Though he'd failed, he was still actively fomenting rebellion. Anne would put out the call to assemble the army any day now.

Henry's own war for influence had experienced both successes and failures. Unsure whom to trust, Richard had placed his northern Neville men in positions of power throughout England, alienating local lords whose titles and honors had been given to strangers. A steady stream of outraged Englishmen had crossed the channel to bolster Henry's ranks.

But Richard had also extended pardons to hundreds of men involved in Buckingham's revolt, and even the entire garrison of Hammes. A few had accepted the offer, sneaking away in the night. Whether they agreed with Grey about working with Lancastrians, disliked relying upon the French, or simply found Henry's cause too unlikely to succeed, he couldn't say. But Henry had to remain in camp to watch them carefully.

A heated argument drifted over the heads of the observers clustered in a ring in the middle of a clearing.

"What's all this, now?" Henry waded through the crowd.

Within, Oxford and Grey turned from each other to Henry. He caught a fading hint of lingering irritation on the face of the former and unapologetic contempt on the latter.

"Well?"

"It is a small matter, hardly worth your concern," Grey began.

Henry addressed the crowd surrounding his commanders, "Gentlemen, might I entreat you for privacy?"

They obediently melted away amid a few frowns and grumbles, leaving only Jasper, Woodville, Grey, and Oxford.

Henry raised an eyebrow. "If you'll join me?" Turning on his heel, he led the group to his tent. Once inside, he crossed his arms across his chest. "If you saw what those soldiers just witnessed, would you respect your leaders?"

No one replied. Most lowered their heads in shame, but Grey met Henry's gaze directly, very clearly unabashed.

Henry sighed. "What caused this argument?"

Oxford spoke first. "Lord Woodville and I were discussing how to incorporate the Hammes garrison into the army when Grey insulted my parentage."

"Only after you called me an antiquated fool," Grey cried. "I refuse to be insulted by a man who only recently escaped from prison."

"I've spent the last fourteen years in a kind of prison." Henry fixed Grey with an unrelenting stare. After Grey turned away, Henry faced Oxford. "But nor do I seek to insult my companions."

Oxford sighed, and his shoulders slumped. "You're right." He turned to Grey. "I apologize for my poor behavior."

Grey darted his eyes from Oxford to Henry. Remaining silent would have been ungentlemanly. "I regret my words as well."

"What did you find so objectionable, Lord Grey?"

Grey jumped on the opportunity to vent his frustration. "You have men of all dispositions in your army." Henry noted the phrasing: Grey had excluded himself from their enterprise. "One man killed the brother of another at Edgecote. One does not simply forget that. Yet Oxford would have them fight side-by-side, be responsible for each other's lives. He doesn't respect where these men came from."

"You're right," Oxford explained. "I don't care a jot why these men fought in the past, only how they fight now. We need to organize based on specialty, not history. Spear with spear, archer with archer, cavalry with cavalry. If that means blending people who fought on opposite sides of some ancient battle, then so be it."

"The men of Hammes are proud of their history of loyalty and the battles they fought. A military man should understand that." To

Henry, Grey added, "They faithfully served King Edward all their lives, putting down rebellions and factions who would see him dethroned." He jutted a finger at Oxford. "He spits on that legacy by making them fight beside Lancastrian traitors."

"Those Lancastrian traitors remained loyal to the true king before he was usurped by the sons of York."

"Enough." Henry could understand why the argument had interested the soldiers. Yet, it also threatened to undermine his efforts to bring these sides together. "York. Lancaster. These distinctions are dead." He turned to Oxford. "The Lancastrians lost. Blame it on deceitful nobles or the excesses of Margaret of Anjou, but they succeeded only in turning most of the country against them."

Henry rounded on Grey, who was smirking at Oxford. "And Yorkist now means the murderer of your half-brothers and uncle and a man who executes the lords of the realm without respect for their positions. It means deeds so vile that even a man who helped him gain his crown sought to unseat him. Is that what you want to honor and defend?"

The tent was silent.

This poison had spread far enough. Henry needed to understand where loyalties lay. "Lord Woodville, you are a soldier and gentleman. Do you agree with Lord Oxford's plans for organizing the army?"

This was the moment. If he coveted Oxford's position, Henry had given him the chance to claim it.

"We must organize as Lord Oxford advises," Woodville said. "To defeat Richard, we will see many more join our ranks. We can't know who they'll be asked to fight beside. Better to settle past grievances now than in England."

"Well spoken." Relief washed over Henry that his judgment of Woodville's character had been accurate. "What matters now is whether a man supports honor and civility or murderous tyranny." He rubbed his temples. "Richard wants us to quarrel with each other.

If we do, our sacrifices will be for naught and he'll keep his crown. Do any of us want that?"

Even Grey shook his head.

Henry nodded, satisfied. "We have an obligation to our country to work together. Now, the regent may soon need us, so let's devote our time to preparing for war." He crossed to his desk. "And let's avoid arguing in front of the men."

Calmed, the group began to file out. Oxford mumbled an apology before ducking through the flap. Woodville led Grey away.

Jasper remained behind. "It'll worsen before it improves."

"I know. But at least I know I can trust Woodville." Collapsing into his chair, Henry rubbed his temples.

"Henry, are you well?"

"I'm fine." Henry offered a faint smile and gestured to the flap. "Check on Oxford for me?"

"He's not the one I'd worry about."

Henry shook his head. "I can't take anything for granted these days."

Jasper nodded and patted Henry on the shoulder before leaving.

But he continued to worry, biting at the inside of his lip until it hurt. If old loyalties ran deep, he needed to apply an even more powerful motivation.

Shifting his chair back to the quill and inkpot he had abandoned, Henry pulled out another sheet of paper and began to write about an incestuous king and a shamed queen.

## HENRY

The Duke of Orléans emerged from hiding in early March and called his allies to converge on Verneuil, northwest of Paris, for another attempt at the city. But Anne had endeared herself to the people. Several copies of the duke's secret letters found their way into her hands.

Henry responded to the muster the day it was issued. Valuing speed over strength, Anne and her husband Peter led their army out of Montargis and up the Seine to intercept the duke before he could summon his full force.

Orléans' plans to steal a march crumbled when Anne's army crawled over the hills toward his rag-tag force. Saddling a fast horse, he abandoned his army and raced for Brittany.

Though the duke had discounted the need for scouts, Anne had not. Expecting more rebels to join the duke, she had sent detachments to the nearby cities to delay any hostile forces long enough for her to defeat her rival. Henry had been assigned Evreux forty miles to the west, and Oxford had surrounded the city in a chain of scouts.

Nonetheless, the Tudor army was as surprised as the Duke of Orléans when the latter came riding into town on an exhausted horse. For a moment, Orléans stared blankly at Henry's troops while the Tudor soldiers admired the gold filigree of his fine armor. Then, when he attempted to wheel his exhausted courser around, William Brandon hauled him off and bound him.

Anne had won her civil war without fighting a single battle.

In Paris, Henry witnessed the fate of the Duke of Orléans. Much as in England, the crown depended upon the strength of loyal nobles. If Anne simply executed a prince of the blood, she could create more enemies for herself and her brother.

Instead, she forced her rival to undergo the *amende honorable.*

It began to the north of the Seine. The duke was stripped of his silk doublet, tunic, and hose and his family crest was cast to the ground before him. Barefoot, he was led by a hooded executioner by a coarse-grain rope about his neck through the streets of Paris. Over the Pont Neuf to Île de la Cité, the very people the duke had hoped to conquer jeered his presumption and arrogance. Feet bleeding, he meekly followed his executioner into the cathedral of Notre Dame. Nearly naked, he passed through the court to halt before the throne of his cousin.

Dropping to his knees, he begged pardon from God, his king, and his country, pledging never again to threaten anyone with such shameful and dishonorable behavior. Damned by his own words and committed to abject humiliation, the duke received his pardon.

Henry immensely enjoyed the magnificent, hideous spectacle as a demonstration of complete supremacy. Anyone with a shred of honor or integrity would have preferred death to such a humiliating debasement. That the duke had chosen to endure it had cost him the rest of his supporters.

Though the victory was Anne's, Henry still appreciated the taste of it.

## HENRY

Upon returning from Paris, Henry gave his men a short respite with their families. Now that Anne's power was undisputed, Henry would insist that she honor her promise. He wanted to sail for England before the campaigning season ended. The reckoning with Richard had waited long enough.

Though he yearned for a hot bath, a pile of letters awaited him in Montargis. New allies, reports of treachery, gossip about the court, demands for repayment, offers for new loans, even Richard's ranting proclamations against him… Each folded missive contained some precious piece of information.

His mother had sent a fat one. Intrigued at the size, Henry cracked open the seal.

*The thirteenth day of April, Anno Domini 1485.*
*My dear Henry,*
*On March 16, Queen Anne Neville died. Her health had been declining for some time. She was the last legitimate child of the Kingmaker and the source of Richard's blood hold over the Neville retainers. Though you may expect this to weaken Richard, the reality is more complicated.*

He leaned forward and re-read the passage with a growing frown. Only Richard's marriage had calmed Henry's fears over the attention the king had been paying to his betrothed. Securing a papal dispensation to marry his niece would be difficult, but it would have been almost impossible for Richard to also arrange an annulment of his marriage.

*I know you were shocked to hear that Elizabeth Woodville left sanctuary. As a mother, I was not. By joining the royal household, she secured dowries for her daughters. She had no other choice.*

*Naturally, the court showed the Woodville girls great attention. Richard wasted no time showing them off. While Catherine and Bridget are still small children, Richard betrothed ten-year-old Anne to the grandson of the Duke of Norfolk as a reward for his assistance against Buckingham.*

*The terms of your oath in Rennes are well known. Edward Woodville participated as the head of his family, or what remains of it. Richard set a precedent by using a pre-contract to claim his throne, and he cannot undermine that now. In the eyes of the English nobility, you and Elizabeth of York are bound together until death. I do hope you intend to honor that agreement, my son. You would anger the majority of the court if you did not.*

Henry lowered the paper and released a breath he hadn't realized he'd been holding. At least his future mother-in-law hadn't repudiated the betrothal. The marriage oath was holding, for the moment.

*Last year, the king's anger was for Scotland. This year, he endlessly declares you a traitor from a bastard line and calls you a coward who first ran to Brittany, then to sanctuary, then to France. He is obsessed with demeaning you, though his attention only increases your support.*

*Richard is no fool. He realizes marrying off Elizabeth would destroy you. And by God, he has tried. One of his creatures married Cecily under the technicality that a pre-contract cannot be made for two people. If you are bound to Elizabeth, you cannot also be bound to Cecily.*

*Many council sessions have discussed a husband for Elizabeth, yet not even Richard's most loyal men will risk marrying your betrothed. Doing so could see that man's children declared bastards by a fickle king, a rival family, or even a cadet branch of their own house. Richard showed everyone it could be done.*

*During one of those sessions shortly after the queen's death, Richard casually suggested he should simply marry her himself.*

God's wounds! Henry dropped the paper with shaking hands. How could his mother not say this at the beginning?

Rubbing his eyes, Henry paced across the room. Had he done enough to galvanize the Yorkists against Richard? It was too soon.

Returning to the discarded paper, he snatched it up to read the next section.

*No one spoke, so complete was the disgust and disbelief. My husband was still outraged at the idea when he told me a week later. Almost immediately thereafter, London was in an uproar about the prospect of blatant incest.*

*Then, the rumors started that Richard had poisoned his wife. The king and queen had not been on friendly terms since Buckingham's revolt. They've barely spoken since the death of their son. He had murdered children, his friends, and his relatives; why not also his wife? He clearly had a replacement in mind.*

*The Neville men were furious. The north breeds hard men, but they are austere and upright. A few approached my husband, asking whether he would support them in revolt should the allegation be true.*

*The rumors were so pervasive that Catesby and Richard Ratcliffe led a deputation of priests and bishops that included our dear Urswick, who remains undisclosed as a member of our cause. In no uncertain terms, they declared that Richard could not marry Elizabeth and keep his head, let alone his throne. The king finally relented when every priest present declared the impossibility of a marriage between uncle and niece under any circumstance. Catesby and Ratcliffe were visibly relieved. They are his closest friends and would lose everything if he fell.*

*And then, Richard abased himself by swearing before an assembly of all London that he had never considered the abhorrent prospect of marrying Elizabeth. His wife, whom he loved dearly, had died of natural causes, not poison. This mollified the public, if only just. The north settled down, and Richard has been quiet these past weeks. Thomas reports that, in council, the king seems to have lost his confidence.*

*It is a very good development for you and will do nothing to advance Richard's cause of finding a groom for Elizabeth.*

*Despite these events, most of the Neville men will likely stay with Richard. They rely on him for their new influence and power.*

*I continue to work on my husband to support your cause. He makes no commitment, but he assures me he doesn't seek a quarrel with his stepson. Write to me about your exploits in France. I hope you are finding more support there than in Brittany.*

*Your loving and faithful mother,*
*M. Beaufort*

Henry laid the paper down gently. Even after some moments of reflection, he could not decide whether he was pleased or disturbed. That Richard had angered some of his most ardent supporters was encouraging, but the king hadn't remained idle. Cecily had already been neutralized, and if Richard found a willing accomplice, Elizabeth, too, would be married off before the poor husband could reconsider.

He exhaled slowly to calm his ragged breathing. It would not do to give in to panic. His alliance with Elizabeth of York remained intact, and Richard's obsession with him had nearly cost him his northern support.

But Henry's own influence was dangerously delicate. Public opinion was the fragile, thin thread keeping his future from unraveling. He could do so little to influence it, merely take advantage of it before it slipped away.

## HENRY

They had been too late at Verberie, and Henry was determined not to fail at Compiègne.

Ears filled with the thumping of his horse's hooves, he focused on the riders in front of him. One of the royal guards had grown up in this part of the country. It was the only real advantage Henry had in this desperate search.

The morning after receiving his mother's letter, Henry had called his small council together to discuss how they could continue to build support. One of them had been missing. Servants were dispatched only to discover that he'd left in the middle of the night.

If the man reached England, Richard would use the defection of one of Henry's most important followers, one who had more cause to hate Richard than most, to destroy Henry's credibility.

Calais was the only possible route of escape. He had come with Henry on the way to relieve Hammes, and the allegiance of the Calais garrison was clearly Ricardian.

Swallowing his pride, Henry had asked the regent for her support. Brilliant as always, Anne had recognized the danger and sent a squad to guide Henry along the most likely route.

"There," Jasper cried as the forest opened to reveal the Oise River.

Behind him, Oxford shouted ahead to their guide, "Where can we cross?"

He replied in French with a heavy Picard accent. "There is a bridge to the west of town."

The bridge was a rickety wooden thing Henry would normally take at a trot. This evening, he charged across at a full gallop. Though the planks rattled with each stride, they held. Henry's party turned along the road and streamed for Compiègne.

The city gates were closing for the night when the party came into sight. "Declare yourselves," demanded the gate guards, leveling their pikes.

"We come on behalf of the king and regent." Their guide slowed to a canter and revealed the crest on his tabard. "Open the gates to us."

"Who are you?" Nonetheless, they began to raise the portcullis.

"I am Henry Tudor, the rightful King of England and ally to the Regent of France, Anne de Beaujeu." He pulled his horse to a halt. "We're looking for a single rider, well-born by his bearing but not necessarily his garments. He would likely sit nobly in the saddle. Delicate features, light brown hair." After a moment, he added, "He would have a fine horse, ridden too hard. And he would speak French with a noticeable English accent."

"Aye, I know the man. He came, not two hours ago."

"You spoke to him?" Henry asked.

The guard nodded. "He asked for an inn. He looked ready to fall out of the saddle."

"Take me there."

The inn was a short ride toward the center of town. As they progressed, they came upon a fine lodging along the main road.

Henry pulled to a stop. "What is this building?"

"Another inn, my lord," the city guard replied.

"And yet you directed the rider farther into the city?"

"Aye."

Henry studied the fresh paint on the sign, the fine wooden walls, and the neatly thatched roof. A roaring fire beckoned from behind the silk curtains visible in the nearest window. "But not to this one?"

The man shifted his eyes from Henry to the inn. "My cousin owns the other, my lord."

Henry gestured to fresh hoof prints visible along a well-trodden path leading behind the inn. "Uncle?"

"Right." Jasper followed the path while Henry and the guards dismounted.

"My lord, I said it's not this one," the gate guard said.

"I know my man," Henry replied. "A gentleman would choose this one."

His uncle emerged, grim-faced. "His horse is in the stable around back."

Henry turned to Oxford. "You have more right than most. Would you please request his presence?"

Oxford grinned like a wolf on the hunt. "It would be my sincere pleasure." Gesturing to the remaining escort to follow him, Oxford strode into the inn.

Henry inclined his head to the gate guard. "Thank you for your help." Reaching into his pouch, he pulled out a gold sovereign and handed it to him. "Would you mind waiting until we confirm we have our man?"

Face lighting up at the glint of gold, he nodded quickly and began tying up their horses.

A moment later, Oxford emerged, flexing his hand and escorting a bound Thomas Grey. The poor man was still dripping, clearly retrieved from his bath. At least Oxford had granted him the dignity of his tunic and breeches.

Grey faced Henry with defiant eyes, one of which was darkening with a bruise. "You have no right to detain me. I am a free Englishman and can go where I please." He gestured with his bound hands to Oxford. "And I expect this one to be punished for assaulting me."

Oxford beamed and exchanged a bemused glance with Jasper. Now that they'd caught their man, Oxford was enjoying himself immensely.

Grey reminded Henry of Vaughn at Chepstow. "I disagree, sir." Henry's voice was calmer than he felt. "You took an oath to support my marriage to your sister and defend my claim to the throne. As a gentleman, you should have honored that pledge."

"You talk to me of oaths?" Grey shouted. "What of your oath to marry my sister? You can't even keep your worst enemy from doing as he pleases with her. Instead, you embroil us in a foreign civil war."

"This will come to battle," Henry insisted. "I'm building an army of Englishmen."

"An army you put in the hands of a Lancastrian who murdered thousands of his fellow Englishmen for that bitch of a she-wolf, Margaret of Anjou. I refuse to follow a traitor."

"Richard deems you a traitor for your mother. He murdered your brother. How can you forgive that?"

"What's done is done," Grey insisted. "My mother says Richard offers me amnesty. He's going to marry Elizabeth, and my family will rise again, while you continue to delude yourself with another exile." He straightened. "Fight French wars all you like. I will return to my rightful place."

"You honestly don't know," Henry muttered in sudden realization. Reaching into his pocket, he withdrew the letter from his mother. "There will be no marriage between Richard and Elizabeth. He proposed it, and the outrage at the concept was so complete that even Catesby and Ratcliffe would not condone it."

Grey's eyes narrowed. "You lie."

"Wait a week until the news of his humiliation spreads, and then tell me that." Henry shook his head slowly. "You are a fool. He would exploit you after abusing your family, and you would welcome it. Worst of all, you aren't even the target of his schemes."

Though Grey gave no response, his face filled with doubt.

Henry turned to the guards. "Chain him. When we return to Montargis, I want him kept under constant watch until I decide what to do with him."

The royal escort moved to bind and load Grey onto his horse. Oxford and Jasper converged on Henry.

"We did it." Jasper's voice oozed with relief.

Pursuer or pursued, Henry's anxiety was the same. "I've had enough of headlong rushes through open country for a lifetime."

Jasper asked, "Do we need to worry about his uncle?"

Oxford shook his head. "Edward is wiser than his years, and he was very fond of his brother Anthony. He will never forgive Richard."

"We can't wait any longer," Henry declared.

"We must. We're stronger than we were in Brittany," Jasper said. "You have an army now, and the freedom to recruit more men."

"We gain more supporters every day," Oxford added. "And Richard grows weaker. He lost Buckingham, Hastings, even his northerners question him now. He won't have anyone left soon."

But Henry was adamant. "Richard undermines me daily. Yesterday, it was Elizabeth of York. Today, it was Grey. If we don't make progress, some of the men here might accept Richard's pardons." He bit at the inside of his lip. "All it takes is one loss to make people question whether I'll ever press my claim. I need to act before anything else changes."

Hope had turned to doubt before in Brittany, and again after Buckingham's revolt. He couldn't risk it a third time. It was time for his reckoning with Richard.

# CHAPTER SIXTEEN

## HENRY

*The twenty-eighth day of April, Anno Domini 1485.*
*To Rhys ap Thomas, honorable lord of Carmarthenshire and*
*son of the gracious and faithful Thomas ap Gruffydd:*
*We greet you in the name of our father, Edmund Tudor,*
*and our grandfather, Owain Tudor, loyal sons of Wales. Twice*
*before, our families served in common cause for the sake of our*
*countrymen. Once again, we ask for your support.*
*Our men are assembling and training. When our forces*
*are sufficient, we propose to deprive Richard, that unnatural*
*tyrant, of the dominion he holds over our brothers. A man*
*who murders his nephews, breaks faith with supporters both*
*noble and common, and shames God himself with incestuous*
*intentions cannot be trusted to vouchsafe the security of*
*the realm.*
*How many of your goods have been ravaged by the pirates*
*enflamed by the usurper? How many of your lands are now*
*occupied by northern interlopers? How many of your honors*
*will he grant to men who do not share our blood?*

*From one Welshman to another, join us in ridding our island of this tyrant. Permit us to reward you as your family's long history of fealty deserves.*

*If you find yourself agreeable to this enterprise, write back with what forces you can bring to bear.*

*God save you, sir. God save Wales, and God save our island.*

*H.R.*

HENRY LEANED BACK, rubbing the cramp out of his thumb and forefinger. After re-reading the missive, he poured sand over the wet strokes to dry them and folded the letter. Rhys—and his father, Thomas, before him—had supported every Lancastrian cause for the past three decades and owned vast tracts of Wales. He could bring thousands to Henry's cause. But he had remained silent during Buckingham's revolt. Had he seen the duke's true nature, or was he, unlike his father and grandfather, a more flexible man?

Dripping some of the melted wax over the fold, Henry imprinted the new seal he'd commissioned, a stylized *HR* below the quartered French fleur-de-lis and the English lions. While it cooled, Henry set the letter on the table on his left beside copies for Thomas Stanley and two dozen other important nobles.

It was time for the lords of England to declare themselves.

He pulled out another sheet and checked the next name on his list, a wool merchant from Plymouth. The sea stood between himself and Richard, and Henry would need transports. From what Jehane had said about her trading ships, they could carry hundreds of soldiers, dozens of horses, and many tons of supplies.

Jehane. Succeed or fail, he would likely never see her again. He hadn't had a chance to tell her how he still felt, how much he still missed her.

Frowning, he pushed aside the list of potential supporters and dipped his pen in the inkwell, scribbling quickly before he reconsidered.

*My dearest Jehane,*

*Since last we spoke, I have left Brittany for France and established myself as a military commander and claimant to the English throne. Though I have gained the power to defend those I love, my thoughts dwell on what I've lost. I am sorry for all that happened. I understand why you left and the impossible choice you faced.*

*My heart yearns for you, my darling. Without you, this world is shaded in darkness and sorrow. The best part of me withers without your love and affection.*

*Come back to me, Jehane. Will you share your life with me, as you once did? Please, come back to me.*

*Your Henry*

Lowering his pen, Henry folded and sealed the missive. There was nothing more he could do; she would either return or not. When he went to England, he would go without regrets.

Assuming, of course, that one more critical meeting went well.

## HENRY

"We thank you for your support against the Duke of Orléans," Anne began in a high alto, addressing only Henry, young King Charles, and a few guards and servants. "Without your assistance, our country would face the evils of a domestic war."

"It is a pleasure to aid a noble and elegant woman in defense of her rights and honors." After a pause, Henry asked, "Can I interpret your comments to indicate that we and our companions have fulfilled our promises to uphold your lawful rights?"

"You can."

Henry bowed his head. "Then I should like to discuss your support for my invasion of England. The usurper has lost the confidence of the realm. Now is the time to strike."

Leaning back, Anne pressed her lips together. "We are aware that Richard of England sought to unite both our friends and enemies against us. We bear no love for him, but though our French enemies are neutralized, we must still deal with the coalition gathered to support him. Brittany, the Empire, even the Spanish."

"Then empower me to strike the shepherd, so you may freely deal with his flock," Henry said. "Richard is the key to your victory as well as mine. Daily, I receive letters from great lords promising their loyalty."

"What support do you request from us?" Anne asked.

"You were gracious enough to advance funds to arm my men before Hammes, and that investment paid you back at Evreux. I ask you to increase your investment, that you may gain for yourself a kingdom as a stalwart ally. We need funds for mercenaries, equipment for a whole army, and whatever soldiers you can spare for our cause."

"How much?" she asked quickly.

"Two hundred thousand *livres* and five thousand men."

Not nearly as schooled in the art of diplomacy as his sister, young Charles sucked in a breath.

Anne gave him a stern look before turning back to Henry. "You ask for much."

"No more than I suggested during our first meeting."

"True enough." Nonetheless, she shook her head. "What you ask is not possible."

After years of studying the wiles of a particular tailor, Henry recognized the opening stages of a negotiation. He waited her out in silence.

"The *Estates General* would never authorize such a large gift. Perhaps twenty thousand, but they would expect something in return. And even against the duke, I did not have five thousand men in the field."

Still, Henry remained silent. He had reminded her of their

agreement. Now he had to remain patient while the thoughts worked their way through her mind.

"A loan would be easier," she said. "I could likely arrange for forty thousand *livres*."

Though the sum was less than Oxford and Woodville required, with royal patronage, Henry could raise the rest through private sources. If he failed, repayment would be irrelevant; he'd likely lose his head. If he succeeded, he could repay the sum by selling off confiscated Ricardian lands.

"And soldiers?"

"We anticipated a long campaign against the duke. In addition to the levies, who will simply disband, we raised a number of regulars. One, perhaps two thousand, fully outfitted." She folded her hands in her lap. "The families of the young maidens around Montargis and Paris will not thank us for leaving them idle to cause trouble. We will loan them to you."

"What of mercenary companies under contract with the French crown?"

Anne shook her head. "The terms of our contracts do not permit us to transfer them to foreign use." She pressed a finger to her lips. "But we can speak to them about suspending their terms of service, allowing you to hire them without damaging our agreements."

It was less than he'd hoped, but about what he'd expected. He would need to have Oxford assess the French soldiers' numbers and quality, but the fact that they already had arms and armor would save money. "I am grateful for your support, Your Highness."

"There is the matter of collateral. My advisors will insist upon something to ensure repayment."

Though he hadn't anticipated that request, Henry seized the chance it offered. "Then I offer two of my nobles as hostages of my good faith: Thomas Grey and John Bourchier, the young Baron Berners. Grey is the half-brother of my betrothed, and John Bourchier is a kinsman of the Archbishop of Canterbury."

She considered for a moment. "That is acceptable. We wish you good luck, Henry Tudor, and look forward to greeting you as King of England." After a brief hesitation, she added, "I trust you understand that this is the extent to which we will support your cause…and that you deem our obligations to you fulfilled?"

This would be his only chance. "I understand."

Anne smiled faintly before ringing a bell to signal the end of the interview. The servants swooped into action, opening the doors at the end of the hall and bringing goblets to refresh the king and regent before their next audience.

Henry struggled not to skip out of the chamber. Forty thousand *livres* was an excellent start. The moneylenders surrounding the court would fleece him, but he might ease the pain by promising opportunities in England after he'd won the crown.

A couple of thousand French soldiers would be a powerful message to the nobles of England. Not just another vague promise. Men for an army. His army, recognized and supported by a major power.

He wished he could see the look on Richard's face when he heard the news.

## MARGARET

The knock on the door broke Margaret out of her contemplation.

"Enter." She regretted not clearing her throat first. She'd had so few visitors since her incarceration that her voice was scratchy from disuse.

Her brother-in-law, William Stanley, entered. Unlike her husband, this Stanley was thick-muscled and tall, a born soldier.

"William." She laid the embroidery she was pretending to care about on a table between her chair and another.

"Lady Margaret," he answered tightly.

"I'm sure you know why I've asked to speak with you."

William settled his weight on his heels, folding his hands behind his back. "Because my brother refuses to give you the answer you seek."

She had hoped her intimate knowledge of Thomas Stanley's nature might help her influence him, but Stanley still refused to pledge her son his support. "He says only that he seeks no quarrel with my Henry."

"I imagine Christmas would be difficult if he did."

She pressed her lips together, refusing to be baited. "Surely you don't trust Richard."

"Whatever my beliefs, I won't endanger my nephew, Lord Strange."

Her mouth twitched. "Will you not speak plainly, even in your brother's home?"

Frowning, William crossed the distance to sit in the open chair beside her. "Do you imagine Richard left you here without eyes and ears to observe you?" His voice was barely audible.

"Surely not…" Voice trailing off, she considered which of her husband's servants might be working for the king. Most had served faithfully for years. But who in Richard's England was above bribery? Nor had Urswick trusted any of them with carrying messages to her son. That was a telling fact.

"It's best not to talk of such things before their time."

"That's your brother speaking," she chided with a voice too strained for her purposes.

"We would all do well to emulate my brother, Lady Margaret. His caution saved us when haste would doom us."

She tried again. "But each time, he eventually chose a side."

"Do you imagine Richard would permit him not to?"

Lord Strange's captivity would guarantee it. "When that time comes, who will he support?"

Rising, William shook his head. "This kind of meddling already cost you much."

"I would pay a far dearer price for my son." Margaret had even considered arranging Lord Strange's death and implicating Richard. But only Urswick could arrange such a scheme for her, and doing so might endanger him. He was her only contact with Henry and the rest of the kingdom.

A frown tugged at the corners of William's lips. "Be careful not to overstep, Margaret. I don't wish for my brother to be widowed again."

She narrowed her eyes. "Is that your answer, then?"

He tossed his arms in the air and abandoned his hushed caution. "God's wounds, woman, do you expect us to ruin ourselves for the sake of your son?"

She only wished they would. "If you had the chance, would you defend or destroy Richard?"

He shook his head. "You're losing your touch, Margaret."

The words struck her like a blow. Losing her touch? She had defied two kings and married a powerful lord despite the taint of treason. When all the men around her had died, she alone had survived. When the entire realm had wished her to fall into ruin, she had defied them all. Even from all the way in England, she had kept her son safe through the years. How dare he make such a claim!

And yet, always in the past, she'd been able to move freely among the court. She'd once told Jasper she could serve her son better by whispering to sympathetic nobles. But now, tucked away in this northern estate, she saw no one but those who made the long journey to visit her husband.

She could feel her patience fraying. She was losing the subtlety and skill upon which she had relied. Day by day, she could feel it draining into the meaningless embroidery and household drudgery that now filled her days.

Her dear son depended on her efforts. Her husband had saved him from capture. Urswick and his agents had carried his messages throughout the realm.

Richard would never again allow her the freedom to mingle among his nobles, not after Buckingham. She would gain no new allies if she couldn't speak with them. Here, she would molder.

This was her last chance to help Henry.

She leaned forward. "William, I must know."

He rose and straightened the collar of his doublet. "You should speak to your husband about these matters."

"William, I beg you." She grasped his sleeve. "Please, tell me where your loyalties lie. I cannot bear it. I fall asleep each night not knowing whether my husband will protect my boy or see him to his grave." A tear rolled down her eye. "Can you imagine the agony of it?"

Something flashed in his eyes, a blend of hurt and longing. He could imagine it. She saw it in his eyes.

But his gaze hardened after only a moment. He licked his lips and rubbed his thighs, glancing around anxiously. Eyes and ears everywhere, he had said. He truly believed Richard had spies in her household.

"Trust in your husband," he pleaded.

She had called upon him for reassurance and could not accept mere platitudes. "How can I trust when those near me show me no faith or honor?"

"My lady…" He took an involuntary step forward, before halting. After a brief hesitation, he slid his leg back and flourished his arm in a bow fit for royalty, not a mere noble lady.

Her breath caught in her chest. Did that reverent bow contain her answer?

"There is a time for caution and a time for action, Lady Margaret."

That elaborate bow could only mean Lord Stanley intended to assist her son. But, she wondered whether he could overcome his famous penchant for delay.

"I only pray Lord Stanley's caution doesn't outlast the chance for action."

# HENRY

Henry certainly hadn't expected to convince every noble to whom he'd written for support; it was inevitable someone would share his letters with Richard. The king was predictably incensed at Henry's temerity.

Suspicious of all his nobles and loath to neglect any of Henry's partisans, Richard posted a public rebuttal in late June:

*A proclamation to the people of the British Isles, by Richard, by the grace of God, King of England and France and Lord of Ireland:*

*Henry Tudor, the traitor of bastard blood who styles himself as Earl of Richmond, is an illegitimate villain who seeks to suborn the good people of England with false claims about his ancestry, lineage, and rights.*

*We, Richard, King of England, will not abide the damnable perjury of this traitor. Our right to the crown is clear, descending through Edward III and his legitimate children to our father, Richard, Duke of York.*

*Henry Tudor has sought to recruit our foreign allies into rebellion and has bargained away English rights to the French throne for the duchies of Normandy, Anjou, Main, Gascony, Guyenne, and Calais—rights that faithful Englishmen have shed blood to acquire.*

*He now threatens to bring war to our realm with foreign invaders—Frenchmen, rapacious mercenaries, and the most sinful collection of attainted traitors, murderers, and adulterers who, having covered themselves with dishonor, have no choice but to turn against their homeland.*

*I call upon all loyal Englishmen to defend their wives, goods, children, and inheritances against this Welsh traitor. Any man who aids his cause is an enemy of the realm, his king, and Jesus Christ himself.*

*R.R.*

# CHAPTER SEVENTEEN

## HENRY

ENRY LEANED OVER the cluttered table, surveying the work of the past few months with his uncle and Oxford. Off to his left sat a ragged pile of letters, bulging where the seals layered upon each other. A map of England occupied the center, with marks indicating regions offering support and confirmed allies. And off to the right, in front of the general, were Oxford's notes about their numbers and frank assessments of the army's capabilities.

"Rhys ap Thomas is with us." Henry selected a long letter atop the pile in front of Jasper. Finding the passage he remembered, he recited, "*Tell me where to meet you on your march and I shall bring my men to support you.* He commands a thousand men."

"He also brings credibility," Jasper said while Henry marked Rhys' holdings on the map. "When the Welsh see him marching with you, they'll flock to you in droves."

"What does he ask for in exchange?" Oxford asked.

Had the question come from any but an ardent Lancastrian with no hope for restoration except through a Tudor victory, he might have suspected jealousy. But then again, if Oxford hadn't been an ardent

Lancastrian with no other hope for restoration, he wouldn't have been in this room.

"Nothing it pains me to give. Ten estates from among the Richmond lands."

"Quite a prize," Jasper breathed.

"It's a small loss if it buys me a kingdom," Henry answered.

"What of Northumberland?" Oxford gestured to the north of the map.

Henry frowned. "I don't believe he'll join us." He thumbed through the pile until he found the right one. "He didn't deny the rumors that Richard's new heir offended him during the latest Council of the North, but he said nothing to indicate support."

"A pity. A rising in the north would make things significantly easier," Oxford said.

Jasper studied the map. "I'm surprised. Northumberland is a Percy, and they were Lancastrian for generations."

"But they supported Edward upon his restoration," Oxford reminded. "And Richard made them wealthy with his wars against the Scots. An insult isn't enough to turn them."

Jasper nodded. "Any word from the Irish?"

"A few promise their support, but by the time they transport their soldiers, it'll likely be too late." After a moment, Henry added, "There is one exception. The Earl of Ormond."

"The Butlers?" Oxford furrowed his brow. "Thomas Butler was Edward's voice in Europe. He agreed to join you?"

Henry shook his head. "He has the same problem; all his men are in Ireland. But he did pledge his nephew, who is in England surveying his lands. Unfortunately, it's his illegitimate nephew, James Ormond."

"So no cups in our ranks," Jasper summarized, referring to their coat of arms.

Henry smirked. "We seem to collect bastards."

They fell silent. A glance passed between Oxford and Jasper before the latter broached the final topic. "That brings us to the Stanleys."

By way of answer, Henry leafed through the pile and selected a long letter on fine-grained paper. Clearing his throat, he began to read:

*The estates of myself and my brother can yield four thousand men at arms, fifteen hundred archers, and five hundred cavalry. But an army is expensive and cannot be long maintained. The king is learning this lesson very well. Hearing rumors of your imminent invasion, he deployed men throughout the country to delay you until he can gather his main force. He is levying taxes and pressing noble and merchant alike to purchase bonds for their provisioning.*

*I will not raise my army until it is required. However, write where you will land and I will hasten to that site, no matter where it may be. Your mother is well. Fear not for her safety. She is far from those who wish her harm.*

*I look forward to meeting you after so many years.*

"Six thousand men." Jasper shook his head in wonder. "He's the new Kingmaker with that force."

"Thomas Stanley has an army he refuses to use. He sat out of every major battle for the past three decades." Oxford pointed to the letter. "Nor is that an outright declaration of support. He didn't say he would usurp the tyrant or put you on the throne, only that he'd march to you. He could do that as either an ally or an enemy."

"I can't imagine Margaret would allow him to sit by while you fight for your life," Jasper said. "He would never allow Bray to aid us if he was against your cause, nor allow Urswick access to your mother."

Oxford and Jasper fell silent. After some time, Henry leaned forward, dipped his pen in the ink, and circled the area on the map that held Stanley's primary estate.

"He will support me," Henry decided. "He saved my life by warning me of Richard's repatriation plans last year when mere silence would have destroyed me. I cannot doubt his allegiance." He turned to Oxford. "He also shared the details of Richard's plan to marry Elizabeth of York, which I've used in my letters to turn several men to our cause."

Oxford conceded the point with a simple nod.

"Where do our forces stand?" Henry asked.

"Our men are well-trained. Of exiles and Englishmen, we have five hundred fifty, including the garrison from Hammes. They're working well together now."

"And the French?"

"Eighteen hundred under Philibert de Chandée, all from Normandy. We also have a force of artillerymen with cannons."

"Cannons." Jasper shuddered. "They're as likely to terrify our own men as the enemy."

"We also have the Scottish mercenaries."

"Did they hear back from King James?" Henry asked.

Oxford nodded. "He hopes you'll remember his support when you are king."

Henry broke a smile. Would he ever grow used to the favors? Would he ever remember them all?

Oxford added, "Their commander and the French captains have been vital in organizing our supply wagons and provisioning." He gestured to Henry. "I'm amazed at the supplies you've been able to arrange, Henry. They just keep coming. How did you do it?"

He shrugged. After Oxford had provided a list of their needs, Henry's work had begun, arranging loans and securing supplies with the skill of a consummate quartermaster. Savvy and cunning, Henry had taken the moneylenders and provisioners of France by surprise. He knew little of warfare, but Jehane had taught him how to wear down a reluctant supplier.

"So we have a little over three thousand," Jasper remarked. "That's not enough to defeat Richard."

"It's more than Edward had when he returned from exile to defeat

King Henry," Oxford said. "The rest came from nobles who supported him in England."

"Oh, true enough." Jasper's eyes glossed over as they did when he contemplated old betrayals.

"We have three thousand committed in England, and then the Stanleys," Henry summarized.

"And their six thousand," Jasper reminded.

Reports from Stanley and other nobles he'd corresponded with over the past several months suggested Richard would have trouble fielding more than six or seven thousand men, and most of those would come from the nobles who depended upon him, like Norfolk.

But it wasn't the numbers that concerned him; it was timing. He needed to move before Richard found someone to marry Elizabeth of York. Before his supporters began to doubt him. Nor could he maintain so many men here in France for very long. Oxford might have been impressed by his resourcefulness, but the money was nearly gone.

Though Henry hadn't had the power to chart his own destiny through his years of exile, neither had he felt the pressure to deliver on the high expectations of his supporters. Now, he had an army, and his countrymen expected him to use it quickly and effectively.

"We're out of time."

His uncle's eyes held anxiety mingled with agreement. Oxford radiated only satisfaction and anticipation.

"Prepare the army. We sail for England."

## HENRY

Though his possessions had already been loaded onto the carrack, Henry checked his room one final time. Henry wanted to leave nothing of value behind for the English ambassador, who would undoubtedly ransack his lodgings at the first available chance.

A letter that hadn't been there before sat on his empty desk. He didn't recognize the seal or family name. Only after he opened it and read the signature did the chill run down his spine.

Jehane.

He sank into the chair. The fact that she hadn't accompanied it hinted at its contents. Heart hammering and breath ragged, he began to read.

> *My dear Henry,*
>
> *I am relieved to hear of your safety. News of your flight created a sensation across the country. You will be pleased to know Landais' enemies forced the duke to remove him from his offices and try him for treason. He was hanged last week.*
>
> *I cannot come back to you. While I am thankful for your success and regret your great torment, my impossible choice, as you put it, abides.*
>
> *I ask you not to write to me again. I am married. His name is Adrien Touvelle, a chevalier. He is a kind, generous man, and he dotes on me. It is all I could have hoped for, and I am content with my choice. Our young son turns one this month.*
>
> *I hope you can respect my decision. I will forever treasure memories of our time together. I wish you fortune and pray you may one day find happiness again.*
>
> *With affection and respect,*
> *Jehane Touvelle*

The paper slipped from his fingers. Henry released a cry of surprise, but no tears broke free to splash the paper. She had taught him how to think like a tradesman, and he had a particular skill at sums.

If her son was a year old, she would have conceived him nine months prior, around the time of Buckingham's revolt. Right around when she had left him.

That boy could be his son.

At the time, he had thought she had cradled her midsection to calm her nerves. She had spoken about the danger their children would face. He had thought she spoke of the future.

It was possible she had met this Adrien Touvelle on the way to St. Malo and had fallen for him instantly. But why would she take such pains to point out the age of her son? Did she intend to taunt him that she could have what she wanted with another man but not him? The Jehane he remembered wasn't that cruel.

Mind lost in a sea of uncertainty, he began to pace. He could not let his son be raised by a Breton country knight. That boy had noble blood. Yet, as Jehane's husband, Touvelle would be assumed to be his father. Henry would have to contest his parentage, and the timing was so close, so uncertain.

He halted. What would the boy's life be like if Henry claimed him? For God's sake, he had pledged to marry Elizabeth of York. He'd taken great pains to ensure the peers of England saw them as legitimately pre-contracted. His son would be another bastard noble.

If his English venture succeeded, his legitimate children would have cause to fear an older bastard. The cycle that had begun with John of Gaunt and his illegitimate family would start all over again. And if Henry failed, Richard would hunt down and kill the boy himself.

As the son of a tailor and a country knight, he would live well. It was no mean fate, certainly not the shame his uncle and mother believed. He could be happy. He would be at peace.

He swallowed and smoothed his hair, unable to believe he was willing to sacrifice so much. The best thing he could do for that boy, for his Jehane, was to keep silent. That child had a father and a mother who would offer him a place in the world. Henry couldn't rob him of that security, of that home.

No, she wasn't his Jehane anymore, and he was no longer her 'dear Henry'. He'd lost her the moment Catesby had fired the first crossbow at their carriage.

That wasn't true. Though he hadn't known it at the time; he'd lost her the day he'd chosen to support Buckingham and declare himself an enemy of Richard.

She belonged to Adrien Touvelle now, and he to her. He hoped the man, whoever he was, recognized what a magnificent and rare woman he had married.

Henry had his own marriage to claim. Rising from his chair, he stuffed the letter into his doublet and headed for the army waiting at the docks.

So little of his life had been under his control. His blood had made him a threat to an anxious king, forcing him into exile. Others had maneuvered and nearly killed him at St. Malo. His only real choice had been to support Buckingham to remove the looming specter of death hanging just out of sight. That decision had provoked Richard's anger and cost him the only person who had given him happiness.

But it had also given him conviction. There was only one way to end the waves of sorrow battering him. If those who feared his claim to the throne would never let him live in peace, then he would force that claim down their throats and choke them on it.

In his heart, he knew he would never see this room again. He had already left all that was sweet and lovely in Brittany. Now he would leave behind the petitions and pleas, the beggar Earl of Richmond, and the Lancastrian threat against a Yorkist king.

He was going back to England after fourteen years. Neither storm nor army would keep him away this time. He would claim either a throne or a grave.

# VI

## BOSWORTH

AUGUST, AD 1485

# CHAPTER EIGHTEEN

## HENRY

THE SLEEPY VILLAGE of Dale on the western coast of Milford Haven in Pembrokeshire had enjoyed an uneventful, relaxing day. Church services had refreshed the souls of the residents, and a cool wind had brought relief from the summer heat. Fishing had been good lately, so the Sunday meal had been bountiful and filling. The troubles of the English had little to do with the simple folk on the farthest tip of Wales.

No one spotted the sails until the whole fleet was visible on the western horizon. Single-masted, double-masted, carracks, caravels, barges… The great variety and sheer number of ships in the motley fleet suggested something more than a trading convoy.

Jasper knew Dale well from his days as Earl of Pembroke, and while docks could be improved or destroyed in that time, the long, sandy beach—perfect for bringing thousands of men ashore—would stay the same.

Henry observed the landing from the deck of his carrack until his seasick men had time to recover fully and erect a basic camp. Only then did he order them to assemble and step into the last boat, accompanied by a pair of rowers.

The tiny craft rocked as the waves licked against it. He had spent fourteen frantic, uncertain years in exile; why should the final few minutes be any calmer?

Yet, he was not alone, and though he wanted to savor the moment in the shallows before stepping ashore, he had obligations to his soldiers. So, he confidently jumped out of the small boat when it ran aground, doing his best to ignore the weight of his new, heavy silver-inlaid armor. Sparing no time for sentimentality, he knelt and crossed himself with sweeping, exaggerated movements so all could observe clearly, even at a distance. He bowed slowly, letting all see the gleaming golden crown fused onto his shaped helm.

No visor impeded his men's view of his face when he pressed his hands together and raised his eyes to the heavens. He pitched his voice high so it would carry. "Oh God, grant me your blessing that I may restore faith and honor to your kingdom."

In addition to the thousands of soldiers, a few dozen residents assembled on the nearby ridge to watch the activity. Someone began singing a Latin psalm Henry had encouraged through the ranks for the past few months:

> *Judge me, O God,*
> *and discern my cause*
> *from an unholy one;*
> *rescue me from a man*
> *unjust and deceitful.*

Henry held his hands in a divine plea as the singing spread throughout the army, sporadically at first but growing in intensity with each repetition.

The spectacle was proceeding exactly as he'd planned.

Kneeling, he thought not of God's blessing but of his allies. He had arrived on the scheduled day. Where was Rhys ap Thomas? Sir John Savage? Lord Stanley? They should've been waiting here for him.

Henry rose when the singing stopped. While Oxford's and Wood-ville's sergeants shouted orders to finish the camp, Jasper approached with a small man who had the same forehead as his uncle.

"Your Majesty." Jasper halted and bowed before him. "I should like to introduce you to my half-brother, David ap Owen. He is a landowner in Pembroke, and one of my old retainers. He has come to swear fealty and join our army."

Henry inclined his head politely and studied the man. As a bastard, this uncle could not claim the Tudor name. That illegitimacy had protected him when Jasper and Henry were forced into exile. Though clearly not a soldier, he bore himself with confidence. His clothing was of a finer grain than anything Henry had possessed in the first years of his exile.

"Uncle." Henry smirked; Owen was roughly Henry's age, born just a few years before his grandfather's death at Mortimer's Cross. "I am pleased to finally meet you."

Bowing, Owen reached for Henry's hand but stopped abruptly. Henry wore no ring of office. After only a moment's hesitation, Owen leaned forward and kissed the back of Henry's hand instead.

"Thank you, Your Majesty. I am honored to meet you after so many years. I bring thirty men to contribute to your cause, and welcome the return of yourself and my brother."

Thirty men. Where were the Welsh who were supposed to be flocking to his banner?

Henry forced a smile. "I thank you for your support, and that of the men of Pembroke."

Owen bowed again. "There is one other gift I bring you."

At his gesture, two of his men stepped forward carrying a thick parcel. After a perfunctory bow, they unfurled the contents. Between them, they held up a battle banner of thick fabric, four times as wide as it was high. The red cross of St. George was closest to the pole, obviously representing the English crown. The rest of the length was divided by green and white fields, representing the Tudor family itself, and white and red roses that alluded to both his and his wife's claims.

But the largest and most striking feature was a massive red dragon with one of its claws rampant. It was a powerful symbol that every Welshman—and even Englishmen who had been raised on stories of Welsh honor—recognized: the Welsh dragon.

"The dragon of Cadwaladr ap Cadwallon is the most sacred symbol in Wales, stretching back a thousand years. Every Welsh champion has flown it in battle, from Cadwaladr himself to Owen Glendower, eighty years ago." Owen extended a hand to caress the fabric as if it were a holy relic. "I and my men wish to present you with this standard so all may recognize the only man with the blood to command both the Welsh and the English."

It was far more than that, Henry thought while admiring the banner. This dragon would remind everyone why they owed him their allegiance. This single symbol fused Yorkist, Lancastrian, Welsh, and English, tying him to a tradition that would demand the loyalty of the Welsh in these lands. Buckingham hadn't had it, and the Marches had abandoned him. They could not refuse to rally behind it.

It was a gift more precious than any company of soldiers.

"Thank you, my Lord Owen. This is a kingly gift."

Owen flicked his eyes from Jasper to Henry. "Your Majesty, I am no lord."

Henry smirked. "You are mistaken. Once I reach London, the nobility in your heart with be reflected in your rank." He stroked his chin. "Will you dine with me tonight?"

Owen bowed again. "I would be most honored."

"Then, please, see Lord Woodville. He will assign your men positions within the army and help you settle in."

Jasper whispered something to his half-brother but remained with Henry as Owen departed.

"Thirty men," Henry repeated too softly for anyone else to hear.

"More will come when they see that banner flying."

"I hope so."

"You'll gain more on the march," Jasper assured. "But we need to discuss another matter before our ranks swell too much."

"Oh?"

Jasper nodded. "You're in England now, Henry, not France. Richard tried to kill you once before, but distance prevented another opportunity." Jasper lowered his voice further. "Not everyone who joins our side actually joins our side."

"Assassins?" He tensed his leg muscles and darted glances at the men nearest to him.

"We must prepare for the possibility. Richard's objective is you, not this army."

Henry mulled over the problem during dinner while David ap Owen shared the latest news of Wales with Henry and his commanders. While most of Pembroke fervently supported Henry's objectives, the country's nobles were waiting for their chief citizens to declare one way or the other. They were waiting for Rhys ap Thomas.

Who hadn't given any word of his whereabouts after promising his support.

While the army assembled the next morning, Henry conducted an impromptu knighting ceremony, naming William Brandon and David ap Owen as the first of his personal bodyguards. In honor of his good service at Hammes and the hardship his family had endured in following him to France, he named William Brandon as his standard-bearer.

Later, after the army had begun its march, Jasper sidled up to him. "That's one way to handle it."

"Those with me in France had ample opportunity to kill me. I can trust them." Henry smirked. "William Brandon brought a pregnant wife with him. His son Charles has never seen England."

Jasper offered a casual nod. "It was just unexpected."

"Listening to Owen talk about the Welsh, I realized that if I want people to start thinking of me like a king, I need to start acting like one. Knighting is just a start."

Jasper studied his nephew's face. "I'm not sure I understand."

"You'll see." A faint smile curled across his lips. "You'll see."

## HENRY

The next day, Henry's army marched to Haverfordwest. Though only a few miles from Dale, it was better for sustaining an army, and Oxford wanted to accustom them to marching in column before they began their route in earnest.

When they arrived, they found James Ormond awaiting them, the illegitimate son of the previous Earl of Ormond. A lightly framed man with a pink complexion and a thatch of bright red hair, he grinned broadly and often.

"The whole country has been wondering when and where you'll land. Richard has been expecting it since late June." Ormond indicated a number of points on the map unfurled in Henry's tent. "He staged men at all the ports, all the way up the coast on either side."

Henry frowned over the map. "Including here?"

Ormond nodded. "Walter Herbert commands a thousand nearby."

"Herbert…" Jasper breathed.

Henry understood the dangerous inflection in Jasper's tone. "After I have the throne," he warned.

"Do you know the Earl of Pembroke?" Ormond asked.

"The Earl of Pembroke!" Jasper choked on the words. "A Herbert—"

Before outrage consumed his uncle, Henry summarized to Ormond, "The Herberts killed my father."

The calmness of the statement surprised his uncle enough to break him out of his burgeoning anger. Henry could feel their eyes studying him for some further reaction. He almost smiled at the thought of disappointing them, before he calmed even that urge. Many would face a reckoning for their past actions, but his focus needed to remain on Richard for now.

"A thousand, you say?" Henry asked again.

Ormond nodded. "There are many more under arms already throughout the country. No doubt Herbert sent riders to warn Richard of your landing. They will begin to converge."

Henry exchanged a nervous glance with Oxford. They had hoped for the early advantage in numbers. That clearly wouldn't happen.

"Thank you, Thomas, both for your information and your support."

Ormond bowed. "My uncle bid me share all the information I can provide on the current state of the country. I'll help any way I can."

"I am genuinely grateful." Henry offered a warm smile. "Accurate information is as important to our cause as soldiers, and you and your family have brought me both. Thank you."

When Ormond left to update Edward Woodville on the position of Richard's garrisons, Henry posed the question they were all considering. "Do we wait for more supporters or march to Richard now?"

Oxford exhaled, staring at the map. "As a rule, smaller armies march faster. Richard will likely muster them at a staging point before engaging us."

"Is that good or bad?" Henry asked.

"Both," Jasper explained. "With so many groups of soldiers on the move, our allies can join us without attracting attention."

"I'll have to prepare another round of letters, then," Henry decided.

"It also means Richard will challenge us before we anticipated," Oxford warned.

"Do we have enough men to contest him now?"

Oxford didn't hesitate. "Our best chance remains striking before he can amass his full strength, even if some of our allies don't reach us in time."

"What of Herbert? Can he slow us down?"

Oxford pointed to a dot along the winding Severn River. "He could if he garrisons Shrewsbury." The town was directly on their planned march; its bridge across the river was the largest in the area and would permit the fastest crossing. "If we can't cross there, we'll lose precious days."

"Then we need to make our way to Shrewsbury immediately," Henry decided. "And I think it's time I send another letter to Lord Stanley. If Herbert does garrison Shrewsbury, the Stanleys can approach from the east to overcome him."

"If he comes," Jasper warned.

Henry glared at him, not for having the doubt but for voicing it.

## HENRY

Instead of settling into a comfortable camp, the army advanced toward Cardigan. While William Brandon was busy selecting members of Henry's bodyguard from among the most skilled of the exiles, his brother Thomas led Oxford's mounted scouts across the region, seeking everything from hostile soldiers and significant obstacles to water and food sources. As the camp settled down for the night, Thomas reported unpleasant news.

"Several bands of Welsh are marching to join us, but we saw no sizeable force within ten miles. However…"

"However?" Henry leaned forward.

"It is a rumor only."

"Spit it out, man."

Brandon swallowed. "A villager told one of my men he just missed a convoy with supplies for Rhys ap Thomas, whose army was assembling to march with the king."

Had Rhys abandoned him? "Are you certain? They were gathering stores for Rhys ap Thomas, and not Walter Herbert or some other noble?"

Brandon nodded. "Though, Lord Rhys could be spreading this story to cover his true intention to join you. If we know Herbert's men are nearby, so would everyone."

*To march with the king.* Henry bit at his lip long enough for his teeth to ache. If Rhys abandoned him, the Welsh would never join him.

He had received so many promises in the weeks leading up to his invasion. So far, none had resulted in meaningful additions to his army.

Could he trust in the honor of English and Welsh lords? He had been confident of their support while in France. Now that he'd committed himself, he began to wonder whether he marched to his destruction.

## HENRY

Henry pushed through the weathered beech church door. The cool air within soothed his skin.

He hesitated at the entrance for a moment. Someone in the distance hammered a pole into the ground. He really should make the rounds while his army made camp, but he needed a brief respite more.

He stepped inside and closed the door behind him, shutting out the noise and the crushing responsibility of holding so many lives in his hands.

Henry's entry drew the attention of a priest. The confidence and strength of stride as he approached belied the thinning hair and sagging skin that marked his age. The priest made the sign of the cross and greeted Henry in heavily accented English. "May the Lord bless you and keep you, my son."

Could he find nowhere with a little privacy? "Amen." Henry mirrored the man's gesture. "Thank you, Father."

"What brings you to this holy place?" The question carried more than a hint of suspicion, and he emphasized the last words meaningfully. Wales had known the danger of English knights.

"The next King of England wishes to pray for God's blessing," Henry answered in fluid Welsh.

The priest's eyes widened, rising to study Henry's helmet. "Who are you, who speaks our language so well?"

"I am Henry Tudor."

Recognition flashed in his eyes, followed by something else. "So, you've come." It was a statement, not a question.

"I've come." Too late, he realized his recklessness in coming alone. His uncle had warned about assassins. Henry searched the recesses for unfriendly shadows that warned of danger.

But the priest was smiling through tear-filled eyes. "You honor us with your presence, Your Majesty. May God bless your cause." He bowed and retreated to the far corner of the church, pretending to occupy himself with lighting candles and giving his noble guest privacy.

*How many battalions would God bring to the battlefield?*

Eighty years earlier, Owen Glendower had assembled his parliament here in Machynlleth, fifty miles west of Shrewsbury among the most rebellious of Welshmen. Henry had been counting on them to swell his army enough to counter Richard. But while men had joined him in a steady stream, they'd come in dozens, not the hundreds he needed. Richard almost certainly knew his location, and Henry was running out of time.

Doubts nagged at him. He had made a terrible mistake. This was turning out exactly like Buckingham's revolt. Far from being the warm blanket protecting him from the bitterness of his enemies, his army was now a weight surrounding him with demands, expectations, and disappointment.

Behind him came whispering, and Henry turned to see the priest muttering with an outstretched hand. Solitude, it seems, was out of reach.

He cleared his throat. "What purpose to your muttering, priest?"

The old priest smiled. "Merely a benediction for a successful march, Your Grace. Please forgive my presumption."

The tender sentiment evoked a smile. Henry gestured for the priest to join him. "Please."

Eagerly, the priest shuffled forward.

"Tell me, Father… Has Wales suffered these past few years?"

"Terribly so, Your Majesty." Sorrow replaced his former eagerness.

"The king's northern creatures stripped our countrymen from even local offices. Now, we answer to harsh-accented men with no Welsh who show no respect for our ways." He turned to the crucifix and inhaled a breath. "They see us as troublemakers. The gauntlet falls harder on us than anyone."

The tyrant's agents had swarmed over the country, supplanting local leaders in any area Richard had deemed likely to revolt. Kent had been overrun, as had Cornwall and Devon. "Do the people believe in my cause?"

"The people want to believe, but we've heard false rumors of your landing all summer. The first said you landed in Cardigan. The next, in Devon. Three weeks ago, a merchant claimed you were landing that day with thirty thousand Irishmen." He licked his lips. "Richard's agents remind us daily that Owen Glendower hasn't been forgotten and that Wales will bleed if we support you." The priest smiled. "We pay them the same attention as all English threats."

Though Henry smirked, his mind lingered on the implications. If the Welsh had been disappointed by false invasions, they would wait to confirm the truth before marching. They hadn't abandoned him, after all.

Of course, the Welsh would never support Richard; he and his brother had done naught but repress and smother them.

And Rhys was on the march. Reason told him Rhys would only need provisions if he anticipated a lengthy campaign. If the Welsh lord had intended to join Richard, he wouldn't have needed the supplies. Henry's march would've been crushed quickly.

"Have faith, Your Majesty. Your cause is righteous, and God will provide."

Henry blinked. Yes, he needed faith, just not in divine will.

Against all odds, he had repeatedly avoided his own execution. He had been wise to take the oath to marry Elizabeth of York and support Anne of Beaujeu. He had been bold to rescue the garrison of Hammes.

He could not doubt himself now. If he believed the words of the men who had offered their support, he must have faith in that judgment.

Patience. He had laid his plans, and they needed time to develop.

He was suddenly grateful that the priest had interrupted his solitude. He had entered this church as a man beset by doubt about nobles who thrived on deception and betrayal, but he would leave with the reassurance that only the common man with no reason to lie could provide.

Rising, Henry smiled at the priest. "Thank you, Father. My spirit is nourished, and my heart lightened." Before the man could respond, Henry marched back toward the doors and threw them open. "God keep you." And with that, he stepped out of the quiet sanctuary and into the bright sun.

He met his bodyguards where he'd left them, on the side of the square opposite the church. Beneath his new standard, Henry marched to his camp just outside of town. The soldiers had completed the temporary fortifications, and here and there they rested with the repose of exhaustion. He met their eyes with a renewed vigor, grinning at each of them.

York, Lancaster, Welsh, Scottish, French… The coalition he had assembled was broader than any that had previously opposed the sons of York. Not he but Richard needed to worry about the loyalty of his men.

His tent was the largest of the motley assortment of colors and styles, situated in the middle of the fortifications where he could be protected from Richard's assassins. William Brandon had already found and discretely killed two of them.

Opposite his tent was the mustering field, where unit captains would assemble for their daily orders. Normally, it was vacant, but now a few dozen men stood beneath banners Henry didn't recognize.

The two bodyguards who preceded him called out to clear a path. While a few of the men in the back ranks fired off annoyed retorts, one glance at Henry's crowned helmet silenced them. A hush descended after the first few men recognized the Welsh dragon standard marking Henry's progress through the newly parted companies. The whispers began in hurried Welsh.

"—must be the Tudor—"

"—didn't know he flew the dragon—"

"—descended from Cadwaladr ap Cadwallon—"

"—it's the legend of Owain—"

"—renamed at birth, as the bards say—"

"—set Wales free of these English monsters—"

Giddiness threatened to overwhelm him. This was what he wanted, what he needed. They saw him as their savior. His uncle David Owen had been right; the dragon called to the people of Wales. He would make that man a prince of the realm for his foresight.

But he couldn't allow them to see his elation; it wasn't kingly. So, instead, he focused on the question of whom they served.

In front of his tent, Jasper, Woodville, and Oxford were speaking with a slightly portly man in new armor attended by his own squire. One look at his features identified him as a Welsh lord, not an Englishman.

"Uncle, Lord Woodville, Lord Oxford." Approaching, Henry extended his hands to them.

The priest's encouragement and the reverent whispering of these soldiers had filled Henry with fresh confidence. It was time to embrace the mantle of kingship he'd claimed since Brittany.

He debated the right tone to use when greeting the newcomer. Francis had been too casual, Anne of Beaujeu too conversational. Belatedly, he wished he'd known Edward more; he was, despite his hostility, the strongest king of their time.

"Who stands before us?" he asked in English.

Taking a cue from the majestic plural, Jasper bowed. "Your Majesty, I should like to present Sir John Morgan of Tredegar, lately in the service of Sir Walter Herbert."

"Lately?" Henry asked with growing curiosity.

Morgan fell to a knee. "Herbert has command in the region. I could think of no better way to assemble my men than by feigning obedience to him."

"To what end do you assemble your men, sir?" He raised his voice so the closest soldiers could hear. "What brings you to Machynlleth, the seat of Welsh honor?"

A few of the soldiers straightened, while others grinned with pride.

"Your Majesty, I come to join your army."

Henry glanced at the paltry group assembled before him. "How many men do you command?"

Morgan smiled. "Five hundred."

Finally, a sizeable force! "We welcome your men as brothers within our ranks and gladly accept your fealty." Henry removed his gauntlet and offered his hand. This time, his index finger bore a knotted gold ring he had borrowed from one of the exiles.

When Morgan kissed it, the assembled soldiers erupted into cheers and began singing Owen Glendower's marching chant.

Henry drew Morgan closer. Over the singing, he asked, "We understand Sir Herbert intends to intercept us before Shrewsbury. What is his strength?"

Morgan grinned. "That was his intention, though I doubt he'll do so now. My men composed fully half of his force."

That was welcome news. "Have you any report of Rhys ap Thomas? We understand his agents are gathering provisions."

Morgan's smile faded. "Sir Herbert demanded that Lord Rhys submit to his authority and coordinate with his forces."

"And, did he?" The next few words would likely determine the fate of his cause.

"He marches separately but is moving in tandem with Herbert."

"I see." Henry swallowed. If Rhys was against him, then these would be the last Welshmen to join.

He somehow managed to conclude the interview and retire to his tent, where his thoughts dwelled on the arithmetic. Even with Morgan, his army was still less than four thousand.

It wouldn't be enough.

## HENRY

The Tudor army stayed at Machynlleth for an extra day while it absorbed Morgan's volunteers, along with a few hundred more Welshmen from the local communities. The trickle had become a steady drip. It wasn't enough, but it was progress.

Yet, Henry was most excited by a single rider, adorned in madras and fine wool, approaching the column the evening of the fourteenth. He was a messenger from Rhys ap Thomas.

"My lord welcomes thee to his lands," the messenger began in heavily accented English as his horse fell into stride beside Henry. "He has watched your progress for some time and expresses his good wishes for your march."

*Good wishes for my march!*

Stunned by the greeting, Henry nearly lost his balance when his horse shifted to avoid a stone. "We are grateful for such a warm welcome and look forward to setting eyes on the man whose words provided such reassurance to us in France."

"My lord feels the same."

Henry's pulse raced. "Where is Lord Rhys now?"

The messenger lowered his eyes. "He and his army are to the northwest." Henry considered asking for more specificity until he recalled his conversation with the priest. If this commoner could have said more, he would have. "He bids me ask what he stands to gain by fighting for you."

Had they not already discussed the price? "I offered him ten valuable estates."

"Indeed, indeed." The messenger picked at the leather of his saddle.

The price evidently wasn't enough. "How many men does your lord command?"

The messenger hesitated for a moment. "One thousand foot and five hundred cavalry."

The cavalry alone would be worth it; Henry had precious few at the moment. "If Rhys ap Thomas joins me, when I am victorious against the usurper, the Lieutenancy of Wales will be his."

The messenger's eyes widened. He evidently understood the value of such a position. Rhys would be the first man of Wales, ruling in Henry's name.

"I will inform him of your words." The man bowed in his saddle, then broke stride and galloped away.

*Fifteen hundred men!* Suddenly, Shrewsbury didn't seem quite so far away, even if the price of Rhys' loyalty was steeper than expected. Well, someone had to have the Lieutenancy of Wales. Why not a man who offered him fifteen hundred men?

Yet, Rhys was renegotiating after having already pledged his support, and he continued to keep his army hidden. Henry couldn't trust the word of any of these nobles; he would count Rhys as an ally only when their armies marched together.

Resolved, Henry rode to the front of the column to find Oxford. They would make a strong camp each night until Rhys made his decision.

## HENRY

Two days later, the army was twenty miles west of the mighty Severn and the gates of Shrewsbury. Henry wanted Oxford to secure the river and town before nightfall if they found it undefended. While his scouts saw no Ricardians, Henry could feel his enemy approaching out there, somewhere in the distance. They needed to move faster.

But as with much of the march, the gulf between what he wanted and what occurred was wide. Henry was shouting encouragement to the men along the column when Thomas Brandon approached at a gallop.

"Your Majesty," he breathed, "come quickly."

Henry reined in his horse and followed Brandon nearly a mile ahead of the army to a small hill just north of the road where Jasper, Oxford, Morgan, and Woodville were studying something in the distance.

Bisecting the road and filling the field on either side, a force of thousands stood in rank and file, prepared for battle.

Henry soothed his mount with a gentle pat when it reacted to the inadvertent tension in his legs. "How long have we known of this?" Thomas Brandon was responsible for scouting the territory ahead of them and should have reported it sooner.

"An hour ago, that field was empty to our scouts. Outriders saw the vanguard approach only fifteen minutes ago."

Henry studied the force. "Why are they here?"

"That's the question, isn't it?" Jasper wondered.

"No." Henry shook his head. "I mean why are they here, standing exposed on open ground, instead of fortifying Shrewsbury?"

"An excellent point," Oxford agreed.

"Is it Herbert?" He shielded his eyes with his hand. "Do we know the banners?"

Woodville grunted after narrowing his eyes. "We're too far away."

"I don't recommend bringing the army up yet," Oxford warned.

"On the other hand, I wouldn't want to be caught by myself," Woodville said.

Oxford shrugged, acknowledging the point.

Henry grinned, pleased that his two commanders had become fast friends. That could only help in the days to come. "Brandon, send the scouts further afield. We need to know who else is approaching." He met Oxford's eyes for confirmation before adding, "I think we should take a closer look."

The army slowed until Brandon's scouts could complete their

search. An hour later, they reported clear terrain in all directions. By the time they had, Jasper had identified the standard waving in the autumn wind: three black ravens on a field of white, divided by a black bar.

A few hundred yards in front of the host, three mounted men waited patiently. Rhys ap Thomas wanted to talk.

Where was Herbert?

Henry's horse whinnied, breaking the silence that had fallen over his command staff. They were looking to him for a decision.

Could he trust Rhys?

He had been so certain his offer would win over the Welsh lord, but seeing this army arrayed for battle filled him with doubt. Should he deploy his men as well? It could be seen as a provocation and turn this man, whom Henry desperately needed, against him. If he stayed in marching columns, his whole army would be exposed and vulnerable. Should he ride out to face him alone, or invite him to camp?

His path had been clear when he'd fled at St. Malo and when he'd escaped Brittany. Then, he'd had no choice. Even when he'd pledged to marry Elizabeth and had begun styling himself as King Henry, circumstances had been forced upon him. But now, here in England, he saw no correct answers, only uncertainty.

Dealing with foreigners had been so much simpler; English and Welsh lords confounded him. They were so timid, so cautious. They moved as if dragging their feet, and always wanted more, more, more.

But he had to deal with them, and he might as well do it on his terms.

Swallowing, he kicked his horse forward a few paces. "William?"

Brandon sidled up surprisingly quickly. "My lord?"

"Choose the fastest dozen riders to accompany the two of us."

"You're not going down there, are you?" Jasper pointed to the army before them. "He was working with Herbert."

"I am, but not alone. You and Lord Morgan will accompany me. A Welsh welcome may make a difference. Oxford, Woodville, draw up the men into a wide marching column. Don't deploy for battle, but be ready to do so at my signal."

"How will I know?" Oxford asked.

"We'll be galloping back for our lives."

"Henry…" Jasper's eyes had narrowed with doubt. "Are you sure?"

"Fortune favors the bold." His bravado faded quickly. "I'm done with doubt. I need to know if I can trust him, and he won't have a better chance than this to betray me."

Jasper pressed his lips together and nodded. "Lead on, my king."

Henry swapped from his riding rouncey to his black courser, though he stripped it of its battle armor. If Rhys did intend treachery, Henry would need to ride light and fast. Intent not to make himself an obvious target, at the last moment he commandeered the helmet of one of the Welsh composing Sir Morgan's vanguard, leaving his crowned helmet with Oxford.

When he called for them to ride out, Brandon halted him. "Follow me, Your Majesty."

"I must be seen to lead the men."

Brandon shook his head. "Until I know Lord Rhys can be trusted, I will not allow you to make yourself a target. My duty is to protect you, at any cost."

He wasn't prepared for the conviction in Brandon's eyes. Battles lay before him, and he had prepared himself to order men to their deaths. But here was a man who was willing to take an arrow for him. Because of his blood. Because Brandon had decided Henry was worth protecting, he would risk never seeing his young children ever again. When had that happened?

Unable to dishonor that loyalty, Henry allowed William to lead the fifteen riders on a canter into the open field between the two armies. He suddenly felt more exposed than during his week at sea.

"We're entering range of their archers," Jasper warned as they reached the halfway mark.

Henry tensed, and his horse snorted and tried to gallop in response.

Henry pulled back on the reins and patted its neck. "Easy, easy," he called over the drum of hooves.

Distracted by his mount, Henry entirely missed the first tense seconds when the other riders searched the ranks before them for signs of aggression. Before he realized the danger, it had passed. No arrows fell upon them.

Henry, Jasper, and Morgan dismounted and handed their reins to Henry's honor guard. Rhys' army lay several hundred feet away, slightly closer than the Tudor army behind. They had gone down a slight valley less suited for battle than it seemed from the ridge; the gradual slopes would make maneuvering difficult.

It would still be a hard ride to get clear if the worst happened.

A tall man with gleaming steel armor bearing the black crow crest stepped forward and removed his helmet, placing it under his arm. Thick, lustrous hair fell in a ragged cascade, and he spared a moment to sweep it back before stepping forward. The slopes of Rhys' face marked his Welsh heritage. He bore himself with such confidence and coiled power, quite the contrast to the casual elegance of the French and Breton nobility. Behind him, two armored knights remained at ease with their hands resting casually on the hilts of their swords.

So, this was Rhys ap Thomas.

Henry removed his own helmet. Too late, he realized his silver armor shone brighter than those of his companions; even from a great distance, the glinting sunlight would have identified him. His scuffed helmet did nothing to conceal him. It only made him look less impressive before this man he desperately needed.

How to begin? As a claimant to the throne, Henry would have to speak first. Confidence and control. "That's a fine army you have, Lord Rhys."

The other man grinned, showing bright white teeth that made Henry self-conscious of his own defects. "Fairness dictates I show it to you after tracking you for so many days."

"Did your messenger return safely?"

"He did."

"Northwest, indeed." Henry gazed across the Welsh to the east.

Now the grin became a full smile. "My apologies about that deception, Your Grace."

"We may have done the same," Henry conceded. "But it does raise doubts about your intentions." When Rhys made no answer, Henry asked, "Will you join or contest our march?"

Rhys licked his lips. "My messenger says you offer the Lieutenancy of Wales."

"And ten valuable estates from among our birthright of Richmond." He almost reminded Rhys that the offer was better than any Richard had granted, but Rhys was a hereditary lord, not a recently elevated one. That tactic wouldn't work on him. "We will be unable to manage them properly once we are victorious and would prefer they be governed by a fellow Welshman."

"Richard is likely to have more men than I see here. How can you be assured of victory?"

Henry grinned. "Further allies await us in England."

"The Stanleys, you mean?"

Henry prevaricated. "Richard's instability has driven many to discontent."

Rhys nodded. "It has, at that." Without any apparent change in expression, he lowered himself to his knee and clenched his fist over his chest. His knights followed suit. "It would be my honor to march with you. By my life or death, I will defend your throne from any who would oppose it."

Behind him, Rhys' captains saw his action. To the rustling of metal and leather, fifteen hundred men knelt, followed by a cheer from the Tudor army behind him.

Fleeting relief was quickly replaced by another, strange sensation. Mouth falling open at the spectacle, Henry savored the experience. Power flowed into him, drawn from the submission of so many men. The feeling was intoxicating. In this moment, he would do anything to hold onto it. Finally, he understood why Edward and Richard had relentlessly pursued him for so many years.

Shaken, Henry realized Rhys was still kneeling in the dirt. "I gladly accept your loyalty, and promise to honor our agreement once it is within my power to do so, so help me God." Henry helped the man stand and offered a heartfelt smile. "It's good to have you with us. Our scouts had me all but convinced you were working with Sir Herbert."

"Your scouts?" Rhys gestured to his knights, who bowed and rejoined his army.

"Your men were heard to say you were marching to support the king."

Rhys' eyes glinted with mischief. "Did they say which king?" He barked a laugh. "I intended to join you at Milford, but Sir Herbert was already in the field."

"Evidently, Richard expected us and staged men near every potential landing site."

Rhys absorbed the information calmly. This was a thoughtful one, a fact not conveyed by his letters. How many more men had Henry misjudged?

Finally, Rhys shrugged. "Richard and his men suspect everyone. Until I had fully mustered, I had to pretend to obey Herbert."

Given the circumstances, that Rhys marched at all should have confirmed his intentions. Yet even this simple truth could not erase a week of anxiety. "I believed your ruse, and Herbert probably did as well. He probably still awaits word from you."

Rhys grinned broadly. "Not any longer."

Panic flared again. "What do you mean?"

"Yesterday, I came upon Herbert's army suddenly."

Henry's apprehension dissolved. "You have a habit of doing that."

Another broad grin. "We had a frank discussion. I explained that his men were as likely to follow me as to remain loyal, and even if they did, I could drum him soundly. The more prudent choice was to return home and hope you chose to forget that your father died in his care thirty years ago. A path he elected to follow. Two hundred of his men joined me as he skulked home."

While he was pleased to hear Herbert had been nullified, a deeper part of him simmered at Rhys' presumption in speaking for him. But Henry needed this man's army. Reprimands would have to wait. Besides, Henry had promised nothing personally and could deal with Herbert later with a clear conscience.

And he would, too; he refused to fight this war all over again in a few years.

Rhys' army was forming up for the march, while Henry's men were quickly coming upon them to a steady drumbeat.

"Why did you choose to support me?" Henry asked as his bodyguard brought his horse around and Rhys swung into his own saddle.

Rhys shrugged. "How could I fight against a fellow Welshman?"

Henry mounted his horse. "You said yourself Richard will likely have more men."

Rhys answered once their horses fell into an easy pace. "Conviction wins wars, not numbers. Margaret of Anjou and King Henry never learned this, at great cost to their cause." Rubbing his chin, he gestured to the Tudor soldiers behind them. "Each man who went into exile with you or marches with you today actively risks ruin and death. That is why I joined you, and not Buckingham or Richard. Your men believe in your cause. Theirs do not."

That was as good a description of the feeling that had consumed him when Rhys' army had knelt before him. "If you decided to join me before the landing, why did you send your messenger for a better offer?"

Again, Rhys shrugged. "I have an army you desperately needed. I'd be foolish not to take advantage of it."

Henry smiled faintly to mask his outrage. His life depended on these nobles honoring their promises to fight for him. And, in one sense, Rhys and Morgan had honored those oaths. But they had done so either in their own time or after attaching fairly significant conditions.

Swallowing, Henry pushed down the doubt yet again. In the

end, they had honored their promises. It didn't matter whether they'd negotiated for a higher price or delayed or whether he respected the baseness of their natures. They had come. That was enough.

It had to be.

# CHAPTER NINETEEN

## HENRY

SHREWSBURY MARKED THE western border of England, forever watching over its unruly neighbor of Wales. The River Severn wound across the land in a sharp curve before turning west farther to the north, surrounding the town on three sides.

Henry was still mulling the trustworthiness of his supporters when the Welsh Bridge, crossing the river and leading into the north of the city, rose up from the horizon. Solidly built on stone arches that would take the weight of his army, it was the fastest route into England. Henry felt the sudden urge to rush across as quickly as he could.

But both ends of the bridge had gates twenty feet high, flanked by narrow towers that had defended the crossing many times in the past. And those gates were shut. On the Welsh side of the bridge, the city garrison lined the walls, watching the Tudor army's approach.

Henry kicked his horse forward. This time, he wore his crowned helmet. Knowing he would approach from the north, he'd had Matthew polish his armor to dazzle and reflect the waning evening light.

More of the garrison had assembled beyond the gate, but they leaned on their pikes. No archers lined the towers. Shrewsbury was offering a measured response, intending to defend without antagonizing. The townsfolk knew he could storm the town if he tried. Hopefully, they didn't realize he could ill afford the time or lives it would cost him.

He stopped his horse close enough that he could read the expressions of the assembled townsfolk. "By the grace of God, Henry Tudor, rightful King of England, orders you to throw open your gates so our army may pass."

"There is only one crowned king, and that is King Richard." The response came from a burgess framed in an embrasure along the battlement who wore fine wool robes and a chain of office. "He has ordered the gates of every town shut to you and your followers."

Henry clenched his jaw. No columns of smoke on the horizon suggested encamped armies, though the bubbling of the river concealed whatever sounds might lurk in the distance. Since joining, Rhys' more capable scouts had reported clear fields for several miles. Yet, something had to be strengthening this man's resolve.

"Who addresses us?"

"I am Thomas Mitton, bailiff of this fair city," the man declared. "I am responsible for shielding this town from the taint of treason and the depredations of rebel armies."

"Then you would do well to aid our cause. We march to punish treason, incest, and murder."

The man barked a laugh. "Lies and rumors. King Richard has ever been kind to Shrewsbury." Leaning forward, he said louder, "I will not provide succor to unrest. By my oath, you will pass this gate over my belly."

The defenders shifted their weight and murmured.

Hoping the glinting sun hid the flush of embarrassment on his face, Henry stood before the locked gates helplessly. He had built a coalition of men to support him, extracted promises from the nobles of the realm, crossed the seas, and suffered an anxiety-ridden march, only to be stopped short by a single town refusing him entry. And it had all happened in full view of the nearly five thousand men of his army.

This was a disgrace.

Though he struggled with having his powerlessness laid bare, he maintained enough composure to avoid arguing with this man publicly. Instead of sulking away, Henry offered a light shrug and cantered back to his commanders with his head held high.

By the time he reached his column, he had decided how to reassure the army about the locked gates. Loudly enough for those nearby to hear, he ordered, "Make camp. The town is concerned about damage from so large an army traveling through it. We will make assurances and proceed tomorrow."

But before he turned, he exchanged an uneasy glance with his uncle.

While the army enjoyed a good rest, Henry candidly discussed their prospects with his uncle, Oxford, and Woodville. They could storm the city, but doing so would invariably work the army up into a fervor that would be hard to control. Henry preferred not to loot an English town in his first significant military action. The closest suitable crossing would cost them a week. Perhaps more damaging, failing to pass through Shrewsbury now that he had revealed his intentions would be a sign of weakness that could doom his cause. Both time and momentum were too precious to waste.

The four nobles entered Shrewsbury the next morning under a flag of truce to discuss the matter in private. The nature of their welcome suggested conflicting forces within the town. Though the bailiffs, the mayor, and several of the important burgesses had a light repast prepared for them, the meeting itself was held at Mitton's home rather than a public or religious building. Shrewsbury clearly understood the Tudor army could overpower their defenses but did not deem it prudent to officially greet three rebel earls and a baron.

Mitton himself was an aging man with a thinning head of flaxen hair that he concealed with as much fine clothing as possible. The sheer quantity of brocade and gold adorning his body suggested new wealth, a supposition only confirmed when he greeted them with eyes widened in awe. It was one thing to stare someone down with hauteur when protected by a gate. It was quite another to meet at arm's length the steel-eyed conviction of those born ennobled and possessing unshakable certainty as to their worth.

Henry would simply need to pretend he was as confident as Mitton believed him to be.

Without removing his helmet like his companions, Henry stepped forward and extended his ring for Mitton to kiss.

Almost immediately, Mitton bent over the offered hand. Halfway down, the significance of his action dawned upon him. But by then, it was too late to abort without giving offense or embarrassing himself in front of his peers. He kissed the ring and quickly pulled back.

"Bailiff Mitton." Henry decided formal titles were probably safer at this point. "Your concern for your people and town is admirable. I see now that you are an excellent steward for their prosperity."

"Thank you, Your—" Written across Mitton's face was the realization that he was being manipulated. But rather than surrender to outrage or panic, he simply…stopped. That surprised Henry. "—my lord."

Henry expected a cold reception after learning last night that Mitton had arranged Buckingham's capture and execution. Richard had rewarded him handsomely and exempted Shrewsbury from taxes, earning the bailiff the gratitude of his fellow townsfolk.

"I should like to bring my army peacefully through your city," Henry began when the assembly was seated around Mitton's dining table.

"With regret, I cannot allow that."

"I seek not to harass your town, only to pass through it."

"I'm sorry. The risk is too great."

"On the blood of my father and grandfather, on the blood of my mother and her ancestor Edward III, I give you my oath," Henry pressed. "Your people will come to no harm."

The other members of the Shrewsbury delegation stirred until Mitton silenced them with a glare. "I cannot permit you entry."

Anger building, Henry rose abruptly and turned his back on them. Behind him, Jasper cleared his throat.

When Henry turned back, he had restored his composure. "Why will you not allow my army to pass?"

Mitton swallowed. "We will incur the king's most extreme displeasure if we permit you passage."

"Surely you cannot support a man who murdered his nephews to seize the crown."

"I cannot support a man in rebellion against my anointed king, particularly one who leads so many Welshmen," Mitton countered. "This city was built to defend against Welsh armies."

"My army is made up of many subjects. Some fought for King Henry, some with King Edward. Some are mercenaries from the continent. Others are Welshmen with connections to my family for generations." Henry folded his hands in front of him. "But they all answer to me."

"Nonetheless, I cannot threaten our prosperity, and even our very lives, by joining a foreign army in rebellion against fellow Englishmen."

"I'm asking you to stand aside, not march with me," Henry clarified.

"In the mind of King Richard, they are the same."

Henry supposed that was true. "Does that not tell you all you need to know about the king you chose to support, that he would punish you for avoiding a sack?"

"You said you would not harm our town," Mitton countered.

"The tyrant need not know that."

Mitton sighed and folded his hands before him. "When Buckingham brought rebellion, he assembled an army consisting entirely of his own people. That fact mattered little when Richard brought retribution and vengeance sweeping down from the north. It was all I could do to spare our fair town. Many others were not so lucky. I will not risk our prospects for any cause."

"Richard will not be in a position to do anything of the sort." Though he tried to govern his tone in this conversation, he could not maintain his poise now. All his hatred for that man poured into the words, filling the room with a sudden hush in the face of such obvious hostility.

"That remains to be seen," Mitton answered.

Henry froze. "Excuse me?"

Mitton licked his lips. "I mean no disrespect, my lord. Consider the situation as I see it. The king can field twenty thousand. Despite his physical ailments, he has proven an able soldier and skilled commander. As you say, his path to the throne was unorthodox. But where you see shameful behavior, I see challenges overcome." He spread his hands out before him. "On the other hand, you are returning from more than a decade in exile and have no nearby lands to draw men and supplies from. While your army is an impressive achievement, it is not large enough to counter the king." He offered a sympathetic smile. "Your prospects do not look favorable."

Jasper, Oxford, and Woodville each tried to persuade him, but Mitton would not be budged from his position. All through the morning, they argued that Richard's actions had undermined and left him vulnerable, yet Mitton saw only the rewards of loyalty already granted.

Henry was beginning to panic at the very real possibility that one man would thwart his entire march. They would have no choice but to find another crossing. By the time they reached English soil, the country would say the Severn had drowned his rebellion much as it had Buckingham's.

An hour into their meeting, the door opened and one of Mitton's servants stepped in. Eyes widening at the assembly, the young man bowed deeply once, then scurried over to Mitton's side and whispered something in his ear.

"Now?" The bailiff's voice cracked as he jumped to his feet. When the servant nodded, he cried, "Send him in!"

"What's this?" Oxford demanded, rising.

Woodville's hand moved toward his sword.

"A knight has arrived from the east under a flag of truce," their host explained.

*Richard has come*, Henry thought. *We've run out of time.*

But when the door opened a second time and the servant ushered the newcomer in, he didn't bear Richard's boar crest. Instead, he wore the green-and-tawny eagle claw of Lord Stanley.

Stanley's man bowed first to Henry and his lords and then to Mitton and the men of Shrewsbury. "My lords and burgesses, thank you for your hospitality. I am Sir Rowland Warburton. I have ridden hard these past few days on behalf of my lord."

"You are most welcome, sir." Mitton bowed deeply. Though respected in his city, Mitton was still a commoner and owed deference to this knight. "May I have the honor of presenting the Earl of Richmond, the Earl of Pembroke, the Earl of Oxford, and Sir Woodville?" He gestured to each in turn.

"My lords." Warburton greeted them with a bow of his own.

"How may Shrewsbury be of service to your noble lord?"

The knight returned his attention to Mitton. "Lord Stanley requests that you open the gates and permit this army to pass."

Oxford thumped the table with his gauntlet. "Good man."

Murmuring with obvious surprise, the city's leaders clustered around Mitton and debated the request.

"Where is your master?" Henry whispered to Warburton.

"Lord Stanley and his brother Sir William are at Atherstone with six thousand men."

Henry grinned openly. "Excellent. And does he wish us to unite with him there, or will he come to us?

Warburton's eyes hardened. "He and his brother will shadow you as you march, but my lord does not wish to combine forces at this time."

Henry frowned. No, this was wrong. He must have misheard him. Looking at his companions, though, he saw the same confusion he suspected was painted across his own face.

"What?" Jasper asked. "Why not?"

Warburton simply shrugged. "I do not know more than this, Your Grace. My instructions were to inform you of his location, do what I could to enable your passage east, and return with any messages you wish to deliver."

Henry's further inquiries were cut short when Shrewsbury's leaders approached, having ended their discussion.

Mitton straightened his houppelande and cleared his throat. "What Lord Stanley wishes, we are pleased to provide." Turning to Henry, he placed his hand over his chest. "By my oath, you may pass."

Stunned and confused by the past few minutes, Henry allowed Jasper to offer the necessary pleasantries to extricate them from the building. Oxford and Woodville peppered Warburton with questions about the Stanleys' strength and composition.

"Why won't they unite with us?" Henry asked his uncle as they cantered over the stone bridge. Unfamiliar with the intricacies of marching armies, Henry felt out of his depth and could think of no tactical reason for the odd decision.

His uncle simply furrowed his forehead in silence.

Before Mitton could change his mind, Oxford and Woodville directed the breakdown of the camp at double time. Suitably fortified by stiff ale back at his tent, Henry led the column across the bridge and into the town within the hour.

Mitton honored both of his oaths. When Henry crossed the second gate and entered the town, the bailiff climbed down to the riverbank and waited beneath the bridge, with the water lapping at his ankles. From that position, he allowed Henry to ride above his belly—indeed, his entire body—while he passed through the gates. It almost expunged Henry's mortification at failing to gain admittance on his own.

Almost.

He had failed to open the gates of a simple town. His march continued only because of Thomas Stanley, a man who now refused to march with him. The anxiety he'd thought banished came surging back.

Exhaling as his horse cantered through the center of Shrewsbury, he tried to remind himself that Rhys had come. The Welsh had risen. Butler had sent his son. Surely, his own stepfather would support him.

Wouldn't he?

And yet, Stanley wasn't a rebel at heart. He had always preferred caution and delay to bold action. That was why Henry needed him, other than his six thousand men; his support would signal for the English what Rhys' support had for the Welsh. Inevitability. Momentum. Initiative.

But he couldn't help but wonder if perhaps Stanley simply wanted the matter to be resolved one way or the other. Stability would come only when either Richard or Henry was dead. Perhaps his stepfather didn't care which.

And so, the army passed through Shrewsbury while Henry fretted over whether he could trust the man who had opened the city to him.

## HENRY

The Stanleys had made a sport of marrying widows of proven fertility, as Henry discovered the next day when the army left Newport. His rebellion of bastards and stepchildren was joined by the eight hundred soldiers of Sir Richard Corbett, William Stanley's stepson.

Later that day, Sir Gilbert Talbot brought five hundred more. Though Talbot shared no relations with Henry, his parents' marriage had ended the Talbot-Butler feud. He greeted his cousin James Ormond heartily.

Though a handful of powerful families wasn't the popular mandate Henry had expected, he reassured himself that his core of exiles would have all brought hundreds of men-at-arms each if they hadn't been attainted. He could, at least, realistically claim that his army consisted of more than just foreigners and Welshmen.

Henry, Oxford, Woodville, and Jasper clustered around a map of the Midlands in Henry's tent while the army made camp at Stafford.

Henry wasted no time with pleasantries. "We're not where I wanted to be at this point. The Welsh didn't rise as I'd hoped."

Jasper smirked. "Rhys ap Thomas would claim his soldiers are all the Welsh you need."

"Rhys doesn't want to share the glory with his rivals," Oxford countered.

"Regardless," Henry interrupted, though he silently agreed with Oxford, "it means we've doubled our numbers since landing. I'd hoped to have twice that."

"Where are Hastings' and Buckingham's retainers?" Woodville grumbled. "Why wouldn't they support you?"

"You overestimate the loyalty of the gentry, Edward," Henry replied.

"I doubt they would have ever risen," Oxford mused. "After Buckingham, Richard crushed them with taxes and seized the lands of those who didn't betray the duke. Not enough time has passed for them to try again."

Henry leaned over the map, drawing their attention. "We have a choice to make. Oxford?"

Nodding, Oxford placed an inkpot on Newport. "We are here." Farther to the east, he placed a cup. "Before he returned to the Stanleys, Warburton said Richard is assembling his men at Nottingham." They chuckled at his choice of a cup as Richard's symbol; every report they received mentioned the king's drinking. "Norfolk is already at Leicester, and Warburton suspects Richard is waiting for word of our movements before joining him."

"Then we have the initiative," Henry mused.

"How large?" Jasper gestured to Richard's army.

"At least ten thousand, if you include Northumberland, who has yet to arrive. More come every day."

They fell silent, contemplating the deficit.

In France, Henry had received letters of outcry from dozens of nobles, clergy, and city mayors shocked by Richard's execution of children and the rumored murder of his wife. Then there was the king's growing paranoia, obsession with Henry, and abuse of the south. Everything pointed to a man who was barely hanging onto his throne.

Yet, Henry had forgotten to consider the value of the crown. Richard could command the presence of his soldiers and deprive any who didn't take the field of their lands with a simple declaration. Henry depended entirely on his supporters honoring their promises and could do nothing to punish those who didn't join him.

There was power in perception, and the crown represented legitimacy, regardless of the worth of its owner. It cowed the meek and enforced obedience on those who might otherwise contemplate treachery. It hadn't seemed like much back in France. In England, it amounted to four thousand extra men.

Henry broke the silence. "We must decide what we do with this army we've collected."

Leaning forward, Oxford pointed to the inkpot. "We have three choices." He shifted his finger back to the west. "We can move back to the Welsh border in the hope that more men will join us." He shifted his hand to the southeast. "We could march on London and claim the government." Oxford shifted his hand to point at the cup. "The third option is to attack Richard directly, despite the difference in our forces."

"Henry," Jasper began in the tone he used when trying to persuade Henry, "I know you aren't satisfied with the size of our army, but we cannot return to Wales."

"Time may bring us more supporters," Henry insisted. "This summer was ripe with rumors of invasion. It's reasonable for them to be cautious. Once they see I've truly landed, they will come."

"Richard will do the same, and his task is easier than ours," Woodville added.

Jasper continued, "By now, everyone knows what happened at Shrewsbury. If we return to Wales, the people you hope to recruit will view it as a retreat." None but Jasper could speak so frankly with his nephew. "Time will make your supporters second-guess their decision."

Henry remembered his despair as he'd ridden to stop Thomas Grey from defecting.

"This enterprise of ours is held together by the faintest of threads," Jasper continued. "If we lose this chance, it will never come again, and Richard will hold the throne until he dies."

Meeting his uncle's gaze, he saw the briefest glimpse of an emotion he recognized all too well: fear. It looked strange on a face he had admired for its courage his whole life. He supposed he understood. Like him, his uncle refused to return to a life of exile. But while Henry refused to live at the pleasure of others anymore, Jasper already knew the pain of regaining his life only to lose it a second time.

Yet the advice, shared by all his closest advisors, contained wisdom, whatever else besides. "Very well, we move forward."

Oxford's shoulders drained of their tension. "That leaves the question of our destination."

"Taking London would undermine Richard's credibility and may encourage some nobles to join us, or at least abandon the usurper," said Woodville, whose mother and sisters were still there.

"But if we can't take the city quickly, we'd appear weak," Oxford added. "It's also possible Richard could descend on us as we lay siege."

"We're not going to London," Henry stated. "We confront the royal army. The crown and London are just spoils. Richard"—he paused, eyes fixating on the cup—"Richard is the goal. This is our only chance, and I won't let him go unpunished for what he did to me." After a moment, he added, "To you, to them out there, to the entire country."

"Do we have the strength to meet him on an open field?" Jasper asked Oxford. "When Edward defeated Henry, he had many more men than we do now."

Oxford considered carefully before answering. "The divisions of our armies were larger, but they operated independently. Some even attacked each other. It was chaotic."

"Perhaps not so different." Henry's thoughts returned to the unreliability of nobles. "Richard has angered many in the realm and cannot draw the strength his brother did. Norfolk, Catesby, maybe Northumberland."

"It comes down to whether we can trust the Stanleys, then." Woodville finally voiced the unspoken question upon which everything depended. "If they fight with us, we outnumber Richard's army slightly."

"He said he would," Jasper reminded.

"Vaguely," Oxford corrected. "His language was not unequivocal."

"His brother's stepson marches with us already," Jasper insisted.

"That's the issue, isn't it?" Woodville asked. "Would they risk the inheritance of their natural sons to support their stepsons?"

"If they intend treachery, then we are overwhelmingly outnumbered." Oxford reached for two scrolls lying nearby and positioned them to the north and the south of the inkwell. "William and Thomas Stanley currently flank us on both sides and can surround us if we engage Richard."

Jasper shook his head. "Or they may be securing our flanks, exactly as they say."

"Why didn't they join our army, then?" Oxford asked. "Marching as one gives us maximum flexibility and protection. If Richard does attack in force, whichever of the Stanleys was closest would either have to let him pass or engage and be overwhelmed."

"There is a third option," Woodville added. "They may simply refuse to do anything."

Oxford nodded. "The Stanley way."

Henry listened impassively, turning the question around in his mind. He couldn't understand why the Stanleys were acting as they were. But he needed to make a decision.

Jehane had once told him she loved him for his heart. His heart had never led him astray. Even the woman he'd loved had been a blessing, despite the way he'd lost her.

"I do not believe the Stanleys will support Richard." Henry put more confidence in his voice than he felt. "Lord Stanley gave his assurances, and his actions have only advanced my faith in him." He raised a hand when Oxford inhaled. "However, I may be wrong. That he keeps his army separate from us is a concern."

"What are you proposing?" Jasper asked.

"Doubt is a powerful thing. We have doubts about Stanley, and it makes us question our strategy. Richard must surely doubt the loyalty of his supporters as he watches our army grow." Gesturing to the map, Henry tapped Richard's army and London. "Is there some route we can take that appears to threaten London?"

"You mean to fool him?" Oxford grinned.

"And the Stanleys as well, if they intend betrayal. I see no reason to inform them of our plans if they won't join our army."

Oxford tapped his chin. "Edward, any thoughts?"

Woodville nodded, pointing to a more southerly route. "If we march to Lichfield by a western approach, it'll seem like we're avoiding Richard on the path to London."

"Forcing him to follow us." Oxford nodded. "He knows the longer you're at liberty, the weaker he appears."

"And we get to choose the ground for battle," Henry added. "It's possible the Stanleys may simply sit by while we engage Richard. Lord Oxford, Lord Woodville, you've trained these men and understand their capabilities. In your opinion, can you defeat Richard with the six thousand we have here?"

The two military men exchanged a long glance. Finally, Oxford turned to Henry. "If we choose ground that protects our flank and mitigates their numbers."

"Richard will have cannons," Henry reminded.

"As do we," Woodville replied.

"Cannons." Jasper scoffed. "Dreadful things. No honor in them."

Henry ignored his uncle's outburst. "Can we do it?"

"After fourteen years, I sure would like to try." Oxford gave a wolfish grin. He was Henry's best weapon and had developed some innovative formations while the army had trained in France. Certainly, his eyes suggested eagerness and confidence.

"And I," Woodville added predictably; he would fight Richard alone if necessary.

"Uncle?" Henry asked.

"It's our best move," he agreed.

Henry nodded and surveyed the map one last time. "These next few days will decide the course of our futures." He met the gaze of Woodville and Oxford in turn. "When we meet the royal army, I will rely on the two of you. Either we reclaim our homes or we see the loss of all hope for ourselves and our countrymen."

After a few moments of silence, Woodville finally spoke up. "Let's go kill a tyrant."

## HENRY

On the nineteenth, the Tudor army marched well into dusk and managed to reach Tamworth before nightfall. It would be the last difficult march of their journey, for the scouts reported that Richard had learned about Henry's route and had joined Norfolk at Leicester, only twenty-five miles away.

The next day, Oxford moved them only eight miles to Atherstone, determined not to fight both Richard and fatigue at the same time. Having spanned the same distance twice over while riding up and down the column beneath his dragon standard, Henry enjoyed a long, deep sleep that night. The silence that night suggested his soldiers did the same. From the freshest youth to the most battle-hardened veteran, they understood what the short march and additional rest meant.

The Stanleys were also camped at Atherstone, though on the other side of the river. The two armies of roughly equal size were close enough to see the smoke from each others' fires. Some of the scouting parties even crossed paths; in one instance, one of Henry's Welshmen warned a Stanley scout about an adder's burrow hidden where the meadow met the road before saluting and riding off.

The next afternoon, Stanley sent a message welcoming Henry to Atherstone and inviting him to his camp to discuss their dispositions.

Accompanied by William Brandon and five of his exile bodyguards, Henry galloped down Watling Street and over the bridge spanning the River Anker. He doffed his armor and crowned helmet, instead opting to meet his stepfather in his red doublet with a green sash at the waist and his white cotton tunic poking out from beneath.

Henry both anticipated and feared this meeting whose outcome would likely decide his fate.

While Henry's command tent could fit a table, bed, and room for his dozen chief nobles, Lord Stanley's tent was a much larger rectangle with three central support poles. And it was made of the finest cotton brocade and the richest colors Henry had ever seen; even Anne of Beaujeu had never worn anything so fine. On a tent!

Two of Stanley's personal guard pulled back the flaps at Henry's approach, revealing a pageant of color within: deep blues, crimson reds, vibrant amber, and even royal purple. Until recently, the Stanleys had styled themselves as kings of Mann; looking at the wealth on display, Henry could believe it.

The man who owned that wealth rose as Henry entered. For the first time in their lives, the charming blue-eyed youth and the white-bearded, long-featured gentleman set eyes upon each other.

Henry marveled that his mother, who had undeniably been in love with the vibrant Edmund Tudor, had chosen to marry this man who looked far older than his fifty years. Her two husbands could not have been more different. His father had been passionate and excitable, but Stanley had made a career out of caution.

Much depended upon setting the correct tone in these next few minutes. Though his mother had told Henry much of Stanley, he had already seen that letters did little to convey the nature of a man. Yet he'd also had some recent success in first impressions.

He smiled warmly. In a flash, he saw Stanley lower his eyes to his poor teeth peeking past his lips. Henry had forgotten his teeth and the ill health they suggested. On the path here, he had planned on offering his ring so Stanley could show his respects. Standing before the man, Henry changed his mind. His health was perfectly fine, and he needed to convince Stanley of it.

He extended his hand, greeting Stanley as an equal. "Stepfather. It is a pleasure to meet you at last."

Eyes widening, Stanley clasped the offered arm, and Henry squeezed firmly, confidently. *Feel the strength in these arms.*

"You have your mother's nose." Stanley's voice carried a hint of reservation. At least he had decided to acknowledge their relationship. That was good.

"She is well?" Henry lowered his arm.

"Indeed." Stanley bobbed his head. "Though my hand cramps from the letters she insists I write to her."

The laugh escaped naturally and started in Henry's belly. "I have the same cramp." Immediately, the room seemed to lighten. Was that a smirk on Stanley's face? "Thank you for the assistance at Shrewsbury."

Stanley waved a hand. "Think nothing of it. Many goods from my lands pass through there on their way south. They would not risk losing my favor." Stepping back, he gestured behind him. "May I present my brother, Sir William Stanley?"

The only other man in the room was a tall, broad man with a pinched forehead. The creases around his mouth suggested he laughed often.

"Sir Stanley" This time, Henry did extend his hand, palm down.

William Stanley knelt and kissed Henry's ring without hesitation, moving with more elegance and fluidity than Henry thought possible from such a muscular frame. "Your Majesty."

Warmed and reassured by the greeting, Henry tapped him on the shoulder and embraced him as William stood. "Uncle."

"Enough of that, William," Stanley chided. "I doubt my stepson braved a dangerous sea voyage to have you dote on him."

"Indeed not," Henry agreed. "And though I apply the royal title when it suits, I'm aware the army to our northeast would take issue with my using it."

"As would several within the realm," Stanley agreed.

"But not those appalled at the murder of Hastings and King Edward's children," Henry said.

"Your army is smaller than I expected," Stanley said abruptly.

Taken aback, Henry nonetheless recovered quickly. "With your help, it will serve to remove a usurper." Boldness had served him well thus far, so he risked a little more. "Lord Stanley, I will not insult you by pretending your support is of no consequence to me. We both know I need it desperately. Your assistance at Shrewsbury, your correspondence, and my mother's assurances led me to believe you favor my claim. It was the critical factor in my decision to invade."

He paused, but Stanley did not argue with these points.

Henry swallowed. "However, as one gentleman to another, I must ask you directly. I will only ask once, and then the matter will be put to rest forever. Do you intend to use this army to help me unseat Richard?"

There it was, phrased directly enough that not even the legendary Thomas Stanley could refuse to answer without, in fact, providing an answer.

William shifted uncomfortably, but Henry kept his gaze fixed on his stepfather. Surely, the bonds of familial obligation would compel his support. William Stanley's stepson was with the Tudor army. He could not possibly think to profit more under an unstable Richard than under his own relatives.

The old man lowered his gaze beneath the scrutiny, and Henry remembered the phrasing of Stanley's letters, which now seemed unconscionably vague. And he had refused to combine armies. It was the sort of thing someone might do if he intended betrayal.

After some time, Stanley answered. "My brother and I support you. My letters were as clear as I dared make them given Richard's suspicions." Henry's eyes widened at this. "Oh, yes, Richard has doubted my loyalty since Hastings' execution. I suppose he suspected it even earlier because of my marriage to your mother. I had to be very careful."

Henry relaxed, yet something in the old man's face prevented a knot of doubt from uncoiling in his stomach. "Then why do you keep your army apart? If we unite, we can overwhelm Richard."

Stanley shook his head. "I cannot do that until the time is right."

"Why not? Lord Oxford knows firsthand that armies operating independently of each other are difficult to manage and can even trade blows accidentally."

"The time isn't yet right," Stanley repeated.

"I don't understand." Henry shook his head. "When is the time right?"

Stanley sighed. "Richard holds my son hostage for my loyalty. If I combine our armies, he will kill him. I must be assured he cannot order my son's execution before I act."

Henry blinked in surprise. Now, the letters, maneuvers, and reluctance made sense.

Stanley stroked his beard, straightening it with a wave of his hand. "We contrived at his escape, but the man who was to provide the horses failed to deliver and my son was recaptured. Richard declared my brother and John Savage traitors and had them attainted."

"Traitors?"

"That's why I flanked you to the north during your march eastward," William Stanley explained. "Any opposition would likely come from that direction, and I have naught to lose by engaging Richard."

"He didn't punish you?" Henry asked his stepfather.

Lord Stanley shook his head.

His thoughts swirled. Richard had nearly killed the woman he loved, but Jehane was now beyond his reach. The same wasn't true of

Stanley's son. The fact that Stanley had marched at all was surprisingly daring. But, then again, he had to. He was one of the richest men in the realm. To stay home would be treason.

With new eyes, Henry studied this man caught between a king and a relative, between a man who threatened his child and another whose actions threatened that child's life.

"Lord Stanley, I understand the difficulty of your position." Scratching his chin, he paced for a few steps. "There will be a battle tomorrow. Will you form up?"

"I must. Not doing so would seal my son's fate."

"Together, we would defeat him," Henry assured. "Every man in my army knows defeat is death."

William Stanley spoke up. "Give me an opening, and I'll take it."

"And you agree as well?" He asked his stepfather.

"Your mother has advocated tirelessly on your behalf, and after Hastings and those boys…" He swallowed and met Henry's gaze. "If you can engage Richard himself, I will bring my forces to bear."

"I'll find a way," Henry promised.

"Will your command tent be satisfied with this answer?" Stanley asked.

"Our strategy will account for the disparity in our numbers, but I confess that your forces openly joining us would reassure them far more."

Stanley stroked his beard again. "Sir John Savage is eager to repay the king for his attainder. He and a number of my knights are spoiling for a fight. Take them and their men. I'll instruct them to signal me when they feel the time is right."

Henry accepted them happily. Any soldiers would reassure the men of Stanley's support. It was hardly the result Henry had hoped for upon crossing the Anker, or even the channel, but it would have to suffice. At least he need not worry about the Stanleys attacking his rear while he engaged Richard.

But as he and his bodyguard made their way back to his camp, Henry began to wonder whether that was strictly true. Was there anything Lord Stanley wouldn't do if it appeared Richard would win the day? If he could buy his son's life—and perhaps his brother's pardon—by joining a rout in progress, would it matter who Stanley had married or what pledges he had provided?

# CHAPTER TWENTY

## RICHARD

O N THE OTHER side of Ambion Hill, Richard's fingers hungered for something to wrap themselves around. A sword would work. That Tudor bastard's throat was better. Or that traitor, Rhys ap Thomas. Even Thomas Stanley would do.

He should have killed that old man when he'd had the chance. Margaret Beaufort and William Stanley had stopped him. Well, he'd separated the one from his title and he'd separate the other from her head once he was done wiping her son off his war hammer.

He now had no doubt that she'd turned Buckingham against him. The duke hadn't been smart enough to arrange a rebellion. And then there were all those rumors Tudor had spread. As if he could afford to murder his wife when he depended so much on the Neville armies! Yet, the lies had been so detailed that someone must have fed him information.

Or many someones.

Just how many of his subjects had betrayed him? That question had tormented his nights and ruined every audience for the past six months. No obeisance seemed genuine enough, no promise given easily enough. And no subject had given him what he had demanded when he needed it. The excuses were endless. Someone was lying. They had to be.

His spine was starting to ache as it always did when he thought about Tudor. His hand crept to the side table and wrapped itself around the goblet. Lifting it, he drank deeply from the cool port within and felt some of the control return. Some, but not enough. He drained the wine and rose to refill it.

It would all be over soon. One more day and he could finally relax.

One of his servants—he didn't recall the boy's name—entered and bowed. At least someone remembered how to show respect.

"Your Highness, Sir Catesby has returned."

"Then send him in," he snapped. The hoarseness of his voice surprised him, and he took another draught of wine to clear his throat.

Catesby entered and dipped into a light bow that would have ruined his temper if provided by any other man. But this was Catesby, and any liberties stemmed from the man's efficiency, not disrespect. His riding cloak was covered in dust, and he smelled of horses.

Another thought forced a scowl. "If they mistreated you, I will march on their camp and slaughter every one of them."

Though Catesby smiled, he shook his head. "Nothing so insidious. My horse reared at a noise and threw me."

"Yes, well…" Richard muttered. "What did Stanley say?"

Catesby inhaled and held the breath. "He declined your order to join the royal army."

"I knew he would betray me." Richard threw his goblet against the tent wall. The muted slap of iron against fabric wasn't satisfying enough, so Richard gave a nearby table a satisfying kick, splintering one of the legs but failing to knock it over entirely.

"He argued that since you already outnumber the rebels, he serves you better by remaining in a position to outflank Tudor and prevent his escape. He said Oxford lives to challenge you today because no one did so at Barnet."

"Barnet!" Richard cried. "We'd have killed them all if my brother had listened to me."

Catesby ignored the outburst. "He proposes that his and your forces, along with Northumberland's, can surround and destroy the Tudors."

"Northumberland, another traitor," Richard spat. His hands clenched and unclenched absently. "He assured me he was ready this past spring, but when I call him, he claims he needs more time to collect his men. He's had ten days already." Richard retrieved the goblet. "I wager he's been communicating with the brat, too. He probably started the rumor that I murdered Anne. He was always trouble up north."

Catesby listened to this diatribe dispassionately. His eyes never left his liege as the king refilled the goblet and took another deep drink.

"And Shrewsbury… They'll learn my vengeance is far harsher than my kindness." He swirled the port in his goblet. "Why did they let that Welsh milksop through?"

Catesby cleared his throat. "Stanley sent a rider to implore the town to open the gates to the rebels."

"He did what?" Richard rounded on Catesby, eyes burning with outrage.

"Lord Stanley claims they are trapped on this side of the Severn now, effectively isolated from further recruits and their only means of escape. He believed the wisest course was to bring them to battle while you still had the numbers to crush them."

"And he expects me to believe that?"

"He said, 'I was a loyal Englishman before I was Margaret Tudor's husband, and I remain so, even if Your Majesty deems my companions treasonous.'"

"Loyal Englishman, indeed. He's a traitor like his brother. Does he forget I can have his son's head at a word?" He should have taken Stanley's brother and wife as well.

"I did remind him, and he was much affected by it. He clearly knew of the failed escape."

"Did he know his son confessed his father's treason to save his own life?" Richard offered a wicked smile. But even while speaking the words, he doubted Lord Strange's confession; under the mildest of torture, he had confessed to a dozen other, utterly unbelievable crimes.

"No," Catesby admitted. "I felt sharing that information would only weaken our hold over him."

Richard took another drink, eyeing Catesby over the rim. "You think Stanley can still be saved? He married the milksop's mother. Both Stanleys have stepchildren with the rebels."

"I don't know his intentions. But he hasn't betrayed us yet, and what he says is true. Tudor is cut off from the Welsh and has no choice but to give battle tomorrow. We still vastly outnumber him. If he withdraws, we'll pursue and destroy him. If he faces us, we'll crush him. That was made possible by Stanley's actions."

Richard studied the man upon whom he had relied. Had the exiled pretender turned his dear friend against him too? "Are you advising me to take him at his word?"

"Absolutely not." Catesby scoffed. "I only advise that we not drive Stanley into rebellion if we can avoid it. Let's plan for treachery but not encourage it." His eyes flashed with the delightful cunning Richard valued. "His brother is attainted already. It will be no great thing to condemn the other Stanley as well."

Catesby. He could always trust his dear Catesby.

He had tried to be a generous king. He had offered pardons, stipends, and titles. How had they repaid him? With treachery. With rumors and whispers. He'd accepted the blame for the deaths of his nephews to keep his wife's retainers, only to have their loyalty shaken by rumors of her murder. Rumors, spread by traitors all around him.

There would be no more kindness or reconciliation. When the last threat to his rule was dead at his feet, he would punish all those who had refused or hesitated when summoned. All those who had whispered their vile slander in the distant corners of the realm.

They would all pay.

## HENRY

Savage and the other knights raised the spirits of the army, which desperately needed it following news that Northumberland had finally arrived with three thousand men. Though he kept his force separate from Richard's, Northumberland had sent Henry no message, and that left little doubt about his loyalties.

Oxford was less sanguine at this news and Henry's meeting with Lord Stanley than expected. "We always needed to kill Richard to put an end to this, so nothing has changed. I honestly expected Stanley to sit back and wait for us to kill each other."

"They outnumber us nearly two-to-one," Henry cautioned.

Oxford offered a knowing smile. "Numbers aren't everything."

"I don't understand."

"Hopefully, Richard won't, either." Looking at the map for a few more moments, Oxford finally nodded. "I can work with this."

Oxford ordered the army to move to White Moors just south of Ambion Hill that afternoon, determined to give battle in the morning. With Stanley remaining separate and the arrival of Northumberland, he felt confident Richard would accept.

But Henry was haunted by visions of his standard dripping in the blood of his men. In the shadow of Richard's army, he couldn't help but think that perhaps trading an uncertain fate for certain death had been folly. Where there was life, there was still hope.

So, as the army broke camp, Henry called Jasper into his tent. Already in full armor, Jasper, like Oxford, yearned for the chance to meet his enemies in battle again. Henry did not look forward to this conversation.

"Uncle, please sit."

Jasper lowered himself into a chair and shifted his armor to settle comfortably.

"The past fourteen years have led me to this moment," Henry began. "My future rests upon the outcome of this battle. But for you, this struggle has occupied most of your life. You've lost two brothers and countless friends to it. I cannot imagine how difficult that must have been for you."

The faint smile Jasper had worn since entering faded. Henry could see his mind racing to understand where Henry was leading him.

"I never knew my father. He died before I was born. But you…" Voice catching, Henry took a moment to find the words for the feelings he had never dared to share. "You remained by my side all these years, keeping me safe. You taught me how to be a man, how to deal with a world that did not wish me happiness."

Now that he'd given himself the liberty to speak, the words came gushing out. "I don't think of myself as an orphan. You were a father to me in every way that mattered. I love you, I trust you, and I value everything you did for me all this time. I am who I am today because of you."

Tears pooled at the corners of Jasper's eyes. "Henry—"

"But I'm afraid there's one more thing I must ask of you."

"A-anything, my boy." Jasper blinked away the tears.

Henry swallowed. "I must ask you not to join this battle."

Jasper shot to his feet. "What?"

"I need you to return to Shrewsbury and garrison the town."

"No." Jasper jerked his head side to side. "I have to be there."

"Uncle—"

"No, Henry. After all these years of feasts and negotiations, conversations with every noble in three countries, two exiles, nearly thirty years of hardship, you don't want me to see it through?"

"Richard has twice the number we do."

"The Stanleys—"

"Cannot be relied upon!" Henry took a step forward. "If Richard remains at the rear, they will not fight. I know this in my bones. We'll be overwhelmed. I need you to secure our way out."

Jasper hesitated. "Then send William or Thomas Brandon. You cannot send me away."

"It must be you," he cried, control slipping. "If the worst should happen, my life will depend on you. I cannot trust anyone else with this." He took a step to the side, wringing his hands together. "Buckingham was betrayed by his own man." Stabbing the air with his finger, he added. "At Shrewsbury. If Richard stands triumphant, who else can I trust not to turn me over for his own safety?"

Jasper fell silent.

"I am here because I refused to put my fate in anyone else's hands. Richard took Jehane from me. His brother took away my life. So, I supported Buckingham to put an end to him. I chose. And I chose to come here, to take his crown and finally, finally make myself safe." He raised his hands, clenched together into a single fist. "I need to know I have options of my choosing, not someone else's. I need to know you're back there, that I have hope. That I have a choice in case…"

This desperate need came from some place beyond reason. It was the frightened, delirious man at St. Malo, running through the crowd in a panic, blindly seeking salvation.

Slowly, the muscles in Jasper's neck relaxed. When he finally spoke, it was a mere whisper. "I swore I would protect you."

Henry wanted to cry out that this request would protect him, that he needed the reassurance of knowing he had a future, had hope.

Before he could open his lips, Jasper spoke. "I will do what you ask."

Muscles shaking with sudden relief, Henry's head fell forward. Jasper was there, hands on his shoulders. When Henry looked up, his own eyes were glistening. His uncle's anger had been replaced by a soothing smile that filled Henry's heart with warmth. Whatever happened, this battle would not be the end. And that was a comforting thought.

"You must do something for me in return," Jasper said. "Don't take undue risks. I'm giving you a way to save yourself. Take advantage of it if the situation warrants." He raised his chin to gaze down at Henry as he had done so many years earlier. "Do you agree?"

"I promise." Henry inhaled deeply to banish the last remnants of anxiety. "Thank you, uncle."

"Anything for you, son." He pulled Henry into a tight hug, and Henry wrapped his arms around the man who had sacrificed his life, his freedom, and now his pride for him.

# CHAPTER TWENTY-ONE

## RICHARD

RICHARD SLEPT LITTLE that night. Just when he would nod off, he would awaken to nightmarish scenes of Stanley and Tudor laughing over his broken body, or his own soldiers turning against him, or his sword breaking in his hand as he reached the enemy line.

The dreams only stoked his anger. Why was he having nightmares? He was prepared to second-guess his dispositions in the tense moments preceding battle. He knew the importance of patience while searching for the seam in his opponent's armor that would let him deliver the death blow. He was a seasoned veteran.

But even those rational reassurances did nothing to banish the anxiety that granted him only short pockets of sleep. He doubted Stanley, not his own abilities. Northumberland. Even Norfolk. The realm had so many traitors. Rhys ap Thomas had betrayed him despite the generosity he'd shown that Welsh villain. And Herbert should have stopped Tudor in Wales.

Most of all, there was Tudor, that Welsh milksop. *He must know something to risk battle despite overwhelming odds.* Unquestionably, he expected Stanley not to oppose him. But who was Stanley lying to? Didn't the man care about his son's life?

Richard's twisted back ached no matter how he positioned himself on the field cot. Fingers instinctively reaching for the wine goblet, Richard halted in mid-motion. Despite his physical agony, he couldn't risk dulling his wits. Not this day. He had to endure.

His armor had always provided some relief, even in the throes of the very worst pain. He shouted for his page to help him. As the breastplate settled into place, he relaxed his muscles and let the metal frame take the pressure off his torso. Instantly rejuvenated, Richard waved the half-sleeping boy away and settled back down on the cot.

But the doubts remained. What did Tudor know that he didn't?

At first light, he roused himself. Before the day was over, he would have his reckoning. On the morrow, he could celebrate and rest as long as he wanted.

The camp was slowly beginning to awaken when Richard exited the tent resplendent in his crowned helmet and shining armor. He knew he looked magnificent. Only a keen eye could recognize the slight dip in the height of his shoulder and the asymmetry to account for his twisted spine.

Collecting the few of his personal guard who were already awake, Richard mounted his horse with a sigh of relief. The rigid structure of the wooden saddle held his torso and banished the remaining pain from his aching back. On horseback, everything was clear, and he could face any problem.

He was about to ride out when one of his scouts cantered up to him and bowed in the saddle. "Your Majesty, the rebels are on the move."

Richard followed the man to the top of Albion Hill. The ridge ran from the northwest to the southeast. Ahead of him lay a wide plain with a swampy marsh in the middle. Far to the south on the other side of the marsh, the Stanley armies separately arrayed on heights near Dadlington.

And to the west, the rebel army waited in the faint morning light, arrayed in a single long line of battle.

Richard grinned. "Find Norfolk. It's time."

He pulled his horse around and took one more look at the oncoming army. Somewhere among it was the man who had spread vicious rumors and fomented rebellion.

Richard looked forward to killing him.

## HENRY

Oxford chose to form a single line of battle, with Talbot and Savage leading cavalry forces on either side. As they moved into position with the marshland guarding their right flank, the royal army settled onto the slight rise of the hill. Norfolk formed the royal right flank to the north, and Richard's retainers formed the center. Northumberland formed the left, angled back from the rest of the army to follow the ridge.

Sitting to the rear of the army amid his bodyguard and a hundred French pikemen, Henry realized Northumberland's position meant Richard feared the Stanleys turning on him. They were drawn up beyond the marsh to the south, William on the left flank and Thomas on the right. While Oxford wouldn't have to deal with Northumberland immediately, Stanley would face a harder time reaching Richard.

If Oxford could force the king to engage.

Henry bit at his lip. He shouldn't have agreed to stay in the rear, helpless while his followers fought for him. His fate was in the hands of others, yet again. Turning in his saddle, he looked to the west. Finding the road to Shrewsbury, he thought of his uncle.

And then the royal cannons fired.

Henry jumped in his saddle. As if a hundred cathedral bells had struck all at once, the loudest sound Henry had ever heard vibrated through his chest. All around him, his bodyguards struggled to control their horses, and some of the pikemen leaned forward to grab the reins and help steady them.

Voice shaking, he soothed his horse. "E-easy. It's…it's fine, boy."

The sound repeated when Oxford's cannons responded. Lines of smoke puffed skyward and iron sailed wildly over the plain to smash into the ground in tiny plumes of dirt and ash.

They were firing at each other as fast as they could reload now, trading smoke and projectiles. Henry had expected the speed of arrow volleys, but cannons fired surprisingly slowly. During the next volley, one of Richard's found its mark, striking a Tudor cannon and consuming its crew in a ball of metal and dirt. A moment later, one of the royal cannons exploded in a ball of flame and smoke, dropping several men in Norfolk's front rank.

Henry turned to William Brandon, who was also struggling to calm his horse. "Did Oxford hit them?"

"No, Your Majesty. They sometimes explode if they're poorly made."

"They do that?" he cried. "But our men—"

"It's no greater a risk than a volley of arrows, my lord."

"A man can survive an arrow. If you're standing next to—"

"Oxford." Brandon interrupted by pointing at their army. "He's starting his advance."

Oxford fearlessly led the men forward toward Richard's center. The cavalry wings began to spread out, seeking room to maneuver. Up on the hill, Norfolk was positioned closest to the Tudor army. As Oxford's first battalion entered range, the Ricardians let loose a volley of arrows.

Raising their shields, Oxford's soldiers compressed around their standards and advanced, flinching as arrows struck their armor obliquely and deflected off. A few men fell to the ground in pain, but the advance continued unabated.

"Hurry," Henry whispered, watching his men struggle under the hail of arrows. "Do it."

A horn sounded from within the Tudor army. At the signal, it shifted its line of approach northward, turning away from Richard's center. Oxford was bringing his full six thousand men to bear on the royal right.

# NORFOLK

It took Norfolk some time to realize the enemy had indeed shifted direction and wasn't simply adjusting to a contour in the landscape. Cool control shifted to alarm. He wasn't arrayed to absorb a charge by six thousand men. He had to do something to blunt their momentum.

His commanders were still standing nearby, awaiting orders.

"Devereux?"

The captain of his vanguard saluted.

"Shift the cannons and archers to fire at the front ranks. Slow them down."

"Yes, Your Grace." The man kicked his horse forward to join his men. The steed moved only two steps before halting.

Norfolk scowled. Time was critical. "Devereux, onward, man!"

But Devereux did not charge onward. Instead, he slumped forward and fell to the ground at his horse's feet. An arrow had struck him dead through the eye-slit of his armor.

A hellish series of eruptions followed. Men fell to the ground all across Norfolk's front line, struck by projectiles. Norfolk searched wildly, his attention drawn to the puffs of smoke rising from across the vanguard of the advancing enemy.

Handgunners! The rebels had handgunners in their ranks!

Rearing back, Norfolk surveyed the scene in horror. His men were watching him for instructions. His eyes shifted from his dead captain to the faces of his nervous men to the advancing Tudor line. If forced to stand and wait for the charge of twice their number, his men would flee.

His job wasn't to fight the main action, it was to envelop their wing and attack them from the rear. The rebels were supposed to be divided into divisions, like the royal army. They were supposed to be terrified of the thunder of his cannons.

These rebels weren't like the Woodville retainers he'd crushed two years earlier, or the Scottish skirmishers the previous year.

Oxford. This was all because of Oxford.

Swallowing, Norfolk unsheathed his sword and raised it in the air. "All ranks, forward. Teach these foreigners the meaning of English honor!"

With a cry, the royal right flank descended the hill.

## OXFORD

Oxford held his shield above him and spurred his horse forward at the rear of the formation. While the royal archers were focusing mostly on the Tudor archers, Barnet had taught him that not every archer followed instructions. As he continued forward, every few feet another arrow struck the ground near him with a whizzing thunk.

But then, a vibration shook the ground, followed by a new sound that rose above the jangling of armor. It was a battle cry, and it wasn't close enough to be coming from his men.

Raising the shield further, Oxford risked a look. A wave of metal was rolling down the hill. Norfolk was advancing from his position.

Forgetting the shield, Oxford raised his helm so his men would hear him. Grinning, he spurred his horse forward and rode along the line. "Brace for impact! Captains, remember your orders."

The captains saluted and began shouting to their men, reminding them of their instructions.

The arrows stopped when Norfolk's men and the Tudor army closed to within twenty feet of each other. Only then did the royalist line begin to charge at full speed, slamming into the Tudor vanguard. With a loud crash, men and metal collided with the shiver-inducing scraping of blades on armor.

But the rebels did not break off to meet them in a jumbled mass of private struggles and churning bodies. Instead, the soldiers followed Oxford's instructions, remaining within ten paces of their standards, clustered together tightly enough to support and guard each other. The captains repeatedly screamed the simple orders, and the soldiers obeyed.

# RICHARD

The noise of the first collision on the right flank reached Richard on the hill. With disdain that slowly grew into apprehension, he noted that the Tudor line did not crumble under Norfolk's downhill rush. The rebels were holding.

Richard scowled. His brother should have killed Oxford when he'd had the chance years ago instead of imprisoning him, France or no France. The fool had actually thought he could turn Oxford to his cause, not realizing that John de Vere wasn't cut from the same cloth as Buckingham, Northumberland, or even the Stanleys.

Richard turned to the south. Stanley hadn't moved and seemed to have no intention of engaging anyone. It was so clear now. He had been the weak link on the Privy Council. Tudor must have escaped Brittany because Stanley had warned the boy.

"Treason," he muttered.

"My lord?" a young page responded, frowning.

Richard blinked and returned his attention to Norfolk. "Tell Brackenbury to take our vanguard and main force to reinforce Norfolk."

The man saluted and rode off to find the king's captain.

Rounding, he found another messenger. "Tell Northumberland to maneuver around the enemy and attack from behind. We'll crush them between us."

The man rode off, and Richard returned his attention to the battlefield. Oxford had surprised him by attacking the right, but what Richard had started at Barnet, he would finish here at Redemore.

Searching the Tudor ranks, finally, far in the back, he saw the Welsh dragon standard waving in the breeze. "There you are."

*I'm coming for you.*

## WILLIAM STANLEY

From his position to the south of the marsh, William Stanley saw most of Richard's center advance. They engaged Talbot's cavalry first, which desperately tried to protect the Tudor right. Overcome by superior numbers, Talbot's riders withdrew, but they did so with only light casualties and formed up again to mount a charge. Rather than pursue them, Richard's men wheeled around to hit the Tudor infantry from the right.

William licked his lips at the screams and clanging of steel. Men were dying down there, far more than were necessary if only his brother would do…something.

Breath coming quickly, William recognized Richard's standard, tantalizingly exposed among only the king's personal guard and a mere three hundred cavalry.

He turned to one of his riders. "This is our chance. Go tell my brother he can strike Richard down if he marches now."

## HENRY

Several hundred feet behind his army, Henry watched helplessly as Richard's center marched into Rhys ap Thomas' men on the right. Talbot chose that moment to charge the Ricardians with his re-formed cavalry, delaying them long enough for Rhys to redeploy his rear ranks and confront the royal center. Rhys avoided being outflanked, but now his lines were dangerously thin and sorely pressed.

Talbot reformed for another charge, but his men had taken heavy losses, and both men and riders moved more sluggishly than before.

Henry gnawed at his lip. Would it help for him to ride out, join with Talbot, and lead another charge? Oxford had used fifty men to devastating effect at Hammes; surely twice that would make a difference, wouldn't it? He knew so little about this type of warfare that he was paralyzed by doubt.

His heart told him to do something to help, that he couldn't simply sit on his horse while his fate was decided. But his reason told him Richard was also holding back, and there must be some purpose to remaining safe in the rear.

Before he could consider further, the need passed. Rhys' men pushed Richard's division back and recovered some of the lost ground. The advance halted, and the two armies remained pressed against each other.

The boar standard fluttered defiantly in the distance, far from battle.

And the Stanleys still hadn't moved.


## WILLIAM STANLEY

The rider returned and ground to a halt before William Stanley. "My lord."

"Did you see my brother?" William asked.

"Yes, my lord."

"And?"

"He says that the time is not yet right. Richard remains unengaged, and Lord Stanley's son is still vulnerable."

William clenched the air helplessly and glared at the tantalizingly vulnerable backs of the Ricardians. The opportunity lay in front of him, but he could do nothing about it.


## OXFORD

Cuts, bruises, and exhaustion were beginning to take their toll on the soldiers. The frequency of charges slowed, pauses became longer, and the armies opened up greater and greater space between them.

And then, Oxford shifted his strategy, taking advantage of a pause in combat to rearrange his men into an unusual wedge formation. Infantry moved to the front and formed a hedgerow of pikes that extended forward, creating a pocket into which he poured his archers.

When Norfolk's men made their next charge, the archers fired just over the heads of the pikemen shielding them. At the extremely close range, the volley speared into the royalists, piercing their armor and killing two dozen instantly.

Surprised and uncertain how to react to the devastating development, the royalists halted. The Tudor army advanced, step by step. Pikemen jabbed mercilessly at the vulnerable spots at the necks and beneath the arms of their adversaries.

Oxford shouted in delight as the royal line fell back.

Amid the shifting sea of bodies, he caught a glimpse of the red, gold, and white standard of Norfolk. The duke himself was strafing the Tudor line, hacking and slashing with his sword.

At Barnet, fourteen years earlier, and Towton, ten years before that, the Yorkists had deliberately targeted Lancastrian nobles in battle. Many of Oxford's friends had died because of that practice. Now, Norfolk saw his chance for retribution.

"The duke!" Drawing the attention of several of his archers, Oxford pointed at Norfolk. "Shoot the duke!"

A nearby archer heard him despite the sounds of battle drowning out his voice. Gauging the wind and the rhythmic rise and fall of the duke on his horse, the young man withdrew a bodkin arrow from his quiver and nocked it. With an inhale, he drew back fully. At this close range, he wouldn't need to worry about too much drop.

He exhaled and released.

A moment later, the duke fell from his horse, gurgling blood and clutching at his throat, where the arrow had penetrated his armor.

A cheer rose up from the closest Tudor soldiers. The duke's household guard fought to recover his body. Two died as they slung him over his horse.

But word spread quickly. The first few companies ran back toward the hill. Only the efforts of Norfolk's son, the Earl of Surrey, prevented a general rout. While Surrey pulled the men back thirty yards and began to reform their lines, the Tudor army advanced again.

# HENRY

"My lord, we are exposed," William Brandon announced in a voice drawn tight. The dragon standard hung limply above him, its pole balanced on his stirrup.

Henry surveyed the battlefield. Though the left flank under Oxford was winning, Rhys ap Thomas's Welshmen were tiring. Richard's veterans were slowly driving them back, swinging the line of battle to the west. Talbot's cavalry responded, defending Rhys' men again and again from the constant royalist attempts to spill around and outflank them. Though he hadn't moved, Henry was now exposed.

He needed to reposition himself. Yet, if he tried to join Oxford, he would pass dangerously close to Richard's division fighting Rhys' soldiers. If they faltered, not only would Henry be riding directly into the enemy, but the entire army could collapse.

He needed the Stanleys.

"Make ready to move."

"Where, my lord?" Brandon asked.

Henry grinned. "For William Stanley."

He couldn't wait any longer. He would force their decision. Stanley would have to either welcome him in full view of Richard or kill him.

# RICHARD

Something had happened to Norfolk's men, and Oxford had started to advance. Yet, to Richard's experienced eye, the Tudor right was on the verge of collapse. Oxford had evidently meant to surprise Norfolk, rout him quickly, and then turn on each of Richard's divisions in turn. But Norfolk had done the unexpected and halted them with the force of his charge. Bless that man. He would shower him with titles for this.

"Your Majesty."

Turning to the south, Richard expected to see Northumberland advancing. Instead, only his messenger came riding up.

"Where is he?"

"The earl says doing what you ask is not possible, for it would expose both himself and you to Thomas Stanley."

"Not possible!" Richard shouted. "Damn that man. I put him there to envelop Tudor, and now he refuses to do it. Curse him, curse that traitor!"

Eyes instinctively turning to the Welsh dragon standard in the distance, Richard gasped. It was moving. Was the brat joining the battle?

No, he was heading south. Toward the Stanleys.

Northumberland's instincts had been right, after all. Stanley had betrayed him.

Mind racing, Richard considered his options. If the milksop convinced the Stanleys to engage, Thomas could circle the marsh to the right and delay Northumberland while William circled left to reinforce the flagging Tudor right.

Nor was he the only one to see the danger.

"My lord," Catesby said, "I beg you to retire from the field and allow your commanders to manage the engagement."

Couched in his fine language was Catesby's true meaning: flee for his life.

Richard looked to the right. Oxford was continuing to advance, and while Norfolk wasn't falling apart, nor was he contesting them. What was that man thinking?

He looked to his left. Northumberland and Stanley hadn't moved. He couldn't rely on help there.

He had faced so many difficult decisions these past two years, just to survive. This was not one of them. He would not live in exile as Tudor and Edward had. He hadn't fled when the Woodvilles had sought to dominate the next king, and he would not flee now before this brash milksop. Henry Tudor was right there before him, begging to be killed.

"God forbid I yield one step." Boldness had served him well in the past. He would have to take matters into his own hands. "I will die a king or win the day."

Reaching down, he grabbed his lance from a waiting page and checked that his war hammer was firmly set in the loop at his saddle.

He charged down the hill.

## HENRY

Henry crossed the plain slowly enough that his pikemen could keep up, debating what he would say to persuade Stanley. Only when he glanced casually to his left to gauge the height of the sun did he see Richard's cavalry descending the hill. At first, he thought Richard was reinforcing Norfolk. But as he watched, he realized with growing alarm that Richard was not skirting the hill. He was charging directly for Henry's small band.

And he wasn't alone. Behind him were hundreds of cavalry that slowly fanned out into a wedge, with the king and his household at the center.

"God's wounds," he cried.

His companions followed his gaze and choked back their surprise.

"My lord, what do we do?" Brandon asked.

None of their strategies had accounted for the outrageous possibility that Richard would race across the field to strike at Henry directly. It simply wasn't done.

A great many cavalry were approaching, and they were coming upon him fast. Talbot was too far away. Stanley was too far away. No one could intervene.

He could dash madly for William Stanley, but his pikemen would never keep pace with his riders. It would be their death sentence. They deserved better than abandonment, and he might not even reach Stanley in time.

Swallowing, Henry studied the faces of his men. John Cheyne, who knew many of the men now stabbing toward them. William Brandon. So many faces had been with him in Brittany.

Had riding for Stanley been the wrong choice? It didn't matter anymore.

"Form a line of battle." He swallowed. "Prepare to receive a charge."

## WILLIAM STANLEY

"My God," William Stanley muttered as the boar banner converged on the Welsh dragon. He had seen charges like this before. Henry was outnumbered by more than two to one.

The Tudor army was about to lose the object of their efforts.

Twisting in his saddle, he sought his brother, who had wanted Richard to engage. Still, his banner did not move.

To hell with his brother.

If Thomas wouldn't save his stepson, then William would. The life of his own stepson and any prospect of retaining his lands depended on Henry's victory.

Besides, it wasn't his son whom Richard held hostage.

"Order the advance, double time." He prayed he wasn't already too late.

## HENRY

At the last moment, Henry's men countered the power of Richard's charge with an advance of their own. A row of oncoming lances met a mixed line of lances and pikes with bone-shattering force. Men went flying and animals crashed to the ground in a tangled mix of metal and mud.

Richard aimed directly for Henry's standard, screaming a war cry as he struck. The king's lance pieced William Brandon through the collar bone. Eyes wide with horror, Henry watched him twitch for a moment before falling still.

Surrounded by the nightmarish swirling of screams and misting blood, Henry watched faces he had known for more than a decade twist in agony and fury. To his right, a knight with whom he and Jehane had dined in Brittany was stabbed through the waist by a lance. To his left, a sergeant from Chepstow fell when an axe crumpled his helmet.

"Protect Lord Tudor!" came a nearby shout. "Rally to the dragon."

Near him, one of his bodyguards retrieved the standard from where Brandon had dropped it and raised it aloft. Henry's bodyguards surrounded him. Most had been unhorsed, but a few, like John Cheyne, were still mounted, hacking mercilessly at the royal cavalry.

The French pikemen remained mostly intact. Professionals trained in the Swiss style of warfare, they backed up gradually, closing into a protective circle around Henry as Richard's men swarmed the perimeter.

But the boar banner continued the attack behind its master, and the dragon standard drew Richard's fury. Again and again, Richard charged with his household, slowly opening a wedge in the pikes. Pushing inward, he brought his war hammer down on the helmets of Henry's pikemen, one by one. Each man who fell created an obstacle for his companions to dance around. The gap grew wider, and more of Richard's cavalry streamed in, forcing the two halves of pikemen apart.

"Tudor!" Richard brought his hammer down again on the collar bone of the last pikeman between himself and Henry's bodyguards. One of the exiles stabbed the king's horse at the neck, and both rider and beast fell to the earth.

For a moment, Henry dared to hope it was over, that the beast had broken Richard's leg and one of his men could finish him off. But the tyrant hauled himself to his feet and continued the assault, unperturbed. Several of Richard's men were dismounting now, using their horses to create a barrier through which more of them could pour.

John Cheyne stepped in front of the king and brought his sword in a heavy chop. Richard sidestepped and, with a mighty swing of his hammer, struck Cheyne in the temple, knocking him to the ground.

Henry stood shoulder-to-shoulder with his guards. Only two separated him from Richard, who continued to quickly rain down blow after blow at Henry with his hammer. Tudor swords knocked each blow aside, deflecting them from their commander. One of his bodyguards took a strike to the arm and screamed in pain.

Henry's rapid breaths echoed in his ears. They had been overrun. It was only a matter of time before every one of them died. Fourteen years of exile and a life spent in fear and anxiety would end in failure. All his sacrifices would count for nothing but a casual reference in the record of Richard's reign.

The mass of men shifted, shoving Henry forward into his guards.

Seeing the opportunity, Richard reached over the men interposing them and swung his hammer downward. "This ends, devil."

This man who had cost him Jehane would never pay for his crimes. That wasn't how the world worked. He had been such a deluded fool to think otherwise.

*I'm sorry, Jehane.*

Henry twisted as the hammer struck. Instead of shattering Henry's shoulder, it merely scratched against his breastplate. Henry lifted his sword to ward off another blow. Richard raised his hammer again and swung laterally for Henry's head.

With a grunt, Henry's bodyguard, still nursing his wounded arm, shoved Richard sharply away. Screaming in fury, Richard struck him twice in the helmet, dropping him to the ground.

Rage burned in Richard's eyes as he turned to Henry and raised his arm to strike again.

But the blow never came.

## RICHARD

"Traitors!" Richard cried when one of his own men jostled his arm. He struggled to remain upright.

The momentary delay was enough for the Tudor bodyguards to yank Henry out of Richard's reach.

"No!" he wailed as Henry was swallowed up by his soldiers. He had been so close! The pretender's head had been within his grasp. "Treason!" he screamed. "Attack, attack. Kill them all!"

But by then, his men were contending with another threat. William Stanley's soldiers had arrived and were quickly swarming Richard's cavalry. In twos and threes, his men were being overpowered.

Behind Richard, Ratcliffe cried out. A billhook caught him around the neck and pulled him to the ground. A moment later, two pikemen stabbed downward onto the seams of his armor and stilled him.

"Your Majesty, we must withdraw," cried his standard-bearer.

Amid the clash of metal and screaming of dying men, Stanley's standard gradually advanced from the south.

Stanley.

"Kill Lord Strange!" he shouted as he and his men fended off a charge by Stanley's infantry. "Do it now." He swung his hammer again. "Someone kill Strange now!"

But they were trapped and surrounded. None of his men could break free for their camp.

Stanley had betrayed him. Rhys ap Thomas had betrayed him. Northumberland had betrayed him by disobeying his instructions.

"Where is Norfolk?" Only Norfolk had remained true.

His men rallied around him and slowly fell back, struggling to fight off the pikemen surrounding them. His foot came down on something wet and stuck when he tried to move it. They were in the marsh. Had they traveled so far?

Someone screamed behind him. A low slash had relieved Richard's standard-bearer of his legs. Propped up by the mire, he leaned against the standard. "My king!" he cried before a pike silenced him.

Richard felt a sharp jab in his ribs. Swinging his hammer around instinctively, he struck and shattered the hand of the man who had stabbed him. Reaching back with a grunt, he pulled a dagger out from his flesh. A sharp pain shot up his back.

He had taken wounds before. This one wouldn't kill him. They could still rally. If Norfolk and his center had routed Oxford, his men would be turning back around to finish off the Stanleys any minute now. He just needed to hold on a while longer.

He had fought his way to Tudor once and would do it again. That boy would die by his hand. This wasn't over. Not yet.

A hard blow knocked him forward, denting his helmet and digging it painfully into the back of his head. His eye slits no longer aligned, so as he swung his war hammer blindly, Richard wrenched the helmet off.

His men were surrounded and fighting for their lives. Of the Welsh dragon, he saw nothing. The pretender was letting Stanley fight for him, the coward.

A pikeman came at him at a run. Richard swung his hammer once to deflect the long spear and again to shatter the cheek of the man wielding it.

"Traitor!" He struck the pikeman again in the skull with a crack, sending him down in a heap. These men deserved death for their villainy. He was a king, a son of a noble house. He would not be brought down by a collection of peasants and commoners.

They were upon him now, slashing with their pikes. He swung his hammer in a circle to clear space and deflected their stabs with his free gauntlet. He had been so close!

A sword caught him in the back of the head, cleaving skin and bouncing off the edge of his skull. A searing pain shot through his head and down his back.

How had it come to this?

He swung his hammer and shattered the hand that held the sword, forcing the man to withdraw. A pike came in toward his face. He turned his head at the last moment, and it slashed across his chin instead of piercing his jaw.

But they were coming in too fast, and mud was pouring into his sabatons, making his movements heavy and awkward. Another slash struck his cheek. Needles of pain burned as blow after blow struck his head. They all wanted to deliver the killing blow on their king.

This was how it would end. All his work, all his sacrifices, would come to nothing. His son was dead. His brother and nephews were dead. The House of York would end with him. Because of him. And a drop of bastard blood would sit on his throne.

Furious, Richard screamed, "Traitors, cowards, all of you!" one last time before a serrated pike broke through the base of his skull and into his brain.

Abruptly, the carnage around him faded to silence. The ever-present pain in his back and the searing sting of his wounds numbed for a moment before death separated him from all conscious thought.

## HENRY

Henry and his battered companions were ushered far from Richard's last stand on Sir Stanley's orders, so he didn't witness Richard's end. However, Henry did hear the great cheer that signaled the king's death and quickly spread through the Stanley ranks.

Oxford, Rhys ap Thomas, and the Tudor army were still fighting to the north, but upon hearing the shouts of elation, both armies halted and counted banners. Henry Tudor's Welsh dragon fluttered unmistakably in the light breeze. Richard's boar was gone. Some surrendered on the spot.

Those who fled toward Northumberland were rudely disappointed, for the earl turned and abandoned the field without ever engaging. The Tudor army, in no mood for clemency after two hours of hard fighting, found the reserves of strength necessary to relentlessly chase down the runners.

Ten minutes earlier, Henry had believed his life would end under the assault of raw fury. He'd thought he'd known hatred after Catesby had attacked his carriage in Brittany. Now, he understood that had only been anger and fear. Hatred, leading a cavalry charge across the open field at him, had been something far worse. And it had been terrifying.

But it was over. The rage, fear, and anxiety had died in a marsh at Redemore, a short distance from Market Bosworth. The exile, the hopelessness… They, too, were over.

Despite all of the odds, despite the insanity of seeking battle with a force that outnumbered him, they had done it. The tyrant was dead.

Finally, he was home. He was safe. His great struggle was over.

## HENRY

A new challenge began immediately, one Henry hadn't anticipated. It started as Henry rode through the ranks of the wounded in his camp. Many of the exiles had suffered injuries during the battle, on top of years of exile and the loss of all they had possessed. Though the tyrant was dead, the legacy of Yorkist rule remained. It was up to Henry to repair the damage.

But before he could do that, he had to do a little more damage himself.

Ratcliffe and Norfolk were dead, and Surrey had already been captured. But Catesby, the worst of the lot, remained. Henry would grant no leniency for the man who'd stood on that Vannes rooftop, washed in moonlight. He dispatched Savage's and Talbot's cavalry and Thomas Brandon's scouts to find the villain and drag him back to face the justice due to an assassin.

Brandon. He remembered William Brandon lying motionless in the mud where Richard's lance had slain him. He had sacrificed himself to protect his king, all because of a spontaneous decision to knight him a mere two weeks earlier. Yes, Richard was dead, but he'd died an hour too late for poor Brandon and his fatherless son. Henry would never forget or fail to repay that sacrifice.

He owed his life to many men who had stood between him

and his enemies, and he would repay them all. Only, not in the way they hoped.

The struggle of his exile was over. Never again would he endure that life. Now began the struggle to bring order to a broken land.

William Stanley led a quartet of his men bearing Richard's body on a purple cloth taken from the king's camp. "Your Majesty." William, giddy with victory, grinned at the honorific. "What do you wish us to do with the body?"

Henry eyed the ruin of a king before him. In exile, every rumor had been his ally. Now, he was determined not to allow others to use the same tactic against him. The people needed to know that the Yorkist cause was dead and that resistance was hopeless.

Henry had won a battle. Now, he would prevent future battles.

"Strip him naked and sling him over a horse," Henry declared. "March him at the front of the army. Let all those we pass look upon his crooked spine and his broken body and know that the tyrant and murderer, Richard of Gloucester, has met God's wrath and King Henry's justice."

William's bright smile faded. Backing away, he gestured sharply for his men to follow the command.

Behind him, Oxford grinned wolfishly and nodded his respect. Of course, Oxford would understand. He had been an exile as long as Henry.

His men parted to reveal an approaching Thomas Stanley holding Richard's crown aloft. A hushed murmur spread as men recognized what was happening. This was something rare and wondrous, something each of them had helped to bring about.

Stanley's eyes contained relief and pride; Lord Strange must have evidently still drawn breath. Henry was glad of it. He had very nearly forced Stanley into an impossible choice, and only Richard's daring charge had spared him tragedy. No, Stanley hadn't fought like his brother, but he'd risked much, nonetheless.

Clearing his throat, Stanley took the last two steps and placed the crown on Henry's head. "Long live King Henry, seventh of that name!"

The weight of the crown settled oddly on Henry's brow. He had never felt gold on his forehead before. The pressure felt strange, and he briefly wondered whether Richard and Edward had shared the same thought. It was a heavy burden that had cost each of them their sleep, their lives, and their legacies.

But the call had already begun, spreading through the ranks of the English exiles. Stanley's men soon picked it up, and he was surrounded by the thunderous chant that seemed to rush across the field to the four corners of England. The ground trembled at the sound.

"King Henry! King Henry!"

*Let it tremble.*

More than anyone, Henry knew the price of this moment. He vowed that none would ever need to pay it again. He would prevent the dark times from returning if he had to crush a thousand nobles to accomplish it.

Another call began from among the Welsh, almost hidden in the cries of his accession like an ominous warning for the few who could hear it.

"*Henry, Y Draig Gymreig!*"

Henry, the Welsh Dragon.

The sound gladdened his heart, beckoning the majesty and terror he would use to impose security on the realm.

His realm.

# EPILOGUE

## AD 1491


## HENRY

"Henry, dear, your guests are waiting for you." Elizabeth of York effortlessly swept into the room.

"I'm just finishing." He was still adjusting the lay of his robe as he turned from the mirror. He had added another tunic to ward off the cold, but it caused everything to bulge awkwardly.

A smile tugged at the corners of his wife's mouth. With quiet efficiency, Elizabeth approached and reached into his robe, tugging at two places.

Turning back to the mirror, he marveled at how she could make him look dignified with so little effort. How could she do that every time?

She hadn't yet withdrawn her hand, and he cradled it for a moment. Their eyes met each other's reflection in the mirror. Now the smile filled her face, and he couldn't help but soften.

"Let them wait," he whispered mischievously.

"Henry!" She slapped him softly, her eyes dancing. "You know we can't."

He reached down, placing a hand on her belly. She had said she could already feel kicking. Try though he might, he felt only her breathing, could hear only her heartbeat. "How are you feeling today?"

"Oh, fine." It was always the same answer, though her tone revealed much. At the moment, it carried no annoyance or exasperation.

Reaching down, she lifted the crown off the desk. Slinging it over one hand, she adjusted the part of his hair. As her fingers moved, he watched those focused eyes, certain she applied more attention to his appearance than he did to the wording of most treaties.

Satisfied, she shifted her gaze to the desk and twitched her mouth before sighing. Taking his cheeks in her hands, she kissed him on the nose. "Don't be too long, dear. It can wait one night."

He watched her dress sway rhythmically as she left. A lesser woman would have insisted that he come with her. How could she understand him so well after a mere five years when she continued to surprise him?

He was almost finished, though, so he returned to the work he'd abandoned. Wool prices had risen again, and the weaver's guild was begging for relief. He had some ideas but wanted to consider them further. Manipulating the economy was delicate work. A heavy hand could cost thousands of pounds.

But his wife was right; it could wait.

Straightening the pile of reports on his desk, he saw the date on one of them and froze. Like a voice calling his name, the past echoed back at him.

It was fifteen years to the day since St. Malo.

Had it been so long? He coughed, remembering the first bite of the chill when he'd thrust open the window of that drab inn. His legs throbbed as he recalled his desperate, frantic race through the city streets, searching for safety with Catesby on his heels.

But that was the past. Now, he was safe and warm.

He finished straightening the letters and shuffled into the hallway. Stillington, Landais, even Duke Francis… Everyone involved in that day, all those men who had held power over him, were dead. So, too, was Catesby. He could forgive them all for their roles—even Catesby, the dog loyal to his master.

But he would never forgive Richard. No one would ever forget Richard of Gloucester's villainy.

Nonetheless, slowly, the stain of unrest and civil discord had been fading. Over the years, Henry had faced challenges and rebellions, but they had let him prune weeds the previous two kings had allowed to flourish.

He straightened his robe again when he reached the doors to the feasting hall. The steward stirred to announce him, but Henry waved him off and instead quietly slipped inside.

Elizabeth had decorated beautifully with holly and ivy beneath the shields of each noble family on the walls and weaving through the candelabras. Mistletoe above the thresholds was already being used to good effect by some of the younger members of the court. Craning his neck, he laughed at the sprigs over their thrones, placed exactly as she'd playfully threatened to do the previous night.

But most reassuring of all was the sound of chattering voices. Fathers presented their daughters to their neighbors, sons laughed and joked with each other, and the only whispering along the perimeter came from noble matrons discussing potential matches for their children.

Noticing him enter, Elizabeth gestured for him to join her near a man in a dark blue doublet who carried himself with the telltale signs of a Breton.

Oh, how he missed the Rieux brothers!

Moving through the crowd, he acknowledged the bows and curtseys with a nod. He sidled up to his wife and kissed her cheek. "Hello, love."

"Darling," she began, "I've just been speaking with the new ambassador from Brittany, the chevalier Adrien Touvelle."

The ambassador dipped into a low bow.

Henry inclined his head in response. "I was sorry to hear of your predecessor's recall. He was an excellent chess player. Do you play?"

The ambassador grimaced. "I'm afraid not, Your Majesty."

"Well, you can learn." He grinned. "Touvelle…" The name seemed familiar. "Is your family of the old nobility?"

"No, Your Majesty," he replied shyly. "My father was only a humble knight serving the Quelennec family."

"Quelennec…" Without his advice to Francis, the Tudors would have died decades earlier. Henry wished Quelennec had lived to see the fruits of his support after all those years. "My grandfather was a yeoman in the queen's household. Great things come from humble origins."

"Yes, Your Majesty."

"Tell me of yourself, ambassador. Are you married? Children?"

"Yes, Your Majesty. I am blessed with a wife who is a force of nature and two little demons running through the house."

He laughed, imagining the scene. "Have you brought them to England with you?"

"Unfortunately, no. My Jehane is in the increasing way yet again."

Henry froze, remembering where he'd heard this man's name.

"Ah, how lovely," Elizabeth added. "You have my congratulations."

"Jehane, you say?" Henry asked.

"Yes, my wife. Her name means 'gracious'."

Henry stared into the eyes of the man who had married his Jehane. Part of him wanted to hate him, but her description of her husband burned in his mind. Those eyes carried no hint of mischief or cruelty, and he had spoken of his family with tenderness and affection.

"Is-is she pleased with your appointment?" he forced himself to ask.

Beside him, his wife tilted her head. She'd noticed the change in his mood. She always did.

Touvelle shifted. "In truth, Your Majesty, she was not. She knew it would take me away from her, though she tried mightily to hide her feelings."

His efforts to smile succeeded only in drawing his lips tight. He could imagine her reaction. Henry knew her well enough to understand what it meant; she had found happiness and wanted nothing to interrupt it.

He wondered if her eldest child had his cheekbones or hair color.

Beside him, Elizabeth stroked his arm lightly, studying him with concerned eyes.

Elizabeth. They had built a life together, and he could hardly imagine facing the struggles of the previous six years without her at his side. "Well, perhaps one day you will entice her to visit you here, and we can meet this impressive wife of yours."

Realizing his audience had come to an end, Touvelle bowed and rejoined the crowd.

"Henry, dear, is everything well?" Elizabeth asked.

Henry's life had taken so many strange turns. Three times, sea voyages had changed the course of his fate, robbing him of an earldom twice and giving him a throne. He had lost the only woman he'd ever wanted, only to gain the only woman with whom he really belonged.

Eyes drifting around the room, he considered the people he loved most dearly in the world. Jasper, who finally looked his age after so many years of hale health, gestured excitedly as he recounted one of his stories for Prince Arthur. His son's eyes contained the same wonder Henry's had during those six months with his uncle during King Henry's reign.

From her seat at the royal table, young Margaret played with a doll in blissful ignorance of everyone around her. She was already a handful, breaking out of the nursery to sit on the throne when no one was watching.

And there was his mother, who had worked tirelessly to bring him home. She was soothing baby Henry, who already possessed a thatch of bright red hair and a scream to pierce the night.

The struggle, the sacrifice, the anxiety... It had been worth it, after all.

He kissed his wife tenderly on the lips, eliciting gasps of surprise from those closest to them. Let them be shocked. Their king wanted to show his appreciation for his queen.

"Everything is exactly as it should be, darling."

# MAJOR CHARACTERS

**LANCASTER**

Henry Tudor, Earl of Richmond, a young nobleman with a weak claim to the English throne

Jasper Tudor, Earl of Pembroke, Henry's uncle and half-brother of King Henry VI

Margaret Beaufort, Henry's mother and the daughter of the Duke of Somerset

Reginald Bray, Margaret Beaufort's loyal servant

John de Vere, Earl of Oxford, an experienced Lancastrian general

King Henry VI, King of England, deposed once before by the Yorkists

Margaret of Anjou, King Henry VI's wife

Rhys ap Thomas, a powerful Welsh landowner

**YORK**

Edward IV, Yorkist King of England returning after a six-month exile

Elizabeth Woodville, Queen of England and Edward IV's wife

Elizabeth of York, Edward IV's eldest daughter

Anthony Woodville, Lord Rivers, Elizabeth's brother and a charming nobleman

Edward Woodville, Elizabeth's youngest brother and the Lord High Admiral

George Plantagenet, Duke of Clarence, younger brother of Edward IV

Richard Plantagenet, Duke of Gloucester, youngest brother of Edward IV

Anne Neville, Richard's wife and the source of his Neville power base

Thomas Stanley, a powerful noble in the northwest of England

William Stanley, Thomas' brother and a military man

Henry Stafford, Duke of Buckingham, a rich nobleman with a legitimate royal claim

Catherine Woodville, Duchess of Buckingham and sister to Elizabeth Woodville

William Hastings, a baron and the wealthiest man in England

William Catesby, friend and supporter of Richard Plantagenet

Robert Stillington, Bishop of Bath and Wells

John Morton, Bishop of Ely

William Brandon, a soldier with the garrison of Calais

## BRITTANY

Jehane de Rousson, a widow and tailor of Vannes

Francis II, Duke of Brittany, a duchy independent of France

Pierre Landais, the treasurer and chief magistrate

Jean du Quelennec, admiral and rival of Landais

Jean de Rieux, a nobleman with whom Henry lived early in his Breton exile

## FRANCE

Louis XI, the elderly and sickly King of France

Charles VII, his young son

Anne de Beaujeu, eldest child of Louis XI

Most of the events depicted in *The Welsh Dragon* are historical, such as the relief of Hammes, the attempted escape of Thomas Grey, and Henry's participation in Anne of Beaujeu's army. Henry did flee for his life in St. Malo and relied on sanctuary to escape his captors. He escaped Brittany by rushing for the French border, reaching it an hour before his pursuers.

There is no historical consensus on the fate of the princes in the tower. However, as the daughter of the most cunning man in the realm—Warwick, the "Kingmaker"—and wife of Richard III, Anne Neville had a front-row seat to every event of the Wars of the Roses. She observed the Lancastrian cause collapse when King Henry VI and his son were executed. Her husband was responsible for Edward's son failing to inherit his father's kingdom. More than most, she understood the difficulty of passing an inheritance to the next generation and had every reason to kill rival claimants to her son's throne.

Jehane, though not historical, is historically authentic. *The Hidden Lives of Tudor Women* by Elizabeth Norton can provide many examples of contemporary women who actively engaged in trade and commerce. Some were even influential guild leaders. Married women ran households and family businesses.

Henry Tudor was a very different kind of English king, blending highly mercantile thinking with an intense suspicion of the nobility. He learned these characteristics in France. Though fictional, Jehane presents a plausible means of combining these elements of his later character with the very human urges and experiences at the Breton court.

While Tudor historians claim the goal of Buckingham's revolt was to crown Henry Tudor, this is likely a product of Tudor propaganda. Buckingham had a better claim to the throne and was better-resourced.

I see no reason why he would let himself be passed over for an exile with a weak, bastardly claim.

Necessity required me to alter or exclude some events for narrative clarity. With these changes, I sought to maintain the spirit of personalities and events. For instance, I make no reference to Margaret Beaufort's first or third husbands because they didn't influence Henry's story. The march to Bosworth is accurate but simplified to focus on Rhys ap Thomas and Thomas Stanley, respectively Henry's most important Welsh and English supporters.

History buffs will note I've excluded two anecdotes about Stanley. The first is Stanley finding Richard's crown in a bramble bush; that's almost certainly fiction. The second is Stanley's famous declaration, "I have other sons," when told Richard would kill Lord Strange. Stanley was a cautious man. I doubt he would have provoked a king who could execute his heir. More likely, this quote was added later by Tudor propagandists to justify Stanley's odd behavior. After all, if Henry's stepfather hesitated to offer his support, why should the rest of the country do so?

I'd like to make one final comment about language. I've opted to convey my characters' sentiments as contemporary 15th-century English minds would have comprehended them, rather than by using the words 15th-century English ears would have heard. Keep in mind that the characters are speaking Breton, French, and Welsh throughout most of the book.

To those interested in a study of the events leading to Bosworth, I strongly recommend *The Making of the Tudor Dynasty* by Ralph Griffiths and Roger Thomas.

Your time is the most precious gift you can give. I thank you for spending it on my novel.

# ABOUT THE AUTHOR

K.M. Butler studied literature at Carnegie Mellon University and has always had an avid interest in history. His writing influences are *The Lions of al-Rassan* by Guy Gavriel Kay and Colleen McCullough's *Masters of Rome* series.

He lives in Philadelphia with his wife and two daughters. His wife is his first and harshest editor, while his daughters always want his stories to feature more blood and talking animals, but never at the same time.

Contact K.M. Butler at kmbutlerauthor@yahoo.com or on Twitter at @kmbutlerauthor.

www.ingramcontent.com/pod-product-compliance
Lightning Source LLC
Chambersburg PA
CBHW021757190726
48290CB00005B/1301